Inheritance
of
Power

Inheritance
of
Power

The House of Medici

A NOVEL

Edward Charles

Skyhorse Publishing

FIRST NORTH AMERICAN PAPERBACK EDITION BY SKYHORSE PUBLISHING 2017

First published in Great Britain in 2013 by Pen & Sword Fiction, an imprint of Pen & Sword Books Ltd.

Skyhorse Publishing books may be purchased in bulk at special discounts for sales promotion, corporate gifts, fund-raising, or educational purposes. Special editions can also be created to specifications. For details, contact the Special Sales Department, Skyhorse Publishing, 307 West 36th Street, 11th Floor, New York, NY 10018 or info@skyhorsepublishing.com.

Skyhorse® and Skyhorse Publishing® are registered trademarks of Skyhorse Publishing, Inc.®, a Delaware corporation.

Visit our website at www.skyhorsepublishing.com.

10 9 8 7 6 5 4 3 2 1

Library of Congress Cataloging-in-Publication Data is available on file.

Jacket design by Erin Seaward-Hiatt
Jacket photo credit: iStock

Print ISBN: 978-1-5107-1783-1
Ebook ISBN: 978-1-62914-994-3

Printed in the United States of America

CONTENTS

Chapter 1
Beginnings
Convento di San Damiano, Mugello, Northern Tuscany
Saturday, 1st October 1457

'Horses.'

The abbess looked down at the little *educanda*'s face. Elena was new; the first boarding girl to enter the convent in ten years. The first and only. They needed more, and with good dowries; the remaining nuns were getting older and money was increasingly in short supply.

Madonna Arcangelica bit her lip, feeling, as she did so often, the burden of her office. Nothing was easy these days. With each year that passed, her uncertainties about her position as abbess seemed to grow. And each time they did so, her self-confidence seemed to shrivel further. Now, deep down, she knew it was beginning to die.

More than once in the past year, she had thought of giving up. Yet somehow, each time, pride and stubbornness had dragged her back. Now she was grateful that they had. Now, for the first time, there was a glimmer of hope. If he had truly meant what he had said, there was this one possibility. This one, tenuous possibility. Now everything depended on him – The Great One. But could she trust him?

She shook her head. What had brought about this growing sense of inadequacy? This feeling she was drowning in a world for which she felt responsible, yet over which she had no control?

It was not spiritual leadership that concerned her. Since the age of thirteen, when, to everyone's awe, she had seen the visions, her belief in God and her assurance that He stood beside her at all times, had never wavered; and she knew the nuns – every one of them – still looked up to her for spiritual guidance.

No, the problem was a worldly one. One she was not sure even God could help her with; shortage of money; diminishing income in the face of increasing costs. One cost in particular – the maintenance of the building that loomed behind her.

Remoteness from the city was part of the problem. Although by climbing to the top of the bell-tower, and looking south, she could see the haze of Florence, already now shimmering in the sun of an unusually hot autumn morning; there were too many other convents to choose from between the city and their hilltop, here, deep in the Mugello. And with the uncertainties of recent years, most parents had, sadly, gone elsewhere.

Instinctively, the abbess looked up at the chapel roof. For many winters now, a number of tiles had been missing and others were cracked and broken. And each winter, the number grew. Beneath them, she knew, the timbers were wet, and in some cases rotten. If they had another hard winter, with rain and frosts, anything could happen. And it was at those times, when she dwelt on such matters, that Madonna Arcangelica wondered whether she was truly suited to the responsibilities of abbess. On bad days, the problems she faced seemed endless.

Unless…

Elena screwed up her face, concentrating, her head turned slightly to one side. 'I can hear horses.'

Madonna Arcangelica looked down and smiled. It was only a month since, on the day of her seventh birthday, the child had entered the convent. Amongst so many aging spinsters, Elena often seemed out of place. It wasn't just a matter of age. By any standards, she was unusual; even amongst a crowd of her own age group, she would have stood out. Her mind was pin-sharp, and now, it appeared, her sight and hearing were the same.

The abbess nodded to herself. *Put your troubles aside. Better to think of happy things; of opportunities rather than of problems.* If Elena said she could hear horses, then surely, he must be coming. And this time, God willing, he would be bringing the new nun with him. And if he did, the road to salvation that she had prayed for might finally begin to appear.

And if not…? She crushed the thought from her mind. She could hardly bring herself to think about it.

Elena tugged at the hem of her robe. 'I can hear carts as well. And jingling. It sounds like soldiers.' Her face fell slightly. 'Do you think men are coming to attack us?'

The abbess smiled at her. *Such beautiful innocence.* The little girl's eyes were wide open, hopefully more in excitement than in fear. Most Florentine childhoods were full of stories about armies and battles, but the Republic had been quiet for many years now – many more than Elena's short lifetime, so God be praised, she was unlikely to have experienced the true horrors of war at first hand.

'In a moment, if I am not mistaken, you may indeed see horses, Elena. Yes, and carts. And liveried servants. A great man is coming to visit us today. In the circumstances, I expect he will bring quite a retinue. And yes, soldiers, too, are quite a possibility.'

She saw the child frown and squeezed her hand for reassurance. 'You need not be afraid. They will not be coming to attack us. They will be our visitors, and our honoured guests.'

She leant down and whispered conspiratorially in the child's ear. 'Cosimo de' Medici is a man of great wealth. He may need the soldiers to guard…' she allowed her eyes to open wide, 'the valuables.'

Elena looked up, also now wide-eyed, but Madonna Arcangelica decided she had gone far enough. She put her head on one side and gave the girl her special abbess' smile; the one that said 'that's enough for now; don't ask any more questions.' Elena gripped her hand once more, then turned away and tilted her head, again listening carefully.

Released from the girl's gaze, the abbess gave a little frown. *If it is them* she thought *they are earlier than I expected*. The community had only just finished the mass after Terce and the rest of the nuns were still at their quiet reading. *It can't be beyond mid-morning. If they have ridden all the way from Cafaggiolo, they must have been up at dawn. Perhaps they stayed at the castle of Il Trebbio and came from there this morning?*

She looked out across the valley, beyond Bivigliano, and felt herself frown. *It's still a good ride.*

The girl heard something new and looked up for confirmation; and this time, the abbess nodded. 'Yes, Elena, I heard it too. It is as you said; horses, and the creak of carts.'

Following Elena's example, she cocked her head to one side, listening harder. 'Yes I think you're right, the chink of armour, also.' She ruffled the little girl's hair. 'Aren't you clever?'

To herself she continued. *Quite a little army, indeed.* She felt her heart begin to beat a little faster. *Surely, it must be him?*

The sound of horses was louder now and Elena, with growing excitement, began pointing. Madonna Arcangelica smiled, with a knowing nod of satisfaction. *So the great plan is to proceed, after all. And now it's beginning. I am sure it is. Everything Cosimo said would happen is starting to happen. Surely?*

At least, she hoped it would.

***

They came suddenly, bursting out of the forest below and along the path beneath them. First four foot soldiers, with helmets and breastplates, still, despite the great hill, loping forward at an exhausting pace, each with a huge grey wolfhound pulling forward on a leash.

Well behind, came eight carts, seemingly fully loaded, but each covered with stout canvas, for privacy and protection. Each cart was pulled by a pair of horses and on each sat a liveried driver and a companion, dressed in Medici colours. Bringing up the rear were ten more soldiers, this time mounted; four pike men and six crossbow men, their heads scanning the route, distrusting the cover of the hillside forest even as they left it behind.

And there, between the foot soldiers and the carts, rode Cosimo himself, dressed in his customary long crimson robe. His face as she had seen it before; long and mournful, yet intelligent; missing nothing. As on his previous visits, he was riding a huge, white mule, its long ears pricking up as the convent walls came into its view.

Beside Cosimo, on a small palfrey, rode a diminutive figure. She was well dressed and rode confidently, straddle-saddle like a man; close to him, as if they were the best and oldest of friends. To the abbess, she seemed many years younger than herself; perhaps in her early forties, with a tiny elfin face and short, jet-black hair. Her hair was so short, and her build so slim and slight, that but for her clothing, and the obvious delicacy of her un-gloved hands, she might easily have been a young man.

Suddenly Elena saw her and her grip on the abbess' hand tightened. 'Is that the new nun?' Her eyes were wide open now and as she pointed with her free hand, she stared at the mounted woman in open-mouthed amazement.

Beside her, the abbess concentrated hard to control her own expression of surprise. There was one thing about the handsome new arrival that held her attention, and for which all her negotiations with Cosimo had left her completely unprepared.

The woman Cosimo appeared to be bringing to their convent, to become a nun, and to live at the heart of their community, was black.

Chapter 2
Arrival
Saturday, 1st October 1457

For the third time, Maddalena felt herself sway in the saddle. This time she was sure she was going to fall.

She couldn't hide it now. It was The Dread, and it was getting worse; the clammy skin, the sweat running down her back, the hands greasy and slipping on the reins. The tight chest; like a bodice laced so hard that she felt the very breath was being squeezed out of her.

'Not far now.' Beside her, Cosimo looked at her searchingly, surely recognising her distress, but nevertheless, as was his wont, refusing to acknowledge any signs of weakness. Instead he lifted his head and smiled, clearly excited by the prospect of arriving at the convent.

But try as she might, this time she could not share his enthusiasm. *It's all very well for him. He will be riding back down this hill before the day is over. He has a future – in the countryside of his estates, amongst the cheering crowds in the city, in the rooms and corridors of his palazzi. He will not be incarcerated for the rest of his life behind those huge, overpowering walls. He will be able to breathe.*

As she, already, felt she could not.

She knew it was the sight of the walls that was making her feel like this. Each attack had coincided with another, closer, view of the convent above her. With each view, the building had looked more forbidding, the walls taller and even more oppressive, and the sense of impending imprisonment and the consequent rising panic worse than ever before.

A wave of nausea swept over her again and she felt herself falling. This time, had she not been riding upright, with a big ceremonial saddle, she knew she would have gone. Down, under the horse's hooves, embarrassing everybody and almost certainly being injured in the process.

Another wave of nausea passed over her. She was sure she was going to be sick. Trying hard to concentrate, she fought to regain control. She made herself breathe deeply, drawing in great gasps of mountain air. Slowly, and to her immense relief, the clean, fresh smell of the pinewoods began to clear her head.

'Maddalena!' Cosimo's voice was sharp. He was not looking at her, but up at the walls, where two faces had appeared; an old woman and a young girl, both in habits and both staring intently.

'We are observed. Come on! You can do it. You've been through worse. Concentrate.'

His voice sounded stern, but she knew, in his way, he was trying to be helpful. And he was right. She had been through worse than this. Childbirth; just as frightening and ten times as painful. She could do it. She had to do it. He had asked her to do it and she, as always, had agreed. Now there was no more to be said. It was too late for regrets; she was committed and there was no going back.

They reached the last bend in the road and turned. Maddalena looked ahead and to her immense relief, there were no great wooden doors, embossed with iron, as there had been at the Murate. Instead there were slim iron grilles; barriers yes, like prison bars, but barriers you could see through; light and airy.

Perhaps, after all she thought *I will be able to breathe.* Pride overcame anxiety and as they drew level with the convent building, she finally felt her head clear.

They entered the gates and rode slowly into a courtyard. It was wide and airy, open to the sky. Those great outer walls, she now saw, had been an illusion; thirty feet high when viewed from the hillside below, but now, when seen from within, looking outward from the gravel platform that was the courtyard, they were barely shoulder high, and not forbidding at all.

They approached the standing woman. Surely, by her stance alone, she must be the abbess. Maddalena noticed a trickle of nuns starting to appear from various staircases around the courtyard. Not an orderly procession, but individuals, drifting independently, singly or in small groups, each trying to look as if her presence was an accident and the arrival of the visiting party a complete surprise.

Cosimo flicked her one last look, a glance and a nod. 'Better now?'

She smiled back, trying to look as confident as she knew was expected. She knew he had noticed everything. He always did. But as always, his iron will had prevailed and despite her apprehension, despite her nearly fainting and falling from the saddle, they were here. There was no going back now. *Perhaps* she thought *there never had been.*

She took a deep breath, lifted her chin and sat as upright as she could. *Come on. Best foot forward.*

***

The abbess stood and waited as the riders approached and then came to a halt. Without moving her head, she allowed her eyes to slide left and right, quietly observing what was happening around her. Although she was more nervous than she had been for years, or perhaps because of it, the sight in the courtyard still made her chuckle to herself. As she had expected, there had been no need for a fanfare of trumpets. No need for an advanced messenger to announce their visitors' arrival. It was amazing how word spread. By the time the riders had pulled up, every one of the nuns who could still walk seemed to have made the decision to leave her morning reading and instead, just for a moment, and on a pure whim, to take a stroll outside.

Now they stood awkwardly as the first men to be seen in many months (apart from their confessor; an old monk from the Badia di Buonsollazzo, who visited them once a week) dismounted and awaited their orders. Only Cosimo and his lady companion remained in their saddles; waiting patiently as their mounts tossed their heads, no doubt in relief that their steep climb from the valley was finally over.

Madonna Arcangelica handed Elena to one of the waiting nuns and stepped forward, looking up at her guests. 'Welcome, Magnificence. Welcome to our holy house.'

As she spoke to him, she could not prevent her eyes from straying to the slight figure beside him. The abbess had never seen a black woman before. This one was tiny; almost elfin, yet she seemed to have an air of intense energy and self-confidence that radiated from her like one of the holy paintings in the chapel behind them. On closer inspection, her skin was not black, but a rich nut-brown, and it glowed, like a freshly opened chestnut, exuding strength and health. Only her gloveless hands, and the corners of her eyes, gave any indication of her age. There was a hint of weariness, perhaps born of life's experiences, in the creases around those eyes. But as for the eyes themselves; they were, against all expectations, a clear, pale blue.

There was no doubt that the woman, whoever she was, still had a radiant beauty, and an exotic presence that owed much to the compelling combination of brown skin and pale blue eyes. Their paleness was perhaps an illusion; her eyes also had an intensity about them that made you want to look deep into them, and having done so, and having seen the gentle intelligence within, to engage her in conversation, to discover what she knew, what she liked, and what she believed in.

'Are you to be our new *Suora*?' She found herself asking the question uncertainly. Cosimo had brought no other woman with him, but yet…. It was such a huge assumption to make and one which, if wrong, in the circumstances, might create such discomfort.

Cosimo seemed to see the predicament, dismounted from his mule and handed the woman down. Her palfrey was only small; but still, with no mounting block, she had to slide from the saddle, and as she did so, he reached up and caught her. She turned, facing him, smiling her thanks, and without hesitation, he planted a lingering kiss on her mouth.

Behind her, Madonna Arcangelica could hear a succession of sighs from the assembled nuns, followed by giggles of embarrassment.

Cosimo looked up. Perhaps in response to the sound, or perhaps to the silence that followed it, he addressed his wider audience first. 'This, sisters, is Maddalena; shortly, I hope, to come amongst you and remain with you, as part of your community in God.'

Around the courtyard, the nuns broke into uncertain, but spontaneous applause.

With an accepting tilt of the head, Cosimo continued, already taking command with an easy assumption of position amongst them. 'But until she does; until she takes her vows and dons the habit of your holy order, she remains part of my family and I need her to help me fulfil one part of my agreement with your Mother Superior, Madonna Arcangelica.'

Brought back into the conversation, the abbess inclined her head and reached out a hand to Maddalena. 'Welcome. I hope you will be very happy here.' Behind her, murmurs of assent from the assembled nuns confirmed her greeting.

Easily now, her position of authority apparently re-established, she started to lead Maddalena towards the door of the new tower. 'Shall I show you to your new room?' As she said it, she looked across at Cosimo. She saw him give a little frown and froze, suddenly and uncomfortably aware that she had made a mistake, uncertain how to proceed further.

'I wonder whether we might complete the more mundane domestic arrangements first, Reverend Mother. Then, once the carts have been unloaded, we can allow them to commence their empty return. I shall remain behind and follow them later, with my soldiers.' Cosimo indicated the carts with a dip of his forehead. She reddened.

'How stupid of me, Magnificence. Of course. Please tell us what you wish to do and what help, if any, you need.'

Having regained control without embarrassment, Cosimo smiled, expansively. 'If my servants could be pointed towards the kitchen larder and the library, they can commence their work.' He smiled again, this time specifically at the abbess. 'I think we three should supervise.'

The ground rules established, and with Cosimo issuing orders, his servants began unloading. Madonna Arcangelica, unsure what else she should do, stood beside Maddalena and smiled at the assembled nuns to indicate that all was well and that everything was as expected.

The contents of the first two carts were uncovered and showed themselves to be destined for the kitchens. Hams, lambs, half-pigs and half-cattle all brought gasps from the watchers. Sacks of flour and barrels of salt, olive oil and wine began to make their way towards the larder and as they did so, surreptitiously, the nuns began to shuffle off in that direction as well. By the time the third cart was uncovered, and open trays of a prepared meal had been carried in, the nuns had all but gone.

With the first task complete, Cosimo turned his attention to the library. The remaining carts were pulled close to the chapel door and men began carrying large wooden cases through the chapel and into the library itself. Within an hour, the contents had been unloaded and the empty boxes returned to the carts.

Now Cosimo took a closer personal command, asking Maddalena to join him in the library. Delicately, he asked the abbess to leave them for a short while and awkwardly, she complied, as servants were dismissed and soldiers summoned into the library in their place.

Madonna Arcangelica sat alone outside in the chapel, praying that everything would go according to whatever plan The Magnificent Cosimo had in his mind. She wondered what Cosimo and Maddalena were discussing in the library, what secrets the soldiers were carrying down those narrow stone steps into the recently constructed vault.

But there was nothing she could do. The building of the library, the carving of a vault and the placing of unidentified objects within it had all been part of her agreement with Cosimo; and now the process was taking place, she could hardly complain. It was hard to watch passively, not understanding what was really taking place. He had never felt the need to explain the purpose of his actions and she had not, in any of their discussions, dared to ask him. *Perhaps* she thought *if I come to know Maddalena better over time, the secret will eventually emerge?*

***

In less than an hour, Cosimo and Maddalena had rejoined her and the soldiers had withdrawn, to wait outside the doors of the chapel. For the first time since his arrival, Cosimo seemed to relax. He smiled at the abbess. 'It is done. The books are in their cases and the vault has been filled and sealed.' He inclined his head slightly. 'I hope you will be content to leave the key with Maddalena.'

His tone of voice did not make it a question and the look on his face did not invite an alternative suggestion. It was clear to the abbess she had only one choice. Graciously, with a returning incline of the head, she complied.

Now, for the first time, Maddalena spoke. Her voice was soft and refined, stronger than expected, and although her Tuscan was fluent, it bore the hint of an accent foreign to the city of Florence. 'We took the liberty of bringing a celebratory feast with us,' she said. 'It was prepared by Cosimo's cooks at Cafaggiolo and his servants have laid it out on your refectory tables. I hope that was not too presumptuous?'

Just presumptuous enough said a voice inside Madonna Arcangelica's head, but her relief overcame her irritation. Unused to visitors, she had not thought about the need to feed them and nothing had been prepared. A bell rang and she realised, with returning embarrassment, that it was time for Sext; the next service of the day in the calendar of their Order.

Cosimo saw the expression on her face. 'I feel we are intruding upon your Order.' He paused and looked around him. 'We would be happy to wait, while you attend service?'

Madonna Arcangelica hesitated. The arrival of all that food had caught her out completely. Perhaps she ought to give a dispensation and allow the nuns to miss Sext? Already they seemed to be hovering excitedly around the refectory door. But then again, Cosimo might not be too impressed by an abbess who put aside a religious service in the interests of mere feasting?

Ever sensitive to protocol, Cosimo saw the hesitancy and made a further suggestion. 'Perhaps, while you attend chapel, I might take Maddalena to her room and see her settled? Then, I think it might be more appropriate if I were to take my last farewell of her and depart? That way, you and your sisters would not be constrained by my presence and could enjoy the dinner as an opportunity to eat together with Maddalena for the first time?'

The suggestion came as a relief. It was a new experience for Madonna Arcangelica to have a major benefactor, and she was struggling to adjust. She had not wanted to be seen putting food before prayer, but if she accepted The Great One's suggestion, she could hardly be criticised. She tipped her head to one side, gratefully. 'That's an excellent suggestion, Your Magnificence. Do you want me to guide you?'

He grinned; a boyish grin, unexpected from a man she knew to be in his late sixties. 'I think I know the way. Let us leave you to your devotions and then I shall take my leave quietly, without disturbing you further. Maddalena will rejoin you in...what? An hour?'

She nodded. 'An hour. Yes, that's just right.' Uncertainly, she extended her hand. 'I'll say farewell then, and thank you. For everything.' He kissed her hand and she found herself blushing.

Suddenly, she felt relieved. She had not known how to bring it to a close; not known the protocol, the appropriate procedure. It was a good solution, doing it his way. Cosimo and Maddalena could say their last farewells in privacy and the convent could return to its daily routine. The nuns became fractious if their routine was upset. Better to get back to the familiar as soon as possible.

She accompanied them to the door of the chapel and beckoned the awaiting nuns to come inside to their devotions. Cosimo and Maddalena stood back and the nuns streamed in, still chattering amongst themselves.

The last she saw of Cosimo de' Medici was his back, as he led Maddalena into the corner of the chapel and through the heavy new door, and into her tower. As they passed through, Maddalena turned and gave the abbess an uncertain smile. She looked hesitant. Perhaps she was beginning to recognise what the implication of committing the rest of her life to God, in this place, really meant?

Madonna Arcangelica saw the flicker of uncertainty on Maddalena's face and hoped they could be friends. Life here could be lonely; especially for an abbess. She had a position to maintain and was expected to keep a certain distance. The young nuns were in awe of her and the old ones – five of them, all in their eighties – tended to live in a little huddle of their own, with their own rules; supposedly dispensations from the previous abbess. She'd never been sure about that, but sometimes it was easier to let water flow downhill than to fight.

As they disappeared from view she smiled to herself. She could learn from that Maddalena, and at the same time, she thought, help her. The dark woman looked intelligent. And surely educated, she must be? She hoped dearly that they could build a working relationship. With God's grace, she could help Maddalena adjust to the slowness of their life here, whilst Maddalena, in turn, might perhaps teach her something of that other world; the world out there, the world her father had taken her from at the age of seven and to which she had never once returned.

What, she wondered, had she missed in all these years? Perhaps Maddalena could enlighten her. An unexpected shiver of apprehension ran down her back. Would finding out make her life here in the convent any easier to bear, or harder? There was no way of knowing. But she must ask. This might be her only opportunity.

Yes, risky or not, she needed to ask.

Chapter 3
Realisation

Saturday, 1st October 1457

'Come. I will escort you to your room and then we must say our final farewells.'

Maddalena stood in the doorway of the new tower, so reminiscent of her favourite tower at Cafaggiolo, and watched as Cosimo began to climb the stone steps. *Judging by the height of the tower* she thought *he will need a few rests before he reaches the top.* But he seemed not to be alarmed by the steepness of the steps and set off, confidently enough, not looking back; no doubt, as always, assuming she would follow him.

And then, suddenly, in an unexpected flood of complete clarity, she realised the truth of the situation. Of course he knew exactly how steep the stairs were, and how many steps he would have to climb. More than that, he knew what he would find when he got to the top. *He has been here before.* And in that moment, she understood for the first time just how carefully, how completely, and how secretly he had planned all this.

For a moment, she felt misled and manipulated. She turned in the doorway, and looked back at the abbess. *How much* she wondered *does that woman know about the reasons for my being here?* It was clear the abbess had met Cosimo before, yet she still appeared in awe of him. Maddalena gave her an uncertain smile, not sure, after all, whether she and Madonna Arcangelica could ever be friends or whether her deep-grained habits from the outside world would be a burr under the saddle of this peaceful and contemplative place.

But already, she realised, it was too late for prevarication. She had been led – he had led her – too far along the path of agreement to this unknown future for her to withdraw now. She turned again and started to follow Cosimo up the steps.

As she began to climb, she knew it was no accident that the tower was like Cafaggiolo. She knew that now and she also knew why. *This must be the new tower he had built. He must have told Michelozzo to make it the same, for my sake. And look at him now. He knows exactly where he's going; he's climbed these steps before. Back at the Palazzo Medici he would not have contemplated a set of steps like this. He would have mentioned his sciatica and had a servant carry him in a chair.*

Slowly, hesitantly, she followed him up the stone steps, pausing after four flights, where the treads narrowed and steepened, changing from stone to wood. He pointed into the small empty room. 'Your storeroom. I have had your chests taken above for the present. No doubt there will be some servant who can bring the empty chests back down later if you wish?'

Of course he has been here before. But to be fair, he is making no secret of it.

They continued up, and like a cook presenting a special dish to the high table, he opened the door at the top of the wooden stairs with a flourish. He propped it open with his outstretched foot, and leaning back, indicated that she should enter before him.

She stepped into the room and immediately her mood changed. She was instantly overcome by its airiness, its light and all-encompassing feeling of openness. The walls had been plastered, smoothly, as if awaiting a *fresco*, but then left unpainted; a soft pale *terra-cotta*. There was a tiny window in the wall to her right and through it, a slim shaft of light shone across the room and splashed the wall just above and to one side of the little bed.

Beaming with relief, she pushed wide the folding chestnut doors and walked out onto the balcony. Immediately, one of her first fears fell away. *I will not feel imprisoned. I will not be walled up. Not in this room. Not with this view.* She looked up the valley, along the ridge of the hill, running due north, towards Trebbio and Cafaggiolo, where she had slept the previous night.

How appropriate. The Mugello was beautiful country and almost everything she could see before her belonged, she knew, to the man standing behind her. The Cafaggiolo estate alone contained fifty-seven *poderi* worked by tenant farmers; all belonging to Cosimo, their estate landlord, to whom they paid their annual rents, either in kind, or if they had special skills, by labour. And in that sense, she realised, that incarcerated as she might be, she would still be amongst his people and part of his world.

'What a privilege to live so much of one's life amongst such country.' She looked back into the room and smiled at him. He reached out a hand to her and she joined him once again. He pointed to something, in the corner of the room.

There, at the foot of the bed and to the right of the huge chestnut doors, was an *inginocchiatoio*; a simple yet beautiful votive table made of rosewood, or perhaps oiled chestnut like the doors. It had a plain flat top and four supports in the twisting design they called *tortiglioni*. The table had a protruding base, so that she could kneel and still place her elbows on the top, in prayer, without fear of tipping it toward her.

She looked at it and smiled. Then, with a glance at Cosimo, she lifted it and turned it round, placing the protruding base against the wall, the flat side towards her. She crossed the room and lifted the plain chair from the other corner and stood it before the table. Then she sat.

Turning to Cosimo she smiled. 'It's lovely. Just the right height for writing and, of course, perfect in its original, intended, role also.' She gave a little frown of uncertainty. 'Is this the one from your *studiolo*?'

Cosimo laid a gentle hand on her shoulder and shook his head. 'A copy. An exact copy. I didn't think they were going to finish it in time. You have written so many entries into my ledgers sitting at that table; I thought you would be lost without it. I hope the nuns won't disapprove if they find it turned, as is so often the case at home.'

He reached into a small chest lying on the floor in the corner. *Another confidence born of familiarity* she thought. He took out a book, its pages folio-sized, like the *Libro Privato* in which she had kept the private records of the Medici Bank; but unlike those great ledgers, the spine was no thicker than the width of his thumb. The book was bound in green leather and in the centre of the front cover it had the embossed *palle* and shield of the Medici emblem.

'You know, my dear, this project of ours is the most important matter to me and nothing is more private. You, and only you, now share my deepest secret. I have finally had to accept the uncomfortable conclusion that neither of my sons, neither Piero nor Giovanni, has the wherewithal to carry the Medici Bank forward as have I, in my time, in respect to my father's memory. On the contrary; between them, they are likely to bring the bank low; perhaps even to collapse and extinction.'

She looked into his eyes and knew how hard he found it to admit to such things.

'There are but two saving graces. The first, and this is a terrible thing to have to say, is that neither of my sons are healthy and both of them are likely to die young. The second, and redeeming feature of this whole episode, is that they will be followed by the one person who can save the bank and the family's long term reputation.'

Sitting at the little table, she nodded. 'Lorenzo.'

Cosimo smiled, as he always did at the mention of his grandson's name. 'Indeed. Lorenzo.'

He tapped the book with his fingertips. 'That is where this whole scheme started. To make provision for Lorenzo. To ensure that even if Piero and Giovanni allow the bank to go to rack and ruin, Lorenzo will have sufficient funds to save it; and with it, the reputation and future of the family.'

He put a hand on her shoulder. 'That's why I gave you your freedom.'

Maddalena took his hand and squeezed it. She did not want him to think her unkind, but she knew it must be said. '*Lent* me my freedom, Cosimo. Lent only. A week ago you gave me my freedom; removed me from slavery and made me a free woman. But today, let us both understand, you are imprisoning me again and in that respect, removing my freedom, for a second time.'

Immediately, she could see deep sadness in his face. It was clear that despite making repeated efforts to tell himself it was otherwise, he knew that what she said was true.

'You can still change your mind. You are indeed now a free woman and if you want to walk away from this place I will not stop you. I will buy you a farm, miles away, as I have recently done for Donatello; somewhere you are not known, and you can live out your days there in privacy. It's not too late, you know. I shall not hold it against you.'

She smiled, but knew immediately it was a weary smile. Weary from spending night after night contemplating the proposal which she had finally decided to accept. But now it was too late. Now she had given her word and now she must stand by it.

'If I did that, I should be separated from you and to no purpose. No. It's too late now, Cosimo. You need me to look after Lorenzo's gold. How else will you know it is safe in that vault and undisturbed? Who else, when the time comes, will tell Lucrezia and Lorenzo where the money is? I have accepted this undertaking in good faith, in respect for you and in thanks for all the Medici family has done for me over the last thirty-six years.'

Cosimo's eyes were wet with emotion. 'Thank you my love. You are right. There is nobody else I could have trusted with this matter. I have told no one, not even my wife.'

'You haven't told Contessina?'

He shook his head. 'How could I tell Contessina that I was planning to hide money from her own two sons because I did not trust them? No. Nobody knows and nobody must know. But already, I must warn you, they suspect. Already people are sniffing around, and not just within the family. Agnolo Acciaiuoli, Luca Pitti, Dietisalvi Neroni, they all have their noses in the air, sensing something is in the offing. They think I don't know about them, but half their spies are paid even more by me to spy on *them*, and to report back only what I tell them to report.'

His eyes looked tired now and for the first time that day, she could see his age showing. 'It's a dirty little world, Maddalena, but I must do what I can. For the future of the family.'

He tapped the book again. 'I shall write to you when I can, and send my letters by trusted servants. But I dare not let you reply.'

She went to protest but he held up his hand. 'No. The situation is too fluid. If you're not there day by day, at Careggi, at Fiesole, at Cafaggiolo, and particularly at the Palazzo Medici in the city, you will never know who you can trust. That's why I must forbid you to write to me.'

He extended the book toward her. 'Instead, I am giving you this journal. When you wish to speak to me, write your words in here. Then, when next I come to visit you, I will be able to read what you have written.'

She took the journal, felt the leather, opened the pages and smelled the clean paper. Then defiantly, she shook her head. 'I shall write my replies in this book, but when you visit me again, I shall not give them to you to read. Instead I shall read them to you myself.'

Cosimo kissed her on the forehead. 'That is even better. Agreed then.'

He walked across the room and opened a simple plain chest beside the wall. Inside was a nun's habit and he lifted it and draped it across the chair. 'It is nearly time. Time for me to depart, and for you to make your vows. Soon they will be waiting, downstairs.'

As he spoke the words, she was seized once again by panic. It had come. The moment she had closed her mind to. The one part of the whole arrangement that she had not allowed herself to visualise. This was the moment of departure. There was no going back. It was so final. So absolute.

'Don't leave me, Cosimo...' She clung to his gown and for a moment her whole world was encased in soft red velvet. Then she felt his arms strong, around her, his body stiffening, his hands, busy, urgent, and familiar yet fumbling in their hurry.

'One last time.' His voice had become husky,

'Cosimo we can't.' As she said it her own hands made a lie of her words. She knew his clothing almost as well as she knew her own. He was naked and soon so was she. Giggling with embarrassment, they climbed onto the little bed. It had not yet been made; just a plain mattress, a coarse blanket folded up on the pillow. She shivered. It was draughty there, with the great chestnut folding doors still wide open.

He reached across the floor and pulled his velvet gown over them. Again, as so many times in the past, since that first time in Venice, they were together.

They clung to each other, relishing the proximity, unwilling to let it end, and as their breathing subsided in unison, briefly, they slept. Silently, the ray of light from the tiny window above worked its way across the wall and shone its meagre warmth on them. And at that very moment, a solitary bell began to chime, and they both knew the time had come.

***

Alone on the balcony, wearing only her silk *camicia*, she watched him walk towards the horses and she knew that the last breath of her old life had just been expelled. Now, alone for the first time since her childhood, she must take the first breath of her new life.

She walked back into the room, and for a moment considered, before rejecting the thought. *No, I must not begin by cheating. I must do this properly.* Regretfully, but resigned to the necessity, she allowed her *camicia* to fall to the ground, picked up her nun's habit, and let it slide over her head, coarse and rough against her skin. Her heart was thumping with apprehension. But she knew it had to be done. She had agreed to enter this place and now, whatever happened, she must make the most of it.

Chapter 4
Settling In
Monday, 3rd October 1457

Maddalena stepped in from the balcony of her room and began to close the double-folding doors. The chestnut wood still smelled freshly planed and the new hinges gave the gentlest of sighs where the oil had yet to seep into place. But like everything else in the room, they had been beautifully executed to a most thoughtful design. She ran her finger down the smooth edge of the door and wondered which of Michelozzo's carpenters had made these doors. It had to be him, of course. Every detail of the tower and her little room here at the top resonated with his style and attention to detail.

She smiled to herself. Cosimo and Michelozzo! What a combination. Was there nothing they couldn't create between them? Cosimo's imagination and his endless money had always seemed able to conjure up one dream after another. But the real credit, she thought, must go to Michelozzo, who seemed to be able to see into Cosimo's head, to pluck the dream from inside, and to turn it into a working reality. Oh the joy and responsibility of patronage.

Before the doors closed completely, she took one last long lingering look outside. Then, decisively, she took a deep breath, closed them and slid the bolts home. *I must stop doing this* she said to herself. *Cosimo has gone. Michelozzo is part of another world; no longer my world. They all are; Piero, Giovanni, Lorenzo, Lucrezia....* She smiled; a wry smile as she realised that she had been about to name Contessina in her list, but Cosimo's wife in full sail was one image she could easily learn to live without. But the others, yes she would miss them. All of them. She pressed her hand against the chestnut doors with a decisive finality and turned back into the room. *I must accept the reality of my incarceration here and learn to embrace it. Every day – every hour I look out there and cling to my old life will make it more difficult.*

Clinging on. Despite telling herself not to, she knew it would be hard to avoid.

She sighed and tried to concentrate. It would not be easy to blank out the memories from almost four decades of living amongst the greatest family in Europe. She shook her head and snorted at her own stupidity. Of course she could not erase the memories; why should she? That was not the challenge she faced.

She crossed the room and put her hand on the votive table, at the exact corner where Cosimo had held it as he helped her turn it round. She nodded to herself, a decision made. Yes she would retain the memories, succour them, enjoy them, and nurture them, as the residual echoes of her former life. But what she did have to do was to remind herself that that is what they now were: memories, not realities. Part of her past – but only in their echoes, part of her future.

Letting go. She was finding it harder than she had thought. Standing on the balcony, she had watched him go. She had stood back from the edge so that he would not see her; but to her disappointment, he had not looked back once keeping his eyes firmly fixed on the rough little ridge between his mule's ears as slowly he disappeared down the steep lane towards Bivigliano and then to Vaglia and the valley road back up to Trebbio and Cafaggiolo.

Try as she did, she hadn't been able to shake off the feelings of that moment. Even now, looking back forty-eight hours later, she couldn't remember which had been stronger; the gut-wrenching feeling of loss as she watched him ride away, or the stifling, claustrophobic fear of the future. Not fear of the nuns, or the endless repetition of the office, spelled out by the pages of the breviary; she was used to regular prayers and her life within the Medici family had always been constrained by the strict protocols of the family's religious responsibilities. No, her fear was more physical; the returning, overpowering fear of enclosure. Of imprisonment. Of confinement in a small space.

She had thought she had shaken it off, but The Dread still returned and at times, still haunted her. But not here. Not in this room. She looked around, remembering the light, the feeling of expansiveness when those great doors were opened and she nodded to herself. *He knew, didn't he? He understood my feelings; my fear of entrapment. It was for that reason, I am sure, that he chose this convent, on a hilltop, with fine views and with an open Rule, allowing conversation, exercise and work out there in the great gardens. Gardens that separate the outer walls from the convent building itself. He even had Michelozzo build this room, this whole tower, just for me. To make it easier. I know he did.*

But then the opposing thought – a clear and terrifying memory, ineffectively suppressed, flashed back into her mind. The sights, the sounds, the smells; they all returned in an instant. Immediately, she found herself panting with apprehension. *I thank the Good Lord he didn't choose Le Murate. Anything – anything but Le Murate.* Her mind went back over thirty years, to the day shortly after Cosimo had brought her from Rome to Florence. The date was still etched in her mind.

***

VIA GHIBELLINA, FLORENCE
14th December 1424

'In for Christmas. Well done! They should be so proud of themselves.'

She turns. Cosimo is smiling enthusiastically, standing at the very front of the crowd and applauding loudly. The crowd is filling the Via Ghibellina, and massing opposite the great doors of the new Benedictine convent of Santa Maria Annunziata. It's a day to remember. She can sense its importance and knows she will remember it for years to come. They have just watched the Walled-In Nuns process from their old building on the Ponte Rubaconte to their new home. All along the route there has been great celebration, the singing of psalms and hymns and the parading of their works of art. And now it's time for the finale.

Cosimo leans towards her. 'The fourteenth of December in the year 1424. You should remember that date, Maddalena. It is important. What an occasion!' Cosimo looks at her and she attempts a smile that echoes his enthusiasm. But now she begins to think about what is to come next and the prospect of it is already filling her with a cold, clammy dread.

It's the same sort of sick, dizzy feeling she gets when Cosimo takes her up to high places, like the top of the tower on the Palazzo Signoria, where he expects her to stand beside him on the balcony, part of his retinue, holding his hat and looking downward, while he waves to the crowd.

But now it is not the fear of falling that she knows will overcome her. Even more terrifying, that suffocating feeling of impending doom. The Dread, as the doors are closed and the entrance to the convent is symbolically bricked up. Le Murate. The Walled-In Nuns. She understands their history and the extent of their faith, but *how can they bear to be enclosed like that?*

The singing of hymns comes to an end. Inside the great archway, the nuns turn outward; facing the crowded street through the great doors, then, in unison, take three steps backward. In front of them, as trumpets play, first one door, then the other, is closed from within. The key is heard turning in the great lock.

'That would suit you wouldn't it?' Cosimo is grinning. 'Not a bad way for a woman to end her days; in the peace and tranquillity of an isolated existence, given over fully to prayer and contemplation?' He has his teasing expression on his face. But today she is not in a mood for teasing. Today it is all she can do to remain on her feet as, horror of horrors, she watches the bricklayers step forward, lay the first line of mortar across the entrance, and then start bricking up the doorway.

It is too much. The crowd surges forward, to watch every moment of this, the climax of the day, and as the crush tightens around them, the claustrophobic thought of being walled-in overcomes her and makes her heart race. Immediately, the dizziness becomes worse and as Cosimo turns to see what the commotion is, she falls, unconscious, to the ground.

***

Maddalena leaned against the table and willed her heartbeat to slow down. Her first instinct had been to rush to the chestnut doors and to fling them open again, but she had not let herself do it. Instead she had gripped the edge of the table and forced herself to concentrate.

She must fight this. She had known immediately what was happening, the moment it started. The memory of that day, thirty-three years before, was triggering the fears all over again. Already the palms of her hands were wet with sweat and there was a strange hollow feeling inside her that she knew, if she couldn't control herself, would soon turn to an increasing and all-encompassing tightness. She bit her lip, concentrating hard, trying not to let her heartbeat climb again, as it had done three times already since her arrival in this place. Each time she had fought the breathlessness and the horror that she would die of asphyxiation unless she ran outside. Each time, she had fought it; and each time, she had not allowed herself to run outside.

Now, once again, she conquered her fear, taking slow breaths as she gripped the corner of her little votive table, her knuckles white, whilst with the other hand she pressed gently with the first two fingers against the great artery on the left hand side of her neck. It was a physicians' trick she had learned from her father when she was still a child, and as always, it began to work. She counted to twenty, and then removed her fingers as her heartbeat began to drop back to normal, as the constriction in her chest eased and she could breathe once again.

Even as she recovered, a thought came to her. *But he still did it didn't he?*

As her head cleared, the thought hit her harder. *Even knowing of my fears. Even having seen them for himself and the effect they always had on me, he still put me in this place. I was right in what I said to him. He lent me my freedom; gave it to me, but as soon as I had it, he took it back again.*

Once more she remembered that last look down at his departing mule, flanked by a line of soldiers either side of him, looking, for all the world, as if *he* was the prisoner, not her.

And then another thought came to her. *Perhaps that was how he felt. Perhaps he, too, felt imprisoned; in his case, by his worries.* What had he seen himself returning to? A great palace, yes. Money, paintings, sculptures, rich food; a world of endless luxury. Yes.

But also a life of loneliness. *Who will he talk to now?*

The truth was, without her, Cosimo was alone. He did not trust his sons' judgement or even, in some cases, their motives. And as for his wife, he may have remained publicly loyal to Contessina for her constancy, and the reliability with which she ran the family and the household. And it was true he respected her good taste when it came to patronage, or filling their buildings with good things; but let's be honest, she was, in the final analysis, a fat, old-fashioned, narrow-minded and uneducated sow of a woman who had never showed the slightest interest in the bank or in affairs of state, other than as part of her narrow circle of social relationships within the noble families of Florence. *He won't be able to talk to her about the big things, the things that matter.* Secretly, she thought, Cosimo despised his wife nearly as much as she did. Contessina was one person she wouldn't miss.

But enough of them. She had left them now and she must address her own situation. Realising that the fainting feeling had abated, she took her hand from the table and shook it until the circulation recovered. Once again, she could stand alone. She did not need support. *Come on. You've been through worse than this. It will not beat you. Cosimo has a task for you to perform; an obligation, an entrustment. Stand upright. Move forward and embrace your new responsibilities. What would Carlo say if he saw his mother wilting like a waterless flower?* The memory of her son – Cosimo's son, and her proudest achievement – gave her strength, and she turned towards the door.

She had been kept busy since arriving in her new home. The abbess must have recognised the signs of her rising panic as soon as Cosimo had departed. No doubt she had seen them many times before. The answer, it seemed, was to remain busy and they had not allowed her any time to think. Not, that is, until now.

Taking her vows had not been as distressing as she had expected. By the time the service began, she had already faced the reality of her situation and to her pleasant surprise she had felt a real sense of welcome and acceptance from the other nuns. Well, most of them; there were four or five old ones huddled in one corner by themselves, who looked at her as if she was the devil incarnate. Their response had reminded her of Contessina's open distaste when Cosimo had first brought her back with him from Rome and announced that she would be living amongst them, in the family home, as his personal slave. She had survived that, and she would survive this.

The abbess had been clever. She had insisted that 'our new sister' took her vows before they partook of the great feast that Cosimo had provided, and she had announced that 'in the spirit of welcome' the daily rule of silence during meals would be dispensed with. The result was that Maddalena, the new *Suora*, had been able to participate in the feast as a full member of her new community and the permission to speak had actively encouraged everyone to talk to her.

It seemed that Cosimo had told the abbess her original family name – Octavia Lanza (how had he remembered that name after thirty-six years?) – and had 'suggested' Maddalena as her 'new' name. Was there no end to his ingenuity?

The first night had not been too bad. Having refused the abbess' offered reprieve from early prayers – *'Thank you, but I am a full member of the community now and I must demonstrate my full commitment to my sisters.'* – she had been dragged from a deep sleep by the Matins bell and had almost fallen down the steps of her tower in her attempt to hurry down them by candlelight.

There had been no point in climbing the tower steps again before Lauds and she had spent the short period between prayers dozing in a spare cell next to *Suora* Maria Benigna; a young nun in her thirties, who, it seemed, thrived on the conspiracy. It was from that same cell that she had seen the dawn break just before Prime.

Her first full day had similarly come and gone, gathered in and absorbed by the hourly ritual of the Office. Refreshment after Prime, then more prayers at Terce, with the second half of the morning, usually absorbed by work, but on this, her first day, instead given over to an explanatory walk round the convent. She had found to her relief that the place had none of the terrifying feeling of confinement that had remained with her all these years after seeing the Murate being walled-in. The chapel was tall, light and open; the refectory similarly spacious (although that may to a degree have reflected the fact that a room originally built for a hundred diners now had only fifty nuns occupying the benches).

They had climbed the bell-tower and enjoyed the views to the south, over Fiesole and the City of Florence itself, then returned to the central courtyard, cloistered on two sides and with a light and airy loggia running the length of the third, west side; already gathering the morning light to perfection.

In the centre of the courtyard was a great *cisterna* – a covered well, strong and functional, yet seemingly now unused. The abbess had seen Maddalena's questioning frown and answered her question even before she had asked it. 'We now have a new well. Over there, in that well-house against the north side.'

Against the north wall of the courtyard she had been shown a large, two-storey lean-to shed, from which emanated the sound and the smell of animals. 'It is Michelozzo's great invention.' The abbess had been animated in her pride. 'Not only does the new well have winding gear, but also donkeys to wind up the water from deep below.' She put an explanatory hand on Maddalena's arm. 'As you will imagine, a convent on a hilltop has to face the endless challenge of obtaining water and both of our wells are very deep. But the architect's master stroke was to have the pump bring the water beyond the surface of the courtyard and lift it up to a great tank, high in the roof of that building. It means we can have running water in all of our ground-floor rooms. Isn't that wonderful?'

Maddalena had agreed, and was even more impressed when the abbess took her out into the gardens to show her how the waste water from the kitchens and the washroom was also being saved, for use in the gardens, which were extensive and as well-cultivated as any of those in Careggi or Cafaggiolo.

Noonday prayers at Sext, the sixth hour of the day, were always followed by dinner, now once again taken in near-silence. It seemed that the abbess' interpretation of the Rule of the convent leaned towards the gentle side and civilised whispers were overlooked. The result was a continuous but unobtrusive murmur, which she found calming after the noisy jollity of most of the well-attended meals she had known in the Medici *palazzi*.

After None at mid-afternoon, there was more time for work or contemplation, before Vespers at sunset, and then a light supper before Compline and retiring. Few delayed the benefit of their beds, as already the spectre of Matins was hovering ahead of them in the small hours of the night, before another day began.

Now, it was mid-afternoon on her third day. None was over, and for the first time, she found herself alone in her room, with time to think, about the past and about the future. Both were dangerous. She knew that. Dwelling on the past would only emphasise what she had left behind and increase her desire to return home. And at the moment, thoughts of the future were so overpowered by uncertainty that they were at risk of turning negative. Better to keep busy and not to dwell too long on her predicament. Instead, she decided to complete the process of organising her few possessions in her room.

She had brought little with her. Allowable possessions were specified by the Order, and the list had been heart-sinkingly short. Some holy books were allowed, even recommended, for those in a position to afford them; and provided by the convent for those who could not. Cosimo had purchased lovely new copies of each for her. Her breviary, containing the words for the celebration of the Office, and her missal, containing the spoken parts of the Mass, were already on the tiny shelf beside her bed, together with the new journal which she had as yet not opened.

Cosimo had also wanted her to have a book of graduals, containing the sung part of the Mass, and an antiphony, with the music and chants for the celebration of the Office, but she had demurred. 'You are asking enough of me to enter the convent,' she had told him crisply. 'It is too much to ask me to sing as well. In all the years we have been together, have you ever heard me sing? And in any case, five books will be far too many to declare. How many new nuns do you think arrive at a convent carrying such wealth? I am supposed to fit in there, not stick out like a sore thumb.'

Later, realising from his expression that he had already had them made, and that her rejection had upset him, she had suggested that he present the book of graduals and the antiphony to the abbess 'for the general use of the convent', and to her relief, he had agreed.

She had brought little else; her simple washing things, the few clothes she had arrived in and which she could not bring herself to give to the poor. Lucrezia, ever sensible and not over-given to the acceptance of rules, had insisted she slip three more *camicie* into her chest, in addition to the one she had worn when she arrived. 'They won't be able to tell if you're wearing them under your habit and cold is still cold, even to the pious.' She had said it with such a wicked grin that Maddalena had left them there.

She was still smiling to herself at the memory when she heard footsteps on the stone steps below. Maddalena looked at the door and frowned. Who would climb those stairs except at her invitation? Unless it was the abbess.

There was a brief pause and she found herself listening, her head on one side. Was the visitor entering the storeroom or pausing to catch her breath? The question was answered as the footsteps resumed; this time louder, their sound no longer a flat slap and more a hollow boom. Her visitor must have passed the stone steps, and must now be climbing the final flight of wooden stairs.

Another pause, then a hesitant knock at the door. 'Come in.' Maddalena waited, intrigued.

'Forgive me. I'm out of breath. Those stairs were designed for a younger woman than I.' Madonna Arcangelica leaned against the door jamb and wheezed. Maddalena looked at her, surprised. For the first time, the abbess' controlled serenity had slipped revealing an older woman that Maddalena had believed, and a frailer one.

'Reverend Mother. You look exhausted. Please sit down and get your breath back.'

Madonna Arcangelica nodded gratefully and took the chair beside her. She looked back at the door, realising she had forgotten to close it, and made a weak attempt to rise. Maddalena waved her down and crossing the room, closed the door herself.

Still breathless, the abbess nodded her thanks. 'Those stairs are steeper than I had realised. You should not attempt to descend them in the dark. Might I suggest you use one of the cells below to sleep in between Offices? You would be closer to the others and it would avoid the risk…I'm concerned that one dark night…if your candle fails…' Each sentence was curtailed as she ran out of breath.

Maddalena stiffened. Was the abbess already trying to take her away from this room? The one airy, bright room that could support her sanity on the claustrophobic days?

'Do not be concerned, Madonna Arcangelica. I like this room. It has special meaning for me.'

'Oh, I did not mean in place of…' the abbess wheezed again, still not recovered. 'I am fully aware that this room was made for you and you alone. I was merely suggesting you use it as a day room and, at least while the winter nights are dark and drawn out, you save yourself a great deal of effort by sleeping below. There's a spare cell next to *Suora* Maria Benigna.'

'Yes I…'

Too late Maddalena tried to recover, but the smile on the abbess' face showed she had already gone too far.

'So I believe.' Her breath now fully recovered, she smiled benignly. 'Few details are missed in our little community and I have my informants. The Watch Sister happened to pass by while you were resting there. It's all right. I told her it was my suggestion. As a temporary measure, of course. To become a permanent arrangement it would have to be agreed in Chapter.'

Maddalena nodded, thinking. She had underestimated this place. After the complexities and subtleties of life in the Palazzo Medici, she had presumed that life in a convent would be simpler. But clearly she was wrong. She had forgotten that fifty women with little to do except pray, sleep and eat have too much time for private thoughts, and for the scheming that inevitably arises.

It was clear also, that Madonna Arcangelica felt less than secure in her position as abbess. Had Cosimo's action created difficulties for her? Was there a conflict of interest between his demands (or as he liked to call them, his 'requests') and the Rule of their Order? Had her own arrival caused disruption in this close little community? Already on a number of occasions, she had felt rather like a heavy stone, lobbed into a small and erstwhile tranquil pool.

She considered how she should respond. She did not want to remain an outsider, always closely observed by the informers. What did they call them? The *ascoltatrici*; the 'listeners' who attended every meeting with visitors from outside and listened in to their private conversations.

Nor should she offend the *discrete*, or discreet ones; the elder nuns who formed the governing committee of this place and without whom the slightest proposal for change was almost certainly to be stifled. No. She must tread softly, and get to know how the land lay. Perhaps her first task would be to get to know Madonna Arcangelica better and to try to get her to open up. Somehow she judged the abbess was lonely, and in need of reassurance.

Now she smiled. 'Thank you for that kindness. I must admit I did have to tread carefully on the stairs last night and I frightened myself descending. I shall pursue your suggestion and try sleeping in that cell again. I'm sure *Suora* Maria

Benigna will not mind.'

The abbess' smile was conspiratorial. 'No I'm sure she won't.' Her eyes roamed round the room, although whether checking for unauthorised personal possessions or something to talk about wasn't clear. 'I see you have your breviary. I was so pleased you brought it down with you to prayers.'

Maddalena's eyes strayed across to the three books on the shelf. She had better make sure the journal did not offend any rules. 'Cosimo had it made for me, together with the missal.' Carefully, she took all three volumes from the shelf and indicated the first and the second.

Madonna Arcangelica inclined her head. 'I can see they are beautifully made. Before he left, the Magnificent Cosimo was kind enough to present me with a book of graduals and an antiphony, both bound in similar leather. I was delighted to accept them. Our choir mistress, in particular, will treasure them, I am sure.'

Her eyes were already on the third volume. 'And the other book? It has the Medici crest on it, I see.'

Maddalena opened it, as if seeing it for the first time, and riffled through the crisp blank pages. 'A pristine new book. Also a present from Cosimo. He suggested I use it to write a journal.' She raised her eyes and tipped her head on one side. 'Would that offend the Rule of this house?'

'Would it be a private journal?' Madonna Arcangelica's eyes had closed ever so slightly. Now she looked like a cat watching movements in the grass and waiting to see the mouse itself.

Maddalena considered her reply. 'Hardly. It would be a poor journal if no one else was allowed to read it.' She raised her eyes and looked direct at the abbess, knowing she must respond and willing her to do so.

'Who else would be allowed to read it?' The abbess' fingers were trembling with anticipation.

'Why Cosimo himself. I have promised to read every word to him at his next visit.' As she said the words, Maddalena saw them hit home.

The abbess took a short intake of breath. 'Of course. Who else? At his next visit? When, may I ask, is that likely to be?'

Maddalena knew the ploy had worked. She shook her head, avoiding the question. For all the abbess knew, she would be using the journal to write a regular report to Cosimo about the running of the convent. She could see that was what the abbess thought and feared. Patronage could come, but patronage could just as easily depart. What had the abbess said? *I have my informants.* Well so did Cosimo, and as far as the abbess was concerned, she could be looking at one of them as they spoke.

The abbess sat back, thinking, her eyes straying around the room but apparently finding nothing else to comment upon. Finally, she returned to Maddalena. 'The Magnificent One. You always refer to him by his first name. You are a member of his family, as I understand it? Are you close?'

'I have known him for thirty-six years.' She saw the abbess' eyes open wide as she spoke and suddenly everything started to become clear. 'It's a long time, I know. How long have you been here, in this convent?' She hoped the question was not too bold.

Madonna Arcangelica steepled her thin fingers. The joints were knobbly with arthritis and the veins on the back of her hands stood out blue against the pale, dry skin. 'Thirty-six years! That is indeed a long time. I have to admit I've been here even longer than that. I came here at the age of seven and I am now in my fifty ninth year. Since I entered this building all those years ago, I have never once stepped outside its outer walls. I expect the world has changed somewhat since I last saw it?'

Maddalena heard the voice lift at the end of the sentence, confirming that it was a question and not a statement. Now she was sure where she stood. For now, she was certain that the abbess was indeed lonely, and fascinated by the world outside. But more than that, she also realised that Madonna Arcangelica saw her, Maddalena, as the way to find out about that lost world, and sensed that in order to find out about it, she would be willing to trade insights into her own world; the world within.

Don't hurry. Take your time. The proposal must come from her. Maddalena made herself slow down.

She smiled, as enigmatically as she could, and looked down at the floor, as if lost in thought. 'Fifty-one years! You are right. A long time. Exactly a lifetime in my case, although I did not know Florence in my earlier years. But yes, this world has changed greatly, even in the years I have known Cosimo. So many things have happened in Florence since first we met; some good, others so uncomfortable I find it hard now to make myself recall.'

She raised her eyes, and looked directly at the abbess. 'You asked if we were close. All I can say is that I have hardly been separated from him for all of our years together, and during that period we were close enough for me to bear him a son.'

She paused for effect, awaiting a response. The abbess' eyes opened wide. 'You had a son by The Magnificent One? You bore his child?'

Maddalena nodded, enjoying the moment. 'Yes, Carlo. He was twenty-nine years old in June of this year. He is Canon of the Duomo in Florence, and also Rector of the Pieve di Santa Maria in Mugello.' She paused, as if trying to remember, then nodded. 'Oh, and that of San Donato di Calenzano also.'

The abbess shook her head. 'Carlo de' Medici. Of course. I must apologise. I had not realised that the Canon was your son.'

For a moment, Madonna Arcangelica seemed overawed. She levered herself from the chair and slowly stood upright. 'I must not intrude any longer on your private time. As you will soon discover, there is precious little of it here. Afternoons like this will be ideal for you to commit your thoughts to paper, for the Magnificent One when next he visits you.'

She put a hand on the door then turned again. 'Our Rule states that we should devote one afternoon a week to personal study, but the interpretation of that Rule is in my prerogative. If you wish to do so, you have my agreement to devote your work and study time to your journal on one afternoon every two weeks.'

She paused, as if deciding, then nodded to herself. 'And perhaps, on the alternative weeks, I may join you here? I hope I can make your life here amongst us both comfortable and fulfilling. And in return...' She paused again; perhaps uncertain that she was advancing too fast, but already Maddalena was ahead of her.

'Yes, of course. I will look forward to our conversations. And yes, in return, perhaps I may tell you something of the world I have lived in all these years; the world outside these serene walls.' She tilted her head. 'And if you wish it, I will do my best to answer some of the questions you may have.'

The abbess's smile as she left the room was almost childlike in its contentment.

Chapter 5
First Meeting
Monday, 17th October 1457

'Would you prefer we met in your room, Madonna Arcangelica?' After hearing her laboured steps up the staircase and seeing her face as it appeared round the door, Maddalena was becoming concerned. The abbess was only seven years older than her, but at the moment she looked at least ten years more than that.

Madonna Arcangelica shook her head. 'Nonsense. I won't hear a word of it. It does me the world of good to climb these stairs once a fortnight. Besides…'

The abbess slumped into the chair, and although her face was pale, there was a wicked grin on her face. 'We shall be undisturbed here.' She spiralled her forefinger, pointing downward. 'I get no peace below. I am sure the *vecchie* are ganging up on me. They have never forgiven me for trying to change the interpretation of the Rule since I took office. They seem to think the place should remain exactly as it was under my predecessor; Madonna Cecilia.'

She tapped her nose, letting Maddalena into a secret. 'I think they have agreed a rota, between themselves, to ensure that at least one of them drops in on me every time I have an afternoon of contemplation.' She paused, catching her breath, and then banged merrily with her stick on the heavy chestnut planking of the floor. 'But I'm safe here. None of them can make these stairs.'

She sat back and smiled. That little triumph seemed important to her. She pointed to the folding doors with her stick. 'Do you think we could sit out there, on the balcony, this afternoon? It should be quite warm until the sun goes over the hill, and by then it will be time for Vespers.'

Maddalena jumped at the chance. 'Oh of course. How silly of me. Let me take your chair.' Between them they carried the two chairs onto the balcony and sat, facing each other. Now that she was rested, Maddalena could see urgency in the abbess's face. It seemed she had a question to ask.

'Having met the great man, and discussed affairs with him, face-to-face, I was intrigued by what you described as your close relationship with the Magnificent Cosimo. You told me you had been with him for thirty-six years. How, then, did you first meet?'

Maddalena had been thinking about these meetings and how to prepare for them. She sensed that the abbess saw her as something exotic, perhaps one of the first black women she had ever seen. So if their discussions were to prosper and continue, and Maddalena fervently hoped that they would, then she must be informative but at the same time, she should also maintain the mystery.

'He bought me.'

'He bought you?' In that one short sentence, Maddalena could see that the abbess was hooked. Her eyes opened wide. 'Where?'

Maddalena considered for a moment and decided to tell the whole story.

***

RIVA DEGLI SCHIAVONE, VENICE
3rd June 1421

'Send out the next one.'

She knows it's her turn and takes a deep breath. They push her out, embarrassed and terrified, in front of a small audience of noblemen and merchants, and immediately a thin-faced man near the front reacts. He signals for her clothing to be removed and to her dismay, as she turns in front of him for his inspection, he nods his approval.

The man makes her flesh crawl. He has a nasty, weasel face; without sign of humanity. He speaks a few words to the slave master, pointing to her, and she sees the trader nod in confirmation, signalling what he thinks is her age with his fingers.

Instinctively, she shrinks back, disgusted by him. Surely she will not be bought by this one? Not him. Please God not him.

She had feared from the time the pirates sold her, in the port of Ulqini on the Dalmatian coast, that this would be her destiny. They had singled her out early; the slave trader examining her carefully before he paid for her, and then warning his men not to touch her. 'This one's worth money' he had said.

On the week-long sea voyage to Venice she had been fed well and not put in chains as most of the others were, and as soon as she was separated from the other slaves on the Riva degli Schiavone and sent to the indoor market, the one for the 'personal' slaves, she had guessed what was going to happen. And there was nothing she could do about it. Once separated from your true family, there is no kindness in this world. Just greed and the power of one man over another.

But now, to her surprise, the thin-faced man leaves hurriedly, and she finds she has been withdrawn from the sale. She is fed and bathed once again, but what fate awaits her, she cannot, dare not, imagine.

In the early evening, the man returns; this time with another; a tall, confident-looking man, a noble to whom the thin-faced man defers like a humble servant.

'A sound virgin, Magnificence. Free from disease and, they say, aged about twenty-one.'

Inwardly, despite her fears, she smiles at that. It is a mistake she is used to. As a child she was always tall for her age, and since she was quite young, the taut lines of her cheeks, the high cheekbones and the thin, aquiline nose – have all given her an air of self-confidence that belies her true age. A virgin she certainly is, and, as far as she knows, as free from disease as anyone, but in truth her age is only just fifteen.

Her parents – both Circassian; her father a doctor, her mother a poet – had treated her like a young adult since she was quite small and the children she had been brought up with in Palermo had all been years older. And then, suddenly,

34

her life had changed. In the middle of a long-planned family voyage from Syracuse to Venice, a pirate ship had struck. Both of her parents had been killed in the vicious attack and she, fearing for her own life, had been taken to be sold into slavery in the Dalmatian port.

And now, within a week, here she is, being sold again, this time in Venice and her body soon to be the property of the highest bidder.

Yet somehow, it is at this, the lowest point of her life, that she finds strength. She remembers her father's voice, speaking to her, just before her last birthday; quietly, yet firmly, in the slow reassuring manner that she treasured in moments of uncertainty. *'Remember, Octavia, when faced with adversity, you must address it with confidence. People will accept you as the person you believe yourself to be. The outcome is never entirely of their making, but also of your own.'*

She looks across the room, where even at this moment, these two strangers are haggling over her future, and she realises she has to face reality. She knows, with a clarity she has rarely experienced before, that there is no point in collapsing in tears, or complaining that the world is unfair, because there is no one listening.

The world is unfair, as her parents recently discovered; her father hit in the neck by a boarding axe, falling, gurgling in his own blood not twenty paces before her. At least he must have died quickly. Her mother, seeing his fate, had screamed and run at the men, clawing at their faces with her fingernails. And the leader of the pirates, the tall one with the scar on his face, had flung her over the side with one half-interested flick of his wrist and hardly bothered to turn and look as, screaming that she could not swim, she had sunk beneath the waves, as the ship, captured but still out of control, sailed on.

And she? She had cowered against the strakes of the ship, her face pressed hard against the rough wood, too petrified with fear to do anything but wonder how and when she was going to die.

But she hadn't died. The pirates, their bloodlust sated, had begun to take stock of their prize. Their leader had seen profit in her young body and kept her for the slave market. And as her first mind-numbing fear had begun to subside, she had reached the lonely conclusion that whatever happened to her now, the only person she could rely on was herself.

It is that thought that she clings to again now as she decides, with a steely resolve that surprises her with its forcefulness, that she must face the harsh reality of the world, must make what she can of the situation as it arises; and that the shape of her future, if she has one, depends on the nature of the man who buys her.

With an eye that feels more like a predator's than a victim's, she looks hard at the newcomer, and she senses wealth and power. Even though he is simply dressed; his coat and his cap are scarlet like those of the group of cardinals she saw crossing the piazza, and she can see they are made of the very best materials. He looks old – not as old as her father had been, but perhaps twice her age, perhaps in his early thirties. Already his face is creased with worry and she thinks he is remarkably ugly. He has a long nose and big ears – not unlike the elephants she had seen being unloaded when their ship first reached the harbour in Venice.

Yet at the same time, there is a paradox to this man. Although ugly, his manner is calm and kindly; his eyes are not hungry like most of the men in the room had been, and as he turns and looks towards her again, his eyes appear considerate and thoughtful.

'Will you remove your clothing please? And turn around, quite slowly?'

At least he said please. His manner of speech is soft, and refined, his accent strange to her Sicilian ear – northern, yet not, she thinks, Venetian. She has met many Venetians in Palermo and she knows their way of speech.

It is clear she has no choice but to stand, naked before this man. But perhaps, as her father suggested, she can influence his response to her. Besides, even in adversity, she has her pride. She will not cower in front of him.

She does as he bids and turns, realising, to her surprise, that she wants to please him. She finds herself standing tall, flexing her back so that her breasts lift. She turns, once, then again and faces him once again. And this time she looks him straight in the eye.

He responds, catching her look, almost falters at the directness of her gaze, then smiles and points to her clothes, lying beside her. She continues to look at him, and again he smiles and nods. And she is aware, somehow, that she has won a small victory.

Gratefully, she regains her clothing, and as she dresses she feels herself smiling back. She does not fear him now, as she had expected she would. Nor, for all his age and ugliness, is she repulsed by him. And he, for his part, keeps looking up at her, and although she cannot read his expression, she is sure he is interested.

The noble turns away from the slave master, leans toward the thin-faced man next to him, and starts to speak. He speaks very quietly, under his breath, and she has to strain to hear what he says.

'You were right. She is a beauty. Much better than that other one you brought to me last year. The combination of dark skin and blue eyes is, as you said, particularly intriguing. And that slender figure – entrancing.'

He lifts his head, turns to the slave master, and for the first time she hears him raise his voice. 'How much do you want for her?'

The slave master bows and rubs his hands together, finally sensing an opportunity. 'Ninety-five ducats, Magnificence?'

She cannot believe her ears. The man's courage must have failed him at the last minute. He has let his voice lift, making his reply sound more like a question than a confident proposal. That's not the way to do it. Even she knows that. She wouldn't have answered that way. Not to such a noble. It's all going wrong; she knows it is.

She watches the noble, willing him to respond. Somehow she knows she will be safe with him. But not if this man makes such a hash of the negotiation. Too late! To her dismay, the noble wrinkles his nose, as if smelling something unpleasant, and shakes his head. He does not even bother to reply, but instead, turns away and begins walking towards the door. Her heart sinks.

'I'll take seventy, Magnificence. That's my best offer.' It is clear that after a day of preparation, the slave master can see his opportunity disappearing. It is also clear he has lost his nerve.

The noble and his agent keep walking, and for a moment, she is sure all is lost. Then, as they reach the door, the thin-faced agent turns and lifts a coin bag. 'Forty. Best offer. Take it or leave it.'

Forty ducats! For the second time in minutes she feels rejected; humiliated. So small a price for a human body. It is a lot of money to her; it would have been a year's income for her father, but it seems that the noble, with all his apparent wealth, does not value her very highly after all.

The thin man shakes the bag once and she hears coins chink inside. The slave master hesitates and the noble, still with his back turned, leans towards his agent. 'Too much,' he says. 'She's so skinny she could be a boy. Withdraw the offer before he accepts it.' He is speaking loudly enough now for all to hear.

'Done! Sold at forty ducats and here's my hand on it.' The slave master is running after them, while she still stands on the platform, her fate seemingly in the balance once again.

The agent looks across to the noble, who shrugs. 'Too late now. You should have withdrawn faster, Antonio. Now you have offered and in good faith he has accepted. A deal's a deal, whether on the Rialto or on the Riva. You'll have to pay the agreed price. The Medici Bank has a reputation to maintain. Our word is our bond, here in Venice as in every one of our branches.'

The noble shakes his head, as if regretting the whole episode, and begins walking through the door, in disgust.

To her surprise, she is disappointed; fearing she must have lost him already. There was something strangely seductive about that man. Is she now to go to the thin-faced man instead?

Pulling a resigned face, the agent turns, slaps the slave master's hand to seal the bargain, and gives him the jingling bag. The slave master opens the bag and pulls out a handful of freshly minted coins. She recognises the lily symbol – florins. Accepted anywhere and valued as far south as Syracuse and Palermo. So that explains his accent; he must be a Florentine.

She looks round, wondering what she should do now. The slave master beckons her to join the thin man and she follows him through the door into the sunshine, where, to her relief, his master has not left, but is still waiting; apparently not angry at all, but now with a smile on his face.

'Meet your new master.' The agent dips his head towards the quiet noble. 'This is Cosimo di Giovanni de' Medici, owner of the Medici Bank.' He leans toward her condescendingly. 'The richest man in the world'.

The phrase makes her shiver. She feels herself standing tall and arching her back again. Wealth and power, it seems, are like a great fire; you can feel their glow as you stand before them.

The noble brushes his agent aside and takes her hand. 'And now, I am the owner of you, too, young lady.' He nods, as if satisfied. 'I hope you will prove to be one of my better investments.'

She looks up at him, surprised that she is unafraid. 'But also, one of your smallest, perhaps?'

She sees him frown, and quickly she continues. 'Although it is a great sum to me, for such a man as you, forty ducats must be a tiny investment to make. It seems the richest man in the world values me low?'

He looks down at her and his face breaks into a grin. 'So! You have a fiery temperament. I like that. I have no time for meek women. Do you have a name girl?'

'Octavia Lanza.'

He nods, considering. 'I shall call you Maddalena, after that most characterful of saints.'

He takes her elbow, leans forward and looks at her closely. 'You will be my personal slave. You do know what that means, don't you?' As he says it, he gives her a knowing nod.

She feels a glow of embarrassment and a tingle of excitement at the same time. 'I think so, master.'

He smiles, but now his smile is serious, and his eyes are on hers as he speaks. 'I am sure you do.'

To her surprise, he pulls back and begins looking at her, appraisingly, the frown entering his face one of consternation, not of anger. 'You are not, I think, a typical slave. You seem educated. Can you read, by any chance?'

'Yes, master. And I can write. My father was a physician in the Kingdom of Sicily. Whilst at sea, we were captured by pirates. My parents were both killed and I was sold into slavery.'

She sees him raise an eyebrow. 'Indeed. So your life has recently taken a tumble?'

He looks away from her and then back again, as if finally making a decision. 'So. I may have an additional task for you. We shall be going to Rome. When we reach there, you will live in my house and be responsible for keeping my *studiolo* clean and tidy. But you must understand; it is a place of business. A place of documents. A place of secrets. Only you will be allowed in there and you will tell no one of what you see there in the course of your work. Do you understand? No one.'

Her heart is thumping now. She can only nod her understanding.

'And you must always tell me the truth.' He leans forward as he says it, and she notices that, despite his age, his breath is fresh and pleasant. 'Always. Do you hear me?'

His eyes are penetrating. But still, she thinks she has the measure of him now. She inclines her head. 'As my master pleases.'

His smile softens into a grin. It seems that having made his decision, he is in good spirits. He lets her go and stands back, then points a finger at her. 'As for value. The man was a poor negotiator. I was ready to pay a hundred; perhaps more. He opened too low, and even then, he hesitated.'

His eyes look deep into hers, and he gives a tiny nod, as if in emphasis of what he is about to say. 'Always remember this. It was *he* who undervalued you. Not I.'

Then, to her surprise, he leans forward and strokes her brow. His fingers are soft and gentle, and so now is his voice. 'Never hesitate. When you are with me, in private, say what you believe, and say it confidently. Do you understand?'

She bows her head, but keeps looking at him. 'Yes, master. Whatever you wish, I am commanded.'

She sees a little grin reach the corner of his mouth and decides to press further. She lifts her head and gives a little frown in return. 'And if we are not in private? What then, master?'

For a moment, he considers. 'That's a good question. The situation will arise frequently. I occupy a position of responsibility; a position of authority.' He raises a forefinger, the decision made. 'In public, and in front of my family, you will always respond to the position, and not to me. We have a reputation to maintain; that of the Medici name. You do understand, don't you?'

Again, she bows her head. Not too much. Not so much as to be fully subservient, but enough to show the respect he is clearly accustomed to. Just enough. And then, meekly, she says, 'Yes master.'

The thin-faced agent turns away, hiding his grin, and she knows she has not overplayed her hand. Nearly, but not quite.

'Come then. To business.' Cosimo de' Medici begins to walk away. And she falls into step; two paces behind him, as she has seen the slaves and servants do in Palermo.

***

The candle guttered in the convent cell next to *Suora* Maria Benigna and *Suora* Maddalena realised she had been daydreaming. The conversation with Madonna Arcangelica that afternoon had brought back so many memories. Memories she had thought long forgotten. Memories that had made her want to speak to Cosimo, to say something to him. Now, strictly against the Rule of the Order, she lit her candle and began staring at the first page of her new journal.

That first encounter. So long ago now; but once resurrected, the memories were still so vivid. This would not do. The Night Mistress would soon be round and by then her candle must be out and the smell of smoke dissipated or she would be in trouble. If she was to write anything, she must begin quickly.

Kritsch. The pen scratched awkwardly on the pristine paper and left a blot of fresh ink ahead of the writing. *Suora* Maddalena gasped, and then, recovering, tutted quietly to herself. Her new journal, the very first page, and already a mistake. Pulling the candle closer and tilting her head slightly to the right for a clearer view, she took a piece of soft cloth and with her left hand, ever-so-carefully began to blot the ink away.

She wiped the end of her quill and tried to look at it. Her aging eyes made it difficult to see in the candlelight, but it was clear that the point was damaged and split; she should have been more careful. She had been in too much of a hurry to start.

Taking the sharp little penknife that Cosimo had given to her, she re-cut the nib and, holding it up to the candle, nodded. *Yes, that's better.* Working slowly and now with infinite care, she tried again.

I dedicate this, my journal, to Cosimo di Giovanni de' Medici.

Suora Maddalena looked at her handwriting and smiled to herself. The very name made her happy, and writing it, here in this convent cell, was, literally, an indulgence.

Cosimo, son of Giovanni di Bicci, of the great family of Medici; the greatest man in the world, and the man who had changed her life. She smiled to herself. That had been the first time she had met him; there, in the slave market in Venice. It had been the beginning of a new life for her. A long relationship – thirty-six years.

She looked at the new journal in front of her. Leather-bound, handed to her tearfully by Cosimo himself; one of his last actions before saying his red-eyed farewell. How many of her memories dare she commit to paper? She grinned to herself. Sadly, some of the best would have to be omitted, even though no one but Cosimo would read these pages. But she knew that he, too, would remember.

She would pause until another day before writing more. The journal was too important to hurry. She must think before she wrote. What to write and what to hold back? It was a difficult question; a question that merited some serious thought.

Chapter 6
Be Strong
24th October 1457

Suora Maddalena sat in her room, high in the tower, and wondered what she should do. Cosimo had been very clear in his instructions.

***

PALAZZO MEDICI, FLORENCE
1st October 1457

'I am relying on you, Maddalena. I am sure it is as before. They dare not attack me yet, I am still too strong, but I fear that my enemies are gathering their forces, waiting for me to weaken.' His eyes widen as he describes his fears.

'In the meantime, they are watching my houses, attempting to bribe my servants, and in all probability, already intercepting my letters. Under these circumstances, it really is safer that you should not write to me.'

Perhaps he sees her face fall. Perhaps there is something he is not telling her. Whichever it is, he continues immediately.

'I know how difficult that will be for you, when you are feeling isolated; cut off from the family which has been your life for all these years. I don't know how long it will be before I am able to visit you again, and it is for that reason that I have given you this journal. Write your words to me in here, that they are not forgotten. Then, when I do visit you, I shall be able to sit with you and to read for myself the words you have addressed to me.'

She looks at him and wonders. Wonders if he really means what he says. Their journey up into the hills from Cafaggiolo has, she knows, been excruciating for him; and although he is talking bravely of visiting again, she wonders how realistic his intentions really are, or whether, whilst caressing her with sweet words, he is already saying 'goodbye'.

If so, he maintains the pretence well.

'When I can, I shall try to write to you; letters that I know can be delivered safely, by the hand of a trusted servant. But unless I give you instructions to the contrary, your replies should always be committed to this journal.'

And with those words, he places the leather-bound volume in her hands and kisses it, before kissing her, for the last time, and departing. Her last view of him is his face, already racked with pain before the soldiers reach the first turn in the road beneath her. He stares fixedly at the tuft of hair between his mule's ears and although she wills it so, he does not look back.

Not once.

All that had been three weeks before. But still the memory kept coming back to her; again and again, that same image. Why was it so persistent? What message lay hidden within it?

At first she had been overcome by the disappointment that he had not looked up at her. It felt as if she was of such little importance to him that he had forgotten her within minutes of their parting. But now, as the image returned, it was not for herself that she found she was grieving, but for him.

That was it. That was the hidden message his departing profile had been telling her. It was that look; not towards her, but towards the scruffy tuft of coarse hair between the mule's ears. She tried to put herself in his position. To imagine it was she who was riding the mule back down the hill.

Of course! It was obvious now. He had not been looking at the mule's head at all, but at…nothing. Had she been able to see his eyes at that moment, she would have seen that they were not focused on the present, or on the mule that was carrying him back to Cafaggiolo and eventually to Florence. No. His attention had already been focused on the future – on the fate that awaited him once he returned, as inevitably he must, to the city.

'Be brave, Cosimo. Be strong.'

She heard herself say the words aloud and realised that they were what she wanted to write. She picked up the quill, checked that the nib was not crossed, and dipped it carefully into the inkpot.

Oh Cosimo!

For days now I have sat before this journal, which you, in your thoughtfulness, presented to me, that I might speak to you through its pages…

Maddalena smiled, her decision made. The first of many steps in her long journey now made and her confidence growing already. She had found her voice, the voice with which to address him. Now she would tackle her first subject. Suddenly she realised how frightening she found the task before her. Not the writing; she could write clearly, in a good hand and with few errors when she concentrated. It was the commitment; the finality. The realisation that once she put pen to paper, knowing (or at least hoping) that soon he would visit her, and read what she had written, it would be too late to change anything without spoiling this expensive and beautiful journal.

She paused, placing the quill in its holder, and walked to the window. She had been about to write 'be brave' but even as she dipped her quill in the inkpot, she knew they were not the right words. What was the spectre that was already absorbing his mind, even before he and his retinue had left the convent courtyard? She thought back to what he had referred to as 'the last time' – it was back in May of 1433, when the people had risen up against the Medici and had tried to arrest him.

She had seen him then, running away from the city, stumbling in fear, too terrified to think straight. He had seen the others being thrown from the tower of the Palazzo della Signoria and was sure the same fate awaited him. On a number of occasions, he had woken at night, screaming and clutching his neck, terrified, his legs kicking outward, convinced he was falling to his final, agonising end. Those had been bad days, with the people running wild in the streets of Florence and the Albizzi family baying for his blood.

But eventually he had made himself secure in the fortress of Il Trebbio, not far from Cafaggiolo, and he had begun to recover his nerve. What he had done then had told her a great deal about the inner man, although at the time, she had hardly recognised its significance. He had not returned to Florence and confronted his accusers. No. Instead, quietly, he had looked, first, to the bank and to the family's financial future, and secretly, he had begun to squirrel the money away: Venetian ducats to the value of 2,400 florins, placed in the hands of the Benedictine hermits at San Miniato al Monte. A further 4,700 florins handed to the Dominicans at San Marco for safe keeping.

At the same time, the branches of the bank had been working overnight: 15,000 florins had been transferred from the Florence branch to the Venice branch in one hectic day, and all the securities at their disposal had been transferred from Florence to the papal branch of the bank, in Rome. Even then, Cosimo had known that his financial power and the reputation of the Medici Bank were what sustained the family's political strength, and his first instinct had been to protect them.

Now, it seems with the same happening again, Cosimo's response is likely to be similar. But whatever specific action he decides to take, there is one thing she can be sure of. He will not be brave. He will be careful.

Back then, twenty-four years before, Cosimo had been proved right. He had been recalled to the city, in order, they said, 'for some important decisions to be made'. But they had lied to him; when he reported to the Palazzo della Signoria for their supposed meeting, the captain of the guard had not taken him into the meeting room, but instead had led him to the *alberghetto* a tiny upper room in the tower of the Palazzo, where he had pushed him in and locked the door. And that time, he had told her later, he really did believe he would never see the stairs again.

The fear had haunted him. Already, he had told her, the sweat standing out on his forehead at the very memory, he could feel himself falling, flung from the tower with only one prospect ahead of him; the final, agonising wrench as the rope pulled tight and broke his neck.

'What can it be like?' He had gripped her hands so tightly as he asked the question that she had winced with pain herself. 'That last brief moment, as you feel your neck break? How intense can the pain be? Does the agony remain with you after death?'

She had tried to reassure him, but of course none of them knew. She had calmed him and tried to lead the conversation away to less unpleasant matters.

And despite his fears, that last time he had won. Almost immediately his preparations had begun to pay off. Although his enemies within the Albizzi had pressed hard for the death penalty, other members of the government, friends of the Medici family, and to a man well-bribed, had refused, and instead he had been exiled to Padua, in the Republic of Venice, whilst his brother Lorenzo had been sent to Venice itself. And Maddalena, eventually, had joined him there.

The Medici had survived, and so had their money. And so, at least outside the city of Florence, by then controlled by the Albizzi family, had their reputation.

Maddalena shook her head. Cosimo was not, in reality, a hero, as labelled by the city on his return, but a careful, subtle thinker; a calculator, a balancer of risks, and, above all, a survivor. Now, she was sure, the same mind, albeit older and more tired, would be following the same path again.

How many times had she sat with him, privately, just the two of them, in his *studiolo*, in the room where he kept all his books, where he did his business and maintained the private ledgers of the Medici Bank? She was no casual visitor, for just as he had promised at their first meeting, Cosimo had put her in charge of his private office.

From the first, she had slept there, in a little truckle bed that was pushed beneath the writing table during the day. She and she alone, had kept the room clean and tidy, and slowly, as he grew to trust her, Cosimo had begun to explain the purpose of the books of account, and allowed her to keep them in order. While he worked, she would sit on a small chair in the corner, and listen, and little by little, bit by bit, he had involved her in the workings of his office and given her tasks to perform.

The *studiolo* had been linked to Cosimo's private bedroom by a small corner room, in which he washed, shaved, and performed what he called 'his personal tasks'. His wife's bedroom had been on the floor above, and although he would visit her sometimes, most nights, he would appear through the privy room, in his nightgown, and signal Maddalena, with a jerk of his head, to join him.

In the early years, he had been lusty, drawing her to him in his great bed with a fiery passion, but as the years passed, although the frequency of his summons hardly diminished, its purpose quietly changed. Now, as often as not, they would lie together, he in his long nightshirt, she next to him and always naked, as he preferred, a sheet covering them in summer and a heavy bedcover in winter; and he would talk. He would tell her of his concerns, of his cares and his worries and she would listen and wait. Wait until he proposed a solution, or made a decision. And then she would support him in his judgement, until his confidence was restored and he felt able to sleep.

And then, her task performed, she would return, to her own bed 'in the office'.

That was how she had learned of his latest concerns. He had written to her from Careggi, in the middle of June, telling her to prepare herself for some important news, and she had nervously awaited his return to the Palazzo Medici. On his arrival he had made no mention of the matter, but, as always, had greeted his family, merely nodding to her as to a servant, as he always did in front of his wife.

But then, on that particular night, he had called her in to his bedroom and told her of his concerns. It was, he said, similar to twenty-four years before, but this time, the forces against them were gathering, not directly against him, but in expectation of the weakness that would follow when he could no longer personally wield power. Already he could be bedridden for weeks at a time when his gout and arthritis were bad. But now, month by month, the good weeks were getting shorter.

The problem was that Piero, his eldest son, was nearly as ill as Cosimo, whilst Giovanni, his favourite, seemed to be eating and drinking himself into an early grave. The words had come as no surprise to her. She had seen the three of them on more than one occasion; all in the same bed, trying to talk business, but all in such pain from their gout and arthritis that none of them could think straight.

But even as they tried, the plates of rich food would still be brought to them and the red wine kept flowing – especially to Giovanni. How often had she thought that they were their own worst enemies? As her father had said to her years ago, back in Palermo, he could not prove that rich living, spicy foods or red wine were bad for you in excess, but the fact was, you didn't see many poor people with gout.

She could see it and, in his own way, she knew Cosimo could see it too. The future lay not with the next generation; neither Piero nor Giovanni was truly suited and neither was likely to last much longer than Cosimo. And then what? She knew what Cosimo thought. He put his faith in Lorenzo. The boy had it all; the brains, the style, the competitive instinct, and at the same time, the ability to charm the birds out of the trees. Lorenzo would, in time, be the answer. But Lorenzo was only eight years old. So the family needed time – ten years at least; ten years in which to tiptoe carefully towards the future. And ten years in which the assets of the bank had, once again, to be preserved for future generations.

And so, through July and August, the plans had been laid and the arrangements made. Cosimo had done his part then, and she hers. Now here she was, and all she could do was to wait. But for how long?

And in the meantime? All she could do was pray, talk to the abbess once every two weeks, think, and write. She returned to the desk and sat, taking up her quill once again and checking the nib before dipping it into the ink.

Oh Cosimo!

For days now I have sat before this journal, which you, in your thoughtfulness, presented to me, that I might speak to you through its pages. Yet I could not decide how, or where, to start. Now, as I remember that last, discomforted look as you rode behind the trees below where I now sit, I know what to say.

I shall, indeed, speak to you through these pages.

I shall write as I would speak, and when, with God's blessing, your pain reduces and circumstances allow you to visit me here again, I shall not allow you to read them, but instead, you shall sit in comfort whilst I read them out to you. And in this way, my journal shall not be made into some poor substitute, some replacement for a conversation between us, but instead, it shall be a temporary repository for my spoken words, a resting place, where they may be saved, until that wonderful day comes when they may be resurrected.

On that day, knowing more confidently than reliance upon an old woman's memory would ever allow, what it was I intended to say to you, I shall be able to address you fluently, my words preserved.

Be strong, Cosimo. Even before you brought me here, when, back in the Palazzo Medici, you first explained your concerns and the reasons you had decided upon the need for my confinement, I could see how great were the burdens you faced.

Now I am here, supporting you, knowing how deeply you have assessed the situation and how carefully you have put your plans in place. Have faith, Cosimo, as I do also. You have done the right thing and when your plan is complete, you will have secured the future as well as any man could possibly do.

I await your next visit in confident anticipation, and remain

Your ever-loving,

Maddalena.

Chapter 7
Being with a Man
31st October 1457

'Is it really a month since you first arrived here? How time does fly.'

It was another Monday; already the end of October, and as they were doing with increasing frequency, Maddalena and the abbess had just met once again. This time it was immediately clear that the abbess had a question she wished to ask, and equally clear from her uncomfortable fidgeting that she could not bring herself to ask it.

Inwardly, Maddalena smiled. If their relationship was to grow and then to endure, she knew she couldn't just pour out her life's history. It was necessary to have a little magic; some fascination that brought the abbess back, time after time; like the secret answer to an unstated question. And in a house full of virgins, she was pretty sure she knew the question that was hovering, unspoken. She could see it in the yearning expression and the girlish hesitation, and in response, she was equally sure that she would delay answering it for as long as she could.

Their private discussions had been going well. So well, indeed, that in addition to their fortnightly assignations high up in the tower, they had also begun to have a number of less secretive conversations in the abbess' private parlour. Already they were comfortable in each other's company and their exchanges had not only grown increasingly warm, but had also become more trustful and as a result, slowly, but steadily, more intimate.

At the first of their 'parlour' conversations, no doubt emboldened by the greater familiarity of her surroundings, and perhaps feeling that it was her turn to offer information; the abbess had shied away completely from questioning Maddalena and instead had taken a new tack, explaining how the convent had come to be formed and how it had changed over the years of its long history. By the end, Madonna Arcangelica had grown quite candid and had made a number of direct references to the financial problems the convent had faced over recent years. She admitted quite openly that Cosimo's recent generosity had almost certainly saved the convent from closure and for that, she said, she would be eternally grateful. But all of the time, Maddalena sensed that she was holding back; waiting to discuss another subject that she was not yet prepared to ask about.

Their next conversation had been unplanned; Maddalena had knocked on the door of the abbess' parlour, intending simply to ask a couple of procedural questions about the operation of their Rule, but to her surprise, the abbess, having answered both questions, and perhaps feeling she had paid her way with the previous week's divulgences, had returned to questioning.

But still she remained on safe ground, asking Maddalena how Florence fared and general questions about life in the city; the sort of questions that would have embarrassed neither had any of the *discrete* interrupted them, or indeed, had one or more of the *ascoltatrici* been hovering and performing their duties as chaperones.

Maddalena had rewarded her with a long explanation of the city's recent history, describing some of the personalities that today dominated its governance, its commercial success and its artistic development. Madonna Arcangelica appeared particularly interested in hearing about religious paintings and sculptures and Maddalena found she could hold her entranced, simply by giving details of the latest works by Fra Filippo Lippi and by Donatello.

In the course of the conversation, it was, perhaps, inevitable that she should refer to some of the scandals that both of these artists seemed to attract, and it was while describing how Lippi had run off with a nun from Prato by the name of Lucrezia Buti, (a nun who, it was well known, had recently borne him a son) that Maddalena finally confirmed her suspicions. Beneath her saintly manner, the abbess' secret preoccupation was with the great unknown: the opposite sex.

But whether it was her natural reticence, their joint awareness of the likelihood of interruption, or simply the inappropriateness of discussing such matters in the austere and formal rooms of the abbess' personal quarters, Maddalena had not been pressed for further details and she, in turn, had chosen not to volunteer them.

***

Remembering this, back in the more remote atmosphere of her own room, Maddalena now made polite conversation about the seasons, and the weather, and waited for the question that she knew must eventually come. Finally, the abbess could hold it back no longer. 'May I ask you a personal question?'

Maddalena inclined her head to one side and waited. Not for her to presume what the question was; the abbess must ask it herself. But after years of flirting with ambassadors and clients of the Medici Bank, she could play this game effortlessly. 'By all means.'

The abbess put a protective hand to her face, as if wondering whether its colour showed the heat she felt rising within. It did. Patiently, Maddalena waited.

'What is it like? Being with a man?' As she said the words, she gasped at her own audacity and immediately, with a flurry of words, tried to explain. 'It is the younger nuns. It is a subject that, despite all our teachings and our example, they return to, again and again. They wonder what might have been, in another life; what they may have missed.' She sat back, appearing embarrassed and regretting her outburst, but despite her discomfort, the appetite in her face for Maddalena's reply seemed undiminished.

Maddalena paused. Although expected, the question surprised her in its boldness. It was a good question; a question that could be answered at two levels: in one short, lascivious sentence, or more fully. And as she chose the latter, Maddalena realised that she had, in her own way, been willing the abbess to take them in this direction for some time. The fuller reply would allow her to explain how, having come into her life, Cosimo de' Medici had taken it over and dominated it, and in so doing, had changed it forever. But more than that. Now she realised that in answering the abbess' question, she might also be able to answer the question that had been growing in her mind ever since she had watched him depart. What had been the purpose of her life with Cosimo and what, if anything had been its value?

It was a question that had never arisen during her many years with him. There had, simply, never been the time to ask it. But now, having arrived here at this place of contemplation, with more time to think than she had ever had in her life before, it was a question that kept welling up inside her and which, increasingly, demanded an answer.

She felt herself nod gently, a decision made. She had steered herself into being asked this question and now she would have to address it, as best she could.

'I shall answer your question as fully as I can. It is a large question, and my reply may be a long one. Due to the nature of your question, my reply may frequently tell of things that are beyond your experience, here in this isolated and holy place. But at all times, I shall try to tell you the truth as I see it, simply and honestly.'

She saw the abbess nod in reply and took that as an affirmation of the path she had chosen. 'The question contains many parts and sometimes I may have to ask myself a question, in order to answer. You ask what it is like to be with a man. In my life, I have known only one. With that one man have I shared experiences, hopes, fears, setbacks and despondency, success and elation, secrets, intimacies, affection, respect, and finally, love. That man is Cosimo di Giovanni de' Medici and it is through my life with him that I shall try to answer your question.'

Madonna Arcangelica was watching her thoughtfully. Her face seemed at once to contain relief, satisfaction, and expectation. Maddalena wondered whether the abbess had already realised the unstated question that lay beside her own enquiry and in so doing, if she had recognised the growing self-doubt that had led her to ask it. There was no way of knowing. Madonna Arcangelica's expression was too bland to tell. She said nothing, but prepared herself and sat back in her chair, her hands in her lap, no longer gripping each other in anguish but at rest, as Maddalena began.

'I have told you how we came to meet, when he bought me, on the slave market, in Venice. Within days, we were on the road, travelling to Rome, where at that time, he was running the *Corte di Roma* branch of the Medici Bank. This was a travelling branch, which followed the pope's court wherever it went. During my time with Cosimo it resided in Florence for three years, spent a year in Bologna, and another in Ferrara, and then finally returned to Florence for another four years before going back to Rome. But at the time of which I speak, it was situated in Rome itself, and that is where I went with Cosimo.

'He had rented a house in Tivoli and that was where, despite one of the

Medici Bank staff rules being "thou shalt not keep a woman in the house" he took me. Perhaps they thought slaves didn't count. I was not the first; he already had another there, another black girl, whose name was Tita. It was short for Titania, but what made Cosimo think she was like a daughter of the Titans I cannot think. She looked well enough. In fact she was very pretty, but I soon learned that she was, to use Cosimo's unkind but sadly apt phrase, "memorable in her stupidity".'

Titania. Perhaps he had had great hopes for her when first he bought her, or perhaps he just liked the name. I know he liked to read Ovid's *Metamorphoses* and I think he may have found the name there. In any event, by the time I arrived, she had fallen out of any personal favour he might have bestowed on her beauty, and seemed to spend all her time cleaning and doing menial jobs. To my relief, she was so useless at everything she did that she made me look competent. But nevertheless, she taught me an early and important lesson; that I must create my own future, and I was determined from the beginning not to finish up like her.

'Cosimo gave me my opportunity to advance. He was as good as his word and as soon as we arrived, he showed me his *studiolo*, where he and his branch manager, Bartolomeo de' Bardi, wrote up the books for the Curia branch. It was nominally the branch of the Medici Bank located in Rome, but the reality was that it had one client: THE client – no less than the central governing body of the entire Catholic Church worldwide, including the personal bank accounts of all the cardinals and their administrators. And all of this lay in the gift of one man and one man alone: His Holiness the Pope – whoever he was at that time. Later the relationship soured, but the bank was ever so close to Pope Martin V and his Curia at this time, and for you to understand how my relationship with Cosimo developed, I must tell you a little of how the Medici Bank worked.

'The church had a special need for us. The cardinals, prelates and clerics, as well as Mother Church itself, had revenues flowing in from all over the known world; some from Scandinavia, Iceland and even from Greenland. These were regular and well-known payments and of course it would have been far too risky for them to send money by ship or mule-train, in the form of coin. So instead, they sent letters of credit, drawn on a bank in, or close to their own country, and these were then paid into the church's coffers at the Apostolic Chamber by the Depository General. Although this was nominally a senior officer of the Curia, in some years, officers of the Bank took on the administrative responsibility direct.

So the Medici Bank effectively managed the Church's coffers, which for the reasons I have explained, contained more wealth in the form of credit accounts in foreign banks than it did in gold coins.

'During my time with Cosimo in Rome, and for some years afterward, Bartolomeo de' Bardi was not only our branch manager, but he also held the post of Depository General. Because most of the wealth of the church was in the form of promissory notes or letters of credit, while the monies being paid out in Rome were in coin, it was the function of the Medici Bank to turn paper into real cash. As you might imagine, we were paid handsomely for this service. By discounting the overseas bills at our own exchange rate, we could claim that what we were receiving was exchange commission, and not interest, and in this way, we were able to get round the usury laws.'

Across the room, the abbess gave a little frown.

'I can see you are asking yourself how the bank was able to continue, turning promissory notes into cash and the answer lies in trade. If a church in, say, Lavenham, which is a wool-producing town in Suffolk in England, were required to make a payment to mother church, it would instruct its bankers in London to issue a promissory note and send it to Rome. Here, after taking its due commission, the Medici Bank would exchange that note for good value in coin.

'But then the reverse was true. When a Florentine wool merchant wanted to import English wool from Suffolk to Italy, he would not travel to England carrying sacks of gold florins. Instead he would draw a promissory note from his credit with the Medici Bank and would send that to England. There it would be presented to the wool merchant's bank in London, who would, (again after taking the appropriate commission) provide the merchant with his coin.

'And then, perhaps, the rich wool merchant would deposit some of his profit with the local church in Lavenham, to thank God for his good fortune and to ask the chantry to pray for his soul. And thus, the church's coffers were replenished and the whole process could start again.

'Those were happy days. Cosimo was learning the business and growing rapidly in confidence. He had the ear not only of the clerics and the cardinals but also of Pope Martin V himself. True, he was away from home and from his wife and two sons. As was customary, his wife, Contessina had remained behind at the Palazzo Bardi, the family home in Florence that she had brought to the marriage, first with their son Piero and later also with Giovanni, who was born some months after Cosimo left for Rome.

'But as compensation, he had me, and I was determined to provide all the compensation he needed.'

Maddalena looked at the abbess, who seemed to have been dozing during the description of the workings of the Medici Bank, but whose eyes had suddenly widened. 'You mean you...? You and he...?' Somehow, Madonna Arcangelica couldn't bring herself to complete the sentences.

'Lay with him? Of course. Regularly. Perhaps I should say frequently. In fact, pretty well every night. As I told you, I was his compensation and I was determined to satisfy him. Rest assured, Reverend Mother, I had no intention of scrubbing floors and carrying wood to the kitchens as Tita was doing by that time.'

The abbess sat up, with a look of admonition on her face. 'But to give your body to him? Outside marriage? That sacred thing...'

Maddalena shook her head. 'Please! You do not understand. You make it sound like a callous decision made after weeks of carefully considering the moral issues; the pros and cons. But it wasn't like that. Not like that at all. When you reach rock bottom, you find yourself in a place unlike any place you have ever been or even contemplated before. A place of abject and utter loneliness. At such a moment, you really do have to decide; are you going to drown, or are you going to fight? It is primal; instinctive: violent in its raw immediacy.

'I had watched both my parents being killed in front of me and had found myself clinging to the rough wood of the ship's deck, snivelling with terror. At that moment, I thought I had only seconds left, before I too had to face the pain of violent death.

'But I was lucky. I clung to life. A life of sorts: one of being sold into slavery. I had no idea what pain or degradation faced me in the future. But I realised one thing; that I was on my own. I decided I must take my father's advice and do what I could to save and protect myself. And in so doing, it was clear to me that the niceties of married life were no longer available to me as I had once expected them to be.'

She shook her head, searching for adequate words. 'Once you decide to fight, you start looking for weapons. I had nothing but my body and my education. They were all I had.'

She lifted her head and looked hard at the abbess, willing her to understand. 'If you are left with nothing, you don't waste what little you do have.'

She saw the abbess put her hand to her mouth 'I apologise. You are, of course, right. I had no idea what it must have been like.'

Madonna Arcangelica sat, looking at the floor, perhaps trying to visualise the events she had just heard described. She looked up. 'Did you hate the pirates? The ones that killed your parents and sold you off?'

'Hate them? Surprisingly, no. In a strange way, in my predicament, I felt close to them. I saw them simply as poor men; men with almost nothing. I thought perhaps they too had no choice; that they were simply trying in their own way to survive, to make a living of sorts along a rough and inhospitable shoreline.

Opposite her Maddalena watched the abbess sitting, thinking, shaking her head. 'And you were so young.' Then she took her hand from her mouth and leaned forward. 'He didn't hurt you?'

Maddalena shook her head. 'Cosimo? Never. From that first night – on the day he bought me, he never hurt me. Instead he was kind, and thoughtful, and gentle.'

Maddalena saw the abbess's mouth open and close and guessed that inside, she was willing her to continue; to go into the details of their lovemaking. It suddenly dawned on her that during all the years the abbess had been in this place, she might be the first person who could really answer her questions; the private questions that any normal innocent woman, pious or otherwise, must sometimes ask herself.

What could she tell her? How could she explain how it had been? How it had felt? The first time, for example.

***

52

GRAND CANAL, VENICE
3rd June 1421

'Yes here. This is it.'

The gondolier leans on his great oar and the boat turns in its own length, leaving a swirl of turbid water beside it in the Grand Canal. He straightens up and leans the other way, and the gondola, with just enough impetus left to complete the manoeuvre, slides alongside the *molo* and stops exactly midway between the tallest of the red and white spiral-painted poles.

Cosimo sits back while servants run to secure it, front and back, and reach willing hands to stop it rocking. As soon as it is still, he climbs out onto the pier and reaches a hand back down to her.

'Come on. This is where we live. At least, while we are here in Venice. In a few days we shall leave for Rome, but for the time being, this will have to do.'

Have to do? Maddalena (she'll never get used to that strange name) looks up at the building. It's huge; a palazzo. It must be one of the biggest. There's a great door standing open and inside what looks like a warehouse, with bales of wool, stacked high on wooden pallets, presumably to keep them clear of the water, which even at three-quarter tide laps dangerously close to the top of the *molo*.

If the tide rose another two feet she thinks *the water would flood in and then those pallets would be needed. Why do these Venetians live so dangerously close to the water?*

A servant helps her out of the gondola and she follows Cosimo across the limestone floor and up the wide stone staircase beyond it. They reach the first floor. 'This is the *piano nobile* – where we spend much of the day and where, unlike my friend Ugolino, the wool trader who owns this house and works below, I do much of my business.'

He points across the room. 'It's a convenient arrangement, which suits us both. You don't need much to be a banker. Just a green-topped table and a reputation.' He laughs; the first time she has heard him do so. 'It's easy really. Two ducats to make the table, and perhaps a hundred thousand ducats to build the reputation.'

She's not sure she understands the remark, but it's clear she's expected to laugh, so she does. The room is huge; like a ballroom, with paintings on the ceiling and on three walls and between them, mirrors, throwing light everywhere. Bright, yellow light from the enormous windows which run the whole length of the fourth side of the room. She walks to the nearest window, opens it and looks down at the water of the Grand Canal. The sunlight sparkling from little wavelets hurts her eyes and she turns back again, entranced and overcome.

He takes her hand and leads her through a door, and up a smaller staircase, to the floor above. A small bedroom, cosy but somewhat dark after the room below. 'You will sleep here.' He points to the little bed in the corner. *My own clean, dry bed.* A great wave of relief floods over her.

But then, almost immediately, she finds herself regretful, as if mourning some loss, and she realises that despite his age and her lack of it, despite his apparent experience and her innocence, despite her fear of the act itself, she is disappointed. Throughout the journey in the gondola, she has been preparing herself; tensing herself in expectation that this noble; a married man by his own admission will take her to his house, carry her to his bed and…after that, she has not been clear, but she has been preparing herself for it.

Now, to her surprise, her initial sense of relief has turned to a feeling of rejection; the fear she had felt already banished, the shame of being turned away, greater by far than the expected shame of being taken by another woman's husband.

Cosimo sees the sequence of expressions on her face and seems to understand. 'Come.' He takes her hand and leads her through another door, into a room somewhat like the room below, although less than half the size. It's bigger than any room she has ever been in until today and as on the *piano nobile*, the light floods in through a wall of windows overlooking the canal.

He sees her looking at the great bed at the other end of the room and squeezes her hand. 'How old are you? Truthfully?'

'Fifteen.'

'Will this be your first time?' Imperceptibly, he pulls her towards him as he speaks.

Instinctively, she knows this is another of those moments her father used to talk about. She tilts her head up to him and leans forward, arching her back. 'Yes it will. You'll have to teach me.'

The expression on his face is tender, understanding. 'I will. I'll be gentle.'

***

Staring out from her balcony, over the valley, lost in her memories, Maddalena turned, looked at the abbess, and saw she was staring back at her. For a moment she could not understand why, but then realised that this time, it was she who was covering her mouth, and tapping her fingers absent-mindedly, as if not trusting her lips to describe the vivid images that were streaming through her head.

Such images. Such memories. Cosimo had been kind to her on that ridiculously sunny afternoon. She remembered how his expression had softened, as he explained exactly how it would be, when they reached his palazzo in Rome. How her room would be close to his, as was the little room here. How he would call for her when he needed her, how she would go to him, in his room, and how he would take her into his great bed, and make love to her, always with kindness and understanding, and not, as he said 'as a beast'. And afterwards, he told her, she would return to the next room to sleep alone.

She had murmured her understanding. She had nodded her red-faced acceptance, and then, in the late afternoon, with the sun still streaming in through the window, the curtains still open and moving in the breeze, the sound of the boatmen calling on the canal below, he had taken her.

And he had been gentle. And he had been understanding. He had, she remembered with an almost uncomfortable clarity, been kindness itself, even removing his own clothing first and allowing her to look at him, to touch him, before encouraging her to remove her own.

One promise he had not kept. She had not been sent to the adjoining room to sleep alone in that tiny bed. Instead, he had kept her. She had not left his bed until beyond dawn the following morning, when they were driven down by hunger of a different sort. By the time they breakfasted, the shy, virginal child had become a knowledgeable and confident woman, and the master of the slave had become her lover, at least in the privacy of his own, great bed.

Three times he had taken her: the first carefully, seemingly holding back, as if afraid of hurting her.

The second had been in the middle of the night. She had lain still, her head full of thoughts, while he had slept, his face soft and guileless, like a baby's. Some time later, in the dark, when most of the boats had gone and her thoughts were drifting comfortably in the warmth of the cosy bed, lulled by the slap, slap of the waves in the canal below, she had sensed his wakefulness and, reaching out, drawn him to her.

This time her response had been more confident, arousal replacing fear of the unknown, and recognising this, he had given way more fully to his passions, his urgency greater; less controlled and, to her surprise and amusement, his efforts considerably noisier.

They had both slept then, until woken by the sounds of the fishermen arriving at first light to sell their wares at the Campo della Pescheria, across the canal. This time he had shown the initiative, teasing her into losing all semblance of modesty, by throwing the bedclothes to the floor, his arousal no secret in the dawn light. They had tumbled together playfully, drowsily, she exploring, he responding, but then, as the power of her position became clear to her, she began to hold back, to tease him, and as she did so, his desire for her – his need for her – increased, and she knew, already, that the rules between them had changed.

They had not stayed long in that great house by the water. Within days, they were on the road, travelling to Rome, and his responsibilities at that branch of the Medici Bank. The journey had been long and arduous. Discomfort and lack of opportunity had kept them apart until they reached Rome and his home-from-home for the next two years. But that was another part of the story. A part yet to be told.

But now was not the time. It was still too soon; too soon for Madonna Arcangelica and too soon for her. Instead, for the time being, she would steer her away, onto safer ground.

'You asked what it is like to be with a man. I can tell you that from time to time, it is many things. When they are powerful, and successful, yet understanding and generous, it can be a great comfort. A strong man brings a feeling of protection. But when they are involved in battles, or political intrigues, they can be a source of deep-seated fear, as you face the prospect of losing everything. When they share their hopes and fears, their thoughts with you, the feeling of inclusion can be like the summer sun coming out. But when they ignore you, or hold you distant from their activities, it feels like being pushed out alone from a warm house into a freezing winter's night. The courage and vision of a good man can be inspiring, yet his endless untidiness can be a source of demoralising frustration.'

The ploy was successful. The abbess smiled, nodding. These were concepts she could understand and their very contradiction seemed to give them verisimilitude in her eyes. 'I can see it must be wonderful to have a strong man close to you at all times. It has been my own source of comfort for all these years, for I know the Blessed Jesus is always there, beside me. Ever since I was thirteen and had the visions, he has always been there. He has never left me.'

Maddalena looked at the beatific smile on the old abbess' face and was pleased for her. Few seemed able to believe so absolutely. Including her. But the lack of faith that she felt creeping up on her was not her faith in God, but that in Cosimo, and his true motivation and intentions.

Chapter 8
Keeping a Man
31st October 1457

'Was The Magnificent One always at your side? He never left you?' Madonna Arcangelica leaned forward as she asked the question.

Maddalena smiled to herself. She crossed the room and opened the little chest on the shelf beside her bed. For the first few weeks, she had left it inside her great chest, covered by clothing, because she knew that strict interpretation of the Rule would not allow a nun to keep personal possessions, lest they remind her of her life before, and cause her to question her faith and her enclosure. But as the weeks had passed, and the abbess' relaxed interpretation of the Rule had become clear, she had gained the confidence to take out the little chest, and even, on occasion, to open it and to read one or two of the letters she kept within. His letters. Cosimo's letters. Mostly written when he was away, to announce his intended return, and therefore comforting in their memory. But the letter she sought now had been quite different.

She had received it in Tivoli, right at the end of their stay there. Cosimo had returned to Florence on business and she had been alone amongst his temporary household, on the outskirts of Rome. And then the news had come.

Maddalena,

You will remember our discussion. Now it is decided. I shall, after all, be returning here to Florence to manage all the affairs of the bank from this house. I have appointed Bartolomeo de' Bardi to act as my General Manager, and he will establish himself in his new position in Rome within the next month.

I shall come back to Rome, to ensure that Bartolomeo is fully established in his new responsibilities, and then, perhaps after a further month, I shall return permanently, here, to Florence. You will accompany me on that journey and continue your duties as before, but this time, here, in the Palazzo Bardi.

In preparation for the intended changes, please ensure that the books and ledgers of the Rome branch are carefully separated from those of the holding company, and especially the Libro Privato, which, as you know, is for no one's eyes but my own.

Cosimo de' Medici
Palazzo Bardi,
Florence
Dated this 7th September 1423

Maddalena smiled at the abbess. 'Please excuse my rudeness. Your question took me back to events many years ago, and I wanted to refresh my memory before replying. After staying in Rome with Cosimo for just over two years, he returned to Florence and soon decided that he would remain there and that I should join him and would live in the family home. This is the letter Cosimo sent me to tell me what was about to happen.

'Reading the lines again, I can remember oh so clearly the chill that his words sent through me, because he was telling me that from that time onward, I should have to share him. Somehow, I had never faced the reality that one day he would return to his wife. Now here it was, in his own hand, and written with such blithe promises. But despite Cosimo's position of power and his all-encompassing charm, this time, I could not believe his comfortable assurances. And in my heart of hearts I wasn't sure he did either.

'How could I live in the same house as Cosimo and his wife without losing the special place I had established during our stay in Rome? *It is a good house and you will find the arrangements similar to our house in Rome* he wrote. *You will enjoy life here. My wife, Contessina, and my sons, Piero and Giovanni, will welcome you as one of the family.* These were his very words. But try as I might, I could not make myself believe them.

'The difficulty was, as Cosimo had told me, the family lived in the Palazzo Bardi, one of a row of palaces built over the years by the Bardi family. The whole street was, he said, still a Bardi family enclave. He had talked about it on a number of occasions. "Via de' Bardi, in Oltrarno" may have sounded grand, but Cosimo did not like it. In his mind, it seemed, the house was not truly his, and lying as it did, between other Bardi *palazzi*, it was dominated by Contessina's family.

'You may not remember the area, Reverend Mother, but it had once been mean and dirty; years before, the road had gained the name of *Borgo Pidiglioso*, or Flea Lane, and Cosimo was uncomfortably aware that the enemies of the Medici still referred to it that way. It was hardly an address that enhanced his reputation.

'Now all I could see ahead of me was a life like Tita's; cleaning the kitchens, scrubbing the floors, remaining downstairs by day and sleeping up under the roof in the hot and clammy servants' rooms by night, while my beloved Cosimo – oh yes I was deeply in love with him by then – led his separate life with his noble wife and his children, and surrounded by her relations, living on either side.

'It was one of the really low points in my life. I had been torn from a loving family by pirates and sold into slavery. I had fully expected to be violated by rough men, but instead I had become the lover of the richest man in the world. I had progressed in his estimation during that time in Rome, and as I did so, my responsibilities had grown. Soon I was not only cleaning and tidying the *studiolo* and fetching and putting away the great ledger books, but actually writing the entries into the ledgers myself. Cosimo checked them, of course, but nevertheless, I was trusted, and I was useful.

'Within months, Cosimo began to let me talk to the clients as they visited the house and waited for his attention. Clerics, bishops, cardinals; they all came and soon I came to know them and they came to know me. Yes, it is true I flirted with them, and why not? It does not take long to recognise when a cardinal cannot take his eyes off your bottom and when he does, well, why not pretend that the ledgers you need require you to lean right over the desk, immediately in front of him?

'By the second year, they were coming early for their appointments, just to talk to me. Even Pope Martin V came in person, three or four times. He was the lewdest of them all and I had to work hard to stop him fondling me. But Cosimo turned a blind eye to it all. He said if I didn't mind, then neither did he, and Bartolomeo de' Bardi happily followed his example. By the time we had to leave Rome, Bartolomeo had even started to allow me to make the deposit entries into the Deposit Book, not for everybody, but for a number of cardinals who knew me well and trusted me to do it properly. And now, in one short letter, it was all about to disappear. Everything I had worked for seemed to be on the brink of collapse.'

'And did it? When you arrived in Florence, was it really as bad as you had expected? Or was the Magnificent One able to keep his word?' Madonna Arcangelica was clearly keeping up and had not lost interest.

Maddalena cast her mind back. Frightening how the memories fade.

***

PALAZZO BARDI, OLTRARNO, FLORENCE
8th October 1423

'Cosimo?'

'Yes, my little one, of course. What is it?' Cosimo gives her his most indulgent smile.

Maddalena judges his mood carefully. It's the look he reserves for the privacy of the *studiolo*, when things are going well; which is most of the time. In public and in the body of the house, he treats her coolly, as just another one of the servants. But here, in the privacy of the banking rooms, their relationship is entirely different.

***

'It's for your own protection, Maddalena,' he had explained yesterday, after a small but uncomfortable disagreement. 'If I were to act familiarly in front of the family, as I do here in the privacy of the *studiolo*, it would embarrass them and there is always the risk they might resent you. If they did, your life here could be quite uncomfortable, and we don't want that, do we?'

It was a bad time of the month, she had been feeling stubborn, and she had taken a chance. Instead of accepting what he said and leaving it at that, she had answered his question with a question of her own. 'When you say the family, you mean your wife?'

'Not just my wife. Others too, might consider it inappropriate.'

Immediately, he could see by her expression that she didn't believe him. He stopped pretending, and admitted she was right. 'Very well, yes, Contessina, especially, sees you as a threat.'

'Because I am your mistress as well as your slave? Because you take me to your bed and make love to me? Because I arouse passions in you that she...'

'Stop it Maddalena. Don't ever talk like that.'

He had raised his finger then, but God be praised he had not admonished her further. Here in the office, he still treated her as a child, with much to learn. Since their arrival, he had been generous and understanding; even allowing her to make mistakes; small social mistakes, from time to time. But never the same mistake twice. 'Once is learning; twice is stupidity,' he had said and she had never fallen into that trap again.

But yesterday she had come close to getting it wrong. He had stopped her in her tracks, with his finger wagging gently. 'Listen. I shall not repeat this. The position we are in here; you, me and my family, it is a delicate one and we must all be careful to make it work. That involves an unspoken agreement.'

She had watched the finger wag twice and known it was time to listen. 'You will never compare yourself to my wife and I shall never openly admit to her that I sleep with you.'

But surely...? She had thought the words and even opened her mouth, but he had not allowed her to utter them.

'No.' He had been adamant. 'Don't say anything else. Contessina understands. Of course she does. She is very far from stupid. But it is understood between us that whatever I may do with you in the privacy of these banking rooms, I will never rub her face in it, never openly admit that I sleep with you and never show you kindness in public, because that might embarrass her and that I shall never do.'

***

The lesson is still ringing in her ears, and is the reason she approaches her question with some trepidation. Because today, once again, she wants to ask a question about Contessina.

It's two weeks now since she responded to Cosimo's instructions and travelled with him from Rome to this, his family home in Florence. He calls it his home but she knows he does not feel truly at home here. Because it's not really his house. It's a Bardi house; brought by his wife to the marriage as part of her dowry, located in Oltrarno, literally across the Arno River, on the south side, and deep in the old Bardi enclave.

Still, in many respects, Contessina's house. And Contessina has been twice as bad as she had expected. Maddalena is now seventeen and Contessina almost twice her age – only a couple of years younger than Cosimo, and she's huge. She's not just fat – although bearing two sons has obviously plumped her up a bit – but large; broad in shoulders as well as hips. She sails round the *palazzo* like some great ship, her ornate gowns inflated like sails. Being so large, and wearing stout leather shoes (no doubt, Maddalena thinks, to prevent her ankles from swelling any further) you can always tell when she is coming; her great clumping footsteps on the stone floors precede even her low, booming voice.

Her true name is Lotta, but everyone calls her Contessina. And that's one of the questions Maddalena wants to ask.

'I hope you don't think me impertinent, and I do not intend to be so, but why do you refer to your wife as Contessina when you call her Lotta to her face?'

To her relief he smiles. 'My wife's given name is Lotta, but we all call her Contessina – the little Contessa; as a sign of respect and in recognition of the fact that her father, Alessandro, was Count of Vernio.'

Maddalena nods, disappointed. *I got that wrong.* She had convinced herself it was a joke – a double joke, partly to reflect Contessina's rigid adherence to what she called 'The Standards of Nobility' (a phrase she seems to use with monotonous regularity, even though, as Cosimo keeps mentioning, she has married into a family which takes a public pride in being *popolari* or commoners), and secondly, the diminutive, used simply because she is so huge.

She knows her other question is a delicate one, but she must ask it, if only to clarify the security of her position in these rooms. She is never sure whether one day, Contessina will come sailing into the *studiolo* unannounced.

'Why does she never enter these rooms? Does she have no interest in banking?'

Cosimo looks at her closely and she realises that he has guessed the reason for her question. Perhaps that is why he seems willing to answer it.

'On the contrary, Contessina is from a banking family. The Bardi Bank has been internationally famous, and a hundred years ago, was considered one of the "Three Pillars of Christian Trade", together with the Peruzzi and the Acciaiuoli banks. But banking, as I have told you before, has always been a risk business, especially if you begin to lend to kings and warriors. All three of the banks I have mentioned made the same mistake and all three failed at about the same time. Her own family bank was brought down by the unwillingness of the King of Naples and Edward III, King of England, to repay their debts. Never trust kings: they think the obligations of honour only flow in one direction.

'Contessina has been brought up in the tradition of *masserizia*; the "quality of shrewd economic management" which has been the creed of her careful family.'

He grins proprietorially. 'She will wring the neck out of every florin in her housekeeping budget. For that reason, we have divided our responsibilities. I look after the bank and have these few rooms as my private empire, where I can remain undisturbed by daily family life and concentrate on business. My wife, meanwhile, runs the household and has the whole of the rest of the house as her domain. And very well she runs it too.'

Maddalena nods, her question not entirely answered. She considers repeating the question, but dare not.

As if to come to her rescue, Cosimo continues. 'I leave her to run the household and look after the family and she and the children give me the privacy I need to manage the affairs of the bank.'

He nods conspiratorially. 'The absolute privacy I need.'

A pause, then he begins to smile. 'Does that answer your question?'

As if to prove the point and without waiting for her reply, he takes the top button of her *gamurra* and undoes it. With his eyes on hers, he runs his finger down to the next button and slowly begins to undo that too.

***

Maddalena smiled at the abbess.

'So yes, in answer to your question, Cosimo did keep his word, although it required the whole household to be turned inside out for it to happen. It didn't take me long to recognise that Cosimo and Contessina were like chalk and cheese; complete opposites. Whilst she was in the kitchens, ensuring the cooks did not waste anything, in the room above, Cosimo would probably be talking to Donatello about creating a grand new sculpture, in pursuit of his own, completely opposite policy; that of *magnificentia*.

'But make no mistake, strong a character as Contessina was, and respectful of her position as Cosimo remained, he was careful to arrange his affairs in such a way that he got exactly what he wanted. And that, I am pleased to say, included me.'

The abbess smiled, benignly. 'So you survived?'

Maddalena nodded. 'It was that difference between them that gave me my opportunity. I soon accepted that while Contessina ruled the house, she played no part whatsoever in the management of the bank or in the affairs of state in which Cosimo was becoming increasingly embroiled. My answer was clear; I would concentrate my attention on Cosimo's *studiolo*, on the books of the bank, and, if he would let me, on talking to the bank's clients. The bank, I knew, was where his heart was, and that was precisely the place where I wanted to be.

'So that was what I set out to do. It was only after about a week, when everything seemed to be falling into place with remarkable lack of difficulty, that I remembered what Cosimo had said in this letter.' She picked up her copy of the letter and read from it, aloud.

'*…You will accompany me on that journey and continue your duties as before, but this time, here, in the Palazzo Bardi.*

In preparation for the intended changes, please ensure that the books and ledgers of the Rome branch are carefully separated from those of the holding company, and especially the Libro Privato, which, as you know, is for no one's eyes but my own.'

She looked up. 'Clever Cosimo. He had, of course, worked it all out, even before writing to me. He had realised that bringing a young black slave into the family home would drive Contessina to despair, and so it did. But by emphasising my position as part of the bank, by setting me up in the *studiolo*, (which as far as I recall, Contessina never did enter in all the years I was with them) he kept us separate; one in one part of his life and the other in the other part.

'It wasn't always quite as easy as he had perhaps hoped. I ate with the family and lived amongst them, as did an increasing number of visiting artists, poets, philosophers and men of ideas who happened to be passing through the city. Contessina accepted her burden with resignation, and was always civil, but the atmosphere was at times brittle, especially when the house was full.

'For all her limitations, and I soon learned they were greater than Cosimo had acknowledged, he was careful to respect his wife, at least in public, and he never placed her in a position of embarrassment. His *studiolo* (where once again he placed my bed) was in a separate wing of the house and his personal bedroom was next to it. His wife had her own, much grander room, in another wing. Between Cosimo's bedroom and the *studiolo*, and joined to each by a small door, was his *bagno*, which was both his "house of easement" and his washroom, and it was through there that he would call for me in the evenings. In that manner, Cosimo could maintain the pretence that I was just a slave, working for the bank and keeping his private papers in order, and Contessina could save her blushes by appearing to accept that fiction as the truth.'

Maddalena sat back and smiled. It was a weary smile, partly driven by long since happy memories, and partly by memories of unhappiness, whose wounds the intervening years had only partially healed.

'And that was how you continued?' Madonna Arcangelica had her professional, benign smile on her face, which suggested she was, once again, hiding a response or suppressing a question. Perhaps, this time, she was simply suspending disbelief, for only those who had known Cosimo, experienced the power of his position and his money, and felt the dominance of his personality, would understand how such a transparency could have been made to work.

Maddalena put her letter back into the casket and as she did so, noticed the next, lying beside it. In an instant, more thoughts flooded back. 'Yes. That was how we continued. Until my son, Carlo came along.'

'Your son. Of course. A somewhat public refutation of the pretence.' The abbess appeared about to ask another question, but then she noticed how the light was fading. Soon the Vespers bell would ring and they would have to descend those steps more rapidly than she liked.

'I am sorry, *Suora* Maddalena, but we have run out of time. Your son, I fear, will have to wait for next time.' She rose to her feet and winced as a stab of pain ran up her back. She rested, holding the back of the chair for support, as opposite her, Maddalena was also taking her time. *Two old ladies, with more behind us now than in front* Maddalena thought.

The thought seemed to strengthen her bond with her guest. *Suora* Maddalena held open the door and the abbess crossed the room. As she reached the door, she paused.

'Thank you Sister, as always, for the clarity and the candour of your answers to my questions. Sometimes they must seem very naïve to one so experienced in the ways of the world.'

She turned back towards the door, and then paused again. 'I have enjoyed this conversation. With your agreement, I should like to continue, over the coming weeks. But I am aware that the world you are describing is so far from my experience that I no longer even know what questions to ask. But you do. You understand the nature of the void within me, I think. You know the questions I would ask, if only I knew them. So perhaps in future, we could dispense with the formality of questions from me, and you, if you would be so kind, can take me straight to the answers.'

Maddalena bowed her head in liking and respect. Despite the enclosure of so much of her life, Madonna Arcangelica had courage, sincerity, gravitas and a deep human generosity. She put a hand on the abbess' forearm and squeezed it.

'With the greatest of pleasure, Madonna. You will have deduced by now, that in replying to your questions, I am also addressing a question of my own; whether my life has had any real meaning and value and whether, in pursuing it, I have acted honestly, truly and with respect for others.'

Madonna Arcangelica smiled. In the cross-light, her eyes alternated between hazel and grey, but always calm, dignified and sincere. She nodded, swiftly, dismissively, just once. 'At our age, that is a natural question to ask ourselves. Let us keep meeting. Somehow I think it does us both good.'

Maddalena patted her arm and nodded back. 'I too, would like to continue. From next week, we shall continue as you suggest; without need of questions.' She closed the door as they passed through and they began the steep climb down the stairs towards the easier stone steps below. Any later and they would have needed a candle.

Chapter 9
Carlo
7th November 1457

'Two weeks ago, on the last occasion we sat here together, and just as the light was fading, I mentioned my son, Carlo. Let me now tell you something about him.'

Suora Maddalena looked to the abbess for confirmation and Madonna Arcangelica put her hands together in agreement and encouragement; her expression a picture of anticipation.

'I had been living with Cosimo in Florence for about four years, and everything had settled down. Contessina had her empire and I had mine, and apart from mealtimes, our paths rarely crossed. Her two sons were growing; Piero was twelve and little Giovanni – the imp – was seven. Contessina did her best to keep us apart, but boys will be boys and the more she discouraged them from talking to me outside her presence, the more they wanted to do so.

'Piero was awkward in my company; always seemingly conscious that being found talking to me might result in his mother's disapproval. He had developed all the mannerisms of a nervous boy; one who is uncertain about life and his place in it. He adored his father, but held him in such high regard that he was almost dumb in his presence. Somehow I think their relationship always suffered from Cosimo's absence in Rome during Piero's formative years. Piero was not quite four when Cosimo left for Rome and was nearly seven by the time he returned. He always seemed to try too hard to please his father and in so doing, never quite succeeded.

'Giovanni was quite different. He must have been conceived immediately before Cosimo left and was born while he was away in Rome. He was a mother's boy; spoiled and indulged and he assumed (quite rightly, as it turned out) that everyone would love him whatever he did. He was a natural imp; relaxed where Piero was stiff, funny where Piero was serious, and gregarious where Piero was reclusive.

'Love Piero as Cosimo did, his high expectations for his eldest son brought out the worst in the boy. For a man who was slow and careful in coming to decisions, Cosimo was remarkably intolerant of hesitation in others. He became increasingly exasperated by Piero's stuttering rigidity and as Giovanni grew in confidence and character, the comparison put Piero in a progressively worse light. Where Piero would wait in the doorway to a crowded room, unsure what to do next, Giovanni would run straight in and jump into his father's lap with a wild giggle.

'Like many younger sons, Giovanni was afraid of no one, least of all, his mother. Oh of course he loved her, in his own way, but over the years, her attempts to favour Piero, not only as her first born, but also to try to compensate for his awkwardness, fed Giovanni's independent spirit, and as far as he was concerned, if his mother wanted his affection, it would be on his terms.

'As he grew older, he began to play the same game with his father. Realising Cosimo's frustration with Piero, and knowing that as second son, he had nothing to lose, he played up to him mercilessly.'

***

CASA VECCHIA, VIA LARGA, FLORENCE
3rd November 1427

'I'm going to be lonely without him.'

Cosimo is staring out of the window, but Maddalena knows he is not looking at anything in the street. Not looking at anything outside his head. Instead, he is looking back, to his childhood.

She's seen this face before; when he takes on that lost look and becomes maudlin. Now, with Giovanni di Bicci on his deathbed, the moods are becoming more frequent. She hopes, once the old man is dead, that Cosimo will be able to accept the fact and to shake off these bouts of nostalgia. It's good to remember the past, but after a while, you have to get on and live in the present.

'He could see it all, you know. Giovanni. He told me exactly what I must do.'

She looks up. *That's interesting. He is already talking about his father in the past tense.*

Despite the unexpected change of tense, she prepares herself for what she is sure is coming next. Soon she will hear (for the thousandth time) the homilies which his father had forced upon his son, about the way he must behave. To be fair, the old man had known that to make real money you needed to be able to predict (and in reality that meant to influence) events. And he had known well that in the Florentine Republic, the nobility were debarred from holding office, lest, like elsewhere, they used their position to grab control. And of course, as she had been reminded so many times, no Medici worth the name would let himself be deterred from rightful action by some minor rule or piece of misguided legislation. So Giovanni di Bicci had taught young Cosimo how to have it both ways. And now Cosimo will spell it all out to her once again.

Yes, she knows what will come next; she can hear the words already. She knows them as well as he does.

Dress like a lord and say as little as possible. How often had she heard that repeated?

Never appear to be a prince or to want to become a prince. That one always makes her smile. Giovanni had, surely, said that cynically to his son Cosimo; the same son he had married into the noble Bardi family, whilst marrying his younger brother, Lorenzo, to an equally noble Cavalcanti.

Do not hang around the Signoria as if it is a place where you do business lest they think you are seeking power. At least that was clear in its understanding, especially when followed by *only go there when you are summoned and only accept offices when they are bestowed upon you.*

Yes, Giovanni di Bicci had recognised, right from the beginning, that in the interests of the bank, you had to control political events. But at the same time, he had known that in the interests of political survival in a self-conscious republic, you must not be seen to be taking control by the masses. How had he reconciled those two necessities? By using his money to buy alliances, partnerships, and agreements with others in powerful positions and to garner political support whilst pulling the strings from the back of the room. That's how.

But the thing that Cosimo never fully faced was that although Giovanni di Bicci had understood the need, he had never really succeeded in making it work. Yes, his generation had built the bank and made a fortune, but they had never really attained political power. During most of Giovanni's active lifetime, that had remained with the old money; the Bardi, the Peruzzi, the Stozzi and the Acciaiuoli, but especially with the Albizzi. And to a large extent, truth to tell, it still did.

There was no doubt that Cosimo, having had it drilled into him over his childhood breakfast table, understood. The question now is, will he, once his father is no longer there, manage to pull the trick off?

She remembers Giovanni di Bicci's final, damning phrase. *To confide in a man is to become his slave.* Can Cosimo be that cynical about the people around him? Perhaps he can. Somehow, she feels the next year or two are going to test him.

There's a gentle tap at the door and Maddalena opens it. Piero is standing outside the *studiolo*, looking nervous and diffident. 'F – Father?'

'Well?' Cosimo glares at him. 'What do you want, Pietro?' The boy is just over eleven years old, but his father is still using the diminutive form of his name.

Nervously, the boy scratches his bottom. 'Are you busy, father?'

Cosimo shrugs. 'Of course I'm busy. I shall soon have the responsibilities of the bank and of the family on my shoulders. Anyone would be busy!'

'Sorry.' Piero pulls the door shut and Maddalena hears his feet retreating slowly down the corridor.

'Cosimo! That was unkind. You shouldn't be so hard on him.'

Cosimo gives an irritated shiver. 'I wish for once he'd stand up for himself and not just stand there, dithering pathetically.' But even as he speaks, he knows he's in the wrong. 'Where was I? Stupid boy. I've completely lost my train of thought.'

'The catechism.'

He looks up at her, frowning.

'The lessons your father taught you.'

He shrugs. 'Well, not to worry. I'm sure you've heard them before. What time is the cardinal expected?'

'Any minute now. But he's always late.'

Cosimo grins, his mood lifting as quickly as it came on. 'Not when he thinks he can snatch half an hour leering at you. I'm surprised he hasn't slithered in here already. What's that?'

From the door comes a scratching noise and a loud snuffling. Maddalena gets up. 'It sounds like the puppy.'

She opens the door. A small black and white spaniel puppy is lying with his nose against the base of the door, sniffing and scratching. Beside him, also lying with his nose on the floor, is a six year old boy. As she opens the door, the puppy runs in and the boy follows in after him.

'Pisellino. Naughty dog! You know you're not allowed in the *studiolo*.' Giovanni scoops him up and gives his father an angelic grin. He's already in the centre of the room and firmly established.

'What are you doing?' Angelic turns to inquisitive.

Cosimo looks at Maddalena, then at his ledgers, and shrugs. 'Nothing much. We were just talking.'

Giovanni hands the puppy to Maddalena and reaches up to his father. Instinctively, Cosimo lifts him up and props him on the high stool next to the writing table. Giovanni stares at the *Libro Segreto* – the private books of account kept solely for the benefit of the family shareholders.

'How are we doing? Have we made a profit this month?' He looks at Maddalena and rolls his eyes. It is only a week since she suggested he try it as an opening gambit when his father looks upset. She turns away, stifling a laugh, but Cosimo doesn't notice. Carefully, for the next half an hour, he takes his younger son through the entries; loans received, income earned, expenses incurred and, finally, the resultant profit.

Giovanni nods sagely, like an old man. 'Yes. Not bad. Looks like we'll survive.'

He lifts his arms, to be lifted down onto the floor again. 'Got to go now, before Pisellino pisses on the floor.' He turns to Maddalena. 'He's incompetent you know!'

She grins again, remembering their recent conversation. 'Incontinent.'

Unfazed, Giovanni picks up the puppy and makes for the door. As he reaches it he turns and grins back at her. 'Yes, that too. Bye.'

And he's gone.

Maddalena closes the door and looks at Cosimo. On his face is a look of pride and amusement. 'He's a wicked little devil isn't he?'

***

Maddalena could see by the abbess' expression that she might need time to learn to enjoy the company of 'wicked little devils'. Her face seemed unsure whether to be amused or censorious. Finally, she seemed to have decided to err on the side of disapproval.

'At the time, it seemed insignificant, but it was not. The first result was that Giovanni became comfortable amongst the ledgers and legal papers when Piero was not, and soon he knew much more about banking than his elder brother ever did. The second result was that Giovanni befriended me; and that, in later years, was to become important.'

She sat back, deciding, in view of the abbess' unsupportive response, to change the subject.

'I became pregnant in the autumn. Cosimo knew and was delighted, but we didn't tell anyone else. I was small, and almost as slim as the boys, and I was sure nobody would notice until much later. It was Giovanni who eventually let the cat out of the bag.

'It was in March of the following year. Quite early one morning. There was snow on the ground outside and nobody had yet ventured out, so the riverbanks opposite the Palazzo Bardi were pristine white as far as the eye could see, in both directions. As usual, we were in the *studiolo*.'

***

PALAZZO MEDICI, FLORENCE
14th February 1428

'Giovanni! Pick that bloody dog up and get him out of here. This is no place for a puppy. I have told you before.'

Cosimo bends and begins picking up the fallen books from the floor, his face for a moment incandescent with rage. The ledgers are his real children; more close to him even than his sons.

Giovanni, unused to being shouted at, runs to Maddalena, who draws him to her and begins to cuddle him. He puts his head against her belly and she cradles his head while he pretends to cry.

Of course it's all a game to make his father forgive him; Giovanni has never to her knowledge cried genuinely in his life. She is holding him close and swaying from side to side when suddenly he pulls back. 'Your belly has grown all hard'.

He looks at her with that searching look that has always allowed him to discover secrets long before anyone else. Then, suddenly, his face goes deathly pale. 'You haven't got what Francesca Maria had, have you? You're not going to die?'

Maddalena takes a sharp breath and looks at Cosimo for support. Francesca Maria had been a neighbour; a Bardi from along the street and a week earlier, she had died of a tumour in the stomach. The whole street had discussed her death in unpleasant detail and Giovanni, who missed little, must have heard them.

Now, to her surprise, Cosimo picks him up, puts him on his knee, and tells him the truth. 'Don't worry. There's nothing wrong with Maddalena. She's going to have a baby.'

Giovanni wipes his snotty nose on Cosimo's sleeve and looks straight across at her. He frowns. A frown of concentration. 'How can you? You aren't married.'

With absolutely no idea what to say, she looks at Cosimo and says nothing.

Giovanni considers further what he has just heard. He looks up at his father. 'Who can the father be, if Maddalena's not married?'

She begins to bluster, but Cosimo simply tousles the boy's head and tells him. 'I am. Maddalena and I have made a baby together. It will be born in the early summer. Until then, it's a secret. Only you know.'

It's a master stroke. In that moment, Giovanni seems to grow five years. He looks at Maddalena, then at his father, and then he smiles. 'Will it be a boy? I would prefer a brother to play with. Girls are silly.'

Cosimo smiles back. 'I hope it will be a boy too. We shall have to wait and see.'

Giovanni's little brain is already moving onward. He looks at Maddalena very seriously. 'Will he be black, like you, Maddalena?'

Then, again, at his father. 'I should like a black brother. Nobody else has a black brother. I'll be special.'

'He'll be Piero's brother as well.' Cosimo is, as always, trying to be even-handed between his two sons.

But Giovanni just shakes his head and looks at his father. 'Don't worry. He won't find out.' Then to Maddalena, in explanation. 'I won't tell him.'

Maddalena looks at Cosimo and wonders what else he might say. Already he has made it plain that he does not intend to disown the child, but now, prompted by Giovanni's question, she finds herself wondering what difference the baby's colour might make. The children of nobles often had convenient parentages attached to them, but there could be little pretence if the baby was her colour.

Cosimo seems to read her thoughts. He grins at his son's directness. 'He will be a brother to both of you. And I hope he looks just like his mother. If he does, I could not be more proud of him.'

He looks across the room at Maddalena and grins again. 'I would not wish my own looks upon any child.'

'Giovanni runs his fingertip down the bridge of his father's nose, and then, still frowning, feels his ears. Satisfied, he nods his head. 'I must take after my mother, then. My nose is not half as long as yours and I haven't got big droopy ears.'

And Cosimo, with a look of complete sincerity, pats his head. 'Fear not, Giovanni. You have the best of both of us.'

***

'Giovanni did much better than I had expected. He kept the secret for three months. When finally the news broke, it was clear that Cosimo had already told Contessina. I suspect he did so in May, while they were in Lucca, because I remembered her looking at me with a particular severity when they returned, although neither of them said anything at the time.

'The boy (yes, it was a boy) was born on the 22nd June, and although I did not know it at the time, it was to prove a significant date. Years later I discovered that Lucrezia Tornabuoni had been born on the same day, but in the previous year. Of course she had not become part of our lives then, but within seven years she was to become a regular visitor to the house, and despite the difference in their ages, was to become very close to Giovanni, before eventually, at Cosimo's command, marrying Piero.'

Perhaps catching some change in *Suora* Maddalena's voice, the abbess looked up, and saw the look of unhappiness on the face opposite her. Maddalena shook her head. 'It was one of the biggest mistakes Cosimo ever made; tragic in my opinion, but at the time I speak of, it was a long way into the future.'

She paused, gathering her thoughts. For a moment she was far away, lost in the past. Then a frown appeared on her face. 'They say it was a difficult birth. That was the opinion of Dr Ficino.'

'Diotifeci Ficino was a good physician, as well as being a close friend of Cosimo, and the midwife he brought with him had as strong a reputation as he had.' She shook her head, remembering. 'She was huge; her forearms thicker than my thighs, and with great dimples in her elbows. It was a long and painful night. I seemed to have been looking at those elbows for an age, through a red mist of agony and growing exhaustion, wishing those strong arms could just drag the thing out of me; but eventually, between us, after a whole night and half a morning, we did it.'

Across the room, the abbess looks horrified.

'As soon as I was told the child would live, I wrote to Cosimo, who was in Lucca once again, and told him the news. Despite what he had said to Giovanni months before, I was uncertain how he would respond. And then, only a few days later, his letter arrived.'

Maddalena looked across the room. 'If you will forgive me, I shall read it to you, for nothing I can say now will catch the true spirit of his own words.'

Seeing the abbess nod her approval, Maddalena opened her little cask and found the letter. She had preserved it carefully, over the years, and it still looked as fresh as the day it arrived at the Palazzo Bardi. With her voice trembling, she began to read aloud.

Dear Maddalena,

I take the greatest pleasure in writing back to you on this auspicious day. This is God's work. It is marvellous in our eyes.

Thank you for our son. I shall call him Carlo and bring him up as one of the family.

I am so proud of you, my dear. Please look after the boy well, and I shall see him on my return, early next week. Then he will be baptised into the church, at the Basilica di San Lorenzo, as my son.

Yours, with pride,
Cosimo de' Medici
At Lucca Wednesday, 16th June 1428

With eyes glistening, she folded the letter, put it back in the cask and closed the lid. Then she looked at the abbess. 'A good letter, I think you'll agree?'

The abbess looked envious. 'A fine letter. A wonderful letter. His pride rings out from every word. And such an appropriate quotation. *A domino factum est istud et est mirabile in oculis nostris.*4 Saint Mark expresses it beautifully.' The abbess smiled contentedly, her eyes closed; the familiar words clearly comforting her. Then she opened her eyes again and her expression was more serious. 'And did he do as he said?' Madonna Arcangelica's face showed just a hint of uncertainty. Perhaps she was wondering how well Cosimo would keep his promises to her, and the convent, in the future.

Maddalena took a deep breath, remembering how she had felt in those ensuing days. First, it had to be said, relief. Then pride and finally, most important of all, inclusion. As her son had been drawn into the heart of the family, so, by association, had she. Legally, of course, she remained a slave; still described as such on the annual *catasto* tax return. How else could Cosimo have described her? He was a married man, in visible public office and with a business reputation to maintain as well as a political one.

But in the Baptistery of San Lorenzo, Carlo had been accepted as a Medici, and so, finally, in a sense, had she. It was the beginning of a new era in her life. Cosimo had indeed kept his word in full. Carlo had been brought up within the family, with Contessina drawing him deftly under her controlling wing. But the boy had proved to be smart; quickly learning from Giovanni how to slide from his surrogate mother to his real mother and back again, under the same roof, without upsetting either.

Perhaps Maddalena thought, looking back *his father's expertise in the same manoeuvre helped guide him too?*

'And where is Carlo now?' Is he still at the Duomo, in Florence?' It was clear from the abbess' expression that she would not have been able to remain completely silent.

'Being Canon is not a resident appointment. At least, not in his case. He's in Rome, with the Curia. Thanks to his father, his position in the Church seems to be progressing, and judging from the last letter I had from him, he is more than content with his life.'

She could say no more, but in addition to his existing appointments, in Florence and the Mugello, she knew he would soon be appointed *Protonotario* to Prato Cathedral. The position had been promised to him and only the formalities were yet to be completed. Even more, a month or so before she had come to the convent, Cosimo had told her that it was now only a matter of time; he now had assurances that Carlo would, eventually, earn his cardinal's hat.

Chapter 10
Exiled
21st November 1457

It was towards the end of November. The season had been progressing quickly and already the clouds were beginning to have that mixture of purple and slate grey that told of the coming of snow to the hills of the Mugello. The snows were beginning early this year. Everyone sensed that it was going to be a long and cold winter.

Maddalena was concerned. It was nearly half an hour since None had ended and there was only another hour and a half before they would have to reassemble for Vespers, yet still Madonna Arcangelica had not arrived. She had seemed in her normal spirits during the None prayers, and afterwards, as they filed out, had made no indication that their fortnightly appointment would have to be cancelled.

Maddalena opened the folding doors and walked out onto her balcony. The air out here was chill, with a bite that cut through her clothes and exposed her inner weakness, but she persevered; knowing if she leaned over the balcony, she would be able to see much of the courtyard below. Still no sign.

And then she heard the familiar step, scrape, step, scrape of the abbess' feet on the stone steps below. The sound changed as the abbess turned onto the steeper wooden stairs and Maddalena made sure the chairs were ready in their customary positions. No need to waste any more time.

Madonna Arcangelica knocked and entered as soon as Maddalena replied. She looked drawn. 'Sorry. A sudden emergency. *Suora* Magnifica had one of her spells as she was leaving chapel and we had to carry her down to the infirmary. I fear she will not outlast this winter.'

Eager to leave the chapel in order to prepare for the abbess' visit, she had not noticed the commotion, but Maddalena knew who she was referring to; one of the old nuns who refused to accept the modest reforms that Madonna Arcangelica was still trying to introduce. Embarrassed at her failure to come to the aid of a sick sister, she felt the need to comment.

'Yes. I thought she was looking weak at prayers this morning.' She frowned. 'How old is she now?'

The abbess shook her head. 'I'm not sure. She says she's eighty-five, but her mind has been so addled for the last five years that I wouldn't trust to her memory. Somehow, she has always seemed old to me. She even seemed like an old woman when I first came here, but if she's right, she can only have been thirty-four then. I shall have to consult the convent records. I'll have a word with the Chapter Clerk after Vespers.'

Wearily, she eased herself into the customary chair and sat back, closing her eyes. 'Do you have a story from your life to comfort me today? I admit I feel in need of comfort.'

Maddalena closed the door and the folding shutters and took her place opposite the abbess. For a moment she considered changing to another chapter of her life, but in the end she decided against it. The subject she had chosen was more than sufficient.

'I hope so. I have told you of living with a man, of its joys and its frustrations. I have also told you something of the difficulties of sharing a man, under one roof with another woman. Today I should like to tell about the agony of losing a man. But before you despair, I promise my story will continue, and tell also of the ecstasy of regaining him and in the process of elevating my relationship with him to a new plane.'

For a moment she thought the abbess had fallen asleep, but then, without even opening her eyes, Madonna Arcangelica smiled, gave a gentle nod and began to circle her right hand. 'Pray proceed. I have heard enough these past weeks to trust you. Even if it must address tribulations, I know your tale will have a constructive outcome in the end. It is not in your nature to stop on a negative. But today, if you will forgive me, I shall simply sit here with my eyes closed, and enjoy the story as it unfolds.'

'Very well.' Maddalena smiled and prepared herself.

***

PALAZZO BARDI, FLORENCE
20th July 1429

'What *is* wrong with them?'

Maddalena keeps her head down, as Cosimo rants. She's heard it all before.

'Does Rinaldo have *no* idea how to run a city?'

'What's he done now, dearest?' Perhaps she can jolly him out of it. A problem when she doesn't really know what he's unhappy about. 'Is it Volterra?'

Cosimo nods. 'The Volterrani are brewing trouble. They have told us if we try to apply the new *catasto* to them they will rebel. It's beginning to look as if we shall have to employ Fortebraccio to keep them quiet.'

Maddalena wrinkles her nose. 'If you ask me, that Fortebraccio's more trouble than he's worth. What will he do? Lay siege to the city? Steal everything he can lay his hands on? One thing's for sure. There'll be no money to pay taxes once he's "subdued" them. The *condottiere* are professional soldiers. They don't like to go home empty-handed do they?'

Cosimo looks weary and uncertain. 'That's true. They say he has his eye on Lucca too, but if we give him Volterra, that should keep both of them employed for some time. Anyway, they've called a Council of Ten and asked me to chair it.'

'The war council? So are we going to war with Volterra now? Do you really want to take responsibility for that, dear?'

'I'll probably chair the council. If we do go to war, I'll be paying for it in any event, so I might as well keep a handle on proceedings. Anyway, Volterra must be kept in order. We can't have them rebelling every time a new tax is announced.'

'But war? The Volterrani are such nice people. Do we have to?'

'It's politics. We need their taxes. It's nothing personal.'

Only war. Nothing personal. Sometimes she wonders what the world is coming to. Best not to pursue that argument. Back to the other subject. 'So what has Rinaldo degli Albizzi done to anger you this time, Cosimo? I thought you and he had found a way to live peaceably alongside each other?'

'He won't leave people alone. That's the problem. He seems to think the *Signoria* should be visibly active on behalf of the people.'

'And shouldn't they? Isn't that what governments are for?'

He pulls a face. 'Well yes, but not all of the time. Not fiddling about with everything. It's the Church that's put him up to it.'

She keeps embroidering, but raises an eyebrow to show interest. When he's angry like this, he never gets straight to the point, but he will. 'Up to what, exactly, dearest?'

'Not content with introducing the *catasto* tax, now he wants a new law, against *cambio secco*. The doctors of divinity have decided that dry exchange is not true currency exchange and therefore it counts as usury.'

'You know yourself, it's sailing pretty close to the wind. You don't really need two bills of exchange, in opposite currencies, to make a single trade transaction. One would do. That way there would be a real exchange risk and a stronger argument against the Church.'

Cosimo shrugs and sneers. It's what he does when he knows she's right.

'So the *Signoria* want to make it illegal?'

He shrugs again, but she knows that deep down, he's concerned. 'It's personal. The Albizzi are trying to kill our business. They know we do more of that trade than any of the other banks.'

'Will it hurt us badly?'

'Not really. I have made a formal commitment that the Medici Bank only deals in *licit* exchanges and for a couple of months we shall have to be a bit careful how we word our bills of exchange, but in the long term, the law can't be made to stick. The woollen trade, copper, tin, silk, spices what-have-you; none of them can operate without bills of exchange.'

'What would you do if it really did start to pinch?'

'Oh I'd get myself voted onto the *Signoria* again and get the law revoked. But it's expensive, oiling all those sweaty palms. Besides, the whole business is irritating and a waste of time. I could be making money.'

Cosimo shakes his head, depressed. 'What a mess. At least my father didn't live to see it.'

***

Maddalena looked across the room to see whether the abbess had fallen asleep. Receiving an encouraging smile, she continued with her story.

'Cosimo was right. Fortebraccio did attack Lucca and as soon as he did so, the

Signoria in Florence decided to back him. The taxes from Lucca would have been a godsend. Of course, it wasn't that simple. Nothing ever is in Florentine politics. Milan sent aid to Lucca in the form of another *condottiere*; Count Francesco Sforza, and in due course, he too, had to be paid off.'

She took a deep breath. 'And once again, it was Cosimo's money that paid him. So now Cosimo found himself paying for the armies on both sides of a war, and getting no thanks from either. The situation had become ridiculous. Sensing disaster, he resigned from the War Committee.

'Nobody thanked him for his efforts (or his money) and by the time an unhappy peace had been signed, the people had turned again from fighting an enemy to fighting each other.'

'Why was that? Were the people not content to be at peace once again?' The abbess looked bewildered.

'The truth was, it had all got out of hand. In the process of all this argument, Florence had become divided between pro-Albizzi and pro-Medici camps, both with a greater sense of who they supported rather than the reasons why. Personalities had outgrown policies and nobody knew what they were fighting for anymore; only that they were fervently against the other side. The problem now was that both had been playing the "behind the scenes" game and now there was no legal way to resolve the contest without the whole democratic façade collapsing.'

Her eyes were half-closed, but by her expression, Madonna Arcangelica seemed to think the outside world had gone raving mad. Perhaps she was better off where she was.

'In the summer, Cosimo retired to Trebbio and stayed there for two months. The truth was, he didn't know what to do either. Then, unexpectedly, he was called to a meeting at the Palazzo della Signoria. I think he half-knew it was a trap.'

Across the room, Madonna Arcangelica sat up and opened her eyes, as if sensing something significant was about to emerge.

Knowing she was right, Maddalena began to speak faster. 'But he went anyway, believing that the *Signoria* were honourable men. As soon as he walked in, he found the meeting of the *Signoria* was already in progress, and instead of being taken to the Council Hall, he was arrested and put in the *alberghetto*; a tiny dark cell high in the tower.

'What a situation! Over the previous two or three years, knowing the government was overstretched and could not repay its debts, Cosimo had lent the city a further 155,000 florins, and in so doing, he had not only saved them from bankruptcy, but had run the Florence branch of the Medici Bank into heavy losses. Yet here he was now, being indicted for treason, on the dubious grounds that he had used his wealth "to elevate himself above all others". It was an indictment that carried only two penalties; exile or death.'

Madonna Arcangelica had her eyes wide open now and took a deep breath. 'I remember that year and how fearful we were that something terrible was happening. Of course, hidden away up here in the hills, we didn't know the rights or wrongs of it, but to hear that the Magnificent Cosimo had been arrested was like hearing that the end of the world was nigh. We had no idea what would happen next, but I know I never believed that the people would find him guilty and to this day, I have never understood how the accusation of that crime came about. Was there any evidence against him?'

Maddalena shook her head. 'None at all. The so-called evidence was a farce. They pointed to a grand *palazzo* that they said Cosimo was building for himself on the Via Larga. But at that stage in his life, he hadn't even started work on it.'

She saw the abbess frown and continued, speaking even faster, knowing she was on thin ice. 'It was true he was thinking of building a *palazzo*, largely to get away from Oltrarno and the influence of his wife's family. And yes, the ground had been purchased and most of it cleared – including the piece of land next to the Palazzo Vecchio. But they had not started building.'

The abbess' frown had become almost a stare of concentration. 'But surely, there must have been *some* basis for the charge? He must have had more than active plans in his head? How else were the people led into finding him guilty? I have never understood that.'

Now Maddalena found herself frowning. She had not expected to have to defend Cosimo over an event that had taken place twenty-five years earlier. 'It was a false accusation; made by the Albizzi. Someone saw Brunelleschi's original, somewhat ostentatious, design for the Palazzo Medici and made it public knowledge. But Cosimo never intended to build that. That was why, on his return from exile, he asked Michelozzo to come up with a much simpler design. But at the time, all that was in the future. You can't blame a man for his thoughts.'

Across the room she saw the abbess was still frowning. She looked unconvinced. 'They were right, though, weren't they? The people who said he was planning to build a great *palazzo*? No smoke without fire?'

The increasingly accusatory tone took Maddalena back. Once again she felt defensive. At the time she had thought Cosimo was going to be found guilty. Her hands started to sweat as she remembered being in that room at the Palazzo Bardi.

***

PALAZZO BARDI
September 1433

'Accuito. You're back! What is happening? Tell us.'

The servant falls into the room, his face registering shock, horror and exhaustion. Maddalena gives him a large goblet of wine, and he gulps it down in one draft. Then he sits and stares at the floor, avoiding their eyes.

Contessina's patience snaps first. 'Well come on! What is happening?'

Accuito puts his head in his hands. 'I have just come from Bernardo Guadagni. The news is not good.'

Did you see Cosimo? Were you able to speak to him?'

Cosimo, they had been told, was being held in the Bargello by the Giustizia, and as a political prisoner, was inaccessible. Desperate, they had sent their most reliable servant to see the *Gonfaloniere*; the leader of the *Signoria*, and until this day at least, a good friend of the Medici. He, at least, might have word of Cosimo's condition – and perhaps news of his future.

Accuito begins to gasp out his words. 'Cosimo is not in a good way. Apparently he has not slept or eaten since his incarceration. I was able to speak to Bernardo. He was brutal in his description. He said Cosimo was shaking with fear, unable to eat or move; hardly able to breathe, so great is his terror.'

Both women put their hands to their mouths. They are anything but friends, but they share one thing; their position in life is wholly dependent on Cosimo de' Medici.

Accuito has tears in his eyes. 'Bernardo says everyone there, especially Cosimo, remembers that the last man found guilty of treason was thrown from the roof of the Palazzo della Signoria, with a rope tied round his neck and the other end attached to a third-floor window below. They keep saying how he was still falling through the air, kicking and screaming, when the rope pulled tight. Those watching said it nearly tore his head off.' He is slobbering as he speaks.

'Cosimo told Bernardo he sees this image every time he closes his eyes. Bernardo says if he falls asleep for as much as a second, he immediately dreams he is falling and wakes up, screaming and clutching at his neck. He says it's terrifying to watch and his screams curdle the blood. But he can't leave him. Not like that. So he has to stay and endure the screams.'

'Did you hear his screams yourself?' Maddalena regrets asking the question as soon as she has asked it. She offers him another goblet of wine. 'Yes. It's true. It was horrible.' His hand is shaking so violently as he tries to take it, that she has to help him. He slurps at it, his head ducking and jerking uncontrollably.

'Have the *Signoria* come to a decision?' Contessina is keeping her head.

He shakes his head, still drinking. 'No. Not yet. The *Gonfaloniere* says they will meet again this afternoon.'

He looks at Contessina with the face of a terrified dog. 'Bernardo says to be brave. We must not give up hope. Cosimo, he says, has many friends on the *Signoria*. He may yet be saved.'

'Here.' She reaches behind her and takes a moneybag from the *credenza* beside the wall. 'Take this to Bernardo. There's a thousand florins in there, tell him. Ask him to do what he can. Tell him there's the same again for him if he secures Cosimo's release.' It appears that, until now, Contessina's endless and simplistic faith in the power of friendship has encouraged her to hope that her husband will be released before the day is out.

Accuito nods, stuffs the bag inside his padded *farsetto* and pulls his tunic around it. The bag contains a fortune and he dares not walk the streets with its presence visible.

'Go now!' Contessina shoos him out of the door. As he leaves, his face looks as if it is he who is going to his execution.

***

Maddalena paused in mid-sentence. Even today she remembered how Accuito's description had frightened the family into a similar condition. None of them had slept that night.

But she would not refer to that. There was no need. Instead, she took refuge in the abbess' earlier question. 'As you know, they found him guilty. You may ask how the people were led into that outcome, especially, with friendly faces on the *Signoria*. I can tell you now how it happened.

'A new *Signoria* is chosen every two months, with the eight priors and the *Gonfaloniere* being chosen by having their names drawn out of a bag. At that time, the *Signoria* was led by Rinaldo degli Albizzi and it was heavily biased towards his followers. For some years before, Rinaldo had resented Cosimo's leadership of the *Signoria*. Now, perhaps for a short while, the balance of selection had swung his way and he had a majority; now he was sure his opportunity had come.

'Since the Medici family, and Cosimo in particular, were his only serious rivals for power, he pressed the charge home. Not only that, but he understood that the Medici could run their banking business from anywhere, so they would not be ruined by exile as landowners like him would have been. Knowing this, he *had* to demand the death penalty, and for that, the accusation had to be treason. So having started the accusation, Rinaldo degli Albizzi had no choice but to pursue it to the bitter end. It was as if his own life depended on it, which I suppose it did. Cosimo's or his.

'But honourable men, even followers of an opponent, do not like supporting a death penalty, and with the two-month life of his *Signoria* running out fast, Rinaldo knew he was running a very serious risk. If his *Signoria* ran out of term and luck went against him, the next *Signoria* might easily be pro-Medici and then he might find himself in the same position as Cosimo was in now.

'So in order to prevent that from happening, he called a *parlamento*. By law, that was the only gathering which could invoke emergency procedures, temporarily putting aside for the moment the bi-monthly cycle of the *Signoria* and instead invoking the *balia*, or emergency committee.

'The *parlamento* should involve all the grown men of the city meeting together in the Piazza della Signoria, but in the event, the Albizzi put guards at the entrances to the Piazza and instead of the whole city turning out, only twenty-three chosen men were allowed in, to form a very limited *parlamento*. The proposal was put to the vote and, of course, it was approved.'

Across the room the abbess shook her head in dismay. 'Such a travesty of the law.'

'Rinaldo now had absolute power and immediately he set about choosing men for the *balia* that he knew were on his side. The future for Cosimo was looking short and uncomfortable.'

Madonna Arcangelica squirmed uncomfortably in her chair. 'I never realised that while we were here, praying that the citizens of Florence should be given divine guidance, the men in power were acting so unlawfully. I hope they got their just desserts in due course?'

Maddalena raised a finger, as if to say 'be patient; all will be revealed' and the abbess, looking satisfied, sat back.

***

PALAZZO BARDI, FLORENCE
26th September 1433

'Maddalena! Accuito is back. I think you had better come and hear this.' Contessina's big voice booms down the stairs, and she runs to respond.

Accuito's face does not look encouraging.

'Well? How did you get on?' Contessina gets straight to the point.

'I spoke to the *Gonfaloniere* and gave him the money. He accepted it gratefully and promised to do what he could. Then I waited until he returned from the meeting.'

'Yes. And…'

'He said that on balance, he was pleased with the outcome.' Accuito does not look as if he's enjoying his role as news-carrier.

'He told me to tell you that Rinaldo pressed very hard for the death penalty to be authorised and carried out this very afternoon. However, in response to your generosity, Bernardo feigned illness and sent a well-briefed deputy in his place. He has been able to stall the proceedings for two or three weeks. Bernardo is confident that during this period, ambassadors will arrive from Venice and from Pope Euganius IV in Rome. Messages have been sent to them both in Cosimo's name and he fully expects them to call for the death sentence to be commuted to exile, and even that for a reasonably short period only. They need the Medici Bank and they need Cosimo at its helm. That's what he said. He asked me to say "courage" to you both.'

'But that all sounds very tenuous.' Contessina's face expresses anything but courage. 'What happens if the ambassadors don't arrive in time?'

Accuito's face is beginning to recover its colour. Now for the first time, he smiles. A thin smile, but it's a start. 'Bernardo did more. Once the full meeting had been put off, he called Palla Strozzi to his house. He told him the ambassadors were on their way, and hinted that they were ready to protest on the strongest possible terms.

'Palla, as you know, has been a close supporter of the Albizzi, but apparently, hearing this news, he caved in. He told Bernardo that he, for one, would not support the death penalty under any circumstances. So the *Gonfaloniere* sent a message to the Albizzi and told them the situation.'

'So Rinaldo is losing support? Does he realise that?' Contessina seems to have a very clear grasp of the situation.

Accuito's expression tells them all they need to know. He is smiling now, the relief on his face obvious. 'Reluctantly, only an hour ago, he accepted the lesser charge.'

'So the ambassadors are only a formality?' Maddalena can't resist saying something. Unusually, Contessina nods her agreement.

'Indeed. Just a formality. That's what Bernardo says. Yes.'

***

'It was in this manner that Cosimo de Medici was taken from me.' Maddalena looked up.

'The ruling *Signoria* was called back to power and on the 28th of September they banished Cosimo to Padua for ten years, his cousin Averardo to Naples for ten years and his brother Lorenzo to Venice for five years. The last I saw of Cosimo was on the 4th of October, when, escorted by an armed guard, he was led north, through the high mountain pass below Monte Cimone and handed over at the frontier.' She paused, distant memories once again hanging heavily over her.

Across the room, Madonna Arcangelica took a deep breath and shook her head. 'Such a crime. Such wicked men.' She looked at Maddalena and lifted her eyes, as if hoping to help Cosimo in the process. 'Did you hear from him?'

Maddalena smiled, turned to her little casket, and selected a letter. 'Yes. Quite quickly. I have the letter here still. Let me read it to you.'

Dearest Maddalena,

I am safely delivered to the Republic of Venice and now in the offices of our Venice branch. Tomorrow I shall, as is required by the conditions of my exile, continue to Padua and remain there until, by God's good grace, I may obtain permission to travel more freely within the Republic (no doubt with the appropriate assurances) and return to Venice.

I have been most heartily surprised and uplifted by the welcome I have received, both in Emilia Romagna, in the Marquisate of Ferrara, and, especially, here in the great Republic of Venice.

The kindness shown to me has been reward enough, but in addition, there is the comfort of knowing that the Medici name has not been spurned and that at every turn, men of wealth and influence continue to support our bank wholeheartedly.

This being the case, I can be confident in continuing our business whilst here and in Padua. To that end, please rescue the papers we discussed, together with the private ledgers and bring them to me at the house of Jacopo Donato, in Padua, where I expect to arrive this very night.

You should bring six armed servants for your protection. I shall have messages for them to carry on their return journey.

Come soon.

Yours,

Cosimo de' Medici

From Venice Tuesday, 13th October 1433

The abbess clapped her hands. 'So it was business as usual? You joined him there, in Padua?'

Maddalena inclined her head. 'I joined him, yes, taking the account books, but not, as I had expected, in Padua. I rode through the mountains, taking the same route he had taken, through Cutigliano in Pistioia, past Fassano in the Marquisate of Ferrara, through Modena and then by boat from Bondeno to Francolino and finally to Venice.

'I fully expected to take the *traghetto* up the River Brenta to Stra and finally to Padua, but when I reached Venice, I was told that Cosimo had already returned there on the 20th, the *Signoria* in Florence having relented under diplomatic pressure from Andrea Donato, the Venetian ambassador. My faith in Cosimo and in the power of the bank was so great that I knew that he would succeed, even when exiled, and here he was, already bettering his situation.'

To her surprise, she saw a knowing grin break out on the abbess' face.

'And as you rode, I am sure you sensed your opportunity. Because you knew that his wife and children had remained in the Palazzo Bardi and that whilst in exile, you would once again have him to yourself, as before in Rome. Am I not right?'

Maddalena smiled to herself. So the abbess had understood more than she had admitted. Much more. In future, she must be careful not to underestimate this woman. Unworldly Madonna Arcangelica might be, but naïve she certainly was not.

'Indeed. How perceptive of you, Madonna Arcangelica. You are right. Even as we rode high into the first mountains, and felt the chill of the lying snows, I promised myself that I would not consider his exile as an adversity. Instead I would see it as an opportunity. And I vowed that I would help him to see it likewise.'

***

MONTE BASTIONE, NORTH OF FLORENCE
22nd October 1433

The saddle creaks as her horse picks its way up the steep mountain pass. The path is narrow and she feels the vertigo; the long sweep of the mountainside drawing her down, as if it is calling to her, inviting her to lean forward and float down, beyond the snow, below the trees, to the distant meadows thousands of feet below them. For a moment, the thought is all-encompassing, compelling, dizzying, she doesn't trust her own legs and feet to keep her to this stony, narrow pathway.

But she isn't walking; she is riding, and the mountain pony is sure-footed. It is that reassurance which gives her a confidence she would never have had in herself. She draws her eyes away from the abyss and concentrates instead on the pathway ahead of them, winding upward to the high saddle which marks the boundary; the border of the Republic of Florence and the beginning of a new life.

They are high now. She had felt the tingle of cold air in her nostrils as soon as they climbed beyond the snow line, entering what to her felt like another world. She looks back down; to where they left the last of the trees, then scans the mountain on the opposite side of the valley and realises that the upper limit of the trees forms a line – a straight line, crossing from one mountain to another; always constant. Why, she wonders? Then, above the tree line, she notices that the lower limit of the snow also forms a line; a second line, a parallel line.

'It's the temperature. Trees cannot grow where the summer temperature is too low. And the snow only lies where there is insufficient warmth to melt it.' Beside her, the captain of her guard leans on the pommel of his saddle and points. 'But if you look carefully at that mountain over there, you will see that the lines, whilst parallel, are not horizontal. The tree line and the snow line are higher on the southern slope – the Florentine side – than the northern, side, in Emilia.'

'Perhaps we give the hills a warmer welcome?' She shakes her head, to show she is joking and he laughs back. 'Perhaps.'

As they rise higher, their road is pushed relentlessly eastward by the huge shoulder of Monte Bastione to their left. They are climbing diagonally now, the ridge leaning on them; their road avoiding direct confrontation with the mountain and instead pursuing the easy option; beyond Pietramala, to the high Passo della Raticosa.

They reach the pass and abruptly, the view changes. Now, for the first time, all the view is before them and instead of craning their necks at the mountain ahead, they are looking down, and into the endless stretch of the northern plains.

'The border is on that next ridge.' The captain points forward, perhaps another two miles, to where a final, lower ridge runs out from the broad peak of Monte Bastione over their left shoulder, and intersects their road, before dissipating, like fingers from a wrist, into the plain beyond.

To Maddalena's relief, there is an inviting taverna at the roadside, but the captain shakes his head. 'Today we shall eat in Emilia. Not far now.'

The final two miles are easy going; a gentle down-slope, then one last, almost imperceptible rise, before, at a sudden and unexpected bend in the road, they reach Filigare, and the border, marked by twin stone towers, two hundred paces apart. Between them, nestled under a protective rock face, is a second, and larger, taverna, where, amidst much laughter, at a long roadside table, the border guards from Florence and Emilia are sharing a relaxed meal.

They are ignored. The food is good. The wine is excellent. The drinking water is clean and fresh. And the view, all the way down to the great city of Bologna, perhaps twenty-five miles ahead of them, is inviting. The captain strolls across to talk to the guards and his own men gather together around a separate table. For a moment, Maddalena is left alone.

She looks across the broad plain, to Bologna, visible on the horizon; and beyond it, somewhere, Venice and Padua, visible only in her mind still a few days' ride away, and she smiles to herself. *This is another world. Contessina has no place here. Now, once again, I shall have him to myself. But now, I am older, I have seen him at work and at play. I have duelled with his wife and I have borne him a son. Now I can move our relationship onto another level and through that, I can achieve the fulfilment my father told me to seek and which I have always craved.*

Slowly, as they ride down into the valley, she works it all out. As a result of Cosimo's exile, she has been given a third weapon. Her body had been her first, many years ago. Her ability with figures her second, as he had slowly drawn her into his *studiolo* and the showed her the secrets that were recorded there. Now by sharing the very experience of exile with Cosimo, she knows she will become even closer to him. She has seen him on the edge of flight. She has seen him fear death. But now, finally, given time, she knows she will see him triumph and when he does, she will share in that experience in a way that Contessina, remaining back at the Palazzo Bardi, will never be able to do.

***

'How long did you finally spend in exile together?' Having shaken off all of her earlier weariness, the abbess seemed to have become energised by the story; she was now sitting upright, her expression attentive.

'A year. Almost to the day. We returned to Florence in the October of the following year.'

'In triumph?' Madonna Arcangelica looked positively excited.

Maddalena smiled as the bell calling them to Vespers began to chime. 'I will tell you next time.'

As she spoke, she glanced out of the window. 'We had better hurry. It's snowing outside and heavily too. The courtyard will be slippery. We must go.'

Chapter 11
Safe Return
5th December 1457

'It was in Venice, almost a year later, that our good friend Antonio di Ser Tommaso Nasi came to Cosimo at the monastery where we had been given rooms, and on behalf of the people, invited him to return to Florence.'

Perhaps predictably, the abbess had taken Maddalena straight back to where she had left off, and asked how, exactly, she and Cosimo had managed to return to Florence from their exile in Venice. The picture, as always, had been clear in her mind, because over the previous two weeks, she had thought of little else.

***

MONASTERY OF SAN GIORGIO MAGGIORE, VENICE
20th September 1434

'Is that his boat leaving now?'

Cosimo and Maddalena are standing on their large balcony, looking out from the Monastery of San Giorgio Maggiore, over the Canale di San Marco. One of the Doge's barges has just pulled out from the *molo* and has started to row across the tide, towards them.

Her question is hardly a guess, perhaps more of an informed guess. Not two hours before, one of Cosimo's informers had already told him that an envoy had arrived from Florence and was at that moment paying his respects to the Senate. It was pretty certain what his message would be.

During the course of the year, word has come regularly from Florence, both through traders and through diplomats. Progressively, it seems, the people have been growing discontented with the Albizzi government.

According to their informants, the softening of attitudes began shortly after Cosimo's departure. Bartolomeo de' Ridolfi had only just taken up his appointment as *Gonfaloniere* of Justice in Florence when Cosimo had sent his request, supported by Andrea Donato, the Venetian ambassador's kind words, for 'an easing, without slackening' of his conditions of exile.

By return letter, the Florentine *Signoria* had accepted, allowing him to travel anywhere within the Venetian Republic as long as he did not approach any closer to Florence than 140 miles (the distance from Florence to Padua). That excluded Bologna and even Ferrara, which was little more than 100 miles from Florence, but it did allow him to visit, and to live and work, in Venice, and that had been the sole intention of the request. An exiled farmer leaves his lands behind, and has not the benefit of them, but a banker exiled to a great trading city like Venice is, as Cosimo said to Maddalena, "unencumbered" and his life and his business can continue, much as before.

Now if the latest private messages can be believed, the tide of opinion is strengthening further in Cosimo's favour. Many of his friends in Florence have written supportively, but Cosimo is being careful. Maddalena knows better than anyone that the fear of death and the shame of exile are experiences he has not forgotten and she understands fully that he does not want to walk into another trap.

They don't have long to wait. Antonio, son of Ser Tommaso Nasi, runs up the steps and embraces him. 'I am to bring you back to Florence, Cosimo. The people cry out for your return. Come with me. I, and my men, will personally escort you, in case of attack.

Trusting Antonio as he does, and grateful as he is for his support, Cosimo cannot afford to take any more risks. Before breaking the rules of his exile (an act which, in Florentine law, would make him liable for the death penalty) and before putting his head back into the lion's mouth (whose bad breath he can still smell) he needs proof.

Maddalena, as always, supports his judgement. 'You know how fickle these people can be. There is no hurry, Cosimo. You are safe here and we are comfortable. And the bank is thriving. Before you return to Florence and put yourself in their hands, you need more than assurances. You need evidence. Solid evidence.'

He nods, convinced. 'You're right. I'll send someone reliable to confirm the situation.'

Cosimo turns to his secretary. 'Go and get Antonio Martelli. Tell him he has to go to Florence. Immediately.'

***

'So I was right?'

Across the room, Madonna Arcangelica sat with her cloak wrapped round her. It seemed to have been snowing for weeks and Maddalena's tower room was freezing. But it was remote and private, and that was worth more than a log fire to both of them. She smiled triumphantly. 'I knew that once you had the Magnificent Cosimo away from his wife you would become closer to him. You spoke of "our rooms" and "many of our friends in Florence". You make it sound like man and wife. Was it like that? Was your relationship with Cosimo now that close?'

Maddalena smiled, not realising quite how much truth her reminiscences had given away, and for the first time conscious of how carefully the abbess has been listening to, and thinking about, her story week by week. There would be no misleading her now. She was so close that she would spot an inconsistency immediately.

'You are right. Perhaps more right than you knew. But we were not like man and wife. We were closer than that. A man of position in the world of affairs rarely shares his thoughts with his wife. Most of them, and Contessina was certainly no exception, are given the household to run and kept well away from "men's work".'

The abbess nodded, accepting, yet clearly disappointed.

'But I had no such diversions. At the monastery, everything was provided for us and I had no household to maintain. And Cosimo, although being treated with the utmost courtesy and friendship by the government and the merchants of Venice, was always aware that he was in a foreign land, and played his cards even closer to his chest than he had before the trauma of exile.'

She smiled. 'But as you say, he needed someone he trusted; someone to confide in. And that person was me. Now I was *more* than his wife: I was his partner.'

'Yes!' Madonna Arcangelica gripped her right hand into a fist of triumph. 'Women can do these things. I have long believed it was so.'

She stood, crossed the room and as she put a hand gently on Maddalena's forearm, her expression softened, becoming secretive and confidential. 'I have long believed it so. Under what right does Fra Benedict presume to take our confessions? What superior knowledge or judgement do the monks of the Badia di Buonsollazzo have, which give them authority over us? And the bishop? Who is he to determine the lives of a group of women living in isolation?'

As the abbess returned to her seat, Maddalena sat back, for a moment shocked by the vehemence of her outburst. She agreed that their confessor was a stumbling old fool and often wondered how someone with so little common sense managed to find his way the two miles along the ridge of Monte Senario every week without a guide.

As for the bishop? She had not met him, but she certainly could understand the resentment an abbess might have against a patriarchal visitor with authority over the minutiae of their activities, yet who knew little of women or their devotional lives. But the real surprise was the extent of the abbess' commitment to her community and the strength of her resentment against interference from the outside world.

Maddalena looked at the abbess and realised that a door had opened between them. The question that had lain unanswered in her mind was finally becoming clear. Now she knew why Madonna Arcangelica had been so forward in developing their relationship during those first few days.

The abbess had believed she could help Maddalena adjust to the life of confinement. And in that, she had been proved right. And Maddalena's own initial assumption that any intelligent, thinking woman would want to make the most of a new arrival, (especially one who brought with her a world of experience and experience of the world); well, that had surely been correct, too.

But until now, she had not realised that the abbess had an undeclared political agenda; she wanted to use Maddalena in order to understand better the world of men; how they thought, how they went about their business, and, no doubt, how they could be prevented from interfering too much in the day to day life of this, most civilised, of places.

For that, she was beginning to accept, had always been the abbess' intention;

to ensure that the devotional purpose of the convent community was never compromised, but at the same time, interpreting the Rule of their Order in a manner that made the lives of the nuns rewarding, when they could so easily be crushed and dispirited.

Across the room, she saw the abbess falter, as if she had said and shown too much. Instinctively, she now stood, crossed the room, and embraced the surprised abbess in return. She felt her stiffen, then, feeling the warmth of a human embrace perhaps for the first time in many years, squeeze her back. For a moment they clung to each other. Then she pulled back, to arm's length, still holding Madonna Arcangelica's elbows in her hands, and smiled. 'Partnership. It is a wonderful thing.'

In front of her, she saw the abbess' eyes moisten, as she nodded her affirmation. 'Indeed. A precious thing. A thing to be nurtured.'

Maddalena felt the abbess' thin, cold fingers close on her forearms and squeeze them gently. Then, slowly and reluctantly, she let go and sat back in her chair, pulling her thick cloak around her. There was something new and personal in her smile now. For the first time, the woman and not the office speaking to her. 'Pray continue. Your story has new meaning now.'

As the abbess spoke, her breath condensed into a little cloud that hung in the air between them. But the cold did not seem to have dampened her enthusiasm for their conversation.

Maddalena resumed her seat and composed herself.

***

MONASTERY OF SAN GIORGIO MAGGIORE, VENICE
29th September 1434

'I have had a reply. From Antonio Salutati.' Cosimo waves the letter, but keeps reading.

Maddalena looks at the calendar. *That was quick.* Hardly more than a week since Cosimo sent Martelli to Florence to confirm the security of the situation.

'He says we should come. He has consulted widely and it is truly safe to do so.'

***

Within hours, Cosimo and his brother Lorenzo set off for Florence, taking Maddalena with them. Cosimo's cousin Averardo has a fever and feels unfit to travel, so they leave him behind, in the safe hands of the monks of San Giorgio Maggiore.

They reach Ponte a Lago near Vignola the following day and stay with the Magnificent Uguccione de' Contrari. He tells them that he and the Marquess of Ferrara have gathered a small army for their protection on the journey, but when they see them, they are surprised to see there are over two hundred horsemen and an even bigger crowd of foot soldiers. They take Mass together, and while they are doing so, a courier arrives, exhausted, from Florence.

Cosimo opens the letter. 'It's from Antonio Salutati. He says Rinaldo degli Albizzi and Ridolfo Peruzzi have heard we are coming. He estimates that they have gathered an army of 600 to stand against us.'

Maddalena feels nervous. 'Should we turn back?' Cosimo shakes his head for silence and reads on.

'Ah! Apparently, their nerve failed them and on the advice of Bishop Vitelleschi, they went to Santa Maria Novella.' He looks up. 'Pope Euganius IV is staying there, as a fugitive.'

He is reading rapidly now, his eyes scanning the pages. Then he gives a snort of derision. 'They remained with him that night, and while they did so, their troops, without leadership, dispersed to their homes.'

Maddalena shakes her head. Some of these nobles have ambition, but precious little skill when it comes to leadership. 'So what's happening now?'

Cosimo waves to her to be silent, as he reads on. Then he starts to laugh. 'The *Signoria* called for troops. Apparently, more than 3,000 infantry, all carrying our colours, came from the Mugello and stood in the Via Larga by the Casa Vecchia.'

Whether because of the letter or due to Cosimo's expression, Maddalena is feeling more confident already.

'The *Signoria* called a *parlamento*, which gathered in the Piazza della Signoria and immediately authorized a *balia*.' His voice starts to rise. 'It says "Immediately, this met, and with no more than four contrary votes, they have annulled all that had been voted against the Medici last year, reinstating Cosimo and Lorenzo to their former positions."'

Cosimo's eyes are triumphant. 'Right. That's it. We continue. We will leave tomorrow, at first light. If we ride steadily, we can cross the border on the 6th of October.'

Maddalena thinks back to her own journey the previous year. 'We can probably do it quicker than that, can't we?'

Cosimo raises a hand and silences her. His mood now is completely changed; strong and decisive. 'No.' He turns to his secretary. 'Write to Venice and tell them. Then we must go and see the Marquess.' He turns back to Maddalena. The sixth it must be. Don't you see? I want to re-enter the Republic on the anniversary of my exile.'

Suddenly the room is full of confident, busy men.

***

Maddalena couldn't prevent a slight quiver from entering her voice. 'Encouraged by this letter, we left the territory of Ferrara the following day and reached Cutigliano and then Pistoia three days later. And that is how, on the anniversary of his exile, Cosimo once again stepped back into the territory of the Commune of Florence. At midday we reached our house at Careggi and paused for dinner. The house was completely surrounded by a crowd of cheering people.'

Across the room, the abbess has her hand to her mouth, but her eyes are shining.

'While we were eating, a messenger came from the *Signoria*, telling us that a great crowd had gathered by the Casa Vecchia, the Medici house in the Via Larga. Fearful of the crowd getting out of control, the *Signoria* asked Cosimo not to ride into the city until they called him in. He agreed and waited, and told me to remain in Careggi until he called for me. What I tell you now is based on what Cosimo told me later.

'At sunset, they were called, and as the main road was blocked with people, Cosimo and Lorenzo, with just one servant and a mace-bearer from the Commune, rode round the walls, behind the Palazzo del Podestà and entered the Palazzo della Signoria quietly, with the noise of the crowd on Via Larga loud in their ears. Here they were welcomed fulsomely, with the news that Rinaldo degli Albizzi and his son Ormanno had been banished, together with Ridolfo Peruzzi and many other citizens who had supported them.

'And in this manner, Cosimo returned to the arms of the people.' Maddalena sat back and smiled. Even all these years later, the memory still moved her.

'Wonderful. *Seldom has a citizen returning triumphant from a victory been received with such demonstrations of affection.* I remember hearing those words at the time.' Madonna Arcangelica nodded her head. 'It was a time of great rejoicing, not only in the city, but throughout the Mugello and even up here on the mountain.'

Her smile began to fade and she looked at Maddalena seriously. 'How were you received back at the Palazzo Bardi? It was to that house that you finally returned, was it not? I hope the return to Contessina's influence did not set back all you had achieved whilst in Venice?'

'Happily not.' Maddalena kept smiling. She reached into her little casket, selected another letter and began to read it out aloud.

Dear Maddalena,

I am safely delivered to our house. All is well here and the city is quiet. My family are safe and well; Carlo is with Piero and Giovanni, who await me downstairs.

Please go to Cafaggiolo and Il Trebbio and collect my private papers. You know where they are hidden. Then bring them, together with the ledgers and papers we brought from Venice, here, to the Palazzo Bardi.

The studiolo here looks as if it has missed your presence. It awaits you in anticipation, as do I. Come soon.

Cosimo de' Medici
Palazzo Bardi Thursday 7th October 1434

'He wrote to you even before greeting his sons?' The abbess' eyebrows were raised in surprise.

Maddalena nodded, grinning. 'Yes. And as soon as I saw the part about the *studiolo* I knew all was well. It was a code between us. I knew my position of trust in the affairs of the bank would continue unaffected by the presence of

Contessina on the floor below.'

'And the rest?' The abbess has a look of concentration on her face.

For the first time in her presence, Maddalena reddened. 'As you have so quickly surmised, it told me that it would be two days before I returned to him in the *studiolo*, and immediately I knew that in that time, after a year away, he would perform his duty with his wife. But I also knew that he was telling me that not only did the *studiolo* await my presence, but so, next door to it, did his great bed.'

'Life as usual. Nothing lost.' There was a look of satisfaction on the abbess' face, perhaps accompanied by a hint of wistful envy.

'Indeed. But more than that. It was life as usual in the sense that we continued the true partnership we had shared in Venice. But more in the sense that we returned to Florence closer than we had ever been before his exile.'

'Sharing adversity?' The abbess' eyes were level and thoughtful.

'Exactly. Although I had lain with him for over ten years and borne him a son, it was that year of sharing adversity that brought us even closer together; in mind as well as body.'

'Because of the fear?'

'In part. Yes. Cosimo had been deathly afraid at the beginning. Who would not be? To him, he faced an imminent and painful death. But once he knew all he faced was exile, that fear went away and in its place he began to calculate how his life might be saved and made to prosper against adversity.' Maddalena shook her head. 'But I cannot begin to explain the pain it had caused Cosimo to be rejected by his people. To be exiled after giving and doing so much for the city.'

She looked hard at the abbess, wanting to press home the point she was about to make. 'The shame and the unfairness of that rejection changed him forever.'

The abbess saw her expression and paused, nodding thoughtfully, before responding. 'Was he vindictive upon his return? Towards those who had led the opposition against him? Those who had pressed for the death penalty?'

Maddalena smiled enigmatically. She knew her answer would sum up the way Cosimo handled his position of power for the rest of his life, with the apparent and the real always running beside each other, but always a convenient distance apart.

'He didn't need to be vindictive. It was all done for him. The city had realised from its short period under the Albizzi that it could not survive and maintain the way of life to which it had become accustomed, without a benefactor. And Cosimo, they knew, was that benefactor. The *Signoria* were so desperate to please him that they hung on his every sign and expression, and acted upon them. The Albizzi had already been banished. Palla Strozzi, although over seventy, was exiled for ten years, despite, or perhaps because of, Cosimo's half-hearted defence; whilst the others were sent away or stripped of power by making them nobles, and therefore ineligible for office.

'But surely, he did not allow everything to continue as before?'

Maddalena shook her head. 'Cosimo said "the democratic process of government will continue" and everybody cheered, but the reality from then on, became quite different. Cosimo had finally realised that the complicated democratic processes which had been designed many years before to prevent one single noble from taking control were, in reality, preventing the city from being effectively governed at all.

'So quietly, over the next six months, he changed everything. The *squittini* ceased; there was no longer anyone to scrutinise the lists of people eligible for office to make sure everyone had a fair chance. As a result, those who supported the Medici remained and their opponents' names simply disappeared from the *borse*.

'These ballot bags, which physically held the names of those from whom positions of authority were chosen, remained under the control of the *Accopiatore*; theoretically, those who bring together the eligible names from which the *Podestà* (the otherwise powerless official representing authority), would choose by blind selection. So once again, only Cosimo's closest supporters found their names going into the bags.

'Once he could be sure that the priors who formed the *Signoria* and the *Gonfaloniere* who led it were all to a man close supporters of his policy, the democratic process could indeed be maintained. And this time, it worked; always coming to the right conclusion, and still by democratic means.'

Maddalena saw an intense look of concentration in the abbess' eyes and wondered which aspect of what had just been described she proposed to adopt.

'Clever.' The expression on Madonna Arcangelica's face confirmed what Maddalena had been thinking.

She nodded.

'And quiet. Very quiet.'

Chapter 12
Casa Vecchia
19th December 1457

'Once things had settled down, did Cosimo's wife make any attempt to usurp some of your position? She must have been jealous of the closeness that had developed between the two of you during his exile?' Madonna Arcangelica had arrived early for their conversation and already she was seated.

Fresh snows had fallen and the convent was deep in snowdrifts. More than once they had considered giving up the tower for their conversations, but each time it had been the abbess who insisted. It was clear she valued the occasional escape from her responsibilities and particularly from the need to be accessible to the other nuns at all times.

Although nothing had been said, there seemed to be a general understanding throughout the convent that when the abbess and the Medici Nun retired to the tower for their private conversations, they were not to be disturbed. There had been rumours, of course. On one occasion, the old nuns had let it be known that Cosimo de' Medici himself had made it a condition of his generosity to the convent that his Black Nun would take over from Madonna Arcangelica in the spring as abbess and that these discussions were their way of handing over the responsibility. But no one had been sure how this shocking fact had been discovered and in any event, none of the young ones believed it. The abbess, meanwhile, had made a mental note.

Maddalena had been thinking of talking about something else, but the abbess' question took her straight back to her years at the CasaVecchia. *Yes* she thought. *That will do. That will do nicely.*

'Yes she was jealous. More so than ever, in fact, and resentful. But in some way, she seemed to have come to terms with the fact that I still slept with Cosimo.'

The abbess raised a surprised eyebrow, and Maddalena shrugged. 'Cosimo slept with her rarely by this time and when he did, it was as a duty rather than a pleasure. I'm sure Contessina knew that. Perhaps, having reached the age of forty-four, and by this time being very large, she saw it more as a duty than a pleasure herself. Or perhaps she no longer saw it as important. Whatever the reasoning in her mind, it had ceased to be an issue between us, perhaps because the other jealousy took over.'

Again the enquiring eyebrow, but the abbess said nothing. She didn't need to. By this time, Maddalena could sense her responses.

'For years she had satisfied herself that she ran the house and family, and told herself that all I did for Cosimo was to tidy his *studiolo* and "scribble in his books" as she once described it. But after the year of exile, it was clear from a number of our conversations over the meal table, which we all shared together, that he and I were part of a world from which she was excluded. Worse than that, the outside world – the excluded world, not only encompassed the dealings and fortunes of the Medici Bank, but the political leadership of the Commune and City of Florence as well. So instead of being left out of one world, she now found herself excluded from two.'

'Two worlds? Why was that?'

'Almost immediately after our return from exile, Cosimo began to call meetings in the Palazzo Bardi and the priors would be seen crossing the Ponte Vecchio in the winter rain to fulfil his wishes. That in turn meant that the *piano nobile* became a public area, with the *sala*, the largest room in the house: Cosimo's *studiolo* and even his *camera*, the private bedroom where we slept together, were used to meet priors, ambassadors and other visiting dignitaries. So slowly, the banking rooms also became the political rooms, and as a result of my position with the bank, that whole floor became my domain and not hers.'

'I'm sure she must have hated that. Being excluded from part of her own home.' Madonna Arcangelica seemed to have developed a strong dislike for Contessina and always appeared to delight in her discomfort in these little conversations.

'She did, but it was worse for her when we moved across the river, to the Medici House.'

'Ah!' The abbess nodded knowingly. 'The Palazzo Medici. I have heard so much about it.'

Maddalena shook her head. 'No. We didn't move to the Palazzo Medici. Not at that time. Cosimo had begun thinking about the Palazzo Medici three years or so before he was exiled, but Michelozzo's redesign was not completed until after we returned from exile, although most of the work took place while we were in Venice. Michelozzo had showed his loyalty to Cosimo by joining him in exile and in response, Cosimo showed his faith in our eventual return by continuing with his design plans while we were in the north. It was, he said, part of his commitment to himself that he would return to Florence one day.

'Even though Michelozzo had completed the outline drawings by the time we left Venice, it took another fourteen years to design the building and the gardens in detail, to buy up all the land, to knock down the old houses along the Via Larga and to complete the construction of the *palazzo* and the gardens. In the end, we did not move there for another ten years, and even then there was work left to do.'

'Where, then, did you live?' The abbess looked confused.

'The Casa Vecchia. Cosimo's father, Giovanni di Bicci, had died four years before we went into exile and his wife, Piccarda Bueri, who we all called Nannina, died six months before Cosimo left the city; so by the time we returned from Venice, the house was empty.

'Cosimo had always felt a slight resentment at living in Oltrarno – on the wrong side of the river and in La Scala, a Bardi *Gonfalone*. The traditional power base of the Medici lay round his father's houses in Via Larga and Piazza del Duomo, and he felt he ought to be there. Now that he was playing an important part in the government of the city, it was important, he said, for him to live in the *Gonfalone* of Leon d'Oro, within the *Quartiere* of Santa Maria Novella.

'So a year after his return from exile, Cosimo moved the family from the Palazzo Bardi, north, across the river, to Giovanni di Bicci's old house, on the Via Larga. His son Piero knocked it down in the end, to complete the gardens of the Palazzo Medici; but for nine years we lived there, on the Via Larga, in what the family referred to as the Casa Vecchia, and we watched and we listened as the new *palazzo* was being built next door.'

***

PALAZZO BARDI, FLORENCE
12th October 1435

'Why don't you put that lip away, Lotta, before you trip over it? Sulking is demeaning in a woman of quality.'

Maddalena pauses as she passes the doorway. She knows she shouldn't eavesdrop, but it isn't often she hears Cosimo berating his wife like that. Rare to hear him use her real name nowadays. She allows herself a smile and begins to make her way down the steps.

'This place is a dump! It's small, it's noisy and it's overcrowded. And worse than that, it's surrounded by ruffians.' Contessina's voice is booming along the corridor.

'Via Larga is not sophisticated enough for your refined tastes?' Cosimo's voice turns silky smooth.

Maddalena winces. She knows what's coming. When Cosimo loses his temper and shouts, she can jolly him round in minutes. But when his voice starts to get cold and sarcastic, she knows it's time to run for cover, because it means he won't stop until he has destroyed you. It's a rare mood and one to be avoided at all costs.

And it only arises if you criticise the family. His family.

Normally hidden, there is, she knows, a deep sensitivity amongst the Medici on the subject of their 'ordinary' roots. Giovanni di Bicci had made a virtue of it and so, on the surface, does Cosimo. But deep down, he is ashamed of not being noble; either as he once admitted, by birth, by example, or by deportment. 'We are,' he once said to her, when in a particularly maudlin mood, 'street traders, by origin and by instinct. It is our strength but also our weakness.'

No accident, then, that Giovanni di Bicci married Cosimo to a Bardi, and his brother Lorenzo to a Cavalcanti. She wonders, when the time comes, who Cosimo will choose for his sons. The girl seems to be an obvious choice. It can be no accident that little Lucrezia has been invited to live amongst the family. A Tornabuoni. Few better, they say, and by all accounts, she is one of the best. Certainly she is one of the brightest.

'It's ridiculous. This house is too small – smaller than the Palazzo Bardi, and with all the visitors we have every day, I feel crowded out in my own home.'

95

Maddalena waits on the top step. She can't miss this. What will his reply be? She knows that Cosimo hated living in Oltrarno. The Borgo Pidiglioso, Flea Lane as they used to call it, was Bardi country. They had been surrounded, Cosimo had once said, 'smothered' by the Bardi, and he had been delighted when the opportunity finally came to move back to his natural environment in the Leon d'Oro.

'Sit down woman, and for once in your life, listen.' The voice is seething, but controlled in its anger. 'It is not *your* home, it is the Medici family home. You are married to me and as such, you are part of it and you will accept its manner of doing things.'

Phew! Maddalena decides she has heard enough. Quietly she creeps on down the stairs. As far as she can remember, it is the only time he has ever contradicted his wife in public, within earshot of a dozen servants at least, and it makes her realise that with the move across the river, things really have changed. Being a Bardi no longer counts as much as it did in the past and it is clear the Medici family now see themselves in a new and more powerful light.

She reaches the foot of the stairs and pauses. Come to think of it, that's not the only sign of a parting of the ways between the Medici and the Bardi. Not only has Cosimo moved his house away from the Bardi enclave, but he has also broken the long-standing tradition of having a Bardi as his General Manager at the Bank.

When Ilarione de' Bardi had died in the January before Cosimo was exiled, he had replaced him with his nephew, Lipaccio di Benedetto de' Bardi. But when they returned from exile and the contracts were renewed, Lipaccio was dispensed with and in his place, Giovanni d'Amerigo Benci and Antonio di Messer Francesco Salutati had been installed as joint General Managers.

None of them had appreciated the fact at the time, but now she realises that that decision had been an indication of the future; that by doing what he had done, Cosimo had begun to break away from the framework of guidance with which his father had tried to surround, and instead started to shape his own future.

Part of that future is to delegate more of the management of the bank to his professional managers and to turn his own attention towards more public involvement in the government of the city. And, she tells herself, in the process, moving the balance of his attention from Contessina, to her.

With that significant thought in her head, she continues down the next flight of stairs. Smiling.

***

'What was his wife's reaction to being told off like that?' Madonna Arcangelica seemed far more interested in the family's private arguments than in the niceties of the management of the Bank or the politics of the city.

Maddalena noted the limitations in her thinking; conscious that the abbess had not fully realised the significance of what she had just been told.

Nevertheless, she allowed her question to lead them forward.

'Contessina went red in the face at so public a rebuke and sulked for two weeks. I knew she would try to get her own back, because she was, deep down, both spoiled and petulant. Soon it became clear how she planned to do it.'

'How?'

'She used the only weapon she had left: the children.'

'How old were they, by this time?'

'Piero was nineteen. Quite grown up in his stuttering, hesitant way, and trying hard but ineffectually to emulate his father, so he was no longer considered one of the children. Giovanni was thirteen and Carlo, my boy, was coming up to his seventh birthday.'

'Quite a spread. Hardly a close group, I suppose?'

Maddalena shook her head. 'They might not have been such good friends had not little Lucrezia Tornabuoni, who was just a year older than Carlo, started to become a regular, almost daily visitor. She and Carlo were like twins and they went everywhere together, always following Giovanni.

'The Tornabuoni were a fine family; rich wool traders who did a great deal of business with the Medici and were considered close friends. Francesco di Simone Tornabuoni was descended from a long line of *nobili de torri* – long-standing landed nobility.

'The original family name had been Tornaquinci, but Francesco's branch of the family had changed their names in order to be able to accept positions in the government, which by this time, they did regularly. Nanna, Francesco's wife, was of an equally old family, and their daughter Lucrezia seemed to have inherited the best of both of them. She had her father's business brain and her mother's sense of style and propriety, despite also having her mother's plain looks.

'They lived a short distance away from us, in the same *Quartiere* of Santa Maria Novella and in addition to their *palazzo* on the road running north from Ponte Santa Trinita, they also owned a row of fine houses beside the river, along the Lungarno, as well as a number of estates in the country. That little Lucrezia was to make a great deal of difference to all of our lives, we did not yet know; but at the time of which I speak, Contessina, who had been told to bring up Carlo as her own, tried hard to keep all three of them from me.'

'And did she succeed?'

Maddalena laughed. 'Absolutely not.'

***

PALAZZO BARDI, FLORENCE
12th October 1435

'Mr Ambassador, I cannot stress enough the importance of what I have just told you.'

'I agree and I accept your assurances completely.' The Milanese ambassador looks at Cosimo and nods gravely. War and the avoidance of war are as important as any subject to a diplomat.

Maddalena sees the relief on Cosimo's face. She knows he had expected more difficulty; prevarication certainly, and even real barriers to progress; perhaps as much as a downright refusal. This reaction is better than expected. Gently does it now.

'There is one small issue…' The ambassador begins, and then pauses as he sees Cosimo's eyes stray towards the open window.

Maddalena follows his gaze as Cosimo turns towards her for assistance.

Just outside the window, rising and falling invitingly within reach, is a small parcel; a box, made of stiff paper, wrapped carefully in ribbon, being lowered and raised gently on a long, thin piece of twine.

Maddalena frowns, although to Cosimo's experienced eye it is an amused and tolerant frown. She shakes her head. 'Ignore it.'

But Cosimo has forgotten what he was saying and besides, the ambassador has now turned and is standing beside Maddalena, facing the window, and examining the small parcel quizzically. 'What is it?'

Cosimo recovers, now grinning. 'I fear I am discovered. I suspect it is a secret message from one of my spies.'

The ambassador steps back and before his consternation can get the better of him; Cosimo reaches through the window, and untying the twine, retrieves the box.

Closely watched by the ambassador, he opens the box. Inside, as Maddalena expected, is a small, slightly overcooked cake. Play-acting somewhat, for the benefit of the ambassador, who is now standing close to him, Cosimo breaks the cake open and reveals a folded piece of paper. He unfolds it; one, twice, then begins to read the spidery handwriting.

He looks furtively at the ambassador, and then hands the box, the cake and the piece of paper to Maddalena. 'It's for you.'

Now she is the centre of the ambassador's attention. She reads the note. *Meet us in the loggia in one hour. (Signed) The Secret Three.*

The ambassador is craning his neck to read the words. But maintaining the play, she walks away from him, takes a pen and writes a reply on the back. *I will be there.* Then she signs it, puts it in the box and, walking across to the window, and ties the string again.

She looks at the ambassador, who is watching the whole charade with silent fascination. 'Our secret code.' Then, slowly and ostentatiously, she tugs three times on the string and lets go. With a series of irregular jerks, the box rises from view and disappears.

Maddalena closes the window and nods silently to Cosimo, who gives a formal half-bow to the ambassador. 'Please excuse the interruption. Now, where was I?'

For a moment, the Milanese ambassador, mouth agape, seems lost for words. Then he shakes his head. 'Avoiding a war, was it?'

'How long did these games continue?' The abbess was still grinning.

Maddalena wondered how long it would be before little Elena was enrolled in cooking lessons. Somehow, she thought, not long.

'Oh, for years, although they changed later. About a year after Lucrezia began to come to us, the relationship was formalised. She became part of our family, on the understanding that she would share the Medici humanistic education, and soon after, she was joined by one of her brothers.'

'Lucrezia had a brother?'

'She had six. Five of them were older than she was, but little Giovanni Battista was eighteen months younger.'

'Six months younger than your son Carlo, then?'

'Exactly. And that's why they all got on so well. Giovanni di Cosimo was the self-appointed leader and Lucrezia, Carlo, and Giovanni Battista formed the rest of 'The Secret Four' who followed him around everywhere. It was the beginning of lifelong friendships.

'Did they remain close, in later years? The children?'

Maddalena looked at the interest on the abbess' face and thought how sad it was that the convent did not manage to attract more children. She obviously adored them and watching her with little Elena, it was clear how well children responded to her in turn.

She nodded. 'Yes, but not, perhaps, as we might have guessed. Giovanni Battista later joined the Medici Bank and ran the Papal branch in Rome, while Lucrezia married into the family.'

'Of course! She married Giovanni, didn't she? Tell me she did?' Madonna Arcangelica looked delighted that it had all worked out so well.

Maddalena shook her head. 'Unfortunately not. It was, in my opinion, the biggest single mistake that Cosimo ever made in his life. But I can hear the bell calling us. I shall have to tell you about Lucrezia another day.'

Outside, the clear sky had been replaced by another torn bank of purple and grey cloud, swirling in from the north. Already the ridge of the hill beside the Badia di Buonsollazzo had disappeared. There would be another snowstorm that night, and by the look of it, a heavy one.

What a winter.

Chapter 13
Salutation
13th February 1458

Suora Maddalena stared at the pristine pages of her journal and realised that she was still afraid of them. For week after week, when she was not sitting with the abbess, she had retreated here, to her tower cell, opened her journal, and looked at it, reading the first words that she had written. But week after week she had been unable to continue.

Now, once again she looked at the words; the first words that she had written. She had been confident then, that he would visit her very soon, and that the final stages of the plan would quickly be confirmed and put into place. But now, after four months of silence, she was not so sure.

Yes it had been the coldest winter for twenty years, and judging by the view from their mountain top, the path between Florence and the Mugello valleys had probably been impassable for weeks. But mere weather had never stopped the Medici before, and any suggestion to Cosimo that a message sent by him had not been delivered because of a snowfall would have been treated with derision.

But if not the weather, then what? Had he changed his mind? Had circumstances changed? Was she, indeed, still part of the arrangements at all? With every silent week that passed, her confidence slipped further, and with it, her indecision as to what to write had grown.

She had even, on occasions, sat in front of the journal and asked herself whether Cosimo had been taken ill or was even – *God protect us from the thought* – dead. Everything was possible; a riding accident (improbable on that ponderous mule), poison in his food (a considered possibility for many years of his life), or, more prosaically, a bad bout of gout, confining him painfully to his bed.

She still felt overawed, because the journal had been a present from Cosimo and, she knew, carefully chosen. She was nervous because the pages were so new, and because she had already made a mistake on the first page. But more than that, she was afraid; because she still hoped that one day Cosimo himself would read what she had written. Yet now, she was no longer sure what to write.

She had felt she had so much to say, so much, now that she was a free woman, to tell him; things she could never have said as his slave. But now, when it came to putting pen to paper, she could not bring herself to do it. And with every passing week, the problem grew worse rather than better.

How should she address him? She thought she had decided that, but now, after weeks of agonising, the question seemed to have become insurmountable once again. Many years ago, in their first months, she had called him 'master' as befitted the relationship between a slave and the man who owned her, but as time went by and as their private intimacy behind closed doors had grown, the word had come to have a different connotation: master as the partner to mistress.

At first, it had been a gradual change, with little said; simply exchanges of expression, movements and mannerisms, and then, one afternoon, as he went to take her in his private bedroom in the Palazzo Bardi in Florence, she had seen him wince with pain; his manhood stolen by the stab of arthritis at the critical moment.

She did not know to this day what had given her the courage to do it. But she had done it, and it had worked. From that moment on, but only when they were alone, he had insisted she call him Cosimo and he, a twinkle of secret satisfaction in his eye, had called her *Fantinina* – his little jockey.

But that had been more than three years into their relationship, and a matter of absolute privacy between them. Maddalena looked at the page in front of her and shook her head. Such thoughts were inappropriate. Here, on the written page, such private memories would always be out of place. Here, she should surely refer to the extent to which he had changed her life. For although he had begun as her master, never once had he treated her as a slave and never once had she felt like one when in his company. Instead, from that first encounter in Venice, he had proved to be her saviour; her rescuer.

She had certainly been afraid on their first night; afraid of the unknown. But to her surprise, he had been gentle with her, recognising her virginity and taking his time, cajoling rather than demanding; guiding her into accepting him. It was an initiation she looked back on with tingling pleasure and gratitude. He had been a good teacher and she had, without doubt, been a more than willing pupil.

His teaching had extended beyond the bedroom, and into the *studiolo*. He had tested her reading and writing and made her practice daily, to improve them both. He had explained his books of account; the concepts of wealth as assets and obligations as liabilities, how the system of double-entry bookkeeping acknowledged that what was an asset to one party in a transaction automatically became a liability in the other's eyes. Recognising that relationship, he had shown her how to set out the inter-branch ledgers in order to keep account of the separate value of each branch of the bank, and yet to calculate its overall profitability from one year to another. He had been her guide; her mentor.

Over the years, his trust in her had increased, and with it, his reliance upon her. And so, through time, she had moved to be his companion whilst he, with all his power and authority, had developed a deep-seated confidence in her, giving her responsibilities in his *studiolo* that she would never have dreamed of asking for. And in this way, slowly but inexorably, he had become her emancipator.

Finally, when the problems arose with the bank and with the family, and he needed her to leave the Palazzo Medici on Via Largo and come here, to the convent, he had acted again. It was known that no slave could become a *Suora* – a sister nun – but only a *conversa* – taking only simple vows and effectively having the status and authority of a servant – and even then, only under exceptional circumstances.

Without hesitation, and taking delight in being able to do so, he had given her back her freedom, issuing a formal certificate to the effect that she was a free woman, and conferring a generous pension upon her for life. And in so doing, he had, finally, become her liberator.

How, then to address him? What salutation to give him in this, perhaps her final communication to him? It was, to her, and she knew to him, important, and as such, so much harder to decide.

She felt a sudden flutter of confidence and picked up her pen again. In her mind she heard the first words and, encouraged, she dipped the pen into the ink. Then, with only a little trepidation, she began to write.

Cosimo, what shall I call thee?

What name shall I give to the ties that bind me to you? How many and varied, indeed, are the knots that may be tied on one chord?

I was your slave, and you my master yet in that capacity, you were also my teacher in many skills and my mentor in life's opportunities.

Yet what slave, this, who was surely saved from a short and brutal life of misuse and suffering and instead made into a comfortable and, I believe, valued companion? My rescuer, then, in this respect.

As for our son, I can only thank you and call you provider. You treated him as your own sons, gave him every advantage and ensured his progress, and for all these blessings, I thank you on his behalf as well as my own.

And in showing me the inner workings of the Bank and allowing me to use my mind, I could name you saviour, for without that I surely would have gone mad.

Later, with learning and experience, you had the courage and generosity to give me authority within the Bank, to receive instructions and later still, to issue them. In this respect, did you not, then, act as my emancipator?

Then releasing me from legal bondage, you were my liberator, making me a free woman. Even then, you did not leave me without position, but, acting as my deliverer, brought me to safety, comfort and serenity within these holy walls.

So what shall I call you?

Saviour would be blasphemous.

I shall therefore call you dearest, and hope you understand the rest.

Your Maddalena.

She wiped her pen clean and returned it to its holder. She put the stopper back in the ink bottle and returned it to its allotted place in her writing case. She dusted the writing and blew on it, gently and carefully, until she was sure it was dry and that she could finally close the book without defacing it.

A wave of euphoria flooded through her and made her shiver. She had done it. She had completed the first full page and in so doing, set the tone – more conversational than she had ever envisaged – for the pages to follow. The rest would be easier from now on.

She looked outside, just at the moment when a shaft of bright sunlight broke through the clouds and hit a bank of snow across the valley at the base of a coppice of dark trees. Immediately what had been an ill-defined amorphous white mass gained form, and contours, edges and slopes, pale blue shadows and sunlit facets almost orange in their warmth appeared.

Was the worst over? Would the winter now begin to abate and allow spring's confident warmth to replace it? She hoped so. It had been a long winter. Now, at last, perhaps someone would come.

Chapter 14
Donatello
27th February 1458

'Spring at last.'

Eyes shut, in order that she would sense every ounce of the experience, Maddalena pushed open the big door which led from her cell to the balcony outside, and felt the sun's rays warm her to the very bones. For a moment, she stood there, her eyes still tight shut, simply sensing the pleasure of the moment; life itself returning and warming every part of her body. How long she seemed to have waited for this moment. What a long winter it had been.

Two weeks before she had sat here, writing in her journal, and the sun had suddenly come out. She had thought then, that spring had come, but the following day it had snowed again and another week or more had been spent hunkered down in the gloom, trying to keep warm.

It had been a long and lonely winter. In the middle of December, just when her conversations with the abbess had reached a new plane of understanding and disclosure, Madonna Arcangelica had suddenly been struck down with a fever. For two months she had been so weak that she could not perform her duties at all, and Maddalena, amongst others, had feared she would die. But slowly, despite the bitter cold, the abbess had recovered. Now her convalescence had at last progressed to the point where they could recommence their meetings. Not only that, but at the abbess' insistence, they were going to meet at the top of Maddalena's tower, as before.

With a pleasurable finality, she fastened back the doors and walked out onto the balcony. Below her, the sun shone brightly onto deep-lying snow. Now, she was sure, the worst of the winter was over. Soon the snow would melt, the streams would run again and everywhere would, once again, be green.

Yes she thought to herself *a long winter.* A winter of cold, of hardship, and for her, in particular, a winter of deep and sapping loneliness. Not only had she been deprived of her weekly conversations with the abbess, but the visit which she was sure Cosimo would make within weeks of her arrival at the convent, had still not materialised. There had been nothing. He had not come, he had not written, and he had not even sent a messenger.

On many dark days in recent weeks, her confidence had failed her. She had even wondered whether the family were still there, at the Palazzo Medici or whether, somehow, the whole edifice had been a dream, a reality now gone. Had there, after all, been another coup and the whole of the Medici family had been murdered or exiled? She simply did not know, and up here, on this little hilltop, beyond the upper valleys of the Mugello, there had been no way of finding out.

During the last two weeks, the weather had been particularly hard. The valley had been snow-bound for eight days without a single day's respite, and no news had been received from the outside world. Not that the nuns' little community had been overly concerned. They were in a sturdy and dry building, with a deep, reliable well that has never once frozen so thickly that a well-dropped bucket could not break through. They had glass in a number of the windows (including the small ones in the tower rooms) to keep out the wind and sturdy shutters on them all. They also had a plentiful supply of cut wood to cook with and to keep them warm, and their larders were as well stocked as expected of any well-ordered house of God. In other words, despite the wintry conditions surrounding them, they had been comfortable.

Against all expectations, no one else had contracted Madonna Arcangelica's fever and since then, there had been no other illness. It could only be, Maddalena thought, because there had been few visitors to bring illness to them, the passes into and out of the valley having being totally blocked with snow.

In some eyes, there had been compensations. The depth of snow had prevented most travel within the valley, and completely up here on the hills. Their confessor, Fra Benedict, had been unable to reach them from the Badia di Buonsollazzo, some two miles away, for many weeks. That, and the enforced laxity of Madonna Arcangelica, had meant that their religious observances had slipped badly. In the absence of discipline, and with the numbing cold a convenient excuse to salve frozen consciences, the nocturnal prayers, at Matins and Lauds, had, somehow, been put aside and for over a week now: they had not prayed before Prime, at six in the morning. Such indulgence! For most of the nuns, therefore, the recent weeks had passed somewhat pleasantly.

But not for *Suora* Maddalena.

Hers was a more demanding nature, and she had found herself fretting that, perhaps, Cosimo was waiting for her to do something important, and that she was unable to rise to the occasion. Perhaps under these circumstances, Fra Benedict's absence had been a blessing, for Cosimo had sworn her to secrecy about his project, and had she been able to take confession, her loyalties might well have been uncomfortably tested.

But now all that was behind them and as the sun warmed her face, and as she heard the familiar dragging footsteps on the stairs beneath, she found herself, for the first time in many weeks, looking forward, and not back.

***

'You were telling me, the last time we met, about living with Contessina and the children at Casa Vecchia. I think you said you were there for nine years did you not? What was happening with the building of the Palazzo Medici? It seems to have been the background to your story for so long. Did it really take that long to build?'

It was as if there had been no break in their conversations, and despite her protestations of the earlier weeks, Madonna Arcangelica seemed once again to be full of questions.

Maddalena smiled. She was more than content to be back in the abbess' company; back in their familiar routine, and this time, the abbess' question led her into, rather than away from, the part of her life she had decided to talk about.

'Work on the Palazzo Medici was continuing. It was all proceeding noisily, next door to us; first a great dusty hole in the ground, then like a great quarry, with blocks of stone everywhere, in what seemed to be utter chaos. But slowly, by some mystical process of organisation that only Michelozzo fully understood, a huge building started to rise out of the ground.

'I saw Michelozzo almost daily, because early each morning he used to drop in to the *studiolo*, unroll his great drawings, and discuss progress with Cosimo. Then, once their business was over, Cosimo would often go into the *sala* a couple of rooms away, to talk politics, and I would be left with the architect.

'By this time, Cosimo trusted me to make all the entries in the special account book we had opened to keep track of the project. Michelozzo would open his own little account book and pull out all manner of slips of paper, and then we would stand beside each other, our books on the writing bench, and write up our entries, making sure the books tallied. And for what seemed like an age, that was my only involvement with the new house.

'And later, when I did have a part to play, it was not with the house itself, but with the garden.'

The abbess shook her head, surprised and confused. 'I did not know you were a gardener? You have never mentioned it.'

'In the garden, but not, I fear, concerned with plants.' Maddalena felt herself smiling at the ludicrous thought.

'It began when Cosimo asked me to meet him and to bring Carlo with me. He wrote to me, from Prato I think it was. One moment, I still have the letter here.'

She reached into her casket and picked her way through the letters. Then, finding the right one, she nodded and began to read it aloud.

Dear Maddalena,
I shall be leaving Prato the day after tomorrow and will be home before the weekend.
On Monday, I shall have a very distinguished visitor, who I should like to introduce to you and to Carlo. Please bring Carlo to the studiolo at ten in the morning, when all will be revealed.
Please ask Carlo to bring his football.
Cosimo.
At Prato Tuesday, 12th April 1440

'Of course, it was an instruction, not a request.'

***

CASA VECCHIA, FLORENCE
18th April 1440

'Maddalena? What are we doing here? And why did I have to bring my

106

football?'

She feels strange, standing, waiting outside the door of a room she would normally walk straight into, but she knows that today's proceedings are of a formal nature and therefore certain protocols will have to be observed. Like her son having to call her by her given name, whilst Contessina is addressed as 'Mother' by all the children, including Lucrezia and Carlo. It hurts, but she takes comfort in knowing that it's a small battle and she's winning all the big ones.

She has Cosimo's letter in one hand and Carlo, now twelve and already as tall as her, holding this huge football and squirming with embarrassment, in the other.

As soon as Cosimo opens the door, Carlo, who, amongst many other things, has learned impatience from Giovanni, speaks. 'What is it, Father? What is your surprise? Your letter said we were to be ready for a surprise. Why did I have to bring my football?'

Ignoring his questions, Cosimo leads them into the *studiolo* and closes the door. Maddalena watches as Carlo looks around him, seeming to be overcome at his first view of the most private room in the house.

She understands. Her son has lived in the Palazzo Bardi from the day he was born there until the age of seven, and in the Casa Vecchia for the five years since; but apart from occasional flying visits led by Giovanni, when the little gang would quickly be chased out, giggling and screaming, he has never before been allowed to enter his father's *studiolo*.

Carlo looks at her, searchingly. *So this is where you two disappear to* his expression seems to say. She reads his look in an instant, and tries to divert it. 'Don't touch anything! These are the ledgers of the bank. Private documents, and of immense value. You must touch nothing.'

By the way Carlo jumps back; she realises she's overreacted.

Carlo looks at his father for confirmation, and again she can read his expression. The boy has such an open manner. It is part of his charm and, perhaps, the reason he is Cosimo's favourite, at least in private. Piero and Giovanni are lovely boys, but they are both secretive and manipulative, just like their mother.

It is obvious the boy has noticed her tone of voice and she is suddenly aware that he has never seen her to be so forthright in Cosimo's presence in the past. Her manner in the public rooms and at mealtimes is always quiet and submissive

As if in confirmation, Carlo looks at her, one eyebrow raised, and she smiles. He really is so wonderfully transparent. His questions might just as well have been written on a large piece of paper. *Is this another of your secrets?* his eyes seem to say. *Behind these private doors? Are you different with him, here? Is this your true relationship and how I came to be born?*

Is he thinking that, or is it just her conscience speaking? She does not reply. How can she? Much of her is dying for an opportunity to tell him, to explain how much she and Cosimo loved each other, but the secret is Cosimo's, not hers, to tell.

Cosimo sees their expressions, reads them in an instant, and responds. 'Your mother is right. These are important documents.' He looked amused. 'But today's business has nothing to do with the Medici Bank or with these papers. We have a visitor.'

He ducks through the small door that she knows leads to his private bedroom and returns, followed by a small, bearded man, of about his own age; perhaps around fifty. His clothing is dirty, torn and ragged, but he does not seem to notice and nor, she is unsurprised to see, does Cosimo. Although she has never had reason to speak to him, she knows the sculptor by reputation and she has seen him in the house and in the streets of Florence on numerous occasions.

Cosimo addresses himself to Carlo. 'Let me introduce you to my friend; the genius Donato di Niccolò di Betto Bardi. He is, of course, a distant relation, through my wife's family.' As he says it, he opens a hand to the visitor. The man nods to Maddalena, bows his head slightly at Carlo and mumbles "Donatello".

He looks at Maddalena levelly, with a detached artist's eye, as if measuring distances and proportions and then he turns to Carlo. Again that long, appraising look. Carlo twists awkwardly, not liking to be stared at in quite so direct a manner.

Donatello seems to think for a moment, and then returns his attention to Cosimo. 'I agree. It would work. Indeed, I would go so far as to say it will work, and it will be a work of historical significance.'

Cosimo pats him on the shoulder. 'I knew you would agree. Can you do it without bringing the whole of the *Signoria* down on our heads?'

Donatello walks round the room, looking at her and at Carlo as he does so. Carlo starts to get alarmed. He whispers to her. 'What is happening? Are we about to be sold? Does this man intend to buy us?'

Reminded uncomfortably of the past, she shakes her head, and then looks at Cosimo as she replies. 'I think he intends to steal us. But then, later, he will give us back. Yes?'

Cosimo grins. 'You are perceptive, Maddalena. And you are, as so often, right. I have asked Donatello to make a life-sized sculpture of you.'

'Of me or of Carlo?' She frowns with uncertainty as she says it, and realises that she may be appearing overly defensive. 'Or of both of us?' She looks at Carlo. 'I think your father is making sport of us, Carlo.'

Cosimo laughs and embraces them both. 'It is a proposal I have had in my mind for some time,' he says. 'A sculpture, but cast in bronze. It will stand in a position of great prominence, in the grounds of the new house. It will be a centrepiece of the garden.'

He looks across at Donatello and winks. 'As far as the city elders are concerned, it will be a sculpture of The Boy David, victorious over Goliath, standing in a posture of dominance. They will see its glory as reflecting their own.' He bends down to Carlo and whispers in his ear. 'I can be confident that they will interpret it that way because I shall tell them that's what it is. And we shall not tell them the truth of it, will we?'

Carlo, proud to be addressed so directly by his father, shakes his head and grins. Maddalena can see a smile appearing on Donatello's face. It is not the sort of smile she is sure she likes, and she has a horrible idea she knows why. 'Which of us is to play the part of David?'

Donatello looks to Cosimo for guidance, and Cosimo indicates with a nod that he should reply. 'Tell them.'

'You both are.' Donatello's face is that of a man with a vision. 'A composite sculpture, an amalgam of both of you. Mother and son, in one body.'

'Unclothed?' Maddalena thinks she is beginning to understand, and she is not sure the thought pleases her.

Donatello nods; almost a bow. 'Of course. In the classical tradition. It will be the first such sculpture for over a thousand years. A masterpiece. Look.' Quickly, he takes a piece of paper from his shoulder bag and makes a small sketch. 'A young boy, standing victorious, his foot resting on the head of his vanquished opponent, a great sword in his hand.'

Carlo steps forward, fascinated, as the drawing emerges. He points to the severed head, lying beneath the victor's foot, and laughs, delightedly. 'I've got it now. That's what the football is for. To stand on.' He takes one more look at the drawing, then drops the football on the floor and takes up the pose, standing dramatically.

Donatello applauds. 'Excellent. Almost perfect. All you need to do now is to take your clothes off and we can start.'

Carlo looks down at his pose, then at Maddalena, and shakes his head. 'I'm not standing naked, not in this position, and certainly not with him.' He points to Donatello. 'I've heard all about him. He's a dirty old pervert. Nobody is safe.'

Maddalena moves to intervene, even if inwardly agreeing with her son. If she has understood correctly, she, too, will have to pose naked in that position, and it is not a prospect that she embraces with any enthusiasm either. But her son, and Donatello? Not alone in the same room. Not if she has anything to do with it.

Her expression must have told them exactly what she was thinking. Nevertheless, Donatello seems quite unconcerned. 'Donna Maddalena, fear not. In your case, you will not be required to pose naked from the waist down. That part of the finished article will be…a boy. Yes, most definitely, a boy.'

She is taken aback. Accepted as she is amongst the nobles and wealthy merchants of the city, none do her the courtesy of calling her *Donna*. 'Madonna. Great Lady.' She thinks she likes the sound of it. And as for the posing, well, yes, she is relieved. But Carlo?

Cosimo winks at Donatello and grins. 'I said we would reach this point quite quickly.' He turns to Carlo, who is looking uncomfortable. 'You are, I know, an outstanding footballer. No brawl in the street would be complete without your participation, so I hear. That is why I suggested this pose. It is victorious; triumphant. Three goals to nil and you the single goal-scorer.'

As he continues, he turns his head toward Donatello. 'Were you not my son, Carlo, I might feel the need to warn you about this man's appetites, but in your case, I am sure, you need have no fear.'

His eyes turn back toward Donatello. 'You know the rules. One false move and I'll have your balls chopped off and fed to the pigs.'

Donatello just grins, looks at Carlo with an exaggerated look of resigned disappointment on his face, and raises his hands. 'Alas, it is true. But I promise I shall leave my private appetites behind when I enter the doors of this house. In any event, you shall have a chaperone, whenever you pose for me.'

He slants his eyes across to Maddalena. 'It is for the best.'

Carlo looks at her, horrified, and then turns to his father. 'Not her? I'm not undressing in front of her, and standing like that, naked, with my leg up, and everything showing.'

Maddalena gives him her most motherly smile. 'Don't worry. I am your mother. I have seen it all before.' Even as she says it, she knows it is the wrong thing to say. Carlo opens his mouth to protest further but Cosimo intervenes before his project can suffer a setback. 'The sittings, or perhaps I should say standing poses, in this case, will take place here, in the privacy of this room, and I personally shall act as chaperone, for both of you. Is that agreed?'

Maddalena looks at her son, and to her relief and delight he smiles, broadly. 'Yes, Father. I shall do as you instruct.' He raises an eyebrow. 'Do you think I could have a new football? A slightly bigger one?'

Cosimo smiles, nodding. He turns to Donatello, who seems relieved that they have an agreement. 'Goliath would have had a large head, would he not? I think a larger football might be appropriate?'

Donatello bows. 'Certainly, Magnificence. Certainly. Allow me to see to it.'

***

Suora Maddalena took her hands from her mouth. She had managed to shock herself with her own memories. 'The things we used to say in those days. And the things we used to do. Without a second thought.'

She looked across the room to see whether her revelations had shocked the abbess, but Madonna Arcangelica looked better than she had for months. 'I knew I would feel better once I listened to one of your stories. I said to myself as I climbed those infernal steps. *Press on; you will be pleased you came, once the story starts.* Tell me, how was it? Posing for such a great, yet as I understand it, deeply flawed man?'

Maddalena cast her mind back.

Donatello had been almost as good as his word. She *had* stood before him; five times, but despite his initial promises, he had insisted it had to be naked. Each time, she had squirmed uncomfortably, sure that her breasts looked like prunes and her bottom like two overripe pears.

But Cosimo had remained present and his calm look had made her feel better. And each time had been less of an ordeal than the last. Then she had sat a further three times, now clothed, although with a loose gown and wearing a great straw hat that Donatello had brought from the market. He had combed her hair forward, bringing it over her shoulders as she had worn it years before.

In due course, Carlo had earned his new football. Cosimo told her he had stood for hours, holding a great sword that Cosimo had called forth from the

110

armoury, and with his left foot placed securely on the football. Cosimo said he had been proud of him. Each time, he said, the boy had stood for over an hour, without rest or complaint, while Donatello sketched and measured and sketched again; from all angles.

She remembered Cosimo had said that the only source of disagreement had been how to place his left hand, in order to balance the great sword in his right. Eventually Donatello had placed him with his hand somewhat provocatively on his left hip, fist clenched, the back of his hand against his hip. She had thought it looked wrong in the sketches, but when the finished article was brought to the house two years later, she had had no reservations about any of it. She had been proud of it then, and she still was.

'It was much less of an ordeal than I had expected. And Carlo later said the same. Although the process was terribly drawn out, with many sittings for each of us. But the end result was, indeed, a true masterpiece.'

'You liked it? Even though it was an amalgamation of you and your son? You did not find that awkward?'

Maddalena tried to remember. She had always hated that straw hat. And Donatello had made her nose too long. Aristocratic perhaps, but too long. Much too long. But for all that, she had loved the sculpture. She loved the fact that it was Cosimo's private bow in her direction. His expression of thanks for her years of loyalty, through the good years and the bad. And his recognition, if only to her, that her son, their son, was his favourite.

In that respect, it had been a poke in the eye for Piero and for Giovanni. And, she liked to think, for both reasons, a poke in the eye for their plump, self-satisfied mother. She had held her tongue for so many years, and victory, when it came, had been all the sweeter for it. What a pity she was not able to tell her.

'Yes I liked it. Very much.'

A supportive smile from the abbess. 'And what was the reaction of the citizens, and of the priors on the *Signoria*?'

'It was a very public test. Donatello's *David* was placed in the position of honour, in the garden of the Palazzo Medici and everyone marvelled at it. I stood at the back of the crowd, quietly, and I listened to their private comments. The younger, unmarried, women were embarrassed yet fascinated, whispering to each other behind their hands, their eyes wide with concentration. The older ones were dismissive. "My husband never looked like that," I heard a number of them say.'

'And the men? What was their reaction?' Madonna Arcangelica is looking out of the window, but her mind, Maddalena can see, is looking at the sculpture as she visualises it.

'Most of them went unnaturally quiet. They studied it with dry lips and concentrated expressions. Then, one after another, they regained their public faces, proclaimed the *David* a masterpiece and agreed that it expressed, as Cosimo had told them it was meant to, the courage of little Florence, standing up to the giants of Milan and Venice. But watching them as they cast final, backward glances as they left, I don't think many of them were left with thoughts of political strategy.'

'Lust?' Madonna Arcangelica's eyes were gimlet-sharp. 'Is that what drove them?'

Maddalena looked at her and nodded. 'Most of the time, although they tried hard not to admit it. Men can't help it. Their minds may travel the world, but a single well-shaped image will bring them back home in an instant.'

'Even bishops?' The abbess was again looking out of the window. Her face was devoid of expression, as if the question were purely academic. But her expression was too vacant. She was concentrating hard to make it so. What did she have on her mind?

Then Maddalena remembered the date. In four weeks it would be the 25th March. The date of the New Year. The date when the convent's annual inspection by their patriarch and the bishops was due to take place. So that was why the abbess had listened so attentively week after week, before she was ill. And that was why she had been so keen to reconvene their conversations, despite her illness.

She cast her mind back to the years in Rome, when Cosimo ran the Curia branch of the bank and she had found herself entertaining bishops and cardinals, who, week after week, seemed to arrive with unnatural punctuality. More than one inappropriate offer had been made to her in those innocent little conversations, and more than one pudgy hand had found itself exploring her clothing while the fleshy face above it remained bland and expressionless.

She nodded, her eyes looking directly into the abbess's own. 'Yes, Madonna Arcangelica. Especially bishops.'

Chapter 15
Everything is Changing
13th March 1458

'I suppose it was soon after Donatello's statue was unveiled that you all moved next door; into the great palace?' The abbess seemed as sharp as ever she was and her eyes were bright with anticipation. So much so that today she had started asking questions even before she had sat down.

Caught off-balance, Maddalena paused. 'Yes it was, but I don't want you to think that our life at that time was all domesticity. Great changes were happening; many of them, at first, inside Cosimo's head.

Madonna Arcangelica gave a decisive nod and settled herself. 'Of course. I am jumping to conclusions when I should be letting you tell the story in your own way. I shall be quiet and let you inform and entertain me in your usual way.'

Inform and entertain? Maddalena repeated the words in her head, looking quietly at the abbess as she did so. She was more than pleased that their conversations had kept the abbess entertained. But informed? She had had inklings that there was more to some of Madonna Arcangelica's questions than she let her expression admit, but this, perhaps, was confirmation that she was using their meetings to prepare herself for something.

She was sure now that the expected visitation by the patriarch and the Bishops was part of it. She had drawn that conclusion at the end of the previous week's conversation. But there was more; a desire to understand how the outside world, and more specifically, the men in the outside world, thought. But more even than that. There had been something very telling in that nod. The abbess had hidden it quickly, but not before its meaning had emerged. Then it dawned on Maddalena. It was Cosimo's mind the abbess really wished to understand.

She took her mind back, quickly; to the very reason he had brought her here. His project, in recognition of his legitimate sons' weaknesses, to put funds aside for Lorenzo. Lorenzo the grandson who would inherit it all: the bank, its obligations and its influence; as well as its profits, and the political power that arose from all that money.

Cosimo had never admitted how many preparatory meetings he had held with the abbess, but to judge by their mutual demeanour; they must have had a number of discussions and reached a considerable rapport with one another. Had she too been tasked with some part of the plan? Was the abbess an undeclared partner in the project that had caused Cosimo to bring her to this convent in the first place?

It was a conundrum; if you were given a secret to keep, how did you respond when you began to suspect that someone else, someone you had learned to like and to trust, already shared that secret? Perhaps she and Madonna Arcangelica were in the same position? Was the abbess, even at this minute looking at her and asking herself the same question?

Across the room, the abbess found her mind drifting. She let her eyes roam around the walls and remembered her last visit here, alone, shortly before Maddalena's arrival. How mistaken she had been then...

***

CONVENTO DI SAN DAMIANO, MUGELLO
Summer 1457

Madonna Arcangelica takes a deep breath. She has been awake since well before Lauds and unlike the others, has not returned to sleep after dawn but instead, has climbed the new tower once again, to make doubly sure everything is as he had requested. Now she smiles to herself. *Requested.* When Cosimo de' Medici requests something, everyone knows it's an instruction.

Four times he has visited; first to consider, then to discuss, then to refine, and finally to confirm his 'requests'. At first with only a clerk present, scratching away, fingers stained with ink, but afterwards, in addition to the clerk, a black-robed lawyer, communicating with Cosimo almost entirely by nods and frowns. Cosimo in red, watching him always as he speaks, modifying his sentences in response to the lawyer's changing expressions, sometimes part way through. A careful man, then; that is certain. Not a man given to instant whims. A calculator of consequences. A considerer of alternatives. And above all, as she knows now, a clever negotiator of outcomes.

She knows he had achieved exactly what he wanted. There had never really been any doubt that he would. She had known that from the outset. But he, in his special way, had been scrupulously fair; slowing their discussions for her benefit, not his own, allowing her, indeed encouraging her, to examine her alternatives, to consider her options, to weigh up the likely consequences from her own point of view and from that of the convent she represented.

That first time, she remembers, he had been tentative, careful, exploratory, 'merely considering possibilities, you understand, without commitment' and he had left her with nothing tangible. But even as he had ridden away, already her mind had been full of thoughts, and deep within herself she had felt a powerful tremble of excitement about what she believed were the possibilities for the future.

What had he said, as he was leaving? 'We neither of us want surprises, do we, Madonna? Nor disappointments at a later stage? Now that I know your circumstances, I shall consider further. When I return, I will make my objectives clear and offer you some specific suggestions. I want you to be fully satisfied that every aspect of what we do shall fully in the interests of the convent. When we are both confident of that, then, and only then, shall we sign an agreement. And thereafter,' he had put his hand on her arm at this point, 'we shall both be content to perform our obligations under that agreement in confidence and serenity.'

the political tension rising and as an interim measure, he appointed Ilarione's nephew, Lipaccio di Benedetto de' Bardi as his General Manager. But he proved ineffective and perhaps even worse. A conflict had arisen between Ubertino de' Bardi in the London office and Gualterotto de' Bardi in the Bruges branch. The disagreement amounted to some 22,000 florins and when, by the New Year, his newly appointed General Manager failed to sort it out, Cosimo decided that Bardi loyalties were being put before Medici interests and he replaced all three of them in the contract renewals.

'It was a telling time and Cosimo could only begin to relax again when he managed to appoint Giovanni d'Amerigo Benci and Antonio di Messer Francesco Salutati as joint General Managers. These were much more able men than the Bardi had been. Between them, they began to run the bank very successfully and when Salutati died eight years later, the performance of the bank improved further. It was that which led me, and others to conclude that it was Benci, more than anyone else, who had been behind the success of the Medici bank during this period.'

For the first time since their earliest meetings, the abbess looked hesitant. She began to twist awkwardly in her chair. 'If you will forgive the impertinence, *Suora* Maddalena, your statement implies that Benci did more for the Bank than even the Magnificent Cosimo had done. Surely I have misunderstood?'

Maddalena shook her head. 'No you have not misunderstood. But perhaps I have not explained myself sufficiently. The significance of my statement is that from the time of these appointments onward, Cosimo began to change the emphasis of his life.

'It was another of the decisions he had reached while he was in exile. He had realised how important professional managers were in running such a venture. And it was that recognition that made him see why the *Signoria* was so ineffective; it was run entirely by temporary amateurs. There was never enough money to do things properly, so it could not afford to employ a permanent full-time *Provveditore* to manage the day-to-day business, as they did in Venice. As a result, difficult matters were avoided and simpler ones never completed.

'By the time we returned from Venice, Cosimo was convinced that the whole system needed changing. It was at that time that he reconsidered his father's advice: advice that had governed his career since the old man's death. What he now recognised for the first time, was that the guidance his father had given him had been wholly cynical; that what appeared to work didn't, and that it was the hidden hand behind the *Signoria* that moved matters along. He also realised that in making any changes, he must ensure that outward appearances remain; it was only the underlying reality that should be altered.'

'A subtle and difficult game?' The abbess was sitting right on the edge of her chair now, alert as a fox.

Maddalena saw her expression and made a mental note. *However little experience this woman has of the outside world, she clearly has an instinct for politics. What battles does she face in her daily life that have so prepared her for this conversation?*

'Did that challenge present The Magnificent One with any difficulties?'

Madonna Arcangelica tipped her head to one side, perhaps to show Maddalena that she acknowledged her question was a difficult one, and potentially embarrassing.

'It did.' Maddalena found herself nodding as the memories returned. 'He had somewhat of a crisis of conscience once he had grasped how he had misinterpreted his father's advice, and in so doing, had made some big mistakes. The fact that he had been rejected by the people and exiled still hung heavily over him. And with a new cycle of discussions taking place within the church about the morality of usury, he was concerned at the amount of money the bank had made for him over the previous ten years.'

Madonna Arcangelica nodded, satisfied. 'I am pleased and relieved he saw the dilemma. How did he address it?' Again she tipped her head to one side. 'I'm sure he did not let such a great moral issue pass him by?'

'Of course not. He spoke to Pope Euganius, who was living in Florence at that time, and the Pope told him to spend 10,000 florins restoring the Monastery of San Marco.'

The abbess raised an eyebrow. 'Did he indeed? That's an awful lot of money.'

Maddalena saw the expression and knew the abbess was trying hard not to overreact. *So that's the direction of her interest* she thought. *She is trying to understand how Cosimo thinks.*

As if to confirm Maddalena's instinct, the abbess continued. 'And did he spend that much, on San Marco?' She was trying to look relaxed, but the knuckles of her hands which had tightened on the arms of her chair had now turned quite white.

Maddalena noticed the shift of interest. *So...whatever arrangement they have made together remains incomplete. Like me, she is trying to guess what he'll do next.* She smiled to herself. *In that case, what I have to say may help her.*

'No. Not immediately. First he set a condition. The Silvestrines, who occupied San Marco at that time, and whom he described as "living without poverty and without charity", were to be replaced by the Dominicans. As he said to the pope: "Replace them with those severe Dominicans. Only the prayers of men whose very identity is grounded in poverty and purity will be of use to a banker with an illegitimate child."'

The abbess looked at Maddalena and slowly a smile broke across her face. 'Brave words indeed.'

She started nodding to herself, the smile broadening. 'And carefully chosen by a man who planned to place that illegitimate son within the church. Without actually saying so, he was, surely, attaching the promise of his son's future progress to the gift? We are talking about your son, I assume?'

Maddalena frowned, feeling affronted by the accusation. 'It was a penance.'

The abbess' head tipped slowly from side to side as she pursed her lips in thought. 'Perhaps I should have said "the expectation of his son's progress"? As I understand such conversations, nobody would be so crass as to demand a specific condition?'

'And nobody would be so naïve as to rely on a promise from a pope!'

Maddalena's voice was shriller than she had intended, but she was finding discussion about the bartering that may have preceded Carlo's success, uncomfortable. Somehow, even whilst being aware of the influence of the Medici name, she had always convinced herself that Carlo's rise had reflected some merit on his own behalf.

Surprised at Maddalena's tone of voice, the abbess jerked back in her chair but then, seeing the pain of the emotion behind it, relaxed and raised a hand. 'Pax, Sister. We are here to tell each other truths and secrets are we not? By their nature, sometimes they will be painful. But we should not, surely, censor them because of that? Since our very first afternoon, I have always regarded the ascent of those stairs as a transition and a personal withdrawal from the regulations and observances that remain below. Do you accept that?'

Maddalena felt her heart lift. It must have taken great strength of mind and independence for the abbess to even contemplate such an idea and to express it so openly: true courage. She rose from her chair, crossed the room, knelt, and placed her steepled fingers between the abbess' own. 'Yes, Reverend Mother. I do accept that. And in deep gratitude.'

For a moment they remained in that position, until Maddalena's knees began to ask for relief. Madonna Arcangelica smiled and opened her hands. 'Rise, Sister, before we both feel the pain and discomfort of our old age.'

Self-consciously, they sat facing each other, yet each looking out of the open doorway at the landscape beyond, perhaps too embarrassed to catch each other's eye.

Finally, in a careful voice, the abbess spoke again. 'Pray tell me about the work at San Marco. I know something took place, but as to the detail…'

Maddalena nodded, released from the grip of the moment. 'The pope acceded to the request. The "rigid Dominicans" were moved from Fiesole and entered the Monastery of San Marco; which in the process was redesignated as a convent. They were led by Fra Antonino. It was he who undertook the work, meeting on a monthly basis with Cosimo, and with the architect Michelozzo, who had shared Cosimo's exile and become his close friend. Together they renovated the monks' cells above the cloisters, maintaining their intrinsic austerity, but at least in the process, making them waterproof and windproof.'

'There is a library, I believe?' The abbess's eyes were attentive, and Maddalena realised that she was thinking about the library that Michelozzo had built at the rear of the chapel here at San Damiano and perhaps of the vault beneath. The vault where the great chests were keeping their secret. She had almost forgotten they were there.

'Indeed there is. Michelozzo designed a fine library, with a vaulted roof and windows along both sides; and being on the upper floor, light coming in from above, as well as from either side. Cosimo contributed a vast collection of books. I have not seen the library myself, but Cosimo's description was avuncular.'

The abbess spluttered. 'Avuncular? Not fatherly? Was the library not his child?'

Maddalena was still laughing as she shook her head. 'No. Don't forget that by this time, Cosimo was applying his new rules. By this time, he was careful to step back and give most of the credit to others. In particular, he praised the book illustrators and Fra Angelico, the artist who painted the crucifixions in the cells and other *fresci* elsewhere.'

She looked up as a memory returned. 'A kind, gentle man. Sadly, he died, in Rome, just two years before I came here. Cosimo was very upset. They had worked very closely together.'

'Is it true that Cosimo built himself a cell there?' The abbess was still concentrating hard.

'Indeed it is. Cosimo grew to love the place so much that he had his own two-room cell built there and would visit regularly, for peace and contemplation. As far as I am aware, he still does, despite his illnesses.'

There was a long pause and then the abbess' voice, very quiet. 'You expected him to return here also, did you not?'

Maddalena looked up sharply. For a moment she felt invaded, as if the abbess had forced herself into her inner world; her private world, the world she never admitted to anyone. But when she looked at Madonna Arcangelica's face, she did not see probing, but a shared hurt.

'Yes.' She paused, for a moment uncertain whether to ask the question that was in her head. 'As, perhaps, did you?'

Madonna Arcangelica considered for a moment, then nodded, her face fallen and clearly disappointed. 'I expected it, yes. He told me that you would be coming here and that one part of your mission was to act as guide and guardian for certain...I was never sure what they were going to be. "Deposits for the future," he said they were. "A legacy for another generation."' She shook her head. 'He told me he would return and that in due course, all would be revealed.'

For a moment, Maddalena was unsure how to respond. Had Cosimo really said so much? It was almost as much as he had told her. 'I still live in hope. I have not lost faith in him.' She found the words sticking in her throat as she uttered them, but the abbess seemed not to have noticed. She too appeared disappointed, but like the strong woman she was, she lifted her head.

'So what changes in government did Cosimo bring about as a result of his change of heart?' Already she seemed to have recovered and her voice was at full strength.

'It was as I spoke of some weeks ago. The *Signoria* had already called a *parlamento* and gained agreement to a *balia* even before Cosimo reached the city. They seemed keen to read his mind and had already exiled the Albizzi. Palla Strozzi was also ready to leave unless, as he hoped, Cosimo reprieved him, but this Cosimo failed to do, so he left, disappointed.

'Over the next few months, Cosimo made good the plans he had drawn in his head. Outwardly, nothing was changed: Florentine democracy continued to support what appeared to be "a true republic", but underneath the smooth-swimming swan, the legs were already kicking out in a quite different direction. The *Accopiatore* were at the core of it: "the gatherers" were as good as their title suggested; it was they who decided whose names went into which bag. From then on, instead of the *Podestà* selecting from thousands of theoretically eligible men, only the most suitable were put forward.'

'But nevertheless, they were seen to be selected as before.' The abbess' voice made clear her understanding of the difference between form and substance. 'And how long did this process continue?'

'Oh it still does. Even today, as far as I know. There were wobbles, of course. After the Battle of Anghiari, the Council of the People and the Commune insisted the *Podestà* select from a full listing again. But then they faced the prospect of the election of those returning after their ten years of exile, and that frightened them enough to authorise another *balia*, which of course put the *Accopiatore* back into the driving seat.'

'And the people don't mind?'

'There were murmurs at first, but we have a better system now. The *Signoria* make sure a good selection of people are chosen for the lesser positions; just once you understand – enough to allow them to buy the robes and be seen by their neighbours. Then their names go back into a large bag in the corner of the room and someone else is given a chance.'

'But for the minor positions only?'

'Oh of course. As Cosimo says, you can't have little people sitting in big men's seats. But at least, as he also says, we have a working democracy, which is more than we had before.'

'With a big difference between the apparent and the real?'

'Indeed.' As she said it, Maddalena felt a chill of understanding. The abbess was not referring to the government of the city. She was referring to herself. Had Cosimo promised her something? Or at least, had he allowed her to have an expectation that in his absence had not been delivered? Or were her concerns somehow to do with the patriarch's review? Only three weeks to go now. She must be concerned.

'And perhaps a large difference between what people thought had been promised to them and that which was actually intended?' The abbess' words appeared to confirm Maddalena's suspicions. She was talking about herself, and probably, although not necessarily, about Cosimo.

Maddalena shook her head. 'I cannot agree. I still live in faith, and hope. But I do acknowledge there may be a difference between that which was indicated and fully intended at the time, and that which circumstances are now allowing to take place.'

She lifted her head and looked at the abbess, perhaps seeking comfort. 'But I still think he will come. One day.'

'Then we both live in hope.' The abbess was looking out of the window, and appeared for the moment to be talking to herself. But then her head turned and she faced Maddalena again.

And smiled. 'Together? Shall we live in hope together?'

Maddalena felt her heart lurch. *So we are on a parallel course. In some manner, as yet undisclosed, she is associated with Cosimo's plan. She must be. Not only that, but she is beginning to probe; to search out the extent and nature of my role. But it's too early to tell her yet. Much too early to share such confidences. Nevertheless, a problem shared…*

Hoping she was not breaking convent protocol too completely, but remembering the abbess' comment about the stairs, Maddalena crossed the room, embraced the abbess and kissed her on the cheek.

'Yes. Together.'

Chapter 16
Stature
20th March 1458

Suora Maddalena rubbed her eyes and felt her heart start to beat faster. It was bitterly cold in the room and she was having difficulty making her hands write at all. Now, in the poor candlelight, she could hardly read what she had written.

It had always been her greatest fear: losing her sight, and being in the dark. Even losing it to the point where she could no longer read and write would, she had always thought, be a terrible blow, removing her one remaining link with the outside world.

She did not resent being incarcerated here in the convent. Cosimo had, as always, made the arrangement with the best of intentions and at the time, she had agreed with them. His fears had been, she was sure, well founded and in the circumstances, his actions had been thoughtful and kind. At least here, she would be safe, he said.

Not that his actions had been entirely concerned with her well-being. A mind as subtle as Cosimo's was always considering more than one aspect of the situation and she knew that originally, at least, he had another objective in mind; one in which he told her she would play an important part, but a plan which, at the time, he had not been prepared to explain.

That, in itself, had not concerned her. At least, not at the time. She had known she could trust him to tell her when the appropriate moment came. But now? She was, she thought, still willing to give him the benefit of the doubt. No doubt he still had other parts of the arrangements to make, other people to inform, preparations to put into place. She was sure he would tell her in good time. Perhaps when he visited her?

She smiled to herself. That would be when he read the journal. She had decided now that it would be better that way, after all. Yes, better than having him sit while she read her thoughts out to him. And when he came and sat down to read her words, she would watch him as he read. Feeling like a silly little girl, she squirmed in her seat; the thought of him being there, in her cell, overpowering. But he would come. She was sure of it. And then the rest of the plan would finally be unfurled.

If she concentrated hard, she could see him now, hunched over the journal, with his eyeglasses on the end of his long nose, reading her words, and occasionally looking up, smiling at what he read. On second thoughts, perhaps it would be better the way she had originally decided: that he would sit over there, in the small chair in the corner, or perhaps even lie on her bed, easing his painful back, whilst she read her own words out to him. Hard to decide, really.

But first she had to write those words, and then, once she had written them, they would remain, and could not be changed. There would be no cutting pages out of this book; what she wrote would be permanent and as such, should be good enough to pass the test of time.

What, then, should she write about him, that would be truthful (it could hardly be otherwise in this holy place), and that would please him? She couldn't be too effusive. Cosimo would see the flattery in an instant, and would simply respond to it by refusing to believe anything else that was written. In all their years together, she had managed to maintain the balance and she knew she must not lose hold of it now.

Cosimo was a man of stature; of that there was no doubt. But what were the sources of that stature? What, over the years, had led her to respect and, yes, to grow to love him? Wealth? Certainly. It would, surely, be unrealistic to ignore that characteristic in the richest man in the world. But what had impressed her more over the years had been the way he carried his wealth, always remaining modest in thought and deed.

His manner, in his dealings with everyone, had always been noble. Indeed, despite his pain, and she knew it troubled him daily, he had always carried himself with the calm and relaxed grace of the nobility. Yet he would never call himself noble, nor allow others to do so, either. What had he said? 'A couple of lengths of red cloth, that's all, and you have your nobleman.'

No, it was not the trappings of nobility that she respected in him, but the fact that, despite his position, he had not let go of his roots. Though wealthy, he had remained modest; although risen high, he still had humility; and although he was the most powerful man in Florence, he still remained accessible, kind and thoughtful to the lower orders, as long as they were honest, industrious and respectful of his position in return.

In all those respects, there was no doubt in her mind. Cosimo was a good man. A family man: one who, years ago, had taken their son Carlo into his family and brought him up as his own, beside Piero and Giovanni. Now Carlo was bishop of Prato, and well on the way to becoming a cardinal. What more could Cosimo have done for her?

Oh Cosimo! How could she sum him up? What could she write in her journal, to tell him how he had influenced her life? What was he – the true, inner man? In some respects, even after all these years, he remained an enigma. Certainly complicated and with many faces, each of them different. By birth and name a Medici, by trade and instinct a banker, but by nature and preference, still, in many respects, a farmer.

She picked up her quill, examined the nib carefully, and began to write.

Dearest Cosimo,

Today I have set myself a challenge: within one page (I have allowed myself no more) I must state, with brevity but clarity, what it is that gives you such stature in my eyes.

Wealth? Certainly, in many men's eyes and a comfort especially as old age approaches.

Power? You are respected universally. Although not always for the same reasons, or in the same manner. By some it is true you are feared, but only by men who have reason

126

to fear. By others you are resented, but only by those less able than yourself or who have already failed when called upon.

After careful consideration (for a nunnery is a place for contemplation like no other, and it has been a long and dark winter) I have come to the conclusion that the source of your stature in so many men's eyes (and some modest women who shall remain nameless) is the contradiction of your attitudes.

Who, for example, except those who, like me, know you well, would expect the richest man in the world to be modest in his way of life? How many nobles would understand a man who prefers chickpeas to venison, and who, when at home on his country estates, dresses so like his workers in the fields that he must be approached to within arm's length before he can be recognised?

Who, amongst those who have seen you raised high, returning from exile in triumph and, in your leadership, gaining the support of every true man on the Signoria would understand your true humility, know the self-doubt that causes you to consider your actions so carefully, to lie awake at night, holding my hand, going over and over again the consequences of your actions?

Who, but those who know you as I do, who have so many reasons to be grateful to you, would expect the most powerful man in Europe (apart, of course, from His Holiness, who is beyond comparison) to be in his private life kindly and thoughtful, the favourite to nephews and grandsons alike, who would cause an ambassador to wait while he whittled a reed whistle for a young boy?

Cosimo, they know you not. Not in the way that I do. And if they, in their ignorance, hold you in such high regard, then consider how I must see you, from my position of greater knowledge.

Cosimo di Giovanni de' Medici, I salute you!

Yours, in awe,

Maddalena.

Chapter 17
Memories
27th March 1458

As the light faded, Maddalena felt a chill and shivered. It had been a beautiful early spring day. The sort of day that offers a wicked promise of summer's arrival, before stealing the dream away again, in a further buffet of icy cold wind. But today that promise had held; the air had remained still, and the valley had echoed to the songs of nesting birds. Now, well beyond four in the afternoon, the warmth of the sun's rays was finally being lost and a bank of cloud was building up on the hills across the valley – a sure sign of more rain to come, and, by the look of it, soon. But at least it was rain, not snow.

***

The calling bell for Vespers chimed and Maddalena cast one last look over her work before putting it away. She had been writing since the end of morning Mass, breaking only for dinner and missing her supper in her frustration; trying and failing to find the right words. Throughout the day, her frustration had been increased by a feeling of exclusion. The patriarch and his retinue of bishops and servants had arrived at mid-morning, and had gone into conference with the abbess. From time to time, certain *discrete* had been called, no doubt to answer questions about their personal areas of responsibility, but there had been no need for Maddalena and she had not been called. And so she had retreated into her old life and back into her journal.

She had loved the journal when Cosimo had first given it to her. In her mind, it represented a link to him; a repository in which to save her thoughts temporarily until such time as he might visit and she could share them. But that had been at the beginning, when she, in her simplicity, had thought he might return within a week, two at the most. Indeed back then, she had even wondered whether it was worth writing at all, if he was going to be with her again so soon. But she had, finally, committed pen to paper.

The days had grown shorter. They had stretched into weeks, and winter had set in, dark and hard and merciless, and still no word.

She had picked up the journal many times, occasionally writing; but now the book had begun to take on a new personality in her eyes. Now the journal represented the absent Cosimo, the man she had begun to think of as the retreating Cosimo. Gradually, she had stopped loving it and had begun, although she barely admitted it to herself, to resent it.

She looked back at what she had written in earlier weeks and wondered what conclusions would be drawn if the pages were read. They imparted no news. Hardly surprising, since there had been no events to be noted and described. Her life now, although safe and comfortable, had become repetitious and, with the notable exception of her regular conversations with the abbess, stultifying. Rereading them, she saw that what she had written were preparatory words, timeless words. Words considering the relationship between her and Cosimo, written, in part she now thought, to convince herself that they not only had once been true, but that they yet remained true.

As befitted their order and God's commandment, the nuns in the convent were friendly enough. But it always felt like the friendship of good manners. With the exception of the off-duty abbess, the conversations contained no warmth, no personal exchange of secrets, no whispers of hopes, or admissions of uncertainties. It was as if each sister had responded to her incarceration by withdrawing ever deeper into herself, becoming encapsulated in a private shell of contemplation or simply, perhaps, of self-absorption.

Worse, Maddalena sensed that her own isolation was even greater than that of the other nuns. Slowly, as the winter progressed, she had come to realise that she was not, truly 'one of them' but was seen and perhaps always would be seen as an outsider. 'The Medici Nun' as she had overheard one of them call her; a tolerated outsider, whose role in their eyes would always be 'the patron's representative' and as such, someone to be gently distrusted; to be handled with care, and with courtesy, but without any real warmth.

The loneliness that had grown with that knowledge had made her need for Cosimo all the greater, and her desire to write to him even stronger. Yet with that growing strength of need, had come a diminished confidence in what to say. No longer did she dare write directly into her journal, but had begun to write drafts, much corrected, on scraps of paper, before finally copying them in a fair hand onto the journal pages. It was as if the very act of writing had attained such importance that everything she thought to say seemed either far too trivial, or else, when it did seem to matter, the prospect of writing it became so threatening, that she hardly dared begin.

And then, this morning, she had woken with a new sensation: an ache born of dreams; of memories of her life with Cosimo that had clung to her when she woke and throughout Prime. She had daydreamed through the Chapter meeting, lost herself during Mass, and as soon as it was over, she had rushed back to her tower thinking she would go mad if her brain filled with more thoughts before she had time to write any of them down.

On her desk they lay; little scraps of paper, each with another scribbled thought, written hurriedly, lest the effort of writing caused the next thought to be lost before it, in its turn, could be committed to paper. Now she stood at the window, looking across the valley, preparing herself. All day the thoughts had come and gone, fighting each other, calling to her to put quill to paper and clarify them; end their argument, bring their battle to a balanced conclusion.

She turned away from the window, smiling for the first time that day. Now she knew why her thoughts had been so embattled; why the two sides of her mind had been in such contradiction.

She nodded to herself, relieved to have come to a conclusion, and pleased with its nature. She understood her error now; she had been using her deep, private knowledge of the inner man to judge the outer man; the public face of Cosimo de' Medici. No wonder, then, a paradox. Indeed it had always been that very contradiction which had gone to the heart of his character; the tension between those two opposing forces, the very essence of the man's life and the strength of character which he had brought to bear in reconciling them, the reason she had loved and respected him for the many years they had been together.

The conclusion was simple: Cosimo had not been born to greatness. Cosimo had had the responsibilities of greatness thrust upon him. And being the eldest son, he had felt himself with no choice but to accept them.

She remembered his description of 'The Medici Creed' given to both him and his brother, Lorenzo, when they had been very young. How many times had she heard him repeat those lessons, with the intention, no doubt, that she, too, would understand the rules under which he laboured?

She could hear his voice now. 'As my father, Giovanni di Bicci, used to tell me, "*Never hang around the Palazzo della Signoria as if it is the place where you do business. Only go there when you are summoned, and only accept the offices which are bestowed upon you. Never make a show before the people, but if this is unavoidable, let it be the least necessary. Keep out of the public gaze and never go against the will of the people, unless they are advocating some disastrous project.*" Those were my father's words and I strive to obey them.'

And there was no doubt that Cosimo *had* heeded his father's words. Although clearly the most powerful man in Florence, he had always been careful to work through others, giving them the credit for the achievement and at the same time, making friends whilst avoiding the envy of others. A clever man, who allowed it to be recognised that he paid more taxes than any other man in Florence, but who, at the same time, kept two sets of books, so that the taxes he did pay fell far below those he ought to have been liable for.

Doubly clever, in that much of the money he avoided paying in taxes, as an obligation, he then contributed to the city anyway, but in the form of personal generosity; generosity which, whilst quietly understated, somehow never failed to be recognised. At Orsanmichele he had contributed more than the other bankers on the committee to Ghiberti's statue to St Matthew and had then followed this with the novices' dormitory and chapel at Santa Croce, and the choir of Santissima Annunziata.

Yet at the same time, he had always been careful to appear modest. He had always dressed well, his *lucco* plain but made of fine cloth; never in the furs and jewellery that smacked of ostentatious wealth. He had not needed to: everyone knew that Cosimo de' Medici was the richest man in the world. Why flaunt the fact and make enemies?

As with clothing, so with buildings. He had always been generous in supporting magnificence for the Church, for such was to the glory of God; but when it came to building his own house, replacing that which had been brought to him by his wife, he had rejected Brunelleschi's original, elaborate design for the Palazzo Medici and instead had asked Michelozzo to shape something that was, at least externally, plainer and much more modest.

So if the outer man was plain, was the inner man more elaborate? Certainly, it was in his less public contributions that the character of the real man sometimes emerged unhindered by considerations of politics. His endowment of libraries – personal, civic and religious – had, Maddalena knew, been a subject of joy to a man whose private studies of humanism had softened his personality over the years.

Many were the wet winter days she had spent with him in the library at Palazzo Medici, talking, and reading aloud to each other. 'Contessina takes no pleasure in books,' he would sigh, 'she prefers the company of people.' He would say it in a way that reminded her how shy and retiring the real man was, and on occasion how hard, he had had to push himself to perform his civic duties.

Introspective, too. The world might have seen Cosimo as 'the great man' who led the world, 'making incisive decisions without fear'. But they had not sat with him for hours on end in his *studiolo*, agonising over the consequences of those decisions before the public process even started.

'How will it affect the people?' he would ask her, and she, knowing that his wife's answer would only have considered the effect on the great families amongst whom she moved and lived her daily life, would immediately think about the *popolo minuto*, those who were perpetually ignored by society, those who held no importance – literally, the small people, undernourished since childhood. They were referred to by Contessina's rich friends as *piagnoni* – snivellers – not because they were always complaining (although God knows they had plenty to complain about) but because, being hungry and poorly clothed, they inevitably had colds and dripping noses. And over the years, Cosimo had listened to her, and taken her views into account, before making his decisions.

And when it came to retreating from the responsibilities of civic life, where better than his country estates in the Mugello – at Careggi or Cafaggiolo. There she knew (although she had rarely been allowed to join them, having to remain at the Palazzo Medici instead 'in charge of the *studiolo*') Cosimo would have been up early, and out with the vineyard workers, pruning his own vines, working quietly and happily in the cool of the morning air, doing what he sometimes referred to as 'real men's work'.

Maddalena looked down at the journal and shook her head. She could not possibly write such things. Not because they were untrue, but because Cosimo knew them all, and did not need to hear them retold.

But then she remembered a phrase; a phrase he had once used with her, after once admitting the extent of his own self-doubt.

They had been sitting quietly in the *studiolo* of his house in Pisa.

***

131

'I must do something, Maddalena. We can't go on like this.'

'I'm sure you're right, Cosimo. But it's up to you to make a decision. Nobody else can make it for you. Your management are there to implement your policies and your choices, but none of them, not even Giovanni, can be expected to make the policy decisions for you. It's not their job.'

Cosimo seems in grumbling mood. 'But what's the use of a General Manager if he can't sort out a little local situation like this?'

'Giovanni Benci is, I am sure, perfectly capable of finding a successor to Averardo's bank if you want to continue that way. But you know yourself that you have talked openly about establishing your own branch and not relying any more on an agency arrangement. Pisa's an important trade centre now and the Medici Bank needs a presence here. You said it yourself.'

'It's a big decision, Maddalena. Choosing partners is as important a decision as you can make.'

'So you keep telling me. And you also keep telling me how you have absolute faith in Ugolino Martelli and in Matteo. What's the problem?'

Cosimo nods, still hesitant. 'Matteo Masi is as good as his father Cristofano. I give you that.'

'And Niccolò Martelli has been equally blessed with his son. I know you always hesitate when giving authority to the next generation, but one day, you'll have to hand the whole Medici bank to your own sons.'

He squints across the room at her. 'That's what's worrying me.'

'They'll grow into it. Give them time.'

Cosimo nods, but appears uncommitted.

'Now, as far as Pisa is concerned, why don't you tell the lawyers to draw up an agreement, on the basis you described to me the other day? Tell them the great man has decided and this is what you want.'

He's still prevaricating. '"Great man". Pah. I wish I were. Nobody understands the loneliness of "great men". The future is so uncertain and the risks are so high.'

'Not if you choose proven men as your partners, and you structure the branch as an *accomanda*. The liabilities will be limited to the invested capital, and if, as you suggested, they contribute 1,000 florins each, then the Florence *tavola* will only have to contribute 4,000 and you can easily afford that.'

Cosimo nods. Then nods again. Then he smiles. 'You're right, as always, Maddalena. I was avoiding making the decision, but in reality, it's already made. I'll speak to the lawyers in the morning.'

Relieved, she smiles and sits back in her chair. 'Shall we ask cook for venison tonight?'

He nods, more confidently this time. 'Good idea.'

Cosimo gets up and throws another log on the fire, then turns towards her and tousles the top of her head. 'Thank you. You're worth three general managers.'

Maddalena shakes her head. 'I just listen to you and remind you what you've already decided.' She smiles. 'Deep down. It's just that sometimes you need someone to help you let go of a decision and pass it on for others to implement. I know your responsibilities don't come easily to you, Cosimo, but your father would be proud of you. You always face your decisions and you always address them with the utmost fairness. You sometimes need time. That's all.'

***

Maddalena nodded to herself; a decision made. Yes, that's what she would write. She would tell him she understood. And that, even today, she still understood. And how, in understanding the difficulty whilst being one step removed from him, her respect for him had grown even higher.

Encouraged by her decision, she sat and began to write, the words flowing more easily as she went, until she had filled a page.

She put down her quill and reread what she had written. But as she pored over her words, a recurring and troubling thought returned, until she had to put the journal down, walk to the window, and address it.

I know what I have concluded. I know what I have written. And yet...

She remembered the way he had responded to the threats against him in 1433, threats which, to be fair, had proved justified, and which had led to his exile for a year; but which could, just as easily, have led to his death. Yet faced with such threats, he had not, she had to admit, shown courage, but fear.

And within that fear, when the deep inner man was finally exposed, he had fallen back on a long-thinking, cold, calculating logic.

Now, faced with the silence of her situation, she could not help wondering. Had he, after all, done all of those things because he believed they were right, or because he knew that in the long term, they would be profitable and productive? Profitable for the Bank and productive for the growing political power of the Medici name?

And thereby hung the question she had avoided asking, never mind attempting to answer. When finally, he reached Judgement Day and St Peter, standing on the steps, how would Cosimo be judged? As a man of vision, courage and greatness, or as a selfish calculator, sitting behind his green baize table, maximising his own position: at the same time, playing the actor; carefully conceiving and then portraying the other Cosimo – the Cosimo who had achieved public adoration?

Was there indeed an imagined Cosimo, an invented persona, a creation formed in part by his father's inherited instructions and in part by his own creative imagination? And did the private Cosimo – the one she knew better than anyone else – don that mantle as he left his front door or as he entered a roomful of visitors?

And how far apart were those two Cosimos? And which, if either, was the true one?

She thought of the plan to protect Lorenzo's inheritance; a plan in which she had believed she was playing a central part. It was a plan for Cosimo to squirrel away money, as he had done thirty years before; this time, because he did not trust the next generation to safely carry the mantle of his memory, and instead wanted to put his faith in his grandson, Lorenzo.

Lorenzo's gold.

Maddalena and Cosimo had brought the first instalment here to the convent, and here it had been hidden, as he had instructed. But what of the rest? Although the bags of coins she had hidden away ran to 20,000 florins, (it was in her nature to count the bags), the final amounts Cosimo had been talking of were much greater; vast sums, more even than the 100,000 ducats – the equivalent of 120,000 florins in their own coinage – that he had spent on the Palazzo Medici.

Lorenzo's secret inheritance should have involved huge sums of money. But where were they now? And more to the point for her in this isolated position, was she still part of the great scheme, or had Cosimo changed his mind? Indeed, as she closed the journal and put it back in the box, the uncomfortable thought came back to her once again.

Her lack of faith made her gasp and she knelt, painfully, her left knee especially uncomfortable, in front of the little votive table in the corner of her room and prayed for forgiveness.

But try as she might, the thought, now it had been planted, would not leave her. *Was I ever really part of the plan?*

That thought, now released, sickened her. She could not leave it there. She had to write. Something that, should he ever return, would tell him of the agonies that had tormented her.

But at the same time, she, like him, had to be careful and calculating. For if her uncertainties proved to be misplaced, and he did, indeed, arrive one day, carts laden with gold, and having done so, read her journal, the last thing she wanted to be disclosed was her loss of faith.

Somehow, like Cosimo, she must find a way to face in both directions at the same time. She must let him know of the agonies she has borne, but at the same time, thank him for the burden of her promised participation, and in so doing, put the responsibility for the outcome back to him.

Yes. She would write. She *will* write. She will write it now.

Dearest Cosimo,

On such a day as this, the very best sort of April morning, when we are all looking forward to the warmth of summer, I should be looking forward also. But instead, I find myself looking back.

It is now more than six months since you brought me here, to fulfil my part in your plans for the future, and I remain prepared. Back then, in October, I thought to hear your footsteps within days and I looked forward to that moment. But now, having received neither visit nor word from you in half a year, I find myself no longer looking forward with such eagerness.

Instead, I am looking back, thankful for the memories, grateful for the many hours we have spent together, but most of all, appreciative of your great generosity towards me.

And for what? For comforts? Certainly. For gifts? Indeed – frequently and generously given. But above all, for the privilege of access; of admission into the private secrets of the inner man. For you, Cosimo, were courageous as well as generous when you took me, not only into your heart, but also into your soul.

And in gaining that insight, I saw how heavily you have borne the trials and tribulations of leadership and position, both within the Bank and in the governance of Florence. Yet always, you have acted courageously, and in the common interest.

Some seek greatness, and in achieving it, merely satisfy the desires of their own greedy appetites, but others have greatness thrust upon them. Amongst these, a few – the so very few – rise to the challenge and give generously of the leadership which others crave.

For doing these things, I salute you. For taking me into your confidence as you did, I shall remain beholden until my dying day.

Yours, ever
Maddalena.

Chapter 18
An Unstable and Public Life
3rd April 1458

It was windy, in that blustery, unpredictable way of March winds, on and off, stop-start, buffeting you when you least expect it, and leaving you irritated and out of sorts. But it wasn't March any longer; the month end had just turned, and with it the New Year and it was now the 3rd of April and the New Year was named 1458.

Another Monday and once again, Maddalena was unsure whether she would hear the abbess' tired feet on the stairs.

The previous week had been spent on tenterhooks; everything in the convent prepared, everything rehearsed, (but of course, rehearsed to look as natural as possible) and the whole building cleaned until the choir nuns were as exhausted as the *converse*. The previous week it had become clear that the servants could not do everything themselves and the abbess had given instructions that for the next two weeks, that is, until the visitation, manual labour was to be considered as worthy as prayer, at least during the mornings.

The patriarch and his three attendant bishops had finally arrived late, complaining about the terrible roads in the Mugello, but had been placated by a meal that just trod the line between adherence to the Rule and entertainment appropriate to the dignitaries concerned. They had visited the chapel, made a short speech in the Chapter House to the assembled choir nuns, walked the cloisters, toured the gardens and peeped quickly into one or two (well-chosen) cells. Then they had retreated to the Badia di Buonsollazzo for the night. And during the whole of that day, Maddalena had sat quietly with her journal, unbidden and feeling distinctly unwanted.

The following morning they had returned and had spent the whole day in conference with the abbess, occasionally calling in those nuns, like the chapter clerk, the procuratrix, the cellarer and the gatekeeper, whose positions of authority were essential to the smooth running of the community.

Finally, to her great surprise, but not, apparently to the abbess', they had singled out *Suora* Maddalena and interviewed her in the abbess' presence. It had been a strange interview. Much of the time was spent summarising the purpose and detail of their visit and they seemed obsessed with the stringency of their examinations. Their questions, when they reached them, had been oblique and their purpose hard to determine, although it appeared from her demeanour that the abbess knew what they were about.

It was only after they had left that she had explained her thoughts to Maddalena. 'I think they were covering themselves; nervously aware of the source of the recent patronage we have enjoyed and presuming that you were The Magnificent One's representative here. They kept talking about his past generosity to San Marco and how one of his conditions had been the replacement of the Silvestrines by the Strict Dominicans. They had convinced themselves you would be reporting back to him in due course, and wanted to assure you of the diligence of their review.' She had giggled as she continued 'They looked so nervous; as if they thought it was you interviewing them.'

They had waved them off with a mixture of relief and trepidation. What would their report say and what would be its consequences? In the past, convents receiving negative reports had been harshly disciplined and their interpretation of the Rule made so stringent that life for many had become intolerable. Maddalena hoped that would not happen to San Damiano. Madonna Arcangelica's light touch in interpreting the Rule was, she thought, what made life here bearable.

***

There was a bang as the door at the base of the tower slammed shut in the wind and then the slow step, scrape of the abbess' footsteps. So she had decided to come, after all. Perhaps, with the departure of her 'torturers' (her word) she would be less preoccupied with men's politics. Maddalena hoped so. She wanted to talk about the family, although, on consideration, it was going to be impossible to describe their lives over those next ten years without referring to the political background that seemed to surround almost every aspect of what they did or said.

A quiet knock on the door and at once she responded. 'Please enter, Reverend Mother. Our chairs await us.'

Madonna Arcangelica smiled as her face appeared round the door, perhaps embarrassed at her red face and breathless expression, but Maddalena had grown used to the manner of her arrival and as always, gave her time to settle. Not that she needed it today. Maddalena had hardly sat down when she began talking.

'During a quiet moment, while our visitors were with us, I was thinking about our last conversation; how the years immediately following the Magnificent One's return from exile signalled something of a change in him and in his approach to life. Did matters settle down thereafter? It sounds as if they were very busy years, presumably for both of you: your involvement with the bank, then the Convent of San Marco and finally, I believe, work at San Lorenzo? And Cosimo's other projects, the new house, and of course, the politics. Did you, I wonder, ever see anything of the family?'

Maddalena smiled inwardly. The family. How strange that their minds should have been travelling on such parallel paths.

'Of course! You have to remember that after our return from exile, almost everything was run from the family home. First from the Palazzo Bardi in Oltrarno, then from the Casa Vecchia on Via Larga and finally from the Palazzo Medici, next door.'

'When did you finally move in there?'

'There was no single date; no occasion when Cosimo said, "Tomorrow we move next door." It wasn't like that. Apart from anything else, the work was not truly finished, and, I am sure, isn't even now. When I left to come here work was yet being done, and no doubt the Casa Vecchia still stands next door. I am sure one of these days, they will knock it down and extend the *palazzo* even further. Cosimo and Piero talk of using that side to build a separate servants' wing, with stables and storage rooms, but there are still other houses to be bought and demolished before that dream can be made into a reality.

'What I can tell you is that as soon as each part of the new house was finished, we started to use it. Perhaps the most significant change took place just over a year ago, when Cosimo decided to move the books of account into his new apartment, because he wanted the visiting dignitaries to start visiting us there, rather than at the old house. That, I suppose, was when the new *palazzo* became acknowledged as the centre of the Medici world.

'I wish you could see Cosimo's apartment on the *piano nobile*. It's on the south side of the house, overlooking Via Gori on the outside and the main *cortile* within. It is magnificent. On the *piano nobile*, and right in the core of the house, he has built his chapel. He wants to call it the Chapel of the Magi. He has great plans for *fresco* walls, and has asked Benozzo Gozzoli to make them; although they were still plain when I left. But the marble floor is complete and so is the carved wooden ceiling.

'That chapel is Cosimo's place of retreat. The right hand sacristy has a secret staircase, giving access to the attic of the antechamber, where the arms are kept for emergencies, and the sacristy on the left has stairs going down on the outside of the *palazzo*, as a secret escape route. It was only when he showed them to me that I realised how little he has trusted people since his exile.

'Along a short corridor from that, are Cosimo's chamber and his *studiolo*. He ordered the servants to put all the books and documents, including the account books, into boxes and carry them there from the Casa Vecchia. Then he sent everyone away and the two of us spent three days just sorting them out, putting them on shelves and organising the layout of the *tavola*.

'Of course, there isn't really a banking table in the Palazzo Medici – the Florentine *tavola* is in the Mercato Nuovo but Cosimo said he felt more comfortable writing on one so he had a similar table installed in the *studiolo*. It even had a green cloth covering, like the real banking tables, just to make him feel at home.

'The other comforting thing is his *camera*, which is not just a bedroom rather a great *salon*, occupying the whole corner of the building above the *loggia pubblica*, where the Via Gori meets the Via Larga. It is a wonderful room with seven windows. If you look out of the windows above Via Gori by daylight, you can see the Church of San Lorenzo across the *piazza*, and at night, if you leave the curtains part open, and when the cresset lamps are lit all along the road, the light flickers in through the windows. It makes the azure and gilding on the coffered ceiling dance like a night sky.'

'And did you maintain your…sleeping arrangements there, as you had at the

Palazzo Bardi?' The abbess had the old twinkle back in her eye. Maddalena was certain now that there was one great, unasked question that returned repeatedly to the abbess' mind, and that one day, inevitably, it would be voiced. Meanwhile, Maddalena thought, there was no harm in teasing her a little longer.

'Of course. That is the whole point of what I am telling you. The *appartamento* – the whole group of rooms I have described – was our private retreat. I was allowed to use the secret ways, to pray alone in the chapel if I wished and given free access to the *studiolo*, where even to this day, my little bed remains. At least, I assume it does. Of course, entrance to the *salon* was by personal invitation only; Cosimo could not have someone, not even me, wandering in there when he was talking business to the pope's representative, or a duke. But all he had to do was cough, and in I would go.'

'Did he...cough frequently?' Madonna Arcangelica's expression was as angelic as her name. It was the closest she had ever come to *the* question, but still, Maddalena thought, too early to answer it.

'By the time the chapel and the apartment was finished and we moved in, I was in my fiftieth year and Cosimo nearly sixty-seven, so there was much less...coughing than there had been back in Rome, or even at the Palazzo Bardi. But I would still join him there and lie naked beside him, under silk sheets. Often we would open the curtains and watch the lights flickering on the ceiling: Cosimo would lay plans for the future and I would lie beside him and assure him that one day they would all come to fruition.'

'You never contradicted him?'

'No. Never once. I knew him well enough to know that it was not my judgement he welcomed but my reassurance. It didn't matter. I had a part to play; a part that was important to him, and I played it to the best of my ability.' Maddalena looked at the abbess with cool, level eyes. 'And in so doing, I was sure I was making as much use of my life as I might have done by following my father and becoming a physician.'

The abbess sat upright, surprised. 'Would that ever have been possible? In Palermo?'

Maddalena smiled wistfully. 'We can all have our dreams and that had always been mine.' She shook her head. 'Until slavery got in the way.'

'But even that, you turned to your advantage?' Madonna Arcangelica's face was motherly, and full of admiration.

'I could have done nothing without Cosimo. Throughout our many years together he has always...' she paused, trying to find the right word, '...he has always lifted me up.' She shook her head, casting her mind back, sifting the unreliable evidence of memory. 'He has never pretended I am anything other than what I am. Yet in every situation I have shared with him, he has always elevated me when another, lesser man, might have sought to diminish my position, if only to show his own superiority.'

Madonna Arcangelica shook her head. 'It never works. Try as they may, the self-aggrandisement of small men always ends up diminishing them even further.'

Maddalena looked into her eyes and saw a lifetime of confessors, of visiting priests, of bishops and of patriarchs. Now it was her turn to shake her head. 'To a discerning audience, perhaps. But in front of the baying crowd, I can assure you, the smallest cockerel learns to strut and so often, is praised for it.'

'Is that the reality of Florentine politics? Is that what it all comes down to? The baying mass?'

Maddalena nodded. In the last twenty years she had watched Cosimo grow weary and cynical. Seen him reinterpret his father's words as a *chimera* of their original meaning. 'If you wish to maintain the pretence of a democratic republic, then yes, it appears it does. All I know is that it has exhausted him. He would have been happier just to be a banker and a farmer, backing his own judgement and living with the consequences. It was the pretence of politics that wore him down. That and the unreliability of other people..'

'But the Medici Bank? Has that not also contributed to the weariness of his old age? Making money on that scale cannot have been easy?'

Maddalena looked at Madonna Arcangelica and once again wondered at her perception. How many times had the abbess met Cosimo? He had never told her, but they could probably have been counted on the fingers of one hand. Yet here, in the quiet isolation of the convent, she managed to feel her way into people's lives with an uncanny sensitivity.

'Cosimo always used to say to me that banking is complex and wearisome except to those who were born to it, and there is no doubt, he was. But the success of the Medici Bank is not just a reflection of personal flair in Cosimo and his father, Giovanni di Bicci.'

'What then?' The abbess really did appear to care.

For a moment, Maddalena felt her heart sink. How could she possibly explain so complex a matter in a few simple sentences? But Cosimo had. Once. To her. He had been troubled by gout and had retired to bed in the middle of the day, 'to ease the pain'. At least, that's what he had said. Maddalena remembered smiling to herself as she climbed into the great bed beside him. *Retired to bed to avoid his wife, more likely*. They had had another of their rows.

***

PALAZZO BARDI, FLORENCE
13th May 1435

'Do you feel happier, dearest, now the new contracts are in place?'

Maddalena wriggles her toes under the silk sheets and wonders whether Cosimo can do the same, beside her. She has seen no evidence that his toes are hurting since he climbed into bed. In fact he seems in remarkably good spirits. His age is showing, though. He keeps repeating himself.

For a moment she wonders whether to slide a hand onto his belly, but decides against. He seems more in a mood to talk. *Perhaps on balance I'll stick to the bank. Safe ground.*

'Very much so.' She knows immediately from his tone of voice that she's in for a lecture. She lies back against the soft pillows. *There are worse places to listen to a speech. And worse ways to spend an afternoon.*

Cosimo folds his hands behind his head and addresses the ceiling. 'The bank owes its success to four guiding principles; established by my father and, I hope, faithfully followed by me ever since. The contracts have, as you have so perceptively recognised, ensured that those principles are, once again, adhered to.'

Beside him, she wonders why the famous principles had been allowed to drift in the first place, but she knows the answer: *parentado* and in particular, an excess of loyalty to the Bardi family. *They may have been good bankers a century ago, but the modern generation are useless. He doesn't want to be reminded of that.*

'First, we must have a team of qualified and experienced people. Now, once again, in every branch, the bank has experienced professional managers to look after the day-to-day running of its affairs.'

Yes she thinks. *It has now. And to your benefit. That means you will be untroubled by the trivia of administration and can concentrate on making the important decisions and policies. More than that: once you have announced a policy, the managers, especially your General Managers, have the responsibility of ensuring that it is adhered to, day-by-day. And now the Bardi have gone, you can be a little more confident that they will.*

'Second, as Director, I must make clear policy decisions, and having announced them, I must allow my managers to manage. I must not keep looking over their shoulders and questioning every action they take.'

She feels herself nodding. *That is one of your strengths. You make judgements about people and situations and then stand by your own judgement. If you are right, the bank is profitable and if not, it incurs losses. And believe me; both have arisen in the years I have known you. Haven't they?*

'The third key is flexibility. The most profitable branch of the Medici Bank is and probably always will be the Rome branch.'

Yes, of course. We call it the Rome branch, but it is only based in Rome when the pope and the Court of Rome are sitting there, as they were when you first bought me and took me there with you.

'In the last twenty years, it has followed the Ecumenical Council; first to Florence for four years, then to Bologna, then Ferrara and then in 1439 it returned to Florence once again for four more years, before returning once again to Rome.'

Yes. I remember. You seem to forget I was there. While the Council was here in Florence, the pope established himself at Santa Maria Novella and we rented a house in the piazza opposite to act as our Curia branch. A charmless and pretentious house I always thought. But you seemed to like it; perhaps because it made us a lot of money.

'That same flexibility applies to the commercial branches. The Medici Bank has opened branches in response to market opportunities and we will not be afraid to close them again if circumstances change or because we acknowledge that we have made a mistake.'

She turns on the pillow. 'You were always good at admitting your mistakes, dearest. To be fair, you have not made many. I'm still not sure a branch in Ancona will work, though.'

She feels him nodding beside her, still addressing the ceiling. 'No I don't think I have, have I. Not too bad, on balance. Not too many errors of judgement. And don't worry about Ancona. I know what I'm doing there. We need Sforza as a friend.'

Beside him, she regrets the implied criticism and quickly changes the subject. 'You said there were four principles? There is one more?'

He falls for it. 'Structure. The way the Medici Bank is organised. That is the fourth, and in many respects, the most important, principle.'

She relaxes, knowing it is a subject he feels strongly about. With a bit of luck, her badly chosen comment about Ancona will be forgotten.

'Giovanni Benci and I have studied the failures of the great banking dynasties of the past; the banks of Orlando Bonsignori in Siena, of Francesco Datini in Prato, and of the Bardi, the Peruzzi and the Acciaiuoli here in Florence. Each of them in their time has made the same mistake; they structured their company as one great partnership. The result was, when disaster befell them, through trade, or the failure of some king or prince to repay his loans, that the whole edifice collapsed. Giovanni and I intend to avoid that risk.'

Maddalena smiles. She knows full well that at the New Year, two months earlier, on the 15th March, when Cosimo formed the new company with Giovanni Benci, they organised it on a different basis. Each of the branches was designed to be an *accomanda* – a special form of partnership, whose liability is limited to the extent of its capital. And each of these branches is now itself affiliated to the senior *accomanda* – the parent partnership. 'And that has many benefits?' *Keep him going a bit longer. He's enjoying himself.*

Beside her, Cosimo presses back on his elbows and arches his back. 'Of course. Consider for a moment. If a branch partnership is an *accomanda*, the liability of its partners is limited to the invested capital. That means as a partner, you cannot lose more than you have invested.'

'You mean the owners cannot be sucked down?'

'Exactly. Local losses are contained locally, and nobody can sue the parent company, or the investors in that parent company, to make good the losses that the branch has incurred.

'And that is legal?'

'Completely. The branches trade with one another, as if they were doing business with independent third parties. They keep independent sets of books and see the results of their actions in the form of local profits.'

Maddalena frowns. She has never been sure about this part. When talking about the methods used by bankers, the word 'usury' is never far from mind.

Looking somewhat pleased with himself, Cosimo rolls onto his left elbow and grins at her. 'The clever part is, the parent partnership gets to participate in all the branch profits, even though, beyond their invested capital, it is protected from their trading losses.'

But by now, she is no longer feigning interest. Now her brain is whirring away, and the thought inside it troubles her. 'What prevents the individual branches from acting greedily? Say in the interests of their countrymen, rather than their parent company?'

Still grinning, he presses the end of her nose with his forefinger. 'Because we rule. The parent company is always the majority partner. And in case that was not enough, the legal partnership agreement with each branch always makes it clear that the interests of the parent company must come first.'

'Can you really make people do that?'

The smile on his face disappears. 'You cannot allow local greediness to take over, and above all you can't have local branches being rewarded for self-interest when their actions have adverse consequences elsewhere. Success can only be recognised if the overall bank succeeds. And in order to do that, you have to maintain mutuality of interest.'

His face is beginning to look serious. Time to play the simpleton again. 'How do you ensure that?'

'Money. Through the way people are rewarded. *Giovane* are recruited to do clerical work and to demonstrate their ability. Those that succeed can become *governatore* and take on management responsibilities. In due course, if they advance even further, they may become *compagni;* in personal partnership with the parent company in the ownership of the branch. So at each stage of the process, they become drawn ever closer to the *maggiori* who own the business.'

To her relief, he's smiling again. Time for some lemon juice with the honey. 'That's all very clever. But doesn't it all boil down to recognising men's inherent greed and then rewarding it?'

'Of course. But I prefer to think of it as enlightened self-interest.'

'Is it enlightened? It's certainly self-interest. Well, it works for you.'

'It works for everybody. If the Medici Bank had not been run so profitably over the last twenty years and more, I would not have been able to devote so much time to the better government of the City and Commune of Florence. Nor to my charitable works, including San Marco, and San Lorenzo.' He rolls onto his back again and she can see that the grin has returned. He's looking very full of himself now. 'Patronage is such an expensive business. But someone has to do it.'

He's definitely feeling better. She knows what he has in mind when he smiles like that. She slides a hand under the silk sheet. 'You always win, Cosimo. '

***

Across the room, Madonna Arcangelica closed her eyes and began to smile, nodding almost absent-mindedly. 'And the family, meanwhile?'

Maddalena recognised she'd had enough of the way banks work. The abbess liked familiar ground; especially children. 'The family? Oh life went on. Contessina continued to pursue the principles of *masserizia*: running the ever-growing households with bigger and bigger budgets; yet still mending clothes, saving scraps, sending food to members of the family from their farms to avoid their paying city prices and organising packed lunches for them whenever they travelled anywhere.'

The abbess began to grin. By now Maddalena knew she took vicarious pleasure in her open dislike of Contessina and had begun to play up to it.

'On Cosimo's instructions, Giovanni, his younger son, followed the Ecumenical Council to Ferrara to study how a branch of the bank worked and to use his not inconsiderable charms to make friends with the members of the Curia. That he did, by all accounts, with great gusto and even greater expense: Cosimo always grumbling that he spent more time at the dining table and the gaming table than he did at the *tavola*. We missed his jovial company around the house. Suddenly it had all gone rather quiet.

'Carlo went off to Rome and pursued his studies there. Occasionally I would hear of this small appointment, then that, and slowly he began to rise through the ranks. By all accounts he worked hard and I'm sure the Medici name cannot have done him any harm.'

She found herself smiling at her own joke; any opportunity to talk of Carlo was always a pleasure to her, although he had become very independent in recent years and she had not heard from him since coming to the convent. In fact, she was not even certain he knew she was there.

The thought chilled her and the smile left her face as rapidly as it had come. And as her mood darkened, she found her story becoming more negative.

'With Giovanni gone, Lucrezia stopped visiting and went back to pursue her studies at home. Her parents had both died by the time Giovanni left for Ferrara and in his absence she seemed to withdraw into her shell. She had been such a bright little girl, always running round the house with Carlo and her younger brother Giovanni Battista, following our Giovanni around like yapping puppies, but now she settled into her books and seemed to have grown up very fast.

'She was the brightest of them all. I know I defend my Carlo, but she was cleverer by far than he, and she had more application than all the boys put together. When she had gone, I found I missed her and I hoped she would come back into our world when circumstances changed.

'Giovanni Battista, her little brother, had made a good impression with Cosimo and as soon as he was old enough, he was sent to the Florence *tavola* and later to Rome, to study banking. His early reports were very good and by the time he was fifteen, he was established in the Rome branch as a *giovane*.'

'You say little of Cosimo's eldest son?'

'Piero? No. That's true. Perhaps because, apart from sympathy, he invoked few emotions in me and left few impressions. What can I say? He had all the burdens of a firstborn son and had been over-mothered by Contessina. I often think he was smothered, not mothered; like a little chick beneath a great, feathered hen, and to an extent, he never came out from under her wing.

'Of course he idolised his father. But he was afraid of failing him and as a result, he was always hesitant and fumbling in his presence. The effect was most unfortunate. By the time he was ten or eleven, Cosimo had lost faith in the boy and I am sure it was that sense of his father's growing disinterest that made his stutter worse as he got older.'

Maddalena found herself shaking her head and staring at the ground. 'Piero has always been a sad character; reticent and, to be honest, uninspiring.'

The abbess sat upright and frowned. 'Oh dear. What an indictment! Surely his father must have planned a future for him? He was, after all, the eldest son.'

'Cosimo had made his decisions quite early and he stuck by them. Piero, he knew, would ruin the bank, so in his mind, he gave that to Giovanni. That left the Church for Carlo, and to Piero went the spoils of politics. Somehow, Cosimo hoped the family name would carry him through. "Most of the *Signoria* are stupid anyway," he once said to me, "so he'll be in good company."'

'Poor Piero. Too much like his mother, and just like his mother, increasingly ignored as the years went by.'

'You really didn't like him, did you?'

'It's worse than that. I can't even make myself care. There's nothing to like or dislike. The harsh truth is, he's a stuttering non-entity. I hate myself for saying it, but it's the truth.'

'But one day, he will be head of the household and, so they say, Prince of Florence.'

'I know. That's what's worrying me.'

The bell for Vespers chimed and they both felt a sense of relief. As Maddalena followed the abbess down the stairs, she shook her head again. *Poor Piero. He always managed to spoil everything he came into contact with; even our conversation today. But perhaps I have been unfair to him. There's not a trace of malice in the man. Sometimes, I wish there were. I shall pray for him and hope I find some basis to praise him more highly, next time.*

Chapter 19
Lucrezia
17th April 1458

'I hope you will bear with me if I am somewhat hesitant this week, but I find myself troubled.' Maddalena felt uncomfortable. She had been agonising over what to say and was still not prepared when, to her surprise, the abbess had arrived early. Now she felt cornered, and as a result, irritable.

The surprise on the abbess' face was obvious. 'Troubled?'

Still wishing she had had more time to compose herself, Maddalena took a deep breath. 'Reverend Mother, since speaking to you last week, I find myself regretful of certain things I may have said.'

'You wish to retract something?' Madonna Arcangelica had her Mother Superior face on: professional, distant, uncommitted. Perhaps she sensed embarrassment and her instinct was to be careful, but after so many weeks of close informal conversation, Maddalena found this apparent withdrawal disappointing and unsupportive.

'Retract? No. But I do feel the need to return to the subject, in order, perhaps, to redress the balance.' She smiled, cajoling. 'In the interests of fairness.'

'That is a gracious thing to do. What is the subject you wish to return to?' The abbess had a particular way of inclining her head that managed to indicate a willingness to listen whilst, at the same time, withholding any commitment to respond.

Maddalena sensed it was still the position of abbess speaking and not the woman who held it. In response, she found herself retreating too; picking her words with more precision than she had been used to in recent weeks.

'The subject of Piero di Cosimo de' Medici. I feel I did him a disservice.'

The abbess shook her head. 'Really? I thought you chose your words carefully and fairly.'

Relieved, yet feeling thwarted, Maddalena smiled, but the abbess shook her head. 'I apologise. I have interrupted you. I can see you are uncomfortable; please continue with what you were going to say and I shall do my best not to interrupt.'

For the first time, Maddalena started to relax. 'I may find this difficult, as I wish to speak of the marriage of Piero to Lucrezia Tornabuoni, of whom I have already spoken and whom, you may have noted, I hold in particularly high regard.'

'And in describing her marriage to Piero you are concerned that you may allow her, in some way, to overshadow him?' It hadn't taken long for the abbess to break her promise.

'Exactly.' Maddalena paused. In opening the door so immediately, the abbess seemed to have made her task doubly difficult.

'You see. That's the problem. She did. In almost every way, and no doubt she still does.'

Madonna Arcangelica seemed to sense the tension in the room and sensed that her interruptions were largely to blame. Now she made an effort to sit back and relax. 'Perhaps you should just start at the beginning. This time I really will hold my tongue.'

Maddalena tried to prepare herself. All week, in quiet moments, she had heard herself speaking in what must have sounded like the most disparaging, indeed worse than that; dismissive tones, about the man who was likely in the not-too-distant future, to inherit Cosimo's position as head of the Medici family. And yet, by speaking of him in the same breath as Lucrezia, she knew she was in danger of reinforcing, if not worsening, the predicament.

'What I am about to describe is the worst decision that Cosimo has ever made. I have spoken before of Lucrezia, from her early days, with her brother, visiting the Medici household, and even at that young age, enchanting us with her vivacity, her wit and her intelligence.'

'You do not speak of beauty? It is normal, surely, in such a eulogy, to put that first.'

This time, Maddalena smiled at the interruption. It was a point she had intended to make. 'No. It is not appropriate, and in her case, not necessary. Lucrezia is a fine young woman, charming and elegant. She carries herself well and her manners, and her consideration for others, are exemplary. But you would not use the word beautiful. Her eyes are too far apart. Her nose is too long; far too long and her mouth is small and for the most part, straight and unsmiling.'

'She is pious? A straight mouth is often a sign of piety.'

'She is, but, if I may say this without any sense of implied criticism, she is pious without loss of humanity.'

The abbess dipped her head in admiration. 'She transcends both worlds? A rare attribute and one to be cherished.'

'I agree. She is liked by most and respected by all; not only for her studious intellect, her respectful piety and her gentle humanity, but also for her capability. She can read; in Tuscan, Latin and Greek and write in the first and second. She can keep and interpret a set of account books. She owns property in her own right, and she writes poetry. In short, Lucrezia is a woman of many virtues.'

'She must be, indeed. To achieve so many things, she must also, surely, be in the peak of good health?'

'Sadly not. That is her one weakness. She suffers badly from rheumatism, eczema, sciatica and stomach pains, yet you never hear a word of complaint from her. Never.' Maddalena looked up in emphasis. 'It's the men in the Medici family that do all the complaining.'

The abbess, with her usual sensitivity, had begun to frown. 'You have built up my expectations for this remarkable woman, yet by your expression, I fear you are about to dash my hopes for her.'

Maddalena nodded, her expression serious. 'As I said just now, it was one of the worst decisions Cosimo ever made. Fourteen years ago, Cosimo married his eldest son, Piero, who at that time was twenty-eight years old, to Lucrezia Tornabuoni. She was seventeen years old and her education had advanced as far as any woman in Florence. I remember it well. I was thirty-eight then, and more than twice her age, but over the years, she had spent so much time in my company that increasingly I thought of her, and responded to her, as a *confidante*, and as a result of her closeness to Carlo, almost as a daughter.

'The wedding was a quiet affair. The political situation at the time was sensitive and Cosimo did not believe that a large display of wealth was appropriate. So they married simply, in San Lorenzo, and afterward, walked across the *piazza* past the early workings of the Palazzo Medici, and back to the Casa Vecchia; our house at the time.

'By that time, everyone had grown used to the idea and the appropriate smiles were to be seen everywhere, but four months earlier, when Cosimo had first made his announcement, it had been very different.

'We all knew that Cosimo had been talking very earnestly with her father Francesco for some weeks and we all, including Lucrezia, thought we knew why.'

***

PALAZZO MEDICI, FLORENCE
13th April 1444

'Come in Lucrezia and sit here where everyone can see you. Your father and I have an important announcement to make.' Cosimo is all smiles.

Maddalena sits quietly at the very back of the room and smiles too. Lucrezia looks so happy and why should she not? Of course, everyone knows why she is here. The secret has been out for days now. Of course, Guillermo who works as a clerk at the Monte delle Doti should never have told everyone. The details of the accounts at the Monte are confidential, but as everyone in the city seemed to be saying, *who needs to keep a happy secret?*

He'd let it out last Friday morning and by the afternoon everyone in Florence knew that the eleven year fixed interest bond that Francesco Tornabuoni had invested with the Monte was going to mature in three days' time. Since the sole purpose of the Doti is to provide the finances for a daughter's dowry, and since his daughter has lodged with the Medici for the majority of the last ten years, it is clear that Lucrezia is going to marry her childhood sweetheart, Giovanni de' Medici.

The brothers troop in and take their allotted positions, Piero looks nervous as always and Giovanni looks uncomfortable.

They close the doors and an excited silence falls on the room. Cosimo beams. 'Today is a happy occasion. Today my close friend, Francesco Tornabuoni and I are delighted to announce the engagement of his delightful daughter, Lucrezia, to my son, Piero.'

There is a gasp around the room. What an embarrassing mistake! Wrong son! People wait for Cosimo to correct himself, but he doesn't. Instead he takes her hand and leads her towards – yes, towards Piero.

This can't be right? Surely? Heads turn in all directions and all eyes turn to the girl. And just at that moment, the murmur in the room is split asunder by a great shriek of horror as Lucrezia, repulsed, pulls her hand back from Piero's, screams and falls to the floor in a dead faint.

Of course, the room is cleared. 'She's overcome! It's the magnitude of the moment! Give her air!'

As Maddalena slips quietly out of the small door at the end of the room, her heart is thumping: with anger.

And ahead of her, in the corridor full of people, is Cosimo.

'Cosimo! How could you?' For the one and only time in her life, she is shouting at him, in public. She, the diminutive slave, is standing chest high in front of the richest man in the world and she is berating him.

'You stupid, cruel, wicked man! May you rot in hell for this, the foulest action of your life.'

And Cosimo, for once, is lost for words. For he, honestly and genuinely, thinks he has made this rather plain, if clever young girl the best offer she could ever have dreamed of: the hand of his eldest son, the heir to the Medici fortune.

***

Maddalena raised her eyes and looked across the room to the abbess. 'It was the one and only time I ever saw her exhibit weakness. She did her best to recover, but for the rest of that day, she glared at Cosimo as if he had stabbed her in the back with a stiletto.

'For Cosimo to have made that decision at all, knowing how close she and Giovanni had been for years, was misguided. But to announce it in public, without warning the girl in advance, was simply unforgivable.' Maddalena shook her head, still appalled at the memory.

Then she lifted her head and her expression had changed. 'But then a remarkable thing happened. She went off for a week, either to Careggi, or to Cafaggiolo; I cannot now remember which, but she went with Giovanni and her eldest sister Dianora, presumably as a chaperone, and with only a handful of servants to accompany them on the journey.

'I suspect Cosimo had asked Giovanni to try to talk her round. Anyway, a week later, she came back, and it was as if all the difficulties had been put on one side. She was light, charming and as attentive as ever she had been; and even though Piero had the courtship style of a farm boar, she fawned in his presence like a dutiful wife-to-be.

'Even though the couple now seemed to have accepted the reality, I was angry with Cosimo for what I thought was a stupid and unkind act and on more than one occasion, I told him so. As always, he had a logical reason for doing what he had done. For some time it had been understood that Piero was to marry

Gualdrada di Francesco Guidi, the daughter of the Count of Poppi. But now, it seemed, he had changed his mind and chosen Lucrezia instead. I told him that it was a bad decision, badly made and even more badly announced, and finally he gave me his explanation.

'He told me he knew Piero was going to find the political challenge ahead of him very difficult, but that he, Cosimo, could not afford to see him fail. He said that Gualdrada was much too like his own wife to be of much support to Piero and instead what he needed was a wife who (quietly and discreetly) could offset all his weaknesses. And that, he said, was why he had chosen Lucrezia. And regretfully, I had to accept the logic of what he told me. He didn't tell me how the Count of Poppi had taken the news and I didn't dare ask him. No doubt there had been some sort of settlement and equally certainly, it had involved the passing of money or favours.

'Nevertheless, I told him that in my opinion, making the announcement in public without previously talking to Lucrezia in private had been an act of extreme unkindness.'

'What was his response?' The abbess' hands were tightly wrung together.

'To my surprise, he agreed with me, and he apologised. And then, to my amazement, he told me he had had no choice. "Had I told her in advance," he said, "Lucrezia would probably have talked me out of it!"'

'So knowing it was an act of extreme unkindness, and that the girl would never voluntarily agree to it, he did it anyway?' The abbess' expression had changed. Suddenly, it was distant, and cold and analytical.

Something about that stare made Maddalena pause, and the thought that came to her was an uncomfortable one. *This was not the only occasion when Cosimo, knowing that the consequences of his actions would hurt someone he loved, had decided to continue in any event. My own incarceration here, within these walls, could be similarly described. Indeed, should be. And the abbess, by her expression, has a similar example in her mind.*

She realised she was biting her lip, looked at the abbess and knew immediately that she had read the thought; perhaps having already seen the comparison herself. There was a brief exchange of glances; in many respects more eloquent than words, and Maddalena decided to continue. This was not a diversion she wanted to follow today.

'In any event, they married, as I have told you, and then settled down to family life; Piero mainly absent, doing his father's bidding, trying to build a reputation as anything but a stumbling fool amongst the priors of the *Signoria*, whilst Lucrezia immersed herself in the family.

'Predictably, and with her innate presumption, Contessina tried to dominate her and took pleasure in giving her "helpful" advice.'

She smiled, knowing she had an ally in what she is about to say. 'But to little effect. It was amusing to see the ease with which Lucrezia let her mother-in-law's suggestions slide down her back without ever seeming to disagree or give offence.'

The abbess nodded vehemently and smiled back. She had met neither

Lucrezia nor Contessina, but as Maddalena had already recognised, that did not prevent her from taking sides in any described confrontation between them. But again, she decided not to become diverted.

'It was not long before Giovanni was back with us, having "served his time" as he called it, in the Bank's 'Roman Court' branches in Ferrara and Florence. Now more and more of his business seemed to be conducted from home, and as a result, we saw more and more of him.

'For some reason, he decided that, in matters of the Church, I was someone he could learn from, and day after day he would slide up to me and ask how he should respond to this bishop or that cardinal. And it was true; I had known many of them for years, often more intimately than I would have preferred, although always well short of their undoubted intentions at the time. I usually knew of a list of indiscretions of which each of them could be reminded if a little pressure was required and between us, we established Giovanni's position as a man to be watched and respected, if not a little feared.

'Increasingly, as Giovanni took on more responsibilities in the bank, the *studiolo* became a private office where we would meet, sit, discuss the business of the day, and if necessary, seek Cosimo's decision. And as we talked and, with Giovanni in our midst, invariably laughed, I began to notice how close Giovanni and Lucrezia still were.

'He had a habit when he passed her chair, of putting his hand on her shoulder, and as he walked on, of sliding his fingers across the back of her neck. And she, in turn, would shiver as his fingertips caressed her and then lean towards him and bump her shoulder against his thigh as he passed. I never saw them do any of that in public places, where they, like the rest of us, were always being closely observed, but in the privacy of the *studiolo* it was hard to ignore.

'Of course Contessina was never allowed into that part of the house and Piero seemed to have developed his own ways of working with his political friends that had no bearing on bank business, and therefore, gave him no reason to visit the *studiolo* either.

'And then, one day, Cosimo set off for Lucca and took Piero with him. I was in the *studiolo* with Giovanni Benci, going through the ledger pages of the *Libro Segreto* in preparation for making a *catasto* wealth tax return (or to be more precise, to make sure we didn't declare too much wealth), and I thought I heard Giovanni's laugh.

'"Was that Giovanni?" I asked and Benci just jerked his head towards the *salon*. "They're in there," he said.

'"Who? I replied, perhaps somewhat naïvely, and Benci, with a grimace, answered, "the terrible twins, who else?"

'"What are they doing in the *salon*?" I asked. Yes, I know it sounds stupid now, but to me that was a private room only used by Cosimo and me, and I could not believe that...'

'But were they?' Madonna Arcangelica had that twinkle back in her eye, but still she couldn't make herself use the words.

Maddalena nodded. 'Giovanni Benci said, "They go in there every time; every time Cosimo is away."

'At first I could not believe it, but then it occurred to me that on most of the occasions when Cosimo was travelling, he would take me with him, to run private errands and to attend to matters too personal to discuss with his hosts; and for that reason, I had not seen what happened in his absence. Initially I took it as a bit of an affront, but then I thought back to our early days together and I wished them good luck.'

The abbess sat opposite Maddalena and nodded quietly to herself. Maddalena could see there was a tension in her. A question unanswered. The question. The one question that had lain dormant since their first meeting but which both of them had carefully avoided. Until this moment.

'I have to ask you, *Suora* Maddalena.' As Maddalena lifted her head, the abbess opened her hands in self-defence. 'You may be the only opportunity I will ever have to answer this question.'

Maddalena sensed the reversal of roles and knew it was her turn to sit back and be helpful. 'Please do not be concerned. Ask your question and I shall endeavour to answer it with as much truth as I can.'

Madonna Arcangelica screwed up her courage. When she spoke, her voice was unusually tense; high-pitched and nervous. 'What is it like? To lie with a man? I mean…the act. The full act? To be…' she swallowed hard before forcing herself to use the words, '…penetrated by him?'

***

For weeks Maddalena had known that one day this question would be asked, and many times she had rehearsed what she would say. But now that the moment had come, all of her prepared answers flew out of the window.

'I can only speak of one man, although I have heard much of the experience of others. I was a virgin when Cosimo bought me and although my parents, being committed to my full education, had explained the matter to me, as you might say medically, I was unprepared for the reality.

'Was it? Is it? Painful?'

'In my experience, no. Hardly at all. And then only at the very beginning of the very first time. I believe it depends on you. If you wish to lie with the man; to have him love you in every sense, then no, it need not be painful and it will not be. But conversely, I have spoken to women who were taken by force; who were raped, and they speak of indescribable pain.'

'He did not…? Even though he had bought you as a personal slave? As his, to use or abuse as he wished?'

'No. Never. Even on that first night, when he took me back to the palazzo in Venice and led me to his bedroom. He asked me then if I was frightened and listening to the tone of his voice and seeing the expression of care and understanding on his face, I answered truthfully "no". And then, he did something that surprised me. I thought he would undress me, as the men in the slave market had done, while they remained clothed and invulnerable. But instead, he suggested that we take it in turns and that he should lead, not me.'

'He undressed in front of you? Brazenly, in the light?'

'Of course. He knew it was important that I saw him and that I was not taken passively, blindly, in the dark. He said we must share the experience and that sharing meant equality.'

'What does it look like?' The abbess' eyes were bright with attention.

Feeling suddenly mischievous, or perhaps to hide her own embarrassment, Maddalena frowned, feigning ignorance and the abbess was forced to try again. 'You know. A naked man unclothed and uncovered? What does it look like?'

Maddalena paused. She knew exactly what the question implied, but still could not bring herself to give a straight answer. 'It's hardly a thing of beauty, although some, I am sure, must be. My own son, as I have seen from Donatello's drawings, is a fine figure of a man and beautifully proportioned. But sadly, the man I know does not have the body of an athlete.'

The abbess sat, still but not at rest, and Maddalena knew she was being unfair. It was time to answer a civil, if embarrassed question with a civil answer, but in view of the abbess' obvious sensitivities, perhaps slowly and gently.

'When the man comes to you, you feel his closeness and his roughness. A man's body does not have the contours of a woman's, nor the texture. It is boar against sow.'

The abbess nodded. 'More angular? More firm?'

'Yes and more hairy, in places where we are not.'

Madonna Arcangelica had her hand to her face and she took a small intake of breath. But no question emerged.

But none was needed. Maddalena knew the question and this time, she answered it.

'He touches you gently, his fingers soft but insistent, and you are on fire; at the same time, wishing he would stop, yet praying he will continue. And when, finally, he enters you, it is as if the two of you are one, and you move together as one person; two bodies fused and entwined.'

The abbess had her eyes shut. 'So it must have been for the Blessed Virgin. The rapture of the moment.'

'The rapture follows, rising within you like a great fire, until you almost pass out with the release of it.'

Maddalena watched as the abbess sat high in the chair, holding her breath, eyes closed, hands gripping the arms of the chair tightly as she pointed her chin skywards. Then she gave a great triumphant sigh. 'Oh yes. Yes. The rapture and the release. Of course, it has to be so.'

For a moment she seemed lost in herself and Maddalena paused, giving her time. Then, almost reluctantly, Madonna Arcangelica took a long slow inward breath, her eyes still shut, as she nodded to herself in confirmation.

For a moment her eyes opened and she looked at Maddalena as if surprised at her presence. 'And after that?'

Maddalena spoke slowly. 'After that comes the great relaxation, as if your whole body has lifted up and is now floating down again. And on the first occasion, and only on the first occasion, comes something else; the knowledge; the understanding that the great secret is out, and that you too, now share in it.'

She smiled at the abbess, 'It is in that moment that the maid becomes a woman.'

The abbess subsided, nodding, her eyes softly shut once again, seemingly exhausted but deeply content. From the expression on her face, Maddalena thought she could see the expectation of a fresh perception of the world, of being able to stand before the paintings in the chapel and the *fresci* in the cloister, and of having a new depth of understanding. She sat like that for five minutes and Maddalena, her day's work done, sat opposite her and observed.

And then the abbess opened her eyes again and Maddalena could see that the impish expression had returned.

'You will no doubt think less of me, but I must ask you one more question.'

Maddalena waited; certain she knew what the question was going to be.

'The thing a man has...the...implement of penetration...I have never seen one, not even in a painting. It is always...covered over. What is it really like?'

Perhaps it was the admission of naughtiness on the abbess' face that made Maddalena decide to tease her at this moment. Perhaps it was the returning recognition that it is always beneficial to leave a little mystery behind; for another day. She tried to look serious, although inside, knowing what she planned to say, she was smiling.

'It is something like a mushroom.'

The abbess shook her head. Her hands went to her mouth and then down again, now indicating a wide dome. 'But...But it can't be. An object that shape could not possibly...'

Maddalena shook her head, the effect she sought more than satisfied.

'No. Not a field mushroom. More like a *porcino*.'

Madonna Arcangelica put one hand back to her mouth and there was a sharp intake of breath. 'But they're enormous!'

Maddalena smiled, knowing that she had, after all, managed to keep something back.

'Yes they are.'

'Sometimes!'

Chapter 20
Coming to Terms with Life
1st May 1458

It had been an interesting couple of weeks. Two weeks in which Maddalena had found herself observing the abbess and seeing in her a new woman; a woman from whom there were now no secrets. Madonna Arcangelica had chaired the Chapter Meeting with a new authority, as if overnight, she had grown six inches taller. Her decisions now seemed to come to her more quickly and she issued them with instinctive decisiveness.

The effect had been immediate. The cadre of *discrete* had stopped being obstructive and all five of the old nuns were now fully behind their confident leader. The Chapter Meeting itself had been only half the length of previous meetings and yet it had made considerably more decisions.

On a number of occasions during the week, Maddalena had caught the abbess' eye and each time she had felt a silent transference of thought, as if to say 'now I know, and I know you know I know. It is our secret, and it will remain thus'.

Now, as the abbess took her customary place in the tower room, Maddalena wondered where their conversations would go from here, for in a sense, at least one of their destinations had been reached. Yet to her surprise, it was Madonna Arcangelica who moved them forward.

'I am sure you have noticed the difference in atmosphere here this last week, and I should, of course, thank you for your contribution. But as to the others, you may not be aware of their own interpretation of events.'

Not sure what she meant, Maddalena raised an eyebrow and the abbess continued.

'They have, it seems, convinced themselves that I have had a letter from the patriarch's clerk, and that its essence is to tell us that we have passed the inspection, that all is well and that there need be no amendments to our interpretations of The Rule.'

She shook her head, amused. 'Is it not enlightening how easily people will interpret events in the light of their own preoccupations?'

Maddalena smiled, intrigued. 'Indeed. How did this perception come about?'

Madonna Arcangelica leant forward conspiratorially and dropped her voice. 'A few days ago, the gatekeeper received a letter addressed to me. As always, I examined it carefully before opening it; I was convinced that she had eased the seal in an attempt to read its contents. In reality, it was a letter from the bishop, informing me that my aunt had died and that prayers were to be said for her in the local chantry. But I am sure the gatekeeper must have seen the signature and spoken to her cronies; and between them, surmised the rest.'

Maddalena smiled again, and found herself leaning forward, towards the abbess. 'I sometimes think the world gives us the authority we presume to take unto ourselves. They had reason to draw such a conclusion, didn't they? Your manner this week has, if I may say so, been much more assured.'

'Tranquil.' The abbess sat back in her chair, smiling benignly. 'That was how I felt and it is how I still feel. As if something long-lost has finally been found.' As she leant back, she began to laugh. 'I hope to goodness that I do not now receive a critical letter from the patriarch. I'm not sure how I would respond.'

'Receiving bad news in good grace is a measure of a person.' Maddalena said it with such vehemence that the abbess looked at her closely.

'You propose to talk of that? Today?'

Maddalena nodded. 'In part, yes. If I may, I will continue to tell you of Lucrezia Tornabuoni.'

The abbess prepared herself. 'Ah! The marriage. And its hidden secrets. Of course.'

'The Tornabuoni are an ancient family. As Tornaquinci they were *nobili de torri*, and Lucrezia had inherited all that their breeding entails. As the announcement of her wedding demonstrated, she, of all people could accept bad news with considerable resilience and learn to live with it with apparent grace.

***

PALAZZO MEDICI
12th July 1444

She feels sick. Apprehensive. There is a familiarity about the day's proceedings that makes Maddalena feel uncomfortable.

Then, as Piero calls the room to order, she realises what it is. She's been here before; in this same room, standing in this same place at the back, with almost the same people present. But the last time was three months ago, and it was Cosimo calling the room to order: Lucrezia, sitting demurely at the front, was about to receive the shock of her life. Lucrezia is still at the front. But this time, her fixed expression displays no doubt, mouth a straight line and jaw muscles pulsing as she grinds her teeth, that she already knows what her husband is about to announce. And by all accounts, she isn't looking forward to it.

Piero doesn't make a very good fist of it; stuttering and stumbling over his words. 'I have called the family together to make an announcement,' he says. 'I am the f-father of a child.'

Of course everyone's first reaction is to look at Lucrezia, who has been married to him for just over a month and is sitting right there. Surely she's not...

But Piero shakes his head. 'No. Not with my wife. I mean another child, born to a woman in the city, who I shall not name.'

As he says these words, which have obviously been rehearsed, the baby is carried into the room and presented to Lucrezia. She takes it and cradles it. 'I shall bring this child up as my own,' she says, somewhat woodenly. 'I shall call her Maria.'

Then she passes the baby, who is very young and quite beautiful, to the wet nurse, who carries her away again.

The whole thing is like a play – scarcely real but dramatic nevertheless. And like a good play, it leaves them all guessing.

Piero nods to Lucrezia as if to say 'well done' and then helps her to her feet and without any further comment; they walk out, holding hands.

As soon as the door closes, a deep murmur, like a beehive, breaks out. Maddalena sits back and observes. *Keep still and you can become invisible* she thinks.

Most of the people in the room seem preoccupied with the identity of the mother. There is much speculation, during which the names of almost all the beautiful and noble women of the city are mentioned.

But to Maddalena, the biggest question remains: How did Lucrezia manage to play her part so coolly?

***

'The child Maria grew into a beautiful girl, with huge brown eyes and curly nut-brown hair.' Maddalena lifted her eyes to the abbess, who had been listening with her eyes closed but who now, hearing the pause, opened them.

'Yes, a beautiful child; bright and charming. So outgoing that everybody took to her immediately.'

She put a hand to her mouth and her voice dropped to a stage whisper. 'It's an unkind thing to say but more than one person expressed the thought: *how on earth did Piero ever father her?*'

The abbess grinned. 'I was just asking myself the same question. And what, pray, is the answer?'

'They contented themselves with the thought that the mother must have been very beautiful, and of course this intensified the speculation about her identity even further.' Maddalena looked steadily at the abbess, who seemed to sense there was a message in her gaze, but had not yet worked out what it was.

'Who was the mother?'

Maddalena shook her head. 'We were never told. She must have been a true noblewoman; the child was so beautiful and intelligent. Names were mentioned later, but never confirmed and it would be speculative and inappropriate of me to refer to them now.'

'Oh.' The abbess seemed disappointed.

'Later, I talked to Lucrezia and asked her why she had accepted the child and agreed to bring her up as her own. Her reply was simple. "You of all people should know, Maddalena. That is how things work round here, is it not? The family – especially the men, get their own way – every time." I remembered the birth of my Carlo so many years earlier and I thought I understood. But even as I thanked her, I sensed there was another part to the story – something that wasn't mentioned; a secret that Lucrezia was holding back.'

The abbess leaned forward, expectantly.

'Whatever it was, Lucrezia seemed happier after the event, rather than upset, and fourteen months later, her own Bianca was born. Piero declared he was delighted to have a daughter and Lucrezia seemed to glow with contentment. Perhaps, everybody said, the child was what she needed, to make her happy. But I wondered.'

'Mm.' Across the room, Madonna Arcangelica seemed to be withholding her judgement.

'Everything seemed to blow over and two years later, in early March 1447, another child, again a girl, this one called Lucrezia, but addressed by everyone as Nannina, was born. This time, Piero seemed openly disappointed. Of course, we said, he wanted a son. But by this time, I had decided there was quite a different story behind what we saw in public.

'My suspicions were increased when Piero and Lucrezia decided to apply to the pope for a *plenaria remissio* – the forgiveness of their sins. Of course, the argument was that there must be some sin which was preventing them from having a son; but although I did not hear of any particularly serious sins being admitted by either of them, I remained convinced that there was still some problem that remained deep-seated within their marriage.

'The pope was generous and replied almost immediately. As soon as they received his document, which reached them within a few days, both Piero and Lucrezia seemed uplifted; Lucrezia especially so. So much so that I decided my suspicions had been wrong and I prayed in private for thinking such unworthy thoughts. Thanks be to God that I had not said anything to anyone.'

The abbess nodded, smiling. 'Quite.'

'Christmas 1448 was hard for Lucrezia. She was heavily pregnant once again, and very tired. But everything changed on the 1st of January, when at last she gave birth to a baby boy – and a strong one. They named him Lorenzo; and this time, Piero was ecstatic. I was not the only one to think that Lucrezia's expression was just like the blessed Mary's – beatific. I had never seen anyone look so happy in my life.

'Lorenzo was an amazing child. Within weeks, everyone seemed to know he was special. He had none of his father's withdrawn earnestness, but instead exhibited a confident and flamboyant love of life. In this respect, he was the very image of his uncle Giovanni, who clearly doted on the boy, and living in the same house, spent time with him and his mother frequently.

'Lorenzo grew strong and healthy and four years later, his younger brother, Giuliano was born. Although not as forceful as Lorenzo, little Giuliano, too, was strong, outgoing and confident; and Cosimo, at last, began to relax. He was, by this time, sixty years of age. Under Giovanni Benci, the Bank had seen the most profitable period of trading it had ever known, and now the future of the family finally seemed secure. Somehow the whole family seemed to have become united by the birth of these two boys, and it was clear now to everyone, including Piero and Lucrezia, that the pope's forgiveness of their sins had worked.'

Across the room, the abbess nodded, as if she, herself, had been thanked. It was a small movement, but one that irritated Maddalena, seeming as it did to her, to be presumptuous. Her experience of bishops and cardinals had tempered her religious conviction with a strong cynicism and now, instantly, the abbess' reaction seemed to bring out the worst in her. She pulled a sour face.

'That or the money.'

Immediately, the abbess' satisfied nod turned into a frown. She stared at Maddalena as if she was about to admonish her.

Realising that she had reacted too strongly, especially in a house of God, Maddalena saw the need to explain. 'It may have been a condition of the pope's pardon, or it may have been a genuine choice by Piero, who was, to give him his due, as religious as his wife. Whatever brought it about; Piero began to make generous donations in support of religious works.

'San Miniato al Monte and Santissima Annunziata both benefitted. Both churches were redecorated and then Piero had marble tabernacles made; one to support the crucifix in San Miniato and the other to encase the *Annunciation* in Santissima Annunziata. The second was made immediately after Lorenzo's birth and inscribed to thank God for the favour he had received, but being Piero, he could not resist adding that the marble alone cost 4,000 florins. He had a little footnote to this effect inscribed into the base.'

'Tut.' Looking distinctly affronted, the abbess shook her head. 'That was most inappropriate.'

Rather than allowing herself to become sidetracked, Maddalena decided to plough on with her story. 'Lorenzo's christening was a great event; treated as an official public ceremony. We all set off from the Casa Vecchia accompanied by eight priors, nine *Accopiatore*, the archbishop of Florence and the prior of San Lorenzo, as well as a number of foreign dignitaries. Of course the direct route to the baptistery would have only taken about two minutes, so instead we perambulated round the whole city, visiting every quarter and even crossing the river to show the child to the citizens of Santo Spirito, before returning triumphantly to our own *Gonfalone* of Leon D'Oro in the quarter of Santa Maria Novella. And so, finally, we found our way to the baptistery, which of course we claimed as our own.'

'A happy outcome.' The abbess now looked delighted.

Maddalena smiled her agreement. 'It was, indeed. And recognised as such. When Lorenzo was a year old, Piero and Lucrezia made a pilgrimage to Rome, and were granted the privilege of owning a portable altar by the pope, then Nicholas V. It was a prized possession and they took it to Cafaggiolo, where it remains to this day. And so, slowly, through time, the married life of Piero and Lucrezia settled down; if not into domestic bliss, then at least into a settled contentment.'

Pleased with the result, the abbess sat back with a satisfied smile.

Maddalena gave her a couple of minutes, and then slipped in her final comment. 'But still, I felt that beneath the surface of their apparent contentment lay a secret. One that, when it emerged, was sure to cause great unhappiness.'

Chapter 21
The Old Order Passes
15th May 1458

The footsteps on the stairs were faster than usual; almost hurried and for a moment, Maddalena wondered whether the abbess was about to call her down. But when the door opened, the abbess, though red in the face and wheezing somewhat, was beaming, her eyes bright.

'I have been looking forward to this afternoon's conversation. The last time we met privately together, two weeks ago, you were telling of the birth of healthy sons and how Cosimo felt able to relax, his life's accomplishments achieved. Since then, I have been thinking. I am sure, now, that I know why Cosimo came here, and spoke to me of endowments to the convent.'

She leaned against the back of the chair, her flurry of words having robbed her of breath. Maddalena felt her heart quicken. Was the abbess about to tell her how Cosimo had first visited her and what indications – promises even – he had made to her? She seemed to have something to talk about.

'It is as before, isn't it? When he was so generous to San Miniato al Monte and Santissima Annunziata. Cosimo wishes to give thanks to God for all his blessings. Doesn't he?'

Maddalena was perplexed. She remembered the abbess only weeks before, laughing at how easily the nuns had misinterpreted her letter from the bishop, assuming that it referred to those matters that dominated their own world. Now, it seemed, the abbess was falling into the same trap. But how to disabuse her without giving away the whole plan? It was a problem.

Perhaps there was another problem? What must Cosimo have said to her? How could he have allowed the abbess to draw such conclusions? She could understand that he did not wish to tell her the detail of his plan for Lorenzo's gold, but to dissemble to the point where she had such deeply held misconceptions?

'Did Cosimo say that? Is that what he told you?'

The abbess was still smiling confidently. 'Good Lord, no. Not at all. I would not have expected him to tell me his secrets. But you, surely, said as much last time we met? At least, I took you to be saying so. You described a family which had triumphed over adversity and for whom God's blessings were boundless.'

Her confidence began to fade and as it did so, a small furrow crossed her brow. 'Did you not?'

Maddalena shook her head. 'I described Cosimo feeling like that when his two grandsons had been born. Yes. But if you remember, I also made reference to what I thought was a secret, hidden beneath the surface of apparent happiness, like a maggot in a shiny red apple.'

The abbess' face fell. 'But the endowments?'

'It was Piero who financed the work at those two churches; not his father.'

'Oh!' The abbess looked even more disappointed and began to wring her hands together. Maddalena thought it too strong a reaction simply to reflect disappointment at the family's imperfect happiness. She began to wonder whether her contradiction had shattered some naïve expectation of further endowments from the Medici. If so, that had not been her intention and still wasn't.

Perhaps it was time to explain more fully.

'To someone who, like me, knew every expression of the family's faces, some of the idyllic events I have described were marred. There were responses that convinced me that something was amiss. Small things; a glance here, a hesitation in a reply there, a smile fading when the person thought no one was looking at them.'

'Who in particular?'

'Lucrezia.'

'But she had married the man who was to become head of the Medici family, and already she had provided him with two sons. What could be less than idyllic in that?'

Maddalena thought for a moment, and then decided she had to be honest. 'I sensed a falsity in the whole thing. Lucrezia was like a racehorse harnessed to a carthorse. She and Piero were as different as two people could be; a poet married to a mute.'

'But I thought you said they had overcome her initial disappointment at marrying the wrong brother? Everything had settled down nicely and they had four children. That, surely, is proof enough?'

Maddalena listened and reconsidered. Perhaps her thoughts had been unworthy.

'They did, and up to and beyond the birth of Lorenzo, I would have agreed with you. But a few months before Giuliano was born, events took a turn that made me wonder.'

The abbess made her way to her chair and sat, preparing herself, and Maddalena, still on her feet, continued. 'Giovanni married Ginevra degli Alessandrini. She was a nice enough girl, from a good family and she would have made an admirable wife had she married Piero, but it was clear even at the wedding feast that Giovanni had little interest in her. She was of the old school; of *masserizia*, just like her mother-in-law, Contessina.'

'Was that such a bad thing?' Madonna Arcangelica looked perplexed; and not for the first time, Maddalena was reminded that, despite the abbess' willingness to share her dislike of many of Contessina's mannerisms, the quiet pursuit of good housekeeping lay close to her own philosophy for running the convent.

'Perhaps not. But Giovanni had rejected that approach to life and instead believed in the pursuit of *magnificentia*. That's why his nephews, Lorenzo and Giuliano, so adored him; he represented the new, modern world, not that of the old generation. Their uncle, they used to say, understood them and was fun, whilst their father Piero, like their grandfather, Cosimo, was old-fashioned and boring.

'The generations were changing. Piero was in many respects the last remnant of the old world, whilst his younger brother, Giovanni, represented the new. And, it must be said, represented it with enthusiasm.'

'But I am sure I have heard stories of how Cosimo and his wife adored the grandchildren and indulged them at every opportunity? Even the patriarch told a story about having to wait while Cosimo made a whistle for his grandson?'

Maddalena nodded, remembering. That story about the Lucchese ambassador and the reed whistle would probably finish up on Cosimo's headstone. 'Oh yes, they loved their grandsons well enough, and the boys were willing to accept every indulgence as their natural right, especially sweetmeats; but behind their backs, the boys had little true respect for them.

'They called Cosimo *Mulo* because he had a long nose and big ears, and looked to them like the mule he always rode. Contessina was always referred to as *Nonna Grassona*; fat grandma. Not to her face, of course, and never in front of Cosimo, or Piero, or their mother, or me for that matter; but Giovanni knew. And it was Carlo who told me.'

'Ungrateful little ruffians!' Madonna Arcangelica's face looked as if she was eating a raw lemon.

Maddalena laughed. 'Not at all. Just boys being boys. They are always pushing against the fences. That's what makes them what they are.'

'Was your Carlo the same?'

'Carlo? Of course he was. In his time. He and Giovanni were little rascals for a few years. They loved nothing better than to play football with the rough crowd in the Piazza di Santa Croce. And tournaments. They loved to go down there and play tournaments and would come home filthy. But that's boys for you.'

Madonna Arcangelica shook her head. It was clear that such indiscipline did not find favour in her mind. As if to demonstrate her own self-control, she dragged the conversation back again. 'How did Lucrezia respond to seeing Giovanni married?'

'Not well. That's what I was going to say to you. In public, she put a good face on everything, as a dutiful wife would. But the hurt on her face when she didn't think anyone was looking was painful to watch. I remember seeing her, sitting in the house, large with child and clearly exhausted from attending the wedding in San Lorenzo, and looking across the room at Giovanni. The grief in that expression still haunts me.'

'And Giovanni?'

'Oh yes. He still loved her, too. There was no doubt about that. Cosimo may have convinced himself that he had done the right thing from the family's point of view by marrying Lucrezia to Piero, and he may have convinced himself that they had both come to terms with the arrangement, but in my view, neither of them has ever really got over it and neither of them has forgiven Cosimo for what he did.'

Maddalena decided to change the subject. She sat down and prepared herself.

PALAZZO MEDICI
12th June 1453

'She shouldn't interfere!'

Maddalena sits beside Cosimo's bed and tries to calm him. He's always grumpy when bedridden with gout and in pain. Understandable really.

But in recent years, the frequency of his illnesses and incapacity has increased dramatically, and in turn, his manner has declined. Now at his best he is sardonic and caustic, and at his worst, almost unbearably miserable and rude.

And, she has to admit, he is increasingly lonely, because she now is the only one able and willing to handle his moods; while the rest tiptoe away and find more congenial company.

But today he has picked on an infrequent adversary, and one, she thinks, he is unlikely to better. The problem is, she thinks Lucrezia is right, and Cosimo, as is increasingly the case these days, is in the wrong.

It's a family issue really. Lucrezia's youngest brother, Giovanni Battista Tornabuoni, has been working with the Rome branch of the bank from the age of fifteen, initially as a junior cashier, and by now as bookkeeper.

It's a responsible job. Bills of exchange are extremely valuable – effectively money – they are holograph documents; always written by hand by the named author, an example of whose handwriting will have been sent under separate cover to whichever branch or banking agent is expected to honour it at the other end. And Giovanni, along with Roberto Martelli, the General Manager and Leonardo Vernacci, the Assistant Manager, are the only named and recognised authors.

But Roberto has been away a great deal of the time, on business, and Leonardo has had the responsibility of running the Rome branch himself. This is a great burden on his shoulders. So effectively, almost all of the bills end up being written out by Giovanni, who feels put upon.

What makes it worse is that over the years Leonardo d'Angelo Vernacci, the Assistant Manager, under pressure from his additional responsibilities, has frequently accused Tornabuoni of slacking, and complained about him to Roberto, and also to Giovanni Benci, the General Manager of the Bank, in Florence. And Tornabuoni, who was brought up running the corridors of the Palazzo Medici with Giovanni de' Medici, who is now – under Cosimo's nominal leadership – Deputy Director of the Bank and more senior than all of them, thinks he is being unfairly criticised.

The latest row began when Vernacci wrote to Giovanni de' Medici, reminding him that the bank's written policy had for years been 'to advance anyone doing well without regard to family connections' and that 'advancement is based entirely on merit'.

Incensed, Lucrezia's brother has written to Piero in his capacity as head of the family and Lucrezia's husband (and not, as he should have done, to Giovanni, who runs the bank) to take issue with the complaints.

That, Maddalena thinks, is outrageous enough, but Piero has been stupid enough to reply, even though the matter was really none of his business. And now Cosimo is backing Piero, (because he knows nobody else will) and who, he says, was only trying to help. But now, to his surprise, Lucrezia, instead of backing her husband, is arguing the managerial case, saying the family is failing to support its professional management. Why? Because she still loves her brother-in-law, Giovanni de' Medici, and always takes his side. And perhaps because what she says is true.

'Lucrezia is being disloyal!' Cosimo, propped up with pillows, is standing his ground as well as a sick man can.

Maddalena has one more go at getting through to him.

'Loyalty is not the case at point. Not even whether Giovanni is any good or not. The point is, whether the bank is going to support its professional management, including Vernacci, or whether, as has happened too often recently, the family always wins. To Lucrezia, the principles of good management come before loyalty – even to her own brother! Can't you see that?'

'Don't shout at me. I'm ill.' He is putting on his quavering voice now; a sure sign he knows he's losing. But she knows him too well to fall for that one. He'll soon recover if she shows signs of weakening.

'Lucrezia is right. It's ridiculous to buy a powerful horse and then pull your own cart. Even the horse will lose respect for you, if you do that.'

And she says it confidently, because she knows it's true. The Bank has branches all over Europe and it's essential that the managers of those branches respect and adhere to the policies set by the head office.

'Piero may be head of the family, but he is not formally involved in the running of the Bank at all. You can't have him supporting Giovanni Battista against the local and central management, even if he is my brother.'

This time, Cosimo nods and subsides into his pillows.

But Maddalena knows nothing will happen and that the argument will persevere, like a festering sore, so long as Cosimo and Piero keep poking their little fingers in. Lucrezia is right. She nearly always is.

***

The abbess began nodding. 'I think I understand. Discipline is, as we know here well enough, essential to maintain.'

Maddalena smiled back at her. She said nothing, but the thought that entered her head was of interpretation, for it was the lightness of touch with which Madonna Arcangelica interpreted the Rule of the convent that made life bearable.

Had the easing of the policy of the Medici Bank in Cosimo's latter years merely reflected a softening of interpretation, or had the family lost its grip on what originally made the bank what it had become?

Somehow, although she had never met him, she knew what Cosimo's father would have said and she had a feeling that Lucrezia would agree with him.

The abbess was looking drawn. It was time for another change of subject.

'Shall we talk about something different?' She had one more story in her mind that she thought worth telling.

The abbess nodded absent-mindedly.

'Now that he was married, Lucrezia may have thought that Giovanni could do nothing else to hurt her. But two years later, he did.'

Once again, the abbess sat up. It was always the same. People, rather than the rules of institutions and organisations, seemed to be her stimulus.

***

PALAZZO MEDICI
Late Autumn 1455

'I'm back.'

Giovanni de' Medici clambers awkwardly from his carriage and looks across the courtyard of the palazzo.

Two floors above, Maddalena hears the cry and looks out of the window. *Lucrezia will be pleased* she thinks. *She's missed him terribly.*

She knows there's no hurry. *By the look of him he's put on quite a lot more weight during his year as ambassador to Rome. He'll take a lot longer to puff his way up the stairs to the piano nobile than I will to drop down one short staircase.* Instead she leans on the windowsill and watches. Arrivals are always fun. There's nearly always some element of surprise.

Down below, she sees him turn and reach a hand back into the carriage. His hand is followed by a long, slender arm. A girl's arm. A black girl's arm. An arm wearing a slave bangle, just like hers.

The girl looks nervous. Well, who wouldn't be? Arriving in an ambassador's carriage in the central courtyard of the Palazzo Medici. Maddalena leans out further, to get a better look. She's beautiful. Not just attractive, but take-your-breath-away beautiful; tall and slender, slim-hipped and, as she crosses the courtyard holding Giovanni's pudgy hand, she is graceful, walking like a dancer, or an athlete.

Ginevra won't be pleased. Maddalena bites her lip. She even feels a twinge of jealousy herself.

Cosimo will like her. He'll like her a lot. She is truly gorgeous.

As she makes her way down the staircase, her head is whirring. *He must have bought her in Venice*

Step, step, step.

Copied his father and found her on the Riva degli Schiavoni.

Step, step, step.

I hope he is looking after her as well as Cosimo looked after me. She can't be more than seventeen. Perhaps the same age I was?

165

She reaches the landing and slows. *It won't do to arrive breathless. They'll think I've been running.*

She takes the first couple of steps down the next flight of stairs and suddenly stops as she hears what sounds like Lucrezia's voice below her. *Oh dear. Now* she *certainly won't like this. Lucrezia won't like it at all.*

By the time Maddalena reaches the great hall, it is half full. Half full with smiling people – people smiling awkwardly, as if they don't know what to say. And the reason they don't know what to say is in the middle of the room, trying to smile, still holding Giovanni's hand, which against her slim brown fingers looks huge and pudgy, like a butcher holding a sparrow.

'This is Titania.' Giovanni breaks the silence by introducing her.

Ginevra, already pregnant from the short visit Giovanni made home early in the summer, gasps and puts a hand to her mouth. You can see she is very upset, but it hasn't taken her long to remember that Giovanni is a law unto himself and that complaining will achieve nothing on his part but the loss of temper, and on her part, further upset and discomfort. So she stands there, until someone brings her a chair.

Maddalena looks around for Lucrezia but she's not there. It must have been another voice – similar, but not hers. Lucrezia, someone tells her, is still in Pisa, on business. *Oh well. Perhaps that's a blessing.*

Slowly, the household settles and adjusts. And once again, all seems quiet. Giovanni, it appears, has got away with it.

Until Lucrezia gets home. Then we'll see.

***

Maddalena shook her head, laughing to herself, lost in her memories. 'To my surprise, within a few hours of Titania's arrival, Ginevra came to see me, by herself, and asked my advice. She seemed to think I would be able to see into the girl's head just because we were both black and had both arrived under similar circumstances. It wasn't a very long conversation and as you might imagine, somewhat inconclusive. I had no intention of taking sides in the matter.

'Then, to my greater surprise, Titania herself caught my eye and asked if she, too, might speak to me. The poor girl was terrified and had no real idea what was in store for her. My mind went back to the early days in Rome when the other Tita had preceded me in Cosimo's favours. She, like me, was still in the household, although as she had been demoted to kitchens duties, even while in Rome, she had never posed a threat to Contessina or, if I am honest, to me.

'I asked her what she was good at. Her reply was so inarticulate that one thing was immediately clear. Giovanni may have brought her back to show Cosimo and Giovanni Benci that whatever they had done in the past, he could do now; but I was certain that, beautiful as she was, he would have no long-lasting interest in her and if she was found useful work in the kitchens, he would soon forget her and the matter would blow over pretty quickly.

'But I had forgotten about Lucrezia and so, it seemed, had Giovanni. Then, the following afternoon, Cosimo, who was having a good spell, and who was again able to walk a very short distance, was helped by the servants to the *Signoria*. While he was there, Lucrezia returned from Pisa. Within the hour I saw her follow Giovanni into the *salon* and shut the door.

'I was in the *studiolo*, almost next door, but I could hear her voice as if they were in the same room. To say she was not pleased would be an understatement. Ten minutes later, Giovanni emerged, as white as a sheet and visibly shaking. No more was said, but by the next morning, Titania was gone; sold, they said, to one of the Portinari brothers for almost nothing.'

'Your Lucrezia seems to be a lady of some character.' The abbess had an approving smile on her face.

Maddalena beamed at her. 'Lucrezia is special. She represents a new generation. She will never be content to be the dutiful wife, sitting at home with her babies and running the household. She has wider horizons than that. Much wider. And if any of them, from Cosimo to Piero to Giovanni, had failed to recognise that before, they certainly understood it now.'

'Did that end the matter?'

'Oh yes. Giovanni apologised to his wife and to Lucrezia. He even apologised to me, although I was not quite clear what for. Titania was never mentioned again, and before the end of that year, Ginevra gave birth to a lovely, healthy, round-faced boy. They named him Cosimo but everyone calls him Cosimino. His birth brought Giovanni and Ginevra closer together again, and although he was never what you might call an attentive husband, he treated her civilly from that time onward.'

'And Lucrezia? Was she jealous of the child?'

Maddalena looked at the expression on the abbess' face and saw that she had missed little. She nodded and smiled. 'Probably. I didn't ask her. We were overtaken by events. Or to be more precise, by one event of such magnitude that in hindsight, it overshadowed all the others.

'In the middle of July, Giovanni Benci died. He had been General Manager of the bank for twenty years, since Cosimo returned from exile, and in that period, the bank had achieved its greatest growth and its highest profitability. I like to think that during that period, and indeed for the years previously, my support and encouragement had also helped, but in my mind, no one played a more important role in the success of the Medici Bank than Giovanni Benci.'

'More important than Cosimo himself?' The abbess was looking at her carefully from beneath lowered eyebrows. It was a question few would dare ask, and Maddalena knew it was a searching one. Slowly, she nodded her head.

'Probably. Yes.'

Already she was casting her mind back, remembering some of the criticisms of Cosimo she had heard Lucrezia make during those last two years at the Palazzo Medici; those final years before she had left for the convent and her new life. Benci had been a huge loss. Cosimo, now no longer a young man, was lost without him, there was no doubt about that. Uncertain and indecisive, issues that once he had addressed remotely, had now become immediate responsibilities and as such, urgent, frightening and personal threats.

Maddalena remembered it all so clearly. *That had been little more than two years before I left the Palazzo Medici and came here, to do Cosimo's latest bidding.* But already the signs had been bad. One of Cosimo's first actions had been to close down the holding company. Now it was a free-for-all. Now each branch was effectively responsible for its own free-standing profit performance, and in the absence of any real interest by Giovanni, the entire onus for making the branches work together lay on Cosimo's ageing shoulders. And in truth, he was no longer up to it.

Maddalena knew now that whatever Cosimo might ask them to do, local profits, in which they participated heavily, would drive the branch managers to put local considerations first. And, perhaps, cause them to take greater risks than they ought. The old rules had gone. Giovanni di Bicci's strict principles had rapidly been allowed to decay. Giovanni di Cosimo de' Medici was now running the bank. He thought it was all good fun, but still he didn't seem in a hurry to learn banking techniques. And in the absence of strong leadership, it had all started to fall apart.

Distant from these events and seeing them with a new clarity, Maddalena had found herself shocked by what she realised was happening. There had been a time, two years before, and under Cosimo's daily influence, when she had wondered why Lucrezia was so cynical about the bank. At the time it had seemed to be doing so well.

But now, with more time to think, she shared Lucrezia's concern for the future. Now she knew why Cosimo had been so concerned. Now she knew why, once again, as he had done back in 1433, Cosimo had begun squirreling away money; but this time for Lorenzo.

And as far as she knows, he still is. *But where is the plan today?*

Suddenly she felt her heart go heavy. She was aware that the abbess was looking at her, perhaps thinking about the implications of her last utterance. And suddenly, a loss of confidence overcame her. And as it did so, a terrifying image leapt into her mind; a picture she had not thought about for two years.

'Up here, in the hills, did you experience the great storm, in the August of two years ago?'

The abbess shook her head. 'We have a number of violent storms every year, but I don't recall a single one having special significance. Why do you ask?'

Her mind now half-distant, Maddalena stood and walked towards the folding doors. She released the catch, opened the first section, and looked out, yet still with no real focus to her gaze.

'They say it was the greatest storm ever seen. That it came roaring in from the sea, passing over Ancona and flooding the whole valley from side to side as it moved inland. Then for some reason, it stopped moving and came to a halt, over Empoli, the lighting filling the sky, the thunder so deafening that afterwards, many people never recovered their hearing. And all the time, they say, the rain kept falling like spears out of the sky and the floods rose higher and higher. Lucca was waist deep, and Vinci was on the verge of being washed away completely.'

***

PALAZZO MEDICI
24th August 1456

'Yes I think we're safe now. It seems to have missed us. Thank God we were only on the edge of it. It must be terrifying over there.'

Michelozzo points his finger towards the horizon, beyond the city walls, some eight miles downstream; perhaps somewhere over Empoli.

At first they had cowered deep in the strongest part of their house as a series of reports of the storm's progress reached them. It had, they said, swept in from the upper sea, at Ancona, passing over Urbino. By the time it was seen crossing the mountains at Pieve Santo Stefano, everyone feared it was heading for the city.

But then, to their relief, it seemed to skirt the city, the eye of the storm passing between the southern walls and the mountains at San Casciano, before continuing downstream. Relieved, the whole family, like others amongst the nobles and richer merchants who had the benefit of a rooftop loggia, climbed to the highest point in the Palazzo Medici; and, feeling distinctly braver than they had an hour before, had prepared to watch it retreat.

'What are the reports from the Ponte Vecchio?' Piero has to cup his hands to the servant's ear to make himself heard against the howling wind.

It is, by a long way, the fiercest, most vicious wind Maddalena has ever seen or heard. Even here, away from the whirlwind that forms the centre of the tempest, tiles are still being ripped off roofs and the streets are littered with debris.

'Full flood, but holding. They have evacuated the shops and houses, and posted the night guard at both ends, but so far the bridge itself has not washed away. It's vibrating with the water pressure, though. I heard it myself; a deep rhythmic rumbling, like a wounded stag; it's horrible; it turns your stomach.'

The servant shakes his head. 'I would not cross that bridge now for a year's wages.' He is soaked to the skin and looks petrified.

Lucrezia looks up, suddenly. 'Can you take a quick message to the Pitti Palace? It's urgent!'

His jaw drops. The Pitti Palace is on the opposite bank of the river, and the Ponte Vecchio the quickest route, the only acceptable one for a servant with an urgent message.

But Maddalena can see that Lucrezia is only teasing. She tousles the poor man's head and lets him out of his misery. 'I'm only joking. Go downstairs and get dry. Then change your clothes and warm yourself in the kitchens. There's food and wine laid out there, so help yourself. Your work is done for tonight.'

Relieved, the man bobs a bow. As he makes for the stairs, Lucrezia calls after him. 'And thank you, Andrea. You have, as always, served us well tonight.'

Andrea disappears in a flash of grateful teeth as the horizon is lit by yet another enormous flash of lightning. They brace themselves for the rumble of thunder, but what they hear is not a rumble, but a splitting, tearing sound; like a tree being torn asunder.

Maddalena flinches and sees Giovanni recoil so hard he spills nearly all the wine from the large goblet in his hand. He puts the empty goblet down, grabs a cloth from the table beside them and begins to dab at his gown. Beside him, Michelozzo is unaware of the commotion: he has his hands cupped round his forehead, shielding his eyes and is staring intently at the boiling maelstrom of black clouds ahead of them.

'It's stopped moving.'

'What?' Piero has his hand to his ear.

'The storm. It's no longer moving away, towards Pisa.'

Piero looks even more nervous. 'Is it coming back?'

Michelozzo signals him to wait and stands, leaning forward, his elbows on the edge of the balcony, his fingers cupped as before. Finally he stands and turns. 'No. It's just standing there, over Empoli. Like some cornered beast.'

'I don't like it. I'm going down.' Piero's face is pale. Cosimo agrees with him. 'Come on, all of you. If it comes back this way, the loggia will give us little protection.'

As they turn, grateful for the instruction, and begin to descend, Michelozzo looks back at the hurricane. 'If it comes directly over here, there won't be a loggia to protect us. That wind will tear the roof off the house and take the whole loggia with it.'

He follows Maddalena to the staircase and gives her a wry smile. 'I should know. I built it. But not for a storm like this.'

***

'In the morning, news came that the storm had flooded Pisa and done great damage to Lucca, to Prato and to Empoli. The roofs of the churches of San Martino a Bagnuolo and Santa Maria della Pace were lifted into the air and thrown down over a mile away. And a carrier and his mules were lifted bodily skyward and found dead a long way from the road they had been on.

'We wondered what it was telling us. Some said it was an omen – the end of something. Now, when I look back, I believe they were right.'

'It was clearly a memorable occasion. One you have never forgotten. There must have been great destruction? But Brunelleschi's dome was saved?'

Maddalena nodded. 'Indeed there was. The Duomo was undamaged. We could see it quite clearly, living almost next door. Nevertheless, it was truly frightening. Terrifying.'

For a moment she stood staring into space, overcome by the memory.

'We rode out from the city the following day to see what help we could give to the people. You could see the path the hurricane had taken. It was as if a great river had passed though, a mile wide, and carried away everything in its path.

170

Nothing in that great channel remained; no crops, no animals, no trees, no walls, no buildings. Nothing. Just rock and smashed debris.'

'But was it an omen? Or purely a great storm?'

The abbess waited for an explanation, but receiving no response, continued her train of thought. 'It seems God's will that night was to threaten, rather than to chastise Tuscany. Had he intended the latter, he would have sent the storm through Arezzo and right through the City of Florence. The death and destruction would have been truly awful. The most terrible ruin and destruction that the mind of man can conceive.'

'Tell that to the people of San Casciano.' Maddalena was too tired to debate the issue. She had run out of nervous energy. Besides, she was aware that the bell would ring at any moment.

She closed the chestnut doors and dropped the hasp back into place. It was no good. The rest would have to wait.

Chapter 22
San Damiano
29th May 1458

'Reverend Mother! Come in. Please sit down.'

As Maddalena opened the door to the abbess, she was shocked by the expression on her face. She looked exhausted, ravaged, as if by some great storm like that they had talked about the last time they had met together.

'I am sorry I'm late. I expect you had given me up for lost? I was waylaid by the Council of the *Discrete*. They insisted we hold an emergency meeting of the Chapter.'

Maddalena frowned. 'Why?'

'They demand that you and I stop meeting like this. They say it is undemocratic and inappropriate. They asked me to tell them what we discuss.'

'And did you?' Suddenly, Maddalena was concerned. She had always spoken openly to the abbess on the understanding that their conversations were privileged and entirely secret. Surely Cosimo's inner secrets were not now out in the convent for open discussion?

'I told them nothing. I refused even to speak of the subject matter. This, of course, increased their suspicions even more. Now they are talking of asking the Confessor to take a Letter of Supplication to the patriarch. Under our Rule they have this entitlement so long as three quarters of the Chapter, in open meeting, vote for it. They can ask the patriarch to have me dismissed. Not just removed from office, but rejected from the convent. If that happened, I don't know what I would do. I have nowhere else to go. This place has been my life.'

She broke down in tears and fell into her accustomed chair. 'I had always expected to die here; I hoped in peace and tranquillity.'

'When is this Chapter Meeting to take place?' Maddalena was trying to think fast, but her mind was in a whirl.

'It is not yet certain. They say if we agree to stop meeting, they will withdraw the demand.'

'Then we should stop. Do you wish to go downstairs now? Immediately?'

Madonna Arcangelica sat up and straightened her back. 'No. I told them I would not give in to blackmail. We shall talk today as we have always done, but after that, I fear our little conversations will have to be less frequent, in my office, and subject to unexpected and malicious interruption.'

'You will let them get away with this?'

Madonna Arcangelica smiled. Even in the short time since she sat down, she seemed to have recovered much of her equilibrium. But the smile was not one of her usual smiles; not the abbess's 'you will learn to accept it' smile; not the 'fear not, God will provide' smile; nor even the 'I understand but there is little I can do' smile. This was an Old Testament smile, a smile that spoke of an iron will, an inner confidence, an unrelenting persistence, and a deep understanding of the ways of a Vengeful God. This smile said, 'give me time, and I will seek them out. And when I have done so, I will wreak retribution upon them, one by one.'

Maddalena nodded. It was like being back in Cosimo's *studiolo*. 'Good. Then we shall begin.'

The abbess, already remarkably revived, sat back and prepared herself.

'Perhaps appropriately for what must now be our last such conversation, I wish to speak to you today of the events which led up to my arrival in this place.' Maddalena nodded to the abbess, acknowledging her part in the story; a part which she recognised took place, but of which she still had no real knowledge. 'You, I know, have personal knowledge of some of these proceedings and where you deem it appropriate, I should be pleased to receive your contribution to the chain of events.'

Across the room the abbess leaned forward and turned her head, in agreement. 'Gladly. I have no secrets to withhold from you.'

'The changes which I have described to you came slowly, so slowly that at the time, few would have been aware of their existence, never mind their significance. But steadily, over the thirty-six years that Cosimo and I were together, both the person and the bank he owned began to change.

'By the early summer of last year, the bank was larger, more profitable and apparently more secure than it had ever been. But inside, within the professional management, but more especially within the owning family, changes had been taking place which only an insider would have recognised. And despite his increasing illness and growing frailty, Cosimo, I knew, could see these things, including his own weaknesses and mistakes, with a greater clarity than anyone else. Possibly with the exception of Lucrezia.

'Cosimo knew that the bank would no longer thrive unless he was followed by a strong hand. And he knew that neither Piero nor Giovanni was going to be that strong hand. The future, he was certain, lay only with one person; and that person was his grandson, Lorenzo.'

'Lorenzo. How old is he now?' The abbess, concentrating, was sitting hunched up, her own recent difficulties having perhaps sharpened her political instincts.

'He will be ten years old on the first of January next.'

'Still very young, then?'

'Indeed. But not as young as age alone might indicate. Lorenzo is a prodigious talent. By the age of eighteen, he will be the match of most men in Italy. And by twenty-one, he will have surpassed all of them.'

The abbess smiled, as if wishing that she had him by her side even now, but she said nothing.

'Cosimo is now ageing, and unhappy. He sees the future and he doesn't like what he sees. He has been unsettled since the Great Storm that I told you about. It has really frightened him. Last summer, he began to lay plans to protect the next generation from his sons' follies and inadequacies.'

'I know. He first came to see me in early May of last year. And then three more times, during the next few weeks.' The abbess, as requested, made her contribution.

'Then that was before he had said anything to me. I knew of his worries, of course, but the first I heard of his plan was in June, when he wrote to me from Careggi.'

Without speaking, Maddalena leaned over to her casket and drawing out a letter, passed it to the abbess. She began to read.

Dearest Maddalena,

We have reached a position of great sensitivity in the affairs of the bank; an issue that requires me to ask for your assistance. For reasons that I will explain when I return to the palazzo, I wish to make you a free woman.

In exchange, and once your freedom makes this possible, I must ask you to take up holy orders and to enter a nunnery.

I am telling you this in advance, so that you can prepare yourself for this great change to your circumstances. Rest assured, you will be well endowed and your position at the convent will be secure and serene.

I ask you this in all seriousness and with grateful expectation.

Yours, humbly,

Cosimo de' Medici.

At Careggi Wednesday, 15th June 1457

The abbess reached the end, with one eyebrow occasionally raised, and returned the letter. '*Humbly.* Few people have received a "humble request" from the Magnificent Cosimo, I would think?'

Maddalena nodded, grinning. 'You are right. It was something of a tease. He had never asked me anything humbly in his life, and I was quite sure he didn't really intend to do so now. But as always, he was calculating. He had realised that you would not accept me into this place unless I were a free woman, but he also knew that as a free woman, he would have to ask me, not tell me, what he wanted me to do next. It is a typical example of the little coded secrets between us; one that says "yes I know, but please do this for me." And of course he knew I would.

'We met a week later, in the *studiolo* and he told me what was going to happen to me and why. He said he didn't trust his sons to manage the bank properly, and as a result, money had to be stashed away to allow his grandson, Lorenzo, to recover the situation on behalf of the family. He didn't tell me everything, but I heard enough on that day to know it was a typical Cosimo plan; subtle, carefully conceived and, I was sure had every chance of success.'

But it was a big decision and I wanted to be sure. I discussed his view of the future, confidentially, with Lucrezia. She said she agreed with Cosimo.

***

'Yes, Cosimo's right. Piero will never be any good at running the bank.' Lucrezia's eyes are level and confident. As is her voice. It's obvious she has thought about the issue many times before.

'But what about Giovanni? Can he not do it? Your husband was never intended to run the bank. Cosimo always saw him as head of the family and in the political role. But Giovanni? Surely he can...?' Maddalena is choosing her words carefully. She knows how close Lucrezia is to her brother-in-law.

Recognising the signs, Lucrezia puts a hand on Maddalena's arm and smiles. 'Giovanni, lovely as he is, is simply not sufficiently committed to the day-to-day grind'.

Embarrassed to hear her say the words, Maddalena shakes her head. But Lucrezia will have none of it.

'Accept it. In a family business you must realise when your family do not have the skills necessary to run the company successfully. In their place, you must hire the best people that you can get, give them positions of authority, with clear policies for how you want the business run, and support them until they make disastrous mistakes.'

She grins. 'They always make small ones. Everyone does.'

She takes a deep breath. 'Piero always gets it wrong. His stupid pride gets the better of him. I keep telling him, but...'

'Cosimo has always been able to get it right.' It is Maddalena's turn to feel defensive.

To her surprise, Lucrezia disagrees with her. 'Cosimo may have run the bank, but he always had Benci working full-time to support him, and he always had you there, too.'

'But I...' Maddalena shakes her head. She knows the limitations of her role.

Lucrezia wags a finger at her. 'Don't underestimate the significance of what you have done. Running a large and complex business is a lonely process. It niggles away at you. Your self-confidence is always on the edge of destruction and in the main, there is no one you can really talk to openly; no one you can trust.

'Cosimo had you.' She grins and once again touches Maddalena's arm. 'The humble slave. The person the family always underestimated. The one they all overlooked. All of them. Except Cosimo. Because Cosimo knew that your judgement was independent, and sound, and honest. And he relied on that.'

'But I never disagreed with him.' Maddalena suddenly feels concerned about all the decisions she may have influenced in the past.

'You didn't have to. On many occasions, Cosimo has joked with me, privately, about your "little trick".'

'My little trick? What's that?'

'Cosimo says you have a hundred ways of saying "Yes Cosimo, I agree with you" and ninety-nine of them mean "no".'

Lightly, she touches Maddalena's arm again. 'No?'

'Well, yes.' Maddalena finds herself laughing, despite, or perhaps because she feels embarrassed.

'But to be honest, your role has only been secondary to someone else.' Lucrezia's eyes are serious now.

'Giovanni Benci and Antonio Salutati? His General Managers?'

Lucrezia's head tilts from side to side. 'Salutati to a small degree, perhaps. During his nine years as General Manager, he was useful, but not, I believe, as influential as you were.' She snorts. 'His hundred words for yes all meant yes.'

Maddalena giggles. She had always believed that too, but had never dared say so to anyone. 'But Benci?'

Lucrezia nods, gravely. 'In my view, Giovanni d'Amerigo Benci was the greatest manager the Medici Bank ever had. And when he died – do you realise, it's nearly two years ago now? – the Bank lost its strongest single resource.'

'Stronger than Cosimo?' It's hard to speak the words, but necessary, if they are really to understand each other.

'Yes, in my opinion. Look at the facts. Since Benci's gone, Cosimo has lost his touch. You must have noticed it? Ask yourself: how much time do you spend nowadays on bank business?'

Maddalena frowns. 'Little.'

'Precisely. That's my point.' Lucrezia is nodding thoughtfully. 'Cosimo has handed over his responsibilities, but the others have not fully taken them up. So nobody is really driving the horses anymore. You and he aren't, Piero isn't and Giovanni is certainly not.'

'Do you have a solution to this problem? It is one thing to identify a problem, but sometimes much harder to overcome it.' Maddalena has never been content to let a problem fall to the floor unaddressed. It's irresponsible, in her opinion. 'What do you think about Sassetti?'

Lucrezia sniffs. They both know that Cosimo has been considering bringing Francesco di Tommaso Sassetti in from the Geneva branch to 'help' Giovanni. 'In my view, he's a crawler; a "yes-man" and not strong enough for the job. Cosimo should find a better solution. That's my opinion.'

Maddalena has to agree. Cosimo is slipping. He's making mistakes himself and seeing others being made without addressing them. Sassetti is ineffective; he won't stand up to Cosimo. Cosimo needs to do something, and fast. And she says so.

Lucrezia shakes her head, as if resigned to the situation. 'The problem is who's going to tell him?'

***

'And did you? Tell him, I mean?' The abbess had that look of utter concentration on her face.

Maddalena shook her head. 'I couldn't. I knew that Cosimo was already aware of the problems. Rubbing his face in it wouldn't have helped him. My task was always to support his decisions and to give him confidence in driving them forward, not to come up with solutions myself, and certainly not to criticise his actions, or sow fear, uncertainty and doubt. But nevertheless, I had grown used to believing that in my position as confidante and supporter, I was, if I may say so without sounding immodest, indispensible to him.

'And so it was, in October of last year, and with that unhappy background, that Cosimo brought me here to the convent.'

The abbess opened her hands, as if in welcome, and smiled. 'I can understand that it was upsetting for you to have to walk away when you could see such important problems remaining unresolved. But for my part, if I may say so, it was a good day for our little community and a great one for me personally.'

As she finished the sentence, her smile began to fade and she ended by looking at Maddalena silently; her eyes searching. Then, after a long pause, she spoke again, this time her voice much lower and unhappier.

'When was it that you realised your faith in Cosimo was slipping? Was it Lucrezia who brought it about?'

Maddalena took a deep breath before replying. 'I suppose Lucrezia must have sowed many of the seeds of doubt, but still I had faith in Cosimo, because it was then that he told me his plan to have Lorenzo save the bank. And at the same time, he asked me to help him in his scheme to provide for Lorenzo. With gold. Lorenzo's gold we called it. And I had faith in that scheme. It was a good plan and I had a central part to play, so I felt involved.'

Maddalena's eyes fell as she finished and she looked at the ground. Even as she spoke them, she was aware that she did not believe the brave words.

'But...? I ask you again. When was it, then, that you realised your faith in Cosimo was slipping?' The abbess' eyes were kindly, but they were also unblinking. This time she wouldn't let go and Maddalena knew it.

Maddalena felt her eyes fill with tears. Not the tears of sadness but tears of frustration; verging on tears of anger. 'It was the day I arrived here. With him. And with all those servants. You remember? We stood at the foot of this very tower, down there, by the side door; where you entered not two hours ago. I can still remember exactly what he said. "Come. I will escort you to your room and then we must say our farewells."'

She stood up and began to pace. Then she stopped and turned, looking at the abbess, who throughout had sat still and silent, waiting. 'It was at that moment, faced with climbing those steep steps to the tower with Cosimo, who would, I knew, struggle to do so, that I knew the magnitude and the finality of what he intended for me, and the extent to which he had been planning it, in his head, on paper and with others, over all those months.'

Angrily, she shook her head. 'But never with me. I had not shared in the preparation of the plan. He had developed it with others.' She lifted her head and stared accusingly at the abbess. 'With you and with the architect who built this tower and who organised the building of the library and the vault beneath.'

Her head fell forward and she found she was addressing the floor between her feet. 'But for all his fine words to me, I realised, then, that I was not a central player in the play, but had simply been given a minor bit part; one in which I was required to walk off stage, never to be seen again.'

Madonna Arcangelica looked at the top of Maddalena's head, bobbing in time with her sobs. She shook her head slowly. 'I think in your sadness, you underestimate your part in all this. Cosimo made it clear to me that you were at the core of his plan. He stated with absolute firmness that he could not tell me of his intentions, but that you, in the fullness of time, would be able to do so. He said he was relying on us both, but that you would hold the key.'

Maddalena lifted her head, looked at her and smiled. 'I could not be more delighted if that were the case. To continue in partnership with you, working towards saving the future of the Medici Bank and the family, would be the final fulfilment of my life. When I first met Cosimo de' Medici I told myself that I could either see him as the end of my happiness or as the beginning of something new.'

Feeling uncomfortable with the abbess' eyes upon her, she stood and looked out of the little window. 'I decided that if I could, I would make it the latter, and in the thirty-six years that I have served Cosimo, not one day has passed when I did not see that as my destiny. I cannot allow myself to believe that my whole life has been wasted.'

She turned from the window, and lifted her head defiantly, the tears gone. 'Would you think I was deluding myself if I told you that I take pride in the great bank that Cosimo built with my humble help?'

The abbess shook her head. 'Not at all. You have, I am sure, played an important part in a creation that will endure for a thousand years.'

Maddalena shook her head in return. 'Sadly, I think you are wrong in that prediction, kindly as it was meant. Somehow, I fear the Medici Bank will not outlive Lorenzo.'

The abbess stood, crossed the room, and took Maddalena's hands in hers. 'That circumstance is far in the future. With the best will in the world, neither of us is likely to be here when that question is resolved. But together we can at least ensure that Lorenzo gets his opportunity.'

'Did Cosimo ask you to be part of this plan? Did he make promises to you too?' Maddalena still found herself balancing on the edge of faith and doubt.

'He told me that I, and the convent, were to play a part in a great scheme. A scheme that would be of immense importance to the Medici and to Florence. He said he could not tell me the nature of the scheme, but that you would know and you would tell me in good time. In furtherance of our relationship, he made a generous contribution to the finances of our convent and he promised to endow the library, which, in your presence, he has now done. Your own conventual dowry and the annuity that accompanies you here will also make a great difference to us until…'

'He promised you more? Are you, like me, holding a promise from Cosimo and wondering whether it will ever be fulfilled?' Maddalena was still teetering on the cliff-edge of uncertainty.

'He said you would be bringing the first part of the secret deposit with you when you came. And I assume the many boxes that entered the library full and came out empty, reflect something important deposited in the vault beneath the library?'

Maddalena nodded. 'Yes. You are correct.'

'But he also told me that he would return later and that the final deposits would be of a far greater magnitude than the first "modest instalment" as he called it. Like you, I await the future with nervous expectation.'

'And does the convent have expectations, when that great day comes?' It is a question Maddalena had wanted to ask since the day she arrived.

'Yes. We live in hope and expectation, for I trust the Magnificent Cosimo's word.' The abbess allowed herself a little uncertain smile. 'To be honest with you, we need it. The chapel roof is in sore need of repair.'

Chapter 23
Reaching Out
11th December 1458

Six months had passed and Maddalena was feeling lonely. Very lonely. In no time, it seemed, a summer had come and gone, absorbed in repetition, and interrupted by precious little else.

Recently, as the winter days had shortened once again, she had spent more and more time in her other cell; the one next to *Suora* Maria Benigna. Her conversations with Madonna Arcangelica snuffed out like a midnight candle, she had had little reason to come up here, to the top of her tower.

She and the abbess still spoke, but infrequently; nowadays always in the abbess' room, and much more formally than they used to. There was awkwardness between them now; perhaps a shared regret that each of them had admitted to questioning, if not losing, their faith in Cosimo.

But she had her memories, she had her thoughts and she had her journal. And today, alone, she had climbed the stairs and, with gloved fingers, had opened the leather-bound journal at the next clean page.

Maddalena sat at the table and stared at the blank page. It was snowing outside and the valley was blanketed in an eerie and unnatural silence. There was no wind, but the brittle cold had permeated everywhere, not least into her little cell at the top of the tower. In summer, she had been the envy of the other nuns, but now, she knew, those down in the cloister, their cells built direct into the thick walls of the chapel, were grateful for the shelter the bulk of the building afforded. But this morning she had needed to think; and to do that, unconstrained, she needed privacy and freedom. And that had meant the tower and her stairs.

Pulling her outer cloak around her tightly, she opened the big folding doors, which led from her room to the balcony outside; the place where she loved to read and to write her journal in the summer months. For four or five months of the summer, these doors had remained open and pinned back, but now she was grateful for the protection they provided. She poked her nose outside; no different. The wide bay of the balcony was encrusted with icicles, many longer than the opened span of her fingers, and the few plants she had tended so carefully in pots beneath the window ledge, had long ago died.

She closed the door and barred it again, as tightly as she could. Although she was wearing a woollen *camicia* under her heavy winter habit, she was still frozen. The fingerless mittens she had fashioned from one of her old pairs of good leather gloves did little to protect her hands from the cold, and she found she could hardly move them. She smiled to herself: under these circumstances, it was hardly a surprise that she was struggling to write her journal.

Over the months, she had developed a routine for Monday afternoons.

Whenever her religious duties allowed (and as the representative of the convent's most powerful patron, she could hardly describe herself as being overworked), and when it was not a day for conversation with the abbess, she would take out her journal from its box, and sit at her little table, in winter months in the corner of her cell, and in the summer in the corner of her balcony from where she could look down at the valley below.

The winter view was a distant one; the tower was the highest point of the convent – her room on a level with the chapel roof. Its window was small and at shoulder height in the wall, so most of what she saw now was far up the valley, towards Tassaia and the Badia. It was a good view – calm and restful, and, being distant, without detail or distraction; the sort of view that encouraged distant thoughts and sometimes even more distant memories.

And there, most of the time, lay the problem. For day after day, she would look at the view, and find memories of her life flooding back. A few were childhood memories. She could still remember growing up in Palermo, although her parents' faces had long since faded from her mind.

But in the main, her memories had been filled with Cosimo; with the things he had said, the things they had done together, and the things she had watched him do. Whilst she had remained in her accustomed place; quietly, almost invisibly, in the background. And therein had always lain her difficulty, for wonderful as those images were; they were not the sort of thing you could write about. Not, at least, to the one man who had said the words and performed the deeds in the first place.

Some of the memories were old now, and, like those of her childhood, were beginning to fade.

But some of the images were quite recent and being young, were still fresh and strong in her mind. There had been a period in the previous year, shortly before Cosimo had brought her to this place, when his spirits had been as low as the terrible days of his trial and exile. Pain had been part of it. His gout and his sciatica had both worsened over recent years. Cosimo could endure discomfort with the best of men, but when that pain endured unending for weeks and months, so that neither sleeping nor waking offered any real hope of relief, then even the strongest of men could become introspective.

It was in those latter years that Contessina had begun to lose her patience with him.

***

CHAPEL OF THE MAGI, PALAZZO MEDICI
Late Spring 1457

'You do look a pretty miserable lot.' Maddalena shakes her head and smiles at the three long faces in front of her. Cosimo, and his two sons, Piero and Giovanni, are lying together in Cosimo's great bed in the *camera*; the huge bedroom close beside his chapel and next to his *studiolo*, where, when he isn't bedridden, most of the work is usually done. But today, and for the past week or so, his gout has the better of him, as it has for his two sons, and all three are suffering. Little work will be done while they are in this condition, she knows, and precious little laughter will be heard until they are better.

For the last week she has done her best to look after them, despite their best endeavours to make matters worse. She has put them on a diet: no offal, no red meat, no pulses and no red wine; all favourites, especially of Giovanni. It's the diet her father used to recommend for gout sufferers, and she knows that if she enforces it firmly, they will gradually improve. But whilst Cosimo will occasionally listen (when what he believes are the 'banqueting obligations of his position' do not contradict the advice), Piero and Giovanni were born to indulge themselves and will treat any sensible advice from her as a sniggering opportunity to do the opposite 'just to spite her'.

In this respect, they're like naughty schoolboys. The moment her back is turned, one or other of them will call a servant to sneak 'a morsel' to them. And it's always the very worst thing; *cinghiale* in thick red wine sauce being their latest favourite, the wild boar season having just started. They like it with Tuscan beans, great bowls of it and however much she tells them it will make the pain worse, they seem incapable of heeding her advice.

There's a tap on the door and she opens it. A servant nods his head. 'Maddalena. Please tell the Magnificent Cosimo that the Milanese ambassador is here for their appointment.'

She turns. 'Did you hear that?'

Piero and Giovanni feign sleep. Cosimo nods and winces as he does so. 'I had forgotten he was coming. He's come to see the new *fresci*.'

She nods. It is only a few weeks since Benozzo Gozzoli finished his fresco work in the chapel. The paintings are good. Very good. The talk of the city and everyone wants an invitation to see them.

Cosimo beckons her closer. His voice is feeble – almost a whisper. 'Can you send someone to fetch Contessina? I'll have to ask her to show him round. Etiquette requires it's someone senior from the family, but look at us.'

Piero keeps his eyes shut, but Giovanni opens one eye, smirks and winks. Then he too withdraws into self-induced oblivion.

She turns toward the servant, who is standing, holding the door open. 'Send him in. I will explain. Then can you find Contessina please?'

He nods and withdraws, returning almost immediately with Nicodemo Tranchedini, the Milanese ambassador.

'Nicodemo!' She knows him well and likes him. He's been ambassador for some fourteen years and has become a family friend. With her responsibilities to the Bank, she sees him regularly and he's not surprised to be greeted by her. She indicates the bed. 'We are indisposed. The gout again.'

Nicodemo steps back. 'I apologise. I've come at an inconvenient time. Cosimo invited me to see…'

She looks at Cosimo, but he too has closed his eyes. She puts a hand on Nicodemo's arm. 'It's all in hand. Cosimo and his sons apologise. Someone will

182

accompany you. Just a moment.'

They walk to the window and converse until the door bursts open. Contessina in full sail. She looks flustered. She's a rare visitor to this suite of rooms and only comes if specifically invited. She notes Maddalena's comfortable stance beside the ambassador and as he turns toward her, breaks into her best welcoming smile. 'Ambassador. Please excuse our disarray.'

But her smile fades as her gaze sweeps over the bed at the very moment her husband and both sons each risk opening an eye. Now, embarrassed, she glares at them. 'What on earth do you think you're doing? The Milanese ambassador is here to see you and not one of you is even able to raise a smile. You should be ashamed of yourselves.'

It's a grave mistake. Cosimo, his face racked with pain, levers himself into a sitting position. His face is white with rage as he speaks, although his tone remains level and seethingly controlled. 'Maddalena? Would you be so kind as to accompany our guest to the chapel? Nicodemo, I will discuss the paintings with you next time we meet. I trust I shall be in better health on that occasion.'

'But I thought...' Contessina is taken aback by the public snub. Her face tells its own story. To be stood down from accompanying an ambassador in favour of a mere slave? It's clearly unthinkable.

But so is talking down to *Il Magnifico* in front of an ambassador. And for that; make no mistake, she will pay.

As Maddalena leads the ambassador along the short corridor to what they are already calling the Chapel of the Magi, Cosimo's voice follows them through the still-closing door. 'Don't you ever do that again! Now get back to your kitchen, where, it seems, you belong. My slave will look after the business in hand. I can trust her not to embarrass me.'

***

Maddalena had never forgotten that occasion. Time and again, she had remembered; and slowly, she had understood. She came to realise that like her, Contessina had always seen Cosimo as the tower of strength. To both of them, he was like the great walls of the Palazzo Medici, or the battlements of Il Trebbio; valued as the means of their protection, yet perhaps, with the passage of time, under appreciated, taken for granted; assumed always to be there. And then, when he began to fail, when he faltered, when he showed weakness, Contessina, like Maddalena, had found herself afraid. But in Contessina's case, her fear, being impotent, had expressed itself as anger.

It was their one commonality: they had both lived their lives in the shadow of a great and powerful man, but as he weakened, they were each, in their own way, afraid of being left alone without him.

For Maddalena it had perhaps, been a little easier; she had already experienced being left alone when her parents were killed and she was taken into slavery. It had been a terrible time; but having endured it and survived, despite the scars which she never mentioned to anyone, she had in some manner gained strength and self-confidence. But Contessina, she knew, had always been cosseted; and now, with an ailing husband and two equally ailing sons, it was clear she feared for her own future as much as theirs.

Strange, how similar yet how different their lives had been. Each had loved Cosimo. Each had recognised him as the source of everything – money, power, reputation, their place in society. And Maddalena had to accept that Contessina had been a good wife – supportive, hard-working and a wonderful mother to the children. But as soon as Cosimo had brought her back with him from Rome, Contessina had recognised her as a threat.

And – she had been right.

Not because Maddalena harboured any unrealistic ideas of usurping her position. A Florentine wife was a permanent feature; as locked into her situation by *parentado*; the complex interlocking alliances between families, as by the pride of husband and wife. No, that was not the reason.

Nor was it love. Maddalena might have arrived in Florence believing that Cosimo had brought her to his bed because he did not love his wife. But if she had harboured that belief, she had soon been disabused, for whilst Cosimo did not look upon his round-faced, middle-aged wife with the evident lust he showed for Maddalena, they had in those early years shared a long-standing bond of mutual regard, liking and respect that the new arrival should never have underestimated.

Maddalena had recognised the power of that lust, but nevertheless, even when she was still young, she had known that it would only be her ally for a limited number of years. So she had sought, and thought she had found, a substitute – a replacement upon which to rely in her later years. As she had become absorbed into the inner workings of the Bank, to Contessina's evident exclusion, Maddalena had thought that it was in this relationship that her future lay: in some manner, Cosimo respected her superior education and – yes, immodest as it was to say it out loud, she had indeed thought it – her greater intellect. Admirable as she was with people, you would never have described Contessina as 'bookish'.

But in the end, the source of her special and enduring position had proved to be neither of these. Slowly, she had come to realise that Cosimo needed her because he had found in her the one thing he could not find in his loving and supportive wife – the ability to accept his weakness, to recognise his uncertainty when facing the difficult decisions he had to make, both financial and political – and the capacity to ease the loneliness of his elevated and responsible position.

Only she understood and accepted that for much of the time, Cosimo was lonely and uncertain, and that sometimes he wanted someone else to take the upper hand. And she, as she remembered so clearly, had been willing to accept that responsibility. It had come about in an unexpected manner.

***

184

'Take me, Cosimo. Make love to me.'

She lies back, naked, luxuriating in the huge bed, captivated by the sound of the sea outside the window. It has been a long journey from Florence but now they are here and will remain, he says, for a month. They have all the time in the world.

Beside her, Cosimo turns and then, abruptly, stops and, with a gasp, falls back.

'What is it? What's wrong?'

'My back. And right down my leg. It suddenly seized up, like a cramp. As I turned it gave a great spasm and for a moment – I couldn't move.'

Is it alright now?'

'I think so. I'm so sorry. I wanted to…I want to…'

'Do you want to try again? It might have gone now?'

Beside her, gingerly, she feels him turn, then fall back. 'I don't think I can.'

'Does it hurt now?'

'No, it's fine if I lie on my back.'

Maddalena rolls towards him and puts an arm across his chest. 'Perhaps if I…' She moves her hand. He groans and she knows he's still aroused. And so is she. She kneels and mounts him, taking the initiative, taking him into her, taking control.

And she feels him respond.

***

'Where did you learn to do that?' He is lying beside her; he sated, she elated, for already she realises the significance of what has just happened.

But she doesn't reply. *That sort of question is better left unanswered* . 'Was it good?'

'Better than good.' He's still grinning.

'Your back? How was that?'

'I don't know. I forgot about it.' He arches his back experimentally and lets himself fall back. 'I think you've found a cure.'

He turns his head, grinning with what looks like admiration. '*Fantinina!* That's what I shall call you. My little jockey. If you're a good girl, I may let you do that again.'

***

Maddalena rubbed her frozen hands together and realised that deep inside, despite the cold, she felt a warm glow; a glow that came from the satisfaction of knowing she had loved and been loved in return. From that day onward, the relationship between them had changed. That afternoon had been the beginning of a new relationship between herself and Cosimo; a relationship in which he learned to let go; a relationship in which the slave who had become a lover, now also became the confidante – the one person to whom Cosimo could admit his weaknesses, his fears and his uncertainties.

She had never told him what to do – and he had never asked her. But in listening to his thoughts, in hearing him describe the alternative courses of action he had to choose between, and in asking gently probing questions as he explored his possibilities, she had given him the courage to make his decisions, and having made them, the confidence to put them into practice.

Her life had not been wasted. Surely? Cosimo in his hour of need had reached out to her and when he had done so, she had given him the strength he needed. Now, looking across the snowy desolation of the winter valley, she felt she was reaching out to him.

Would he come? Was she still part of his great plan for the future of the family? The plan that had been his sole reason for her arrival at the convent?

Her hands begin to chill again as the afternoon light started to fall. Maddalena scanned the darkening snow, just waiting, for a sign. She would write something today. She must write something. Something that reaches out to him, in the gathering gloom. And then, perhaps, he will finally come.

Dearest Cosimo,

It is winter. The middle of December, and cold, yet still; my candle burns clearly, without flickering. Dusk is falling, and I am standing at my window, that I can look out into the gloom and know you are out there, somewhere.

She rubbed her hands. He would not mind a little poetic licence. She could hardly write standing up, and he, of all people would know that the imagery of her words was more important than absolute precision.

I am looking across the valley, toward the west, and still there is a glow from the last of the sun's rays. Perhaps they are falling on you now; in Cafaggiolo, or in the Palazzo Medici?

Do you remember how many times you reached out for me, Cosimo? I was always there, in times of trouble, or loneliness, or pain. I understood your need for a strong hand and I offered it whenever you asked.

Now I am troubled. I am lonely, and I am in pain. Now I am reaching out for you, Cosimo.

Please be there for me, as I was there for you.

Your truly ever-loving

Maddalena.

As if knowing that she had finished her work for the day, a sudden gust of wind blew out the candle. She closed the journal. Would her prayer be answered? Would he come? How could she be sure?

Chapter 24
Cosimino
Convento di San Damiano, Mugello
19th November 1459

Maddalena stopped pacing up and down and looked, once again, at the letter in her hand. Hardly what you might call an immediate response? Not after eleven months. But still; a reply. And for that, certainly, she was grateful.

Dearest Maddalena,

It is with the greatest sorrow and regret that I must inform you of the death of my beloved grandson, Cosimino. He died three days ago, late at night, here at Cafaggiolo, of a sudden and unexpected fever. He went from a healthy young boy to a corpse in less than two days. I can only thank God in his infinite mercy that the boy, when he had to be taken from us, did not suffer for longer.

You knew the boy well and you know how much I loved him. Even now, as I look from my window, I can see the toy wheelbarrow that he used to push in front of him when he came to the fields to help me. Now I cannot bear to move it, so it sits, forlorn, in the yard.

The timing could not have been worse. The villa at Fiesole is nearing completion and Giovanni and Ginevra were so looking forward to taking the boy there in the springtime.

There was a speck of dust on the letter and absent-mindedly, Maddalena swept it away with the back of her hand. She had been so excited as the messenger had approached. She had spotted his Medici livery as he rode laboriously up the zigzag path beneath her balcony. A desire to intercept him, perhaps even to talk to him just for a short while, and discover what was happening in the Medici world, swept over her.

But running like a young girl was not the way of the Order, and by the time she had slipped fast but furtively down the stone steps, walked rapidly if unobtrusively across the courtyard, and just 'happened' to pass by the gatehouse, her enquiring look at the gatekeeper had been rewarded only with this note.

'For you. He said he did not expect a reply and had not been told to wait for one. So I told him to go.'

Maddalena looked at her and wondered if this was another of the tiny but painful slights that she occasionally had to endure, but had finally decided that the gatekeeper was, simply, doing what had been expected of her.

Still, she had her note. Nobody could deprive her of that. The contents were, however, a disappointment.

Two years! How time flies. She shook her head. And little Cosimino, of all people. She remembered him so well. He had only been four years old when she left the Palazzo Medici. Now, he was dead. Ginevra must be out of her mind. She and Giovanni had doted on that boy.

Giovanni and Ginevra have asked that he should not be buried in the family tomb in San Lorenzo, but instead should have a tomb erected in his honour inside the walls of the Badia. It was his favourite place, where he liked to hunt rabbits with his falcon. Such a lovely boy. Such a great loss.

Automatically, Maddalena turned and looked out of her window and up the valley, to where the walls of the Badia di Buonsollazzo were almost visible. Although their confessor, Fra Pietro, walked the two miles to hear their confessions every week, he saw his role as listening and forgiving, not in imparting information, and even today, she knew little about the place.

She had only been there once, many years before; the only time in her life she had attended a hunting party.

***

BADIA DI BUONSOLLAZZO, MUGELLO
6th May 1457

'Maddalena, look. Sure-flight has caught a rabbit!'

Against all her instincts, Maddalena makes an effort not to turn away. She is sure the sight of a hawk gripping and no doubt ripping a rabbit to pieces will be revolting. But the boy sounds so excited and the last thing she wants to do now is to spoil his moment. He has been looking forward to this hunt for weeks.

'Oh well done, Cosimino!' She does her best to sound enthusiastic.

Cosimo turns his head towards her and away from the youngster, who is standing in his stirrups like a hardened huntsman and staring across the hillside. 'Thank you, Maddalena. You've made his day. He was so keen that you should see his first kill. Try to keep up the pretence when they bring the kill to him. It will almost certainly be a mouse or a vole. I've never seen a kestrel kill a rabbit before. Unless, perhaps, it's a very young one.'

He turns and rides over to the excited boy.

Maddalena sits back in the saddle and takes in the scene. They will, no doubt, talk about this great event for days, if not weeks. Cosimo has chosen the location well. The hillsides below the Badia are steep and covered in moorland; wild enough and distant enough from their castle at Il Trebbio for the boy to know he's had a real adventure. And beneath them, the deep cut made by the Torrente Carza has forced them to climb steeply for two hours, so that now they really do believe they are on top of the world.

She looks south, along the mighty whaleback ridge of Monte Senario towards Fiesole, where, with more than a little help from the architect Michelozzo, Giovanni is building a great villa, overlooking the hillside and beyond that, the basin of Florence itself. In the distance she can just see the bell-tower of a building, and assumes it is the Convento di San Damiano. It's said to be one of the remotest convents in the Mugello, and perhaps for that reason, one of the most pious.

The falconer returns to Cosimino with the hawk on his wrist, and the boy lets out a great yelp of excitement. Everybody looks up. He has taken Sure-flight onto his own wrist now and is holding him up proudly, on his new leather gauntlet, as he stands tall in his stirrups.

Maddalena smiles. He rides well for a four year old; sitting straight in the saddle and looking every inch the young noble which, to all intents and purposes, and despite the traditional Medici protestations, he is. He's a lovely boy. The prettiest of all of them. His hair is a great bubbly mass of curls and his tiny snub nose has yet to develop into the long Medici beak that his father and his uncle Piero have both inherited from Grandfather Cosimo.

He's a happy boy and why should he not be? It's a rare day when his father is not laughing, while his mother, Ginevra degli Alessandrini, dotes on him. It's she who bought him the pony and his father who provided the two small hawks and the expert falconer to make them (and the boy) look skilful.

She turns and waves to Ginevra, who is sitting side-saddle on her pony, a short distance below them. Ginevra waves back and points to Giovanni, who, pursued by four pointers, is riding at full gallop along the ridge and towards his son, keen to see what all the fuss is about.

A happy family enjoying a happy day.

***

Maddalena smiled at the memory and shook her head. Little did any of them realise that day how short-lived their pleasure would be.

Almost reluctantly, she returned to the letter in her hand.

His death has made me concerned about our plan, but Lorenzo seems to remain strong.

Perhaps it was because her mind had slipped away with its memories, but she had trouble following that line of argument. What significance might Cosimino's death and burial have for the work that had brought her here? Unless Cosimo was afraid that Lorenzo, too, might die before he reached adulthood?

We have had difficult circumstances in the bank since you entered the convent and I have judged it inappropriate to make the further withdrawals we discussed. But now Cosimino's death has brought a sense of renewed urgency to the arrangements, and as soon as I am feeling stronger, I shall return to them.

I will write again when circumstances permit. In the meantime, I remember you daily in my prayers as in my dreams. May God preserve you and keep you safe and well.

Her eyes caught upon this line and suddenly her mood changed. So Cosimo had not forgotten her. Nor had he abandoned his scheme for Lorenzo. In fact, quite the opposite, if 'renewed urgency' meant what she thought it did. So now the truth was emerging, and with it, an indication of why the news was so sensitive that he had not written before. The bank was experiencing 'difficult circumstances'. That would explain everything. She turned back to the end of the letter.

Yours, this dark day and always,
Cosimo.
At Cafaggiolo Friday, 18th November 1459

Did that mean a dark day because Cosimino has died or because the bank was ailing? Perhaps both? With Cosimo it was sometimes hard to know.

The sense of rejection that had clung to her for months suddenly began to slide from her shoulders. She was still important. Still wanted. It was just the difficult circumstances at the Bank that had been the problem. She was sure, now, that they would soon blow over.

Even if the messenger had not waited for a reply and had, so it seemed, been told none was expected, nothing could stop her from replying through her journal. She fetched it from its hiding place in the small chest and opened it at the next page.

Dearest Cosimo,
Your messenger came and went with such haste that I could not catch him with a note. Sufficient unto the day, therefore, must be the pages of this journal.
I was saddened by your news, as I am sure the whole family has been. Though I know little of falcons or of rabbit hunting, I can see the adjacent hillsides from here and I am filled with a sense of freedom. Do not grieve for your grandson, Cosimo, he is out there now, his falcon on the wing, and he is happy.
From my own eagle's nest, I have a good view over his hunting country. I shall keep an eye on him. Never fear.
Your loving
Maddalena.

She blew on the writing to dry it and smiled to herself. Aware of the expression, she did it again, facing the journal as if it were looking at her on Cosimo's behalf. The smile, she knew, was more like a smirk; forced, cynical. There was, she was sure, a great deal left unsaid in Cosimo's letter and the same applied to her reply. As an afterthought, she added one more line.

Still awaiting your intentions, and now with renewed vigour.

Were they growing apart? Becoming distrustful of each other? She closed the journal in case it was watching her, and put it away.

Chapter 25
Resignation
17th December 1462

It is three years later. Just before Christmas.

Once again, it is cold and snowing hard. A messenger arrives, looking as exhausted as his horse, the two of them covered in snow and following the path purely by instinct. The nuns have to take him in and put him in the infirmary – very much against the Rule, but exciting for them, as the boy is young and, by common consent, handsome.

Maddalena paces up and down in the freezing cloister, hoping and praying that the Medici livery means that the messenger has brought a letter for her. But she has no responsibilities in the infirmary and the door is closed to her.

Finally, after two hours of ministrations: hot soup, bread, brandy and an insistence on removing and drying his cloak and quilted *farsetto*, the five nuns vying for his attention are able to ask the reason for his visit, and Maddalena is called into the room.

***

Inside it is stifling. The fire has been stoked up and his clothes have finally stopped steaming. As soon as she speaks, the boy, red-faced from the effects of the fire, the food and the brandy, recognises her and rises to his feet.

'Maddalena! Is it you?' He pauses, as if afraid that he has made some terrible mistake, and she puts a hand on his forearm and bids him return to his place by the fire.

He twists in the chair to face her. 'I would not have recognised you in your…habit. But as soon as I heard your voice…It is so good to see you again. Do you remember me? I am Antonio. In your time at the Palazzo Medici I was still at the Casa Vecchia, looking after the mules. Last year I was promoted by the Magnificent Piero and now I am a messenger.'

Maddalena stands with a hand lightly on his shoulder. 'Of course I remember you, Antonio. How could I forget?'

'You said I was the worst pupil you ever had for reading and writing!' He makes it sound like an achievement. 'But I kept on, as you told me I must, and now I can read many things. I can sign my name and write a letter.' He tips his head on one side. 'Well, a short one. With simple words. But it's a start isn't it, Maddalena?'

She pats his shoulder. 'It's an excellent start, Antonio. I am so pleased you persisted with your studies. I always knew you would succeed and now you can see the benefit.'

He frowns, confused.

'Through your elevation to the position of messenger. Your mother must be very proud of you.'

His face falls. 'My mother died, last year. She never lived to hear about my elev…my new job. I was told just a week after she had died.'

She nods, embarrassed for both of them. 'Have you brought any messages? In your new capacity?'

Antonio puts his hand to his mouth and gasps, then reaches for his bag. He takes out a package, wrapped in waterproof cloth. 'I was told to hand this to you personally, Maddalena.'

She takes it and nods her thanks.

'I did not realise how difficult the job could be. I got lost four times. It has taken me two days and a morning to come from the city.'

She opens the package and withdraws a letter, carefully folded and sealed. It is dark in the infirmary; the only light a single candle and the flickering flames of the fire. Too dark to read, especially when your eyes are as old and tired as hers are now. She takes the letter outside and stands in the cloister, feeling twice as cold after the heat of the infirmary, tilting the letter against the light. She does not recognise the handwriting on the outside, but Cosimo often had his clerks write the addresses and it does not concern her,

She begins to open it. The paper is still cold and she opens it carefully, afraid it will tear. The handwriting is awful – barely legible, yet clearly, to her experienced eye, it is Cosimo's.

My beloved Maddalena,

My apologies for not writing for so long. As you can see, my hands now serve me with difficulty and some considerable discomfort. I hope you can read this scrawl.

I had hoped to visit you, but travel has become impossible. I can no longer bear the journey to Cafaggiolo or even to Careggi, and instead I am now confined to the Palazzo Medici, where most of my days are spent, here in my private chapel. There is no light – no windows to let me see the fields and the hills – it is as if I have been blinded by my own possessions. Forgive me for my failing. I can do no more. I am resigned to my fate and believe I will soon meet my maker.

No doubt you are wondering what has happened to our great plan, why you have not heard from me since last I wrote, more than a year ago. It is a good question.

For many months after little Cosimino's death, we argued about his tomb. Although Giovanni and Ginevra wanted him buried at the Badia, as indeed, he was, it has always been my hope that eventually they would agree to move him to San Lorenzo.

Now, after much discussion, I have come round to their point of view, and have agreed to leave him at the Badia. We shall build him a tomb there – a proper one, as befits a man in his position. This decision has created an opportunity that I cannot miss and as a result, I shall change part of our proposal.

Donatello is recently returned from Siena and he has agreed to look after this matter for me. I shall write to you when it is completed. Rest assured, your part remains, and I continue to rely upon you to ensure the next generation are properly looked after. You know what I mean.

For myself, my various ailments have worsened considerably this last twelve months and I am now resigned to my growing weakness. Now I sit here, in my chapel, grumbling and telling others what to do. I can do no more.

I send you my everlasting love and grateful thanks for everything you have done for me, over the years. No more for now. My hand grows weak.

Yours, in weakness,

Cosimo de' Medici.

At Palazzo Medici.

Dated this 14th December 1462

Maddalena lifts the paper to her lips, and with her mouth open, inhales. She hopes that somehow she may catch the fragrance of Cosimo's hand as he wrote. But the paper is cold and there is nothing.

She considers writing a reply, but then, as before, remembers how strong Cosimo's insistence had been that she should not. Well at least she can talk to the boy and find out what is going on in the family. She walks along the cloister and into the little side door of the infirmary.

'Where is he?' The boy is missing.

Suora Simpatica shakes her head. She is very young and her expression is bewildered. 'He thought you had gone and weren't coming back. He asked me to say thank you for all your kindness to him and he hoped if there were any more letters he would be allowed to bring them. Now he knows the way. He was afraid to stay longer as he wanted to get back down to the valley road before the light went. He said the snow was drifting heavily further down, beyond the trees. He seemed nervous about his return journey.'

'But I wanted to give him a message; to take back with him.'

Suora Simpatica shakes her ahead again, this time more decisively. 'I asked if he should wait for any message from you and he said the Magnificent Cosimo had told him to his own face that there was not to be a reply.' She gives a girlish grin. 'He seemed uncomfortable here; I got the impression he could not get away quickly enough.'

Maddalena takes a deep breath and stamps her foot in frustration. 'I'm not surprised; with you and the *converse* fighting to remove his clothing, he must have thought he was in a house of depraved women.'

Suora Simpatica's laugh is like a high-pitched bell. 'Only Cora. It would be unfair to call the rest of us depraved. But we did hope she would uncover something interesting.' She rolls her eyes, her grin making little dimples in her rosy cheeks. 'I must admit we were all watching like hawks.'

'That will do!' Madonna Arcangelica's voice echoes round the small room like a whip. Everyone stiffens. She must have slipped into the room like a wraith. 'I will have no such conversation in this convent. '*Suora* Simpatica; one hour of silent prayer. Now.'

The girl runs from the room, her face crestfallen. She has only been in the convent a short while and still has much to learn. The abbess jerks her head at

Maddalena. 'And you should not encourage the younger ones. You know they all look at you as if you had spent many years in hell itself and returned.'

'But not to tell the tale.' Maddalena knows the rebuke is, as much as anything, an apology that they have had no opportunity to talk recently. She follows the abbess into the cloister and they fall into step beside each other.

'A message from Cosimo?' Madonna Arcangelica gets straight to the point.

'Yes. He is frail and ailing.'

'He has been frail for some years, surely?'

Maddalena nods her head. 'Yes but now it seems, his spirit is failing him. He seems diminished.'

'And the plan? The great scheme? Does that remain alive?'

'The Chapel Roof Fund?' Maddalena allows herself a little grin. It has become a private joke between them; an acknowledgement that they share an interest in Cosimo's proposals for Lorenzo.

It is a reminder that she knows sometimes prickles the abbess like a thorn, but although they have fallen into an understanding of their respective parts in Cosimo's great scheme, she is unwilling to drop back into the passive role in their partnership. At the back of her mind, the fact that Cosimo had had a number of conversations with the abbess before he ever spoke to her of the matter still rankles.

And now, it seems, Donatello too, is to be involved. Does that mean that her involvement is to be diluted? At least his letter gave her some encouragement. What had he said? *Rest assured, your part remains, and I continue to rely upon you to ensure the next generation are properly looked after.*

Encouraged, she replies to the abbess. 'He says the scheme is still alive and moving forward.'

But she can't bring herself to tell the abbess about Donatello. Nor, at this early stage, about the Badia. *Information is power.* Lucrezia had said that once, and she was right. Cosimo had said he would write again when the plans he was developing with Donatello were completed. That would be the time to tell the abbess more. Then and only then.

She looks across at the abbess who notices her glance and returns it.

'Good. I am glad things are moving forward.' Her expression shows that she has also sensed that something is being held back. But the glance is not sustained and they fall into step with each other once again; their thoughts perhaps travelling in parallel, as are their feet.

Chapter 26
Death of Giovanni
5th October 1463

Another nine months have gone by, and still no word of Donatello and his part in Cosimo's great scheme. Twice, in the course of the summer, parties of servants have come from Cafaggiolo, bringing produce from their fifty-three farms.

Generous produce: live pigs, to be fattened up on the local acorns and chestnuts before being slaughtered by the butcher from Bivigliano, a barrel of last year's wine, now ready for drinking, two milk-cows, tied to the back of the cart and led all the way up the hill, and flour and salami and a half-barrel of last year's olives, together with two casks of olive oil.

Each time, Maddalena and the abbess managed to find time to assist them, to thank them and to talk to them, and although they spoke openly about events in Cafaggiolo, in Careggi and in the city, there was nothing that hinted at Cosimo's scheme, even to a ready and waiting ear.

And then, on a warm and lazy October afternoon, another messenger, and another letter; again from Cosimo.

The handwriting is even worse than before; almost illegible, except to the most practiced eye. Except to Maddalena's.

Blessed and beloved Maddalena,

My servants tell me you are still alive and that they have spoken to you, and found you well. I pray they speak the truth, for I no longer have any prospect of verification with my own eyes. The journey would, now, be too much for me.

Our world is coming to an end. Giovanni is dead. He died, last week, on the 23rd of September, unexpectedly, of a heart attack. He was forty-two years of age, and although, I know, you chided him daily about being too fat, and too self-indulgent, he did not deserve to die this young. That joy for life; and until his son died, that laughter. I can still hear Giovanni's laughter echoing through the rooms of this house, as it did in the old days.

We buried him in San Lorenzo. They carried him there in his coffin and me there in a chair. I think he had the more comfortable ride. Never again; the ignominy of it worse than the pain. Who will be next now, me or Piero? Have you ever seen two bedridden men racing each other? I can tell you, it's a slow business.

I am now resigned that I will never see you again. I thank you for your forgiveness of my selfish urgency as a young man. What I would not give to be young and lusty and to have you in my bed just once more.

I thank you, also, for your understanding when troubles surrounded me in my middle years, and again, for all your patience as I grew old, frail and forgetful. You have, quite simply, been a lynchpin of my life, and with your continuing responsibilities, you will, I know, continue to be so.

The process continues, albeit slowly, but under Donatello's safe hand. I shall send you

word when it is done.
   Yours, forever,
   Cosimo.
   Palazzo Medici Monday, 3rd October 1463

                    ***

In the convent, Maddalena reads the letter and immediately, she thinks of the others. Ginevra will be distraught; it will be a terrible shock to lose Giovanni, even though they all knew his days were numbered.

Lucrezia, of course, will miss him terribly. They were always very close. More than close. Much more.

She wonders about the things she heard Lucrezia say about the running of the bank. Giovanni was Deputy Director of the holding company. Who now? Surely not Piero? Francesco Sassetti may be able to manage the day-to-day things, rather like Benci did for Cosimo years ago: but Benci did so much more – he would argue with Cosimo and often he was in the right. But Sassetti is not of the same material at all. Sassetti never argues. If you are a member of the family, Sassetti always says yes, even when he knows you're wrong.

She wonders how Lucrezia will cope. It was obvious that she loved Giovanni and that he loved her too. Knowing that, she had once asked Lucrezia whether she considered that marrying her to Piero was an act of unkindness. Lucrezia's reply was: 'No. Cosimo was not an unkind man. But he was brought up with such a strong sense of family and duty to it, that he put family before individual without thought and without even considering that, in so doing, he was being in any way unkind. Do not blame him for being what he is.'

She respected Lucrezia even more after that. Kindness and understanding in the face of adversity; unusual and impressive.

Lucrezia had told her that she had learned to love Piero as a dutiful wife should; loving him more than anything else 'for his weaknesses and inadequacies, which were not his fault and not of his own making'. But now she's not sure she believes that. The racehorse and the carthorse. Could they really run in harness? Perhaps yes, with training. But in total harmony? Surely not.

What will happen to them now she thinks? Ginevra has nobody. Nobody of her own. No son or grandson to cling to; no reason to live for the future. She will probably continue, with Contessina as her model, perhaps living alone at Fiesole? No. She will be too alone there and the reminders will be too strong. She will return to the Palazzo Medici and become drawn into The Family; duty calling.

And Cosimo? How much longer will he last now? With Piero the daily disappointment (what a thing to have to admit to anyone) he had always concentrated his emotions on Giovanni. In the last letter, his voice, coming from the Chapel of the Magi, had sounded hollow. Losing Cosimino had been like losing an arm. Now losing Giovanni will be like losing a leg as well.

And the scheme? *The process continues, albeit slowly, but under Donatello's safe hand. I shall send you word when it is done.* That sounded positive enough. Donatello had always been competent. But he had also always been unreliable. After all their scheming and planning, was the whole thing going to wither away?

Suddenly an image comes into her mind; a huge cart; a hay-wain, with steep, curved sides, piled high with treasure, yet trundling downhill, out of control, while Piero sits in the driving seat, hands wavering, undecided what to do, and Donatello lolls on the back, fondling some young boy, blissfully unaware that they are headed for a cliff-edge.

Is it all to come to nothing?

***

The abbess sees Maddalena sitting on the wall outside the main doors of the chapel, facing north, up the valley; looking along the great ridge-top towards the Badia and beyond that into the Mugello, toward Il Trebbio and Cafaggiolo. She indicates the letter in her hand and raises an eyebrow. Perhaps she is wondering about the chapel roof?

Maddalena shakes her head.

'Giovanni's dead. It's all coming to pieces.'

Chapter 27
Donatello's Visit
8th December 1463

It begins with shouting. Elena, now thirteen and well on her way to becoming a beauty, still clings to her self-appointed role as the convent lookout.

It's a day of great stillness. A day of benign winter; cold but without any air movement, almost comforting. There is just the slightest hint of snow falling; not enough to carpet the ground. Not even enough to cover the track down to Bivigliano and the valley beyond, but enough, already to soften the sounds of the valley as it falls. And if it continues to fall like this, by tomorrow the valley will be silent.

Even the squirrels in the woods below them seem to be moving quietly. The softness of the day has brought them out of hibernation and they are scurrying at the base of the trees; searching for their caches of acorns and chestnuts, pattering about silently. And above them, on the high wall, where she prefers to stand, wrapped only in a stout cloak, and with her hood down so that her ears are not covered, stands Elena, her head tipped slightly back, watching and listening.

Fifteen minutes ago, she was sure she heard horses and a cart, and excited, for little has happened in months, she let out a yell. But then, to her disappointment: silence. Perhaps, further down, the snow is lying heavier and has drifted across the road, muffling the sound of the wheels?

But Elena's hearing is like a dog's. She can make out the high-pitched sounds that no one else can hear. The choir mistress finds her talent upsetting, for although she appreciates the need for precision, to have Elena endlessly telling you that as they echo around the chapel roof that *Suora* Simplicita's top notes are slightly sharp, when in truth you can no longer hear them at all, is to say the least, frustrating.

Elena starts to smile. Yes. She can hear it again. It's the same cart; she's sure of it. That squeak, intermittent and high – very high, but still, just audible. It's the small cart that they occasionally send from Il Trebbio. The wheel has been squeaking like that since she was a child; for two years at least. Can no one else hear it? Each time the cart comes, her first reaction is to offer the carter some olive oil, to lubricate it. But then that would take away her advantage; her gift. And nobody in their senses gives gifts away, especially God-given ones.

The squeak gets louder and she yells again. Two *converse* appear and then three choir nuns. Word is spreading. Slowly, the courtyard fills with nuns, *converse* and lay-servants, all walking nonchalantly towards the wall and looking down. Now *Suora* Maddalena appears. She's usually one of the first to respond to the promise of a visitor.

The cart appears and it is indeed the Medici cart with the same old driver. But this time, next to him, is an old ragamuffin. The cart enters the courtyard and everyone moves forward, until the wastrel starts to climb down. Elena steps backwards. He's ancient; he must be seventy years old, and his clothes! They are little more than rags. And he doesn't smell too good either.

All round the cart, the nuns are backing away, until only *Suora* Maddalena is left, her face radiant and welcoming, as she steps forward.

'Donatello! How wonderful. Have you come to see me?'

'Maddalena. You haven't changed.' He reaches back into the cart, opens a leather bag and takes out a palm-sized gold crucifix. 'I made this for you.'

'Donatello. But it's...wonderful.' To the nuns' surprise and Elena's evident disgust, Maddalena embraces the sculptor. 'This must have cost a fortune?'

Donatello shrugs. 'I'm retired now, to one of the farms on the Cafaggiolo estate, so I have plenty of time.' He grins sheepishly. 'Cosimo provided the gold. He asked me to make you something appropriate. Something the Rule of the convent would allow you to keep.'

Maddalena holds the crucifix up and shows it to the abbess. Madonna Arcangelica nods deeply. 'Of course. With such provenance, how can I refuse?' She looks at Donatello. 'You have come to speak with *Suora* Maddalena?'

He nods and she turns to Maddalena. 'It ought to be the *parlatorio*,' she sees Maddalena's face fall, 'but in the circumstances, perhaps the tower room? On special dispensation?'

Relieved, Maddalena thanks her. The Rule states that when visitors are entertained in the *parlatorio*, the nun should remain on the outside of the metal-grilled windows, while the visitors sit within the room itself, having been accompanied there by two *discrete*, or in the case of a male visitor, three.

The problem is that they do not withdraw to allow a private conversation to take place. On the contrary, they do not, as their name suggests, even withdraw to a discreet distance. Instead they hover, close enough to hear the words being spoken; they are not called *ascoltatrici* or 'listeners' for nothing.

Maddalena turns towards the door to her tower, but Donatello pauses, standing awkwardly. 'I have brought items from the farms, for the convent; foodstuffs, and some beeswax candles.'

Madonna Arcangelica steps forward with due authority. 'We thank you and the Medici family for those. Perhaps we may relieve you of your burden and then, perhaps, provide some hospitality of our own to your driver?' To Maddalena she adds, 'I shall have a *conversa* bring food to you in the tower. That way you will not be disturbed.'

She turns to the hovering crowd of nuns and addresses herself in particular to the two old *discrete* who are sucking lemons at the back. 'Ser Donatello is here on official Medici business. The Magnificent One will expect his envoy to be given the privacy that such business merits. I trust none of you is considering raising an objection? Any such will of course be referred to the bishop. And he, I have no doubt, will make reference to the cardinal.' At the mention of the cardinal, she gives a knowing nod.

Maddalena smiles. It is one piece of news that has reached them recently. Carlo, her son, has recently earned his cardinal's hat and with it, authority over the region. She has never thought fit to say anything to anyone, but somehow, it appears, word has got through.

***

'How is Cosimo?' It is the first question Maddalena asks Donatello. He shakes his head with a dejected expression. 'Not good. He has more worries than a man in his position should have. By now, Piero should be showing the strong leadership that is expected from the family, but still, matters fall back to Cosimo. And the deaths of Cosimino and Giovanni have taken a terrible toll on him.'

'And yourself?' He looks at her with the same searching eye that had made her so uncomfortable, years ago.

'I am comfortable here. It is a place of relative serenity.'

'Only relative?'

'I have been awaiting your news for some long time now.' She tries not to make it sound like a criticism.

'Then let me put you out of your misery. The second stage of the plan was well advanced, but held back by weaknesses within the bank. For many months, the opportunity could not be found to withdraw such large sums.' He lifts his head in explanation. 'You and Cosimo originally deposited 20,000 florins in the vault, here, I understand. But Cosimo's intention is to provide ten times that amount; 200,000 florins, for Lorenzo's salvation.'

Maddalena shakes her head in amazement. 'That's a huge amount of money. He could build the Palazzo Medici three times over for that amount.' Donatello nods, smiling. 'Including the statues.'

'But the position of the bank has now improved?' Maddalena is keen to lead him on. She knows from the past that it is not easy to get Donatello to the point in a conversation.

'Yes. It is all in place. The money has been withdrawn from the bank and we have buried it.'

'But…' Maddalena is completely thrown off balance. 'I thought the rest of the money was to come here? Otherwise, why am I in this place?'

'There was a change of plan. An unexpected one. In Cosimo's mind, a new opportunity that overcame some of the problems he faced. There had always been three huge practical problems with his plan. One, how do you draw out of the Medici Bank enough money to found a new bank without anyone noticing? Two, how do you hide that amount without anyone seeing you do so, and three, how will Lorenzo eventually release such a huge sum from its hiding place without being discovered?'

Maddalena is nodding now. 'The first, I think I understand. The *Libro Segreto*, which I looked after for many years, maintained the overall summary of assets and liabilities as seen by the holding company, or, when that was disbanded, by the family. So all you had to do was to make a transfer from one of the branches to the centre and then to make an entry in the books saying it has been loaned to someone else. The obvious name is Sforza in Milan. But of course, they never saw the money. It went to…where did it go to?'

Donatello smiles and takes a leather folder from his pocket. From inside, he draws out a slim piece of paper. 'It's here. The solution to both the second and the third problem.'

Maddalena takes the piece of paper and reads. The writing is unmistakeably Cosimo's.

Beneath the goldsmith's secret
Possession, lover, son
There lies the stone of destiny
Whose answer is but one
Ten quarrels equidistant
From where that once we lay
My final diminution
Holds Lorenzo's destiny

'What does it mean?' Maddalena shakes her head.

Then, line-by-line, Donatello explains, and as he does so, the grin on Maddalena's face gets broader and broader. Now, finally, she knows where the gold is hidden. Better still, Donatello has suggested a way for Lorenzo to retrieve it without his actions attracting attention.

'That's clever. That's very clever. Cosimo always looks ahead; this time, he has recognised that at the very time he is likely to need the money; Lorenzo might be under the most extreme political pressure. The last thing he would thank his grandfather for would be an opportunity that turned itself into a problem. So retrieving the money secretly becomes the key to it all. This way, Lorenzo can draw the money from its hiding place under the maximum public gaze, yet without attracting the attention of even the most suspicious observer. Whose idea was it?'

Donatello tips his head from side to side, implying that the matter hangs in the balance. But finally, he stops moving and smiles.' I have to admit, it was Cosimo's. But I can take the credit for the way we hid the gold. It took some doing, but eventually it worked out extremely well.'

He takes out another piece of paper, this one folded and creased. 'I have done a calculation. Two hundred thousand florins, at nine to the troy ounce is nearly three quarters of a ton of solid gold.'

Maddalena nods, absent-mindedly; her mind already beneath the chapel. Already she sees that her dreams of presiding over all the money in that little vault beneath the Medici Library will never now come to fruition. But the new plan is better. Much better, and with Donatello only a couple of years younger than Cosimo, she knows she remains its guardian. He loves her after all. He trusts her after all. How could she ever have doubted it? There was just a little uncertainty, that's all. Because of the delays. A problem of communication. Understandable now.

By the time their food has been brought and eaten, by the time she has told

Donatello what she wants him to say to Cosimo on her behalf and by the time Donatello and his driver are ready to take the empty cart back down the valley, the full burden of her responsibility is beginning to make itself felt. Now, at last, she, and she alone, is responsible for the gold; for Lorenzo's gold.

She hopes she is up to the responsibility.

Chapter 28
The Earthquake
Convento di San Damiano
1st February 1464

It is the first of February; barely eight weeks since she was given her great responsibility, and Maddalena has still to decide how much to tell the abbess. Of course she had to confide that Donatello had brought news of the change of plan. And yes, she had admitted that the new plan was already in place; and no longer, except as far as the first deposit was concerned, involved the Convento di San Damiano. But so far, she has not brought herself to show the abbess the poem nor to tell her what secrets it represents.

Madonna Arcangelica has taken it stoically. 'The repairs to the roof will have to wait, I suppose. It's God's will. We shall struggle on, as we always have.'

Now it is nearly midday and they are all walking quietly into the chapel for Sext. Stomachs are rumbling, for all they have eaten was the lightest refreshment after Prime and the main meal of the day is still nearly an hour away.

As Maddalena takes her seat and places her breviary in front of her, there is a thunderous roar, deep underground. Her first thought is for the vault. Did they dig it too deeply? Has the work Cosimo instructed, somehow weakened the foundations of the chapel? As if to share her concern, a small piece of timber comes away from its long-established place somewhere amongst the roof beams and falls, crashing down, a few feet away from her.

Maddalena flinches as dust and tiny splinters spatter her habit. She looks around her but nobody seems injured. And then she notices Elena, sitting forward in her pew, holding her head. Instinctively, Maddalena leaves her position and walks quietly and with due reverence, but nevertheless quickly, to where the girl is sitting. She leans over her and reaches out to stroke her forehead.

'Elena? Did something fall and hit you?'

Elena lifts her head and Maddalena sees blood on her forehead, and on closer inspection, a small splinter of wood still sticking out.

'Here. Let me help you.' She reaches forward and with great care, draws the splinter out, gripping it carefully between her fingernails. Instinctively, Elena pulls back and puts her hand to the blood and at that very moment, there is a second rumble; now many times louder and the whole building begins to shake violently. Elena ducks and as she does so, Maddalena reaches across her, as if to protect her head from any more danger.

The roof beam is long, and although it is rotten at one end, where rain has been infiltrating the joint for many years now, it is still heavy. The grinding noise as it tears itself away from its neighbours and from the stone buttress that holds it in place is lost in the general cacophony, and now it falls, freely and silently, until it hits Maddalena in the small of her back, crushing the backs of the pews in front of, and behind her.

All round the chapel, timbers and pieces of masonry are falling. The altar receives a direct hit; the crucifix thrown to one side disrespectfully by the heavy stones before they bounce forward, into the body of the chapel.

There are screams as nuns run directionless, trying to escape from the maelstrom, yet everywhere they look there is carnage as the chapel tries to shake itself to pieces. And then, with one throaty roar, the vibration ceases; the shaking ends, and the only sounds are the coughing and whimpering of terrified women, the creaking of timbers as they still swing precariously, fifty feet above the ground, and the hiss of sand as it slides from joints in the stonework and falls, in a perfect arc, through the dust below, to make little pyramids in the marble of the chapel floor.

What is it? Elena's voice sounds even smaller than usual. There is a tremor in it; although she is trying to be controlled.

Elena and Maddalena are on their knees, between two crushed pews; the roof beam across at right-angles. Its weight has smashed the backs of the pews down almost to seat level and the pews have been tipped towards each other, making a small dark church of their own.

'I think it's an earthquake. It seems to have stopped now but there may be more. You can never be certain. We had one in the city, years ago that repeated five times.' Maddalena's face is inches away from Elena's and they are whispering to each other, as if afraid of causing more roof falls.

'Can you move?'

The girl nods her head. 'Yes. The pews are jammed together above my head but I can wriggle backwards.'

'Then release yourself and crawl to the area where you see the least debris on the floor. That should be the strongest place and therefore the safest.'

'What about you?'

'I don't think I can move. I'm trapped. I think I'm caught beneath the broken pews and the beam itself. It's hard to tell. I can move my arms but my hips appear to be jammed.'

'Can you push with your toes?'

'I can't…feel my toes. Or my feet. Or my knees. I can't feel anything below my waist. Don't worry, Elena. Forget about me. Make yourself safe.'

Gingerly, Elena wriggles backwards and finds she can stand. Apart from the original cut on her forehead, she is unmarked and uninjured. She looks around. In front of her is a great pile of timbers, including the one that is trapping *Suora* Maddalena, whilst above, there is a great hole in the roof. On the edges of the hole, timbers are sticking out, torn sheets of lead are twisted grotesquely, and pieces of masonry are balancing, precariously, still ready to fall at any minute.

'Quiet Sisters. Take command of yourselves. We have had an earthquake. There may be further tremors, and as you can see, the building is not safe. Make your way outside and stand across the courtyard by the old well. You will be safe there.' The abbess' voice is soft but commanding.

'Elena. What are you doing girl? Don't just stand there! Make your way outside with the others.' The abbess is pointing towards the door.

'But *Suora* Maddalena is still under here. She is stuck fast.'

***

From her position beneath the pews, Maddalena can see two pairs of feet, facing each other. That Elena can be a defiant little soul when she wants to be. One pair of feet turns toward her and she hears a familiar voice.

'*Suora* Maddalena. Can you hear me? Are you injured?'

Maddalena tries to ease her back. There is a growing pain now, as of bruising to her upper back. But the overpowering sensation is lower down – an all-encompassing numbness.

'I believe my back is trapped.' The words come out as a hoarse whisper. 'I can't move.'

'I will send for help to the Badia and down to Bivigliano. We will need men with lifting gear. Builders or farmers.'

'Is anyone else injured?' Maddalena's first instinct is to think of others.

From her entrapped position between the smashed pews, she sees the abbess' feet turn one way, then the other as she surveys the sorry scene. 'There does not appear to be anyone else left in here. They must all have made their way outside. I saw few injuries around me, but I cannot be sure. Your predicament appears to be the most serious.'

'Then see to the others. I cannot come to greater harm here and you can do nothing until this beam is lifted away. I shall be alright.'

'If you say so, Sister.' She sees the abbess' feet turn, at first hesitantly, and then more decisively, and disappear towards the door.

There is a sudden crash as yet another block of masonry falls from the roof, and then silence. Maddalena uses her elbows to try to change position, but she cannot break free from the half-kneeling position in which she is trapped. She brings her elbows beneath her, and tries her best to relax, her forehead on her crossed wrists.

It is quiet now. Outside she can hear the murmur of voices, but around her the broken chapel appears to be sighing, as timbers twist and moan in resentful response to their new-found positions. She closes her eyes and concentrates on relaxing.

***

It is growing dark when she is woken by the patter of feet. The abbess once again; there is a rough tear in the leather of her right shoe. She noticed it before. The feet approach and stop, at the end of the pew-tunnel; two yards from her face. With difficulty, the abbess kneels and her face appears.

'How are you, Sister?' Only the outline of her hood can be seen, but the familiar voice is comforting.

205

'I have been in more pain. Childbirth was much worse than this.' As she speaks, she feels a fullness in her lungs, and an overpowering desire to cough. She does so, and to her dismay, tastes blood. 'I wish I could lift myself upright. This position is not helping me.' She tries to keep her voice bright, but the taste of blood has frightened her.

'The men say they will come as soon as possible. They have other fallen buildings in the village and the monks are in the same position as us.'

It is now so dark she cannot even make out the outline of the abbess' hood. Only her voice remains to ward off loneliness. Maddalena coughs again and this time feels the blood run out of the corner of her mouth. Her breathing is becoming shallow. She sees her father's face and hears his voice. *You have internal bleeding. If you cannot get upright, your lungs may fill and you may drown in your own blood.*

'I think you may have to prepare yourself for a night here.' The abbess has wriggled forward and her face is now close; the voice a whisper, almost conspiratorial.

'I do not think I will survive until the morning.' With great difficulty, Maddalena turns her left elbow under her and rests on the elbow and shoulder. The change makes her breathing ever so slightly easier and she rests, trying to regain her strength. In front of her she can sense the abbess breathing. She knows Madonna Arcangelica is willing her to hang on but at the same time, knows that platitudes will not help, so she does not speak.

Maddalena sees Carlo's face. Her greatest achievement; if only the cardinal could wield his authority now. But she knows life is not like that.

Now Cosimo's face appears, and she smiles. *Hello Cosimo! You have come to say goodbye, haven't you? As I have nearly done to you on more than one occasion since entering this place of too much contemplation. Many is the time my faith in you has slipped and faltered, but I never lost it completely; and finally, as part of me had always known you would, you sent word, and all was well after all.*

Many times in her life she has wondered what death would be like. Now, with a calmness that surprises her, she thinks she knows. While there is hope, you fight. But once the reality, the certainty of the situation reaches you, the need to fight goes and instead, knowing you can do no more, you relax and prepare to go to that other place. Whether it exists or not (and over the years, ever since her slavery, she has harboured recurring doubts) now no longer seems to matter. She can go into oblivion knowing she has done all she can; that she has made the best she could out of a situation that many would have considered impossible.

And then she feels her heartbeat begin to quicken. But she has not done all she can. Lorenzo's gold! Her task is incomplete. Cosimo believed in her, relied on her and she has accepted his trust. She cannot now let it fail. Not just because of a roof beam.

With the clarity that she normally only experiences in those first thoughtful moments after waking, when everything is calm and ordered and before the detritus of the day begins to clutter her mind, she knows now what she needs to do. She has two tasks. Two things she must do before she allows herself to let go.

First, she must tell the abbess everything; interpret the poem, explain exactly what Donatello and Cosimo have done, and ensure that when the time comes, Lorenzo will be able to find his money and put it to good use.

And second, through her journal, she must tell Cosimo what she has done.

'Are you there?' Her breathing is so shallow now that speech is becoming difficult.

'I am here. I shall not leave you. Not unless you ask me to do so.' The abbess' voice is controlled, although Maddalena can hear the quavering emotion behind it.

'I have little time. I must tell you everything that Donatello told me when he visited me here. I cannot die and take the secret with me. You must now carry it on, until the time comes for Lorenzo to inherit his salvation. And after that, I must write to Cosimo; one final entry in my journal.'

'Are you sure you can write? In that position?'

'I must find a way. I have no choice. I owe Cosimo everything. He gave me my life. And I owe him a debt of honour…as well as…of love.' Her breathing is becoming so difficult she can hardly get the words out.

'I understand.' To Maddalena's relief, Madonna Arcangelica does not try to tell her that her fears are unfounded. She knows there is no time for such insincerities. They both know there is work to be done.

'Can you bring me my casket? The journal is inside it and so are my letters from Cosimo and the guide-poem that Donatello brought with him. And my writing materials?'

'Yes, I will fetch them immediately, and a lamp. Are you *sure* you can write in that position?'

'I have no choice.'

The abbess struggles backwards and with a groan, regains her feet. Maddalena hears her footsteps retreating and rests. She must hang on until the work is done. She dare not fall asleep, but she can rest. She must rest.

***

The sound of the abbess' footsteps wakes her and she is aware that something is different. A full moon has come out and is shining directly through the great hole in the roof and onto the floor around her. Even here, close to her and beneath the shadow of the broken pews, there is enough light to see.

'I have brought them, as you asked.' The abbess pushes a small lamp and the casket forward into the little tunnel before her and follows behind, sliding them forward as she comes. She pushes the lamp to one side and places the journal in front of Maddalena. Then she opens the casket and waits. 'Ready.'

'The small note, folded once only, on top of the pile.' Maddalena watches her unfold it and nods. 'Can you read it by this light?'

'I think so.' The abbess reads the poem aloud.

'Yes. Good. Now I shall tell you what it means.' She is finding it increasingly hard to speak.

Quietly, lying on her side and occasionally pausing for breath, Maddalena explains the whole plan, until the abbess declares herself satisfied that she understands it all.

She lies, panting on her left shoulder. 'Now the journal, if I may.' Madonna Arcangelica slides the journal forward and arranges pen and ink beside it. She moves the lamp until Maddalena nods, and then gives her the pen.

Maddalena writes.

Dearest Cosimo,

God has, it seems, chosen to punish me for my lack of faith. I should never have doubted your word. Now it is too late and I am doubly damned, for in my weakness, I fear I may fail you again.

You put your trust in me, on behalf of Lorenzo, but now I cannot deliver my side of the bargain, for I have not long to live. I have asked Madonna Arcangelica to accept my part and she has agreed to do so. I put my trust in her.

It came at midday, as we were at our devotions. A great roar and shaking of the ground, until part of the building fell asunder. Mercifully everyone was saved, except your sinner, for a great timber hit me and my back is broken. The timber lies on me still, too heavy for the sisters to lift. Now I truly know what it is to carry the cross.

I shall not endure this coming night.

All my love,

Mad...

Gently, the abbess reaches forward, lifts the pen from the page, and places it, together with Maddalena's other possessions, back in the casket. Maddalena is asleep now and appears to be at peace. She prays that they will come early in the morning, but nevertheless, to be on the safe side, she administers last rites.

That done, Madonna Arcangelica folds her own arms, rests her head on her forearms and allows herself to drift into sleep. She will not leave *Suora* Maddalena here alone. Not tonight.

By her elbow, the candle in the little lamp comes to its end, gutters and goes out.

***

Maddalena senses the candle's last flicker, and opens her eyes. In the moonlight, she can see that the abbess has stayed with her, and she smiles. Knowing she is not alone, she allows herself to slip back into sleep. Eyes closed, she says a last prayer, thanks her parents for giving her life, and Cosimo for making her life what it has been. As she slides away she thinks about her life and coming to terms with death. For everyone it comes too soon, but for everyone it comes, and she knows she must accept it.

To fight death is to lose all dignity.

Chapter 29
An Abbess Alone
Convento di San Damiano
2nd February 1464

It is dawn. The abbess wakes; cold, stiff and disoriented. She begins to lift her head, confused as to her whereabouts, and the back of her head hits the pew above her. It is then that she looks ahead of her; at the dim outline of *Suora* Maddalena.

'Sister?'

There is no reply and already Madonna Arcangelica's heart is sinking.

She reaches out and feels the forehead, still resting on the clenched fists. It is cold. Cold as the stone of the floor, and so are the hands. She clasps the two hands in hers, gripping them; hoping somehow to change the truth she knows is unassailable. But it is not to be: like it or not, *Suora* Maddalena is dead.

The abbess has lost many nuns in the course of her life, but none has left the hole in her side that she now feels. *Suora* Maddalena had been special. Perhaps it was because she had come late in life to the convent; bringing with her a lifetime of experience of the outside world, so that the presumed superiority of the Mother Superior was, without any specific agreement between them, put aside in place of…what? Mutual respect certainly. Friendship also, measured by their willingness to address the sometimes uncomfortable, but respectful disagreement. But most of all, warmth; the radiant glow of one human being felt by another. Maddalena; in whom, she now realises with the aching regret of those who are too late, there was no malice.

She finds herself unwilling to withdraw from the special closeness that she still feels for the body in front of her, as if knowing that as soon as she wriggles backwards, as soon as she stands, as soon as she begins to look around her at whatever the new day has brought, she will finally be forced to admit the separation between them, brought about by Maddalena's death.

Already her head is beginning to fill with things she had meant to tell Maddalena and had not found the time or the opportunity to mention. Already the questions are starting to pile up; how did this remain unclear, how could I have failed to ask that? But most of all, what do I do now?

For a moment she feels a sense of panic as the magnitude of the responsibility that she accepted the previous night dawns on her. What specifically is she supposed to do? Should she write to the Medici family, and if so, to whom? What are the protocols with such people? At the meetings they had had together, the Magnificent Cosimo had been easy to talk to, but on every occasion the step-by-step process of their conversation had been driven by him, and she had only, as she now appreciates, been a passive participant.

Perhaps it is Lorenzo she should inform? The whole scheme, as she understood it, was intended for his benefit. But if that is the case, why has he not been told already? He is, of course, still young. What age now? Fifteen. But at what age should he be informed? At what age was it intended that he should inherit the money? She had forgotten to ask, and Maddalena, for all her care, had omitted to tell her.

Lying on her face, she looks through the gloom toward the body of her friend and wills her to provide the answers. With some last glimmer of hope, she calls out her name and once again clasps those freezing hands in hers. But it is hopeless. Maddalena is now alone. And so, in a sense, is she. But she has made a promise and she must fulfil it.

The essence of the scheme, of course, is the avoidance of the next generation. It is that which creates the secrecy. The whole reason Cosimo had to go to such great lengths; sending Maddalena to the convent, was to allow his secret to walk round Piero and Giovanni. And, presumably, their mother and their wives? Now Giovanni is dead. But Piero: the one Maddalena had always dismissed as useless; the future head of the family, Lorenzo's father, he is still alive.

Of course, if Cosimo is still alive when Piero dies, then she will not be needed, as Cosimo can hand the money over to his grandson himself. He would inherit anyway, so there will be no problem. So there, then, is the essence of this hard-faced scheme: the active avoidance of Piero after Cosimo's death. She shakes her head. What degree of disappointment in his son would a father need to make him design such a scheme? And how much must he have trusted Maddalena, to entrust her with its fulfilment, actively avoiding Contessina, Piero, Lucrezia, Giovanni and Ginevra?

Madonna Arcangelica squeezes Maddalena's cold hands. 'Thank you,' she whispers. 'I knew you would tell me what to do. Now I can say farewell to you in the knowledge that I can carry the burden you passed on to me and fulfil Cosimo's wishes when the time comes.'

Awkwardly, she creeps forward on her elbows and kisses Maddalena's forehead. 'Goodbye old friend.'

As she begins to shuffle backwards, voices appear from the door to the chapel. 'I think she's in here. She came back last night to stay with *Suora* Maddalena and comfort her in her imprisonment. They must both be here still; under these timbers.'

She recognises the voice of the gatekeeper and as she finally escapes from the clutches of the crushed pews, she rolls over and, painfully, sits up.

'I am here, Sister. I have bad news. *Suora* Maddalena is dead. She died in the night; I believe peacefully and reconciled to her God. I was able to administer last rites in a form. I trust, in the circumstances, it will suffice.'

Suora Fidelita, the gatekeeper, helps the abbess to her feet. 'These men are from the village, Reverend Mother. They have brought ladders and lifting equipment; levers, a tripod, and block and tackle.'

Six men stand awkwardly, moving their weight from side to side, embarrassed and perhaps overcome by their surroundings. 'Where do you want us to start?'

The abbess points to the great roof beam and the crushed pews beneath it. 'Here, if you please. One of our number is beneath that beam. Perhaps you can release her?'

The men look hesitant. 'That beam is very heavy. If it rolls, it could injure her further. We are not specialists; just farmers.'

Madonna Arcangelica puts a hand on his shoulder. 'She is dead. You cannot injure her further. But I should be grateful if you would treat her body with as much respect as you can.'

She takes one last look at the mass of timbers, heaped together like a funeral pyre. 'She was very special.'

She makes herself stand fully upright for the first time; her back painful after such a long, cold and constrained night. Then, for the first time, she starts to look around her. *The future can wait, and so can Lorenzo's gold. Today I have other, more urgent, responsibilities; here, in the convent.* The thought goads her into action.

'I will leave you men here, to do what you can. The nuns from the infirmary will bring a stretcher to take our dear *Suora* Maddalena to a place of safety until we can bury her. Once that is done, perhaps you could look at the roof? I understand you cannot repair it, but if you could make it safe, then at least we can use one of the side chapels as a place of worship until the skills and the resources are found to rebuild the main roof.'

She begins to walk towards the door, looking from side to side, assessing.

'Now sister, how much damage is there elsewhere?'

Author's Note

The rapid rise and the equally rapid collapse of the Medici Bank (which was effectively all over in less than a hundred years) is a remarkable story – not least because there are so many parallels with the banking crisis of the present period.

Cosimo de' Medici, always strongly guided by the safe judgement of his brilliant General Manager, Giovanni d'Amerigo Benci, built a powerful organisation whose structure ensured that the main shareholders (the *maggiori*) were protected from ruin when (inevitably) problems arose in distant branches. It was an organisation whose accounting systems and banking documentation allowed one bank to operate and control events all over western Europe; and whose management structure ensured that the managers of those distant branches were motivated to act in the best interests of the whole and not just of their own branch.

Unfortunately, things changed in mid-July 1455 when Giovanni Benci died.

By this time, Cosimo was sixty-six years old and no longer the man he had once been. Sadly, neither of his sons, Piero nor Giovanni, was really suited to running a global bank. The bank had been organised as an *accomanda* – a special form of partnership with limited liability, and it was this top company which then entered into a series of separate, tightly-worded partnership agreements with the individual branches, from London and Bruges to Ancona and Lyon. With Benci's death, as one of the *maggiori* partners, it was necessary to sign a new partnership agreement, and it was here that everything began to go wrong.

For those who wish to understand these features in detail, I recommend Tim Parks' *Medici Money* for an outstanding and clearly-written overview and Raymond de Roover's *The Rise and Decline of the Medici Bank 1397-1494* for a detailed textbook analysis.

What I have tried to do in the series *The House of Medici* is to tell the story from a human point of view. What was it like to live through these great events, to face the great opportunities offered to successive Medici sons, but also to manage the problems that regularly occurred in a rapidly changing world and to suffer the disappointments when people let you down?

And in all of this, to try to answer the question: 'How did it all go so disastrously wrong?'

The problems the Medici faced were not only concerned with running the bank. Running the country was also troublesome and unlike the bank, gave little reward. Once again, the problems faced by those who sought to govern the Republic of Florence in the 1400s were remarkably similar to those that politicians all over the world face today. The people wanted provision of services but moaned and pleaded poverty when they had to pay for them. And when one of the rich families, such as the Medici, did fund civic activity, the people turned on them for trying to become princes and take over the much-lauded Republic.

The early Medici played reluctant saviours, pretending they had become drawn into this position; whilst in reality, behind the scenes, they had always sought power and influence. But for the reason described above, they always worked hard not to appear as princes, and instead, always presented themselves as members of the common *popolani* .

Cosimo's father, Giovanni di Bicci de' Medici, had drilled into him a series of mantras on this subject, and these were in due course passed on to his sons and to his grandson, Lorenzo the Magnificent. This framework of thinking, accompanied and influenced by Cosimo's enthusiastic adoption of the new humanist ideas – ideas that were beginning to form the birth of what we later named the Renaissance – made the Medici advanced and creative thinkers; and that, combined with hard work and a little sprinkling of good luck, resulted in immense financial success.

But as *The House of Medici: Inheritance of Power* shows, whilst Cosimo passed on the rules given to him by his father, his own actions seemed to break those rules more often than they reflected them.

The new partnership structure introduced in 1455 no longer protected the *maggiori* from losses incurred within the widely-spread branches. Cosimo's choice of managers broke all his father's rules of promoting the best and not necessarily just the family. The new partnership agreements with the branches motivated the branch managers to act foolhardily and in their own local interests, whilst slippage in maintaining Giovanni di Bicci's strict systems of annual audit meant that the centre did not recognise problems until it was far too late.

It was the same with politics. Cosimo presented the family as commoners, yet he married 'Contessina' – not only a Bardi but (as her common name tells us) the daughter of a Count. Later, he did it again, marrying his elder son Piero to Lucrezia Tornabuoni. She was of good family: major land and property owners, active in the wool trade between Florence and Bruges; and in due course, members of her family successfully held important jobs in the bank for many years.

Lucrezia herself was not only a poet but also a successful businesswoman in her own right; owning shops and a hotel in Pisa, and the medicinal baths at Bagno a Morba, south of Volterra. Uncomfortably for both her and her husband, she was considerably brighter and more able than Piero. Not only that, but she was in love with his younger brother – her childhood hero, Giovanni – and this was to have dramatic consequences, as we shall see in *The House of Medici: Seeds of Decline*.

Later, Piero and Lucrezia were to break one of the golden rules again – marrying their son, Lorenzo the Magnificent, to Clarice Orsini; not only from the nobility, but from the Roman nobility.

To be fair to Cosimo, he had seen much of this coming and as this series of stories describes, he hid a fortune – 200,000 Florins – deep beneath a convent, in order to bypass his useless son and to give his grandson, Lorenzo, the opportunity to salvage something from the mess he knew Piero would inevitably leave behind.

Raymond de Roover quotes the weight of a single Florentine Florin as 0.1143 Troy Ounces, making the hoard 22,860 Troy Ounces of gold. At the time of writing the world gold price is £1,055 per Troy Ounce. This values the hoard in 2013 at over £24 million.

What Cosimo was not to know, was that in her resentment over her marriage, Lucrezia would bring up her precocious son, Lorenzo, in direct opposition to the Medici Creed. She used all her power openly to make him a Great Prince; and between them, in the process, they let the family bank go to the dogs.

But that, as they say, is another story.